WICKED
DREAMS

Books by Lisa Jackson

Stand-Alones
SEE HOW SHE DIES
FINAL SCREAM
RUNNING SCARED
WHISPERS
TWICE KISSED
UNSPOKEN
DEEP FREEZE
FATAL BURN
MOST LIKELY TO DIE
WICKED GAME
WICKED LIES
SOMETHING WICKED
WICKED WAYS
WICKED DREAMS
SINISTER
WITHOUT MERCY
YOU DON'T WANT TO KNOW
CLOSE TO HOME
AFTER SHE'S GONE
REVENGE
YOU WILL PAY
OMINOUS
BACKLASH
RUTHLESS
ONE LAST BREATH
LIAR, LIAR
PARANOID
ENVIOUS
LAST GIRL STANDING
DISTRUST
ALL I WANT FROM SANTA
AFRAID
THE GIRL WHO SURVIVED

Cahill Family Novels
IF SHE ONLY KNEW
ALMOST DEAD
YOU BETRAYED ME

Rick Bentz/
Reuben Montoya Novels
HOT BLOODED
COLD BLOODED
SHIVER
ABSOLUTE FEAR
LOST SOULS
MALICE
DEVIOUS
NEVER DIE ALONE

Pierce Reed/
Nikki Gillette Novels
THE NIGHT BEFORE
THE MORNING AFTER
TELL ME
THE THIRD GRAVE

Selena Alvarez/
Regan Pescoli Novels
LEFT TO DIE
CHOSEN TO DIE
BORN TO DIE
AFRAID TO DIE
READY TO DIE
DESERVES TO DIE
EXPECTING TO DIE
WILLING TO DIE

Books by Nancy Bush

CANDY APPLE RED

ELECTRIC BLUE

ULTRAVIOLET

WICKED GAME

WICKED LIES

SOMETHING WICKED

WICKED WAYS

WICKED DREAMS

UNSEEN

BLIND SPOT

HUSH

NOWHERE TO RUN

NOWHERE TO HIDE

NOWHERE SAFE

SINISTER

I'LL FIND YOU

YOU CAN'T ESCAPE

YOU DON'T KNOW ME

THE KILLING GAME

DANGEROUS BEHAVIOR

OMINOUS

NO TURNING BACK

ONE LAST BREATH

JEALOUSY

BAD THINGS

THE BABYSITTER

THE GOSSIP

THE NEIGHBORS

Published by Kensington Publishing Corp.

SA JACKSON

WICKED DREAMS

NANCY BUSH

KENSINGTON
PUBLISHING CORP.

www.kensingtonbooks.com

KENSINGTON BOOKS are published by

Kensington Publishing Corp.
119 West 40th Street
New York, NY 10019

All Kensington titles, imprints, and distributed lines are available at special quantity discounts for bulk purchases for sales promotion, premiums, fund-raising, educational, or institutional use.

Special book excerpts or customized printings can also be created to fit specific needs. For details, write or phone the office of the Kensington Special Sales Manager: Attn. Special Sales Department. Kensington Publishing Corp, 119 West 40th Street, New York, NY 10018. Phone: 1-800-221-2647.

The K with book logo Reg US Pat. & TM Off.

Library of Congress Card Catalogue Number: 2022943473

ISBN: 978-1-4967-3401-3
First Kensington Hardcover Edition: January 2023

ISBN: 978-1-4967-4335-0 (trade)

ISBN: 978-1-4201-5325-5 (ebook)

10 9 8 7 6 5 4 3 2 1

Printed in the United States of America

WICKED
DREAMS

PROLOGUE

Declan Bancroft stood at the bottom of the stairs, listening hard. His eighty-plus-year-old ears played tricks on him sometimes, but those creaking boards upstairs had been plaguing him for days now. He wanted to see what was making the noise himself, but it was difficult for him to navigate those confounded steps. Seven up to a landing, then seven more to the top floor of his seaside home.

"Ach," he muttered, annoyed with his tired old bones.

He'd called Hale, his grandson, who'd promised to stop by. But the boy was a man now, with a wife and a child and another on the way, and though Declan and Hale were in business together, they spent less and less time after hours in each other's company. Hale was too busy, and Declan was too old.

It hadn't always been that way. Declan had a moment of fondness and rueful musings over the tyrannical woman who ran that cult in Deception Bay. Oh, she didn't like him calling it a cult. "Would a women's prison be more accurate?" he'd asked her once, which had really twisted her tail into a knot. But he loved her . . . loved her still . . . even though she acted like they'd never been together, never created a beautiful child between them who'd grown into an even more beautiful adult.

No, his days with Catherine Rutledge were long over. Distant memories. But sometimes they seemed so close, closer than the wonderful afternoons he sometimes spent with his great-grandson, Declan, named for him. Five years old and full of vinegar that boy was. Everyone had taken to calling him Declan right away, and that meant they called his old, tottering great-grandfather Declan Sr., just to keep them both straight. Declan wasn't really a senior. He had no son, just two daughters, but there'd been a time he'd been kind of confused about the whole thing; he could admit that now. Still, the old noggin was pretty damn sharp. Even Hale commented on it, which had made him act like it made no difference to him, when in reality it tickled Declan pink. He still had it. And if Catherine would deign to drop her knickers just one more time . . .

He chuckled a bit, realized he sounded like a dirty old man and stifled his amusement, although that darned smile wouldn't quite leave his lips. If he—

Crreeeaakkk.

There it was again. Footsteps . . . he was almost sure of it. Should he call Hale? Would he just hear excuses again? His wife was pregnant and about ready to drop. Not an especially good time to bother his grandson, but who else was there? Neither of his daughters lived in the area.

His cell phone was in his pocket. He fished it out and poked in Hale's number but didn't hit SEND. Thought about it a moment, then put the phone back in his pocket. How hard was it to make it up the stairs and check for himself? He used to run up those blasted steps.

Determined, he placed a hand on the newel post. His cell phone was with him, should he find himself in trouble. Carefully, frustrated that it required so much effort, Declan moved up the first step and placed his hand on the banister. Just six more to the landing. He kept his eyes on the steps, watching his feet, carefully placing one foot, then the other on the next step. He was almost jubilant when he reached the landing.

He looked up, and there was a young man standing at the top of the steps. His heart galumphed. "Who are you?" he demanded, but his voice quavered a little.

"Who do you think?" he responded, grinning like a devil.

Declan's mind was a blank. "What are you doing in my house?"

"Should be my house."

Arrogant SOB! "Go away! Get out!"

Fear had hold of him as he shuffled himself around to go back down the steps to the first floor. He tried to shake it off. This . . . *thief* . . . didn't scare him. His house? He was delusional, probably insane. Declan slipped a hand in his pocket for the phone, and suddenly the bastard was right there! Spinning him back around so that they were facing each other. Declan started to tip, but the invader grabbed him by his arms.

"It's me, Dad. Your loving son."

"I don't have any sons . . ."

The man slowly moved him around so his back was to the downward steps. Afraid, Declan gripped the sleeves of the man's jean jacket. He was scruffy. Long hair. All in denim. Grinning. *Chuckling!* Declan's heels were over the edge of the top step. He teetered precariously.

"Stop," he moaned.

"You don't know me?" the man accused.

Declan looked into his eyes. Blue as the sky and . . . crazy. He suddenly knew he was going to die. No, he didn't know him. But whoever he was, whatever he was, he knew this man was going to kill him.

As if reading his mind, the man said, "You die, and I inherit."

"You're—you're mistaken. I have two daughters!"

"I was here before, *Dad*. Five years ago. You remember? I kept telling you I was your son. I kept coming to the house."

Declan blinked. Yes. He remembered. "I was just confused," he denied. Then, as realization flooded through him in a hot wave, "You're Charlie! You're not my son. There is no Declan Jr., no matter what you were named. You're Charlie!"

The man's face tightened, and the blue eyes grew bluer, if that was possible, pinning him with an unholy light. "I am your son," he insisted through his rictus smile.

"No, no . . . DNA will prove you're not . . . !" he gasped.

"Goodbye."

Charlie slowly peeled Declan's hands from his sleeves and stood back. Declan flailed wildly, trying to hold onto his balance, grappling for the rail.

Touching a finger to Declan's nose, Charlie gently pushed.

It was all the momentum needed. Declan went over backward, flying over the first few steps, crashing down the last. His head hit the stone floor, and he saw stars.

Immediately, Charlie was beside him, bending down, staring into his eyes. Declan squeezed his eyelids shut tight.

A wild howl filled his ears, and he felt Charlie trying to forcefully open his lids.

Then he saw a glowing light . . . the pearly gates?

With a soft exhalation of breath, Declan Bancroft died, his ears closing one final time, muffling Charlie's screams of frustration that he couldn't steal the soul of the man he mistakenly assumed was his father.

CHAPTER 1

Funerals . . .
Detective Neville Rhodes sat in one of the back pews as the minister gave a glowing review of Henry Wharton's accomplishments and the character of the older man throughout his fifty-eight years as if he knew him, which he clearly did not. Nev had known the man all his life, and Henry was obdurate and a little mean-spirited, and the father of Nev's one-time best friend, Spencer. One time. A long time ago. Fifteen years ago.

The woman seated beside Nev stirred in her seat. He could sense her shooting him looks, but he kept his eyes straight ahead, as he wasn't ready to engage in conversation. Lana had been Spence's fiancée. They'd gotten engaged just before the accident that had taken Spence's life, and when she'd seen Nev sitting alone in the pew, she'd slipped in beside him. He didn't think they'd spoken more than ten words to each other since Spence's death, but then Nev didn't talk about the accident. If he could have, he would have erased the memory of that day entirely, but it was always with him. And Duncan's death too. It didn't take everyone blaming him for the accident that stole his two closest friends to make him feel guilty. He could do that all by himself, even though he knew it wasn't true, even though he'd been the one who'd tried to stop the harebrained and dangerous, alcohol-fueled plan to row out to Echo Island and confront the harridan who lived there, even though he'd been the one to point out that numerous boats had been capsized or sunk in the treacherous waters that surrounded that godforsaken, one-mile-wide, rocky island.

The fact of the matter was Spence and Duncan had died, while Neville Rhodes had survived. That's all anyone cared to know. That's what had happened.

Lana's fingers tiptoed across the pew to clasp his hand, giving it a squeeze. He finally glanced her way and saw her ragged smile. *I'm sorry*, she mouthed.

Nev nodded, not wanting her sympathy. He didn't want to be here, but if he'd stayed away, he wouldn't have been able to live with himself. If he had forgone Henry's funeral, he wouldn't have had the stomach to face Spence's family with that show of cowardice.

So, here he was . . .

The small chapel was located on Tillamook's south side, perched on a scraggly hill, with a view between several houses to the bay beyond. Through one of the tracery windows, Nev caught a glimpse of a cool, gray October sky. The weather had just turned, summer shedding into autumn, winter promised. With day upon day of sunshine and heat, Indian summer had prevailed, then there was a sudden temperature drop so precipitous the people inside the church had been forced to wear coats for the first time this season, those coats now hanging open over the back of the pews, as the interior of the building was warm. Nev tugged at his collar but kept his coat on.

". . . Henry loved his family. His wife, Candy, and his sons, Andrew and Spencer . . ."

There was a slight stir in the room as Spencer's name was invoked. The perfect son. The one destined for greatness. Several heads turned to look at Nev, and he had to fight a reaction. Years of being in law enforcement had given him an implacable expression, but not today. Not when it came to Spence. Even now, years later in this austere little chapel, Nev could hear his friend's voice.

"C'mon, Rhodes," Spence had urged when Nev had resisted taking out the boat and heading toward Echo Island, the cursed piece of rock and dirt tantalizingly outside of Deception Bay, so deceptive itself, seemingly benign and untouched. But a crazy lady lived there, apparently one of that odd cult of women who resided in that weird lodge on the mainland, which was protected by hedges and high fencing.

All the adventurous kids his age wanted to brave the tide and go out and spy on the unhinged woman who lived on the island, although they all knew about the unpredictable crosscurrents surrounding Echo, how it was only safely accessible in late summer, and that even then, you really needed to be an expert boatman to approach it. Echo's shore was inhospitable, and the tiny dock was washed away practically every year, to be mysteriously resurrected, then washed away again.

The whole place was eerie and unwelcoming.

"We've still got time to get there," Spence had assured him, looking out the window of his bedroom. It was the middle of October that year, almost the same time of year as now, but the weather had been worse.

"It's too late. A storm's coming," warned Nev.

"A storm's coming next week. This is our chance, now."

Duncan Wicklund had yawned and said, "You've got a hard-on for that place, Spence."

The three of them were in their last year of college at Oregon State University in Corvallis. They were home for the weekend, or at least Spence and Nev were; Duncan was from northern California but had become a fast friend over the past three years. Whereas Spence was lean and dark, Duncan was redheaded and muscular. Nev was somewhere in between them. Not as dark as Spence, not as fair as Duncan, not as whip-thin as Spence, and not as filled-out as Duncan.

"How many times have we said we're going to go there?" Spence demanded of Nev. "A hundred? A thousand?"

"It's you, man, not me," said Nev. "Duncan's right."

"Duncan's never right," responded Spence with his trademark sideways, evil grin.

Nev's mom had always thought Spence was bad news, and she was maybe right, but Nev had loved the guy. He made everything brighter, wilder, better. Nev knew Duncan was enticed by Spence's schemes and plans as well, no matter what he said.

"I'm right this time," said Duncan, to which Spence snorted.

Duncan's eyebrows drew together. "Isn't this the same place you said was cursed or haunted or something?"

"Local gossip. Old bitches talking, that's all," Spence replied, and both were right. The stories about Echo were never-ending and all wrapped up in curses, bad luck, and hauntings. Who really could separate fact from fiction?

Nev couldn't recall exactly how Spence had talked them into it, but somehow Nev was renting the rowboat, and Duncan was trying to borrow a coat from him as they were going straight into the teeth of the coming storm and were in trouble if they didn't get away from the island in time, though Spence assured them there was "no way, absolutely no way we'll fail! If we see the old witch, we try to get something from her, something to show that we were there, like some of her hair, something with her DNA on it, but we gotta be fast."

Now Lana leaned toward him, breaking into Nev's uneasy memories as she whispered, "I don't know what I'm doing here. I haven't seen any of the Whartons since Spence died. They didn't want him to be engaged to me. You remember?"

Nev nodded.

"I wasn't good enough for him. Never was good enough for him." Tiny tears filled the corners of her eyes, and she seemed to shrink into the pew.

It was Nev's turn to be the comforter. Quietly, he said, "They just didn't want Spence distracted."

"From the great things he would achieve? I know. But that wasn't Spence. Not really."

"Well, it wasn't about you."

She'd been facing forward, chin jutted, trying to hold back her emotions. Now she threw him a look. "It wasn't about you, either."

Hah. Neither of them would ever convince the Whartons of that.

After the service, Nev stuck around to meet and greet with the other gatherers for a few minutes inside the church. Henry was to be buried in the family plot in the centuries-old graveyard in the foothills of the Cascades, above the flood zone, but Nev wasn't making that pilgrimage. Henry and Candy had made it clear someone needed to be blamed for extinguishing the bright flame of their son, and that someone was Neville Rhodes. Lana may have expressed support for him, but Spence's mother wouldn't feel the same. Nev had come to the service in duty to Spencer and his father. Now it was time to leave, and he followed a group of mourners outside.

Heading down the concrete steps, the breeze off the ocean whipping his hair and stinging his eyes, he didn't realize he was going to pass by Spencer's mother until it was too late to take a different route around the group of friends gathered near the bottom of the steps.

A weak sun threw slanting strips of light through the limbs of a tortured pine, crowning the circle of mourners with undulating illumination.

Nev's sleeve brushed Candy's elbow. She glanced up, saw it was Nev, and stiffened as if struck by a freeze ray.

Nev and Candy locked eyes, and Nev drew a breath, flooded with those memories he tried so desperately to keep locked away.

In that split second, he remembered that awful night.

"I'll go first," Spence had yelled as they'd neared the island. Nev's arms ached from rowing. They should have rented a power boat, but none of them had extra cash, and there was a good chance whatever craft they'd chosen would get smacked around in the currents and grounded on the rocky shoal surrounding the decrepit dock. None of them could afford to pay for that kind of damage.

The front of the rowboat hit the dock and shuddered.

Spence ignobly tumbled onto its grayed planks, feet and legs dangling in the water. He scrambled to his feet just as another wave hit. Hard. The bow swung violently and slammed into a post, narrowly missing Spencer. But Spence was already climbing up the pebble-strewn hill.

"Jesus!" Duncan swore over the roar of the surf.

Nev paddled frantically.

No good!

The hull crashed against some slick black boulders whose barnacle-crusted crowns showed above the waterline, dark bergs whose main bodies lay beneath the waves.

"Lemme," Duncan ordered.

"I've got it," ground out Nev.

"No, you don't!"

With an effort, Nev swung the boat back around, close to the dock on the undulating water. He was breathing hard. "Thought you were following Spence," he managed.

"Who wants to see some old witch?" Duncan started working his way toward the stern, as had been the original plan, to trade places for the trip back to shore.

He wobbled, the wind lashing, frigid ocean spray slapping at both their faces.

Duncan was stronger than Nev, but not as experienced with oars. Nev had grown up on the ocean. Had fished and swum and worked along its shores, whereas Duncan had been a city boy. Nev reluctantly switched to the middle, a trick that took all their concentration, given the heaving boat. Spence, on his return, would man the aft.

When Nev and Duncan were finally in their spots, both of their chests were still rapidly rising and falling from the exertion.

There was no sign of Spence.

"Where is he?" Duncan said, his teeth chattering. "I mean, the island isn't that big, right?"

Nev shrugged. He'd never been on Echo.

They both waited.

How long had it been? Five minutes? Ten? Longer?

Nev ventured a look at the sky, as dark and foreboding as the ocean, storm clouds hovering over the roiling water.

"Did you see him go up there? To her house?" Nev asked tensely. All along, he'd thought Spence would bag out, that he'd bail at the last minute, but now he'd disappeared, and Nev was staring at the overgrown trail leading away from the water, willing him back.

"'Course he did! He's crazy, man!" Duncan steered the boat away from the dock and into the relative safety of a large eddy. Even so, the wind was rising, and the rowboat was being tossed about. Duncan literally had his hands full.

In those minutes Spence was gone, Nev and Duncan were both inside their own heads. Nev was worried. Counting seconds. The storm he'd mentioned wasn't just coming; it was here, its infantry a cold, chopping wind. He knew they shouldn't have come, but they were committed now, and the mainland seemed more distant than ever. If they ran out of time, would it be better to seek shelter on the island? Though it was mostly a rocky tor, there was a house somewhere, supposedly, where the old woman lived. Maybe they should try to pull the boat ashore, find Spence, find a safe place to wait out the storm?

They'd made a foolish mistake, Nev thought grimly. They'd listened to Spence, and they were in trouble.

Duncan's expressive face was sphinxlike, jaw set. His arms were working the oars, keeping the boat from being tossed around like the proverbial cork on the water.

Then Spence suddenly appeared again. Sliding down the hill from the crest of the island. Pebbles flying in front of him as he half-rode on his butt, hands in the dirt and rocks, trying to control his slide. Duncan steered grimly toward the dock, gritting out swear words, the same words inside Nev's head.

Spence reached the dock and flopped onto it, his palms scraped and bloody. "Shit!" he cried, the oath thrown away by the wind.

Only Duncan's strength got them near enough to the dock to allow Spence to clamber in before they were swung around, away from the island but aiming toward the sea, not the shore.

"Why'd you stay in the boat?" Spence demanded of Nev, yelling to be heard above the wind.

"This was your plan, not ours!" Nev yelled back. "Let's go!"

Spence laughed, his eyes wide, his color high. "I got her hair!" he screamed in delight, balancing precariously. "She invited me in and cut it off for me herself!"

"What hair?" Duncan demanded, shooting a glance at Spence.

"The fuckin' witch's! In my pocket. She wanted me to fuck her! Can you believe it? And man, I wanted to! I really wanted it. She made me feel it! If I'd only had more time—"

"For Christ's sake," Duncan said. "Sit the fuck down!"

Spence half-fell in by Nev's feet.

"That freakin' witch, Mary, she wanted me. And man, I wanted her," he repeated, as if he couldn't help himself. Spence was still flying high.

Duncan kept fighting the tide and the currents. He got the rowboat turned around, and Nev and Spence both barked directions at him, coaxing him to guide her to the mainland and the safety of the beach.

But it was a long way off, and the sea was roiling in white caps and waves. Angry gray water reached toward a dark, ominous sky.

"Hurry up!" Spencer ordered, finally grasping how grave the situation was.

From the corner of his eye, Nev saw the monster first: the huge, rolling wave that rose up and came down on them like a fist. His heart lurched hard. He knew they were going to capsize before it happened and screamed at his friends in warning.

"Watch out!" cried Nev.

Duncan's eyes showed white with fear, but he held on.

SLAM!

One hard thunk, and they were overboard, tossed out of the boat and into the sea.

Nev felt the frigid ocean close over his head. Immediately he stopped fighting, letting himself float upward.

As he broke the surface, he tossed wet hair from his eyes and gulped air.

Spence?

Duncan?

Where were they?

Alarmed, he rode the waves, bobbing on the frothy surface, frantically searching for his friends. Oh. God. But the storm was only playing with them. Its full thrust was yet to come.

Shivering, he frantically scoured the sea. There was no swimming in it. No making it straight for shore. The riptide wouldn't allow it. Freezing, Nev spied the capsized boat, swam for it, and grabbed wildly, clinging to the ever-moving rowboat, literally for his life.

"Spence!" he yelled, his voice caught in the screaming wind. "Duncan! Jesus!" Again he scoured the angry ocean.

Duncan surfaced, looking dazed.

"Duncan!"

Nev spied a huge knot in his friend's head, but Duncan saw the boat and swam for it, desperately holding on. Blood stained his forehead, and his short hair was plastered to his head. His eyes were open, but spaced out.

"Hold on!" Nev screamed. "Shit, man, hold on!"

The wind shrieked.

Spence's head surfaced, dark hair visible. "Spence! Oh, God!"

Spence blinked, and gulped.

"Here! Spence!" Nev was frantic.

The boat bucked wildly.

The bow slewed around and slammed into Spence's face with the force of a fighter's knock-out punch.

"Spence!" Nev screamed. Oh, no. Oh, God no! "*Spence!*"

His friend surfaced again, and Nev flung himself away from the boat to grab him and help him to grip the splintered hull. Spence groaned, but his hands clutched the side of the boat.

Blood ran from the blow that had split the skin of his forehead.

Nev looked across the boat to the space where Duncan had been clinging to the overturned hull. He wasn't there.

Shit.

"Hold on. Can you hold on?" Nev demanded in Spence's ear as he searched the surrounding sea.

Spence didn't answer, but his hands clutched on to the hull with a death grip. Nev tried to circumvent the upside-down boat to find Duncan. "Duncan! Duncan!" he screamed and screamed, treading water, circling, shivering, frantic. Where the hell—

He saw the top of Duncan's head beneath the water. He grabbed wildly. Tried to haul him up by his hair. He failed, the hair sliding between his frozen fingers. No. *No.* He tried again and again and again . . .

But Duncan disappeared beneath the churning dark surface.

"Duncan. Dunc—" Salt water slammed into his mouth, choking him. His arms were leaden. He had to give up. Exhausted, holding onto the boat for what felt like hours and sick at heart, Nev hoped for rescue. He'd tried and tried to save his friend, but he'd failed.

As it turned out, someone had seen their capsized boat and raised the alarm. The Coast Guard came to save them, but by then Nev was dealing with hypothermia, his brain and body numb. It was too late for Duncan; his body was found the next day washed up against the shore on the mainland, still in sight of that deadly island.

Spence was alive but had been unconscious as he was dragged from the sea.

Though he didn't remember it, Nev had made his way back to his friend, making certain Spence wouldn't slip back into the water like Duncan. He would die with Spence rather than let him drown. He was half delirious himself when they were rescued.

Spence hovered in a coma for three long days and then succumbed to a brain hematoma.

Nev was examined, treated for mild hypothermia with warm blankets, hot tea and broth, and observed before being released.

Nev tried to talk to Henry and Candy, but they cut him dead. "You rowed him out there," Henry snarled, and Nev, brokenhearted, couldn't seem to explain that the whole thing was Spence's idea. Duncan's parents came for his body and spoke to no one, apart from an angry television interview in which they blamed all of Deception Bay for "giving kids dangerous ideas about that godforsaken island!" Duncan's father had been pale and had glowered into the camera, his one arm draped around his wife, a short woman who huddled close to her husband and avoided looking into the camera.

It all had been hell.

Now Nev broke eye contact with Candy and took a step back, giving her a nod of acknowledgment before turning toward his Ford 150. He'd made it to the truck's door when he heard the fast footfalls behind him. He turned just as she came upon him.

"You bastard," she said, tears standing in her eyes.

"Mrs. Wharton—"

"Why do you get to live? Why does *everyone* die, but you get to live?" Her chin trembled.

"I'm sorry about Mr. Wharton."

"Are you sorry about Spence? You took away the best thing in my life. You took away my favorite . . ." She stumbled, even in her agony hearing the truth of her remark, glancing over at her other son, Andrew, tall, too thin, his hair snapping around his face as he hurried up to his mother. She held her tongue, but Andrew's shuttered expression said he knew all too well what she'd been about to say.

Candy's face was pale and drawn, her lips tight, her hair coming loose from its tight chignon.

Nev said, through a dry throat, "I miss Spence every day."

She slapped him flat across the face. Hard. The blow came so fast he had no time to react. His face stung, his cheek on fire. "You don't know what grief is!" she cried.

Nev was too surprised to do more than take a step back, stumbling against the door of his truck.

"Mom," Andrew said miserably.

Nev felt his color rise, his muscles tighten.

"You're a curse on our family!" she shrieked at him, her blond and gray hair flying all around her head like a corona. People on the steps turned to look as she shook from head to toe, her black lace dress whipping in the wind.

"I'm sorry," he said tersely, wanting to say more, knowing there were no words.

"You should be in jail, not working as a policeman!" she spat. "Henry wouldn't want you here!"

"*Mom!*" Andrew's voice was the crack of a whip.

Neville turned back toward the truck.

"You should have been the one to die!" she screamed after him as he opened the driver's door.

Yes, ma'am.

The rest of the night Neville spent nursing a beer—a few beers, actually—at an out-of-the-way bar near his rented house in Sandbar, a small hamlet south of Tillamook. Rationally, he knew Candy and Henry were wrong. Spence's death wasn't his fault. But at times like these, it was hard to remember. He might know it in his head, but it still hurt his heart. Rarely did he let it get to him any longer. Time had numbed, nearly erased, the pain. But it was always there. Lurking just below the surface. Even though life had gone on, the sorrow and the guilt never really left him.

"Girlfriend?" the bartender asked sympathetically, pointing to the left side of Nev's face. Candy had really nailed him. He could feel the bruising and now knew it was evident to others too.

Nev just shook his head.

"Line of duty?" The guy knew Nev was a detective with the Tillamook County Sheriff's Department.

"Something like that," he said, not wanting to get into it.

He went home and looked at himself in the mirror over the bathroom sink. The handprint had disappeared, but the discoloration made it clear he'd run into something. Tomorrow he was going to have to forgo shaving in the hopes that the beginnings of whiskers might shadow some of the evidence.

He was still feeling the lingering pain of Henry Wharton's and Spencer's and Duncan's deaths the next morning when he rose before dawn, showered, dressed, and headed north past Tillamook toward Deception Bay. He wanted to view Echo Island this morning. The crazy woman who'd lived there was dead, and the island still lay just out of reach. The sea was restless and gray, white caps evident through the trees lining the winding road. He felt the muscles in the back of his neck tighten, as they always did whenever he drove past that section of cliff where the firs gave way to vast ocean, a vista with the black rocks of Echo Island rising above the surface, breaking the line of the horizon. Today, he threw a glance at the island. It was, as always, left just the way it wanted to be: alone, inhospitable, empty.

There was a place to park on the west side of the highway, space enough for about three vehicles. As he'd been heading north, he yanked on the wheel, crossed the highway, and pulled into the wide space, turning around so that he was facing south, nose out, ready to take off. Stepping outside the truck into a biting wind, he yanked the collar of his lightweight jacket tighter as he faced the ocean, then walked to the guardrail mounted on the cliff face, high above the stretch of sand that looked toward the sea and Echo.

The only way down was a treacherous trail of switchbacks that kept would-be sun worshippers searching for a different beach, which was just as well because it wasn't safe to—

Wait.

He froze, his gaze scouring the sandy strip below.

For the love of God, was that a body on the beach? Up away from the water?

Yes.

The hairs on the back of his neck raised, and he squinted down the steep terrain.

Sure enough.

Alive, or . . .

"Hey!" he yelled. "Hey!" His voice caught on the wind, and as he expected, the person didn't move.

"Damn it." He glanced down at his shoes. Sneakers. He was in jeans. Hadn't gotten dressed for work yet. The sun was barely cresting the mountains, and that biting wind . . .

He grabbed his phone from his pocket, planning to call into the station to report the body, then hesitated. Instead, for now, he shoved the device into his back pocket. Hell with it. He was going down.

He climbed over the guardrail and stepped onto the trail, head bent to the wind, as he eased past rocks, roots, and weeds, slipping in several places, remembering how Spencer had slid down the island hillside to the boat as Nev tried to keep from bloodying his own palms. The trail had nearly washed away at the beach, and he jumped down the last couple of feet, landing with a jar, then running across the packed sand toward the man.

He was on his back. Bending down, Nev checked for a pulse, but there was none. No hint of breath. He was clearly dead, but his eyes were open, an arresting shade more silver than blue as they seemed to stare at the sky.

What the hell happened?

Straightening, Nev threw a glance toward the island, feeling a rise of fury in his chest. It looked like Echo had claimed another victim. What else would this man have been doing on this stretch of beach?

Don't go there. Anything could have happened. Keep your own demons locked away.

And yet he felt a finger of dread slide down his spine as he narrowed his eyes on the horizon and the island.

Hunching his shoulders against the wind, wishing the sun would beam down some heat, he placed a call to the Coast Guard, explaining the situation.

Then he called into work, after which he sat down to wait as the surf pounded and seagulls cried and wheeled high above.

Though his eyes were drawn to the formidable rocky outcropping on Echo, he turned his gaze back to the John Doe. Something was peeking out from beneath the man's jacket. A piece of paper? Glancing around, he found a small stick and then carefully lifted the edge of the man's windbreaker to find a note pinned to the dead man's shirt.

He leaned over the corpse. The writing had bled down the page, barely legible.

Gazing down at the message, he frowned, his eyebrows drawing together.

He could just make out a phone number. But the words beside it were easier to read, and they caught him up: NEXT OF KIN.

He quickly looked at the man's face again, then back to the island, then back to the corpse. Whose next of kin? His? Had he written the note and pinned it to himself?

Nev's skin prickled as he carefully set down the stick, slipped his phone from his back pocket, and took a picture of the note. He thought about it, then he unpinned the note from the body and slid it into his back pocket. It took several hours for the Coast Guard to appear, the craft plowing through the currents, damn near crashing against the southern rocks and cliffside. Nev heard crew members swearing and smiled grimly. He knew exactly how they felt about this stretch of sea and land.

The body was collected and hauled into the boat. Nev watched the boat leave, heading directly out to sea before turning far from the riptides surrounding the island, its course heading south toward Tillamook. Then he climbed back up the hillside, once again clinging to roots and vines and finding toeholds in the rock where the trail failed. He reached the crest, legs aching, heart pounding, and got into his vehicle. His hands were numb, and so was his butt from his long wait sitting on the sand. He started his engine and waited for the cab of his truck to warm. As he sat there, he pulled out the note he'd unpinned from the corpse. He should have left it for forensics, but he hadn't. He would have liked to give himself an excuse, say he'd felt it might disintegrate, the information lost, if he hadn't moved it, and maybe there was some truth in that. In reality, he'd wanted the note and number for himself.

He looked out at the island—desolate and forbidding as ever, then placed the call to the dead man's next of kin.

Bzzzzz . . . bzzzzz . . .

Ravinia's cell phone rang. She was driving and was halfway from Portland to the beach, deep inside the Coast Range, where tall firs and hemlocks rose on either side of the winding road. She slid her eyes from the road to glance at her phone as it buzzed away, secure in its cradle attached to her dash. Who was calling? One of her sisters? If it was someone trying to hire her, they would likely call her office phone, not her personal cell. Reception was iffy in the mountains. Nonexistent in spots. So even if she answered, she might be cut off, and it sometimes took twenty minutes or more before a faint signal could be reached again, so a whole lot of calls were dropped as soon as they went through.

Bzzzzz . . . bzzzzz . . .

It wasn't a number she recognized. Not any of her sisters, then. Someone else. Should she answer it? She was feeling tense already. Didn't really want to make this trip in the first place. She had stuff to do in Portland. A missing wife . . . surveillance on someone with a suspicious employment background check . . . Her fledgling PI business could already use another operative, as she couldn't be in two places at once, but she couldn't afford to pay anyone a salary. At least not yet.

Could a potential client have gotten hold of her personal cell number? She rarely gave it out, if she could help it, but sometimes it was necessary.

Bzzzz . . . bzzzz . . .

Well, hell.

She was west of the summit, so cell reception might actually work.

She hit the ON button, and then SPEAKER. "Hello?" she answered brusquely, not giving anything away.

"Hello," a male voice answered back. She detected a slight drawl, but the voice held tension. "I'm Detective Neville Rhodes with the Tillamook County Sheriff's Department. An unidentified male body washed up on a small beach just north of Deception Bay, with a note attached to it with this phone number and the handwritten message 'next of kin.'"

"Excuse me?" Ravinia said. What had he said?

"The note was . . . uh . . . gripped in the decedent's hand."

"With this number? My number? And it said . . . 'next of kin'?"

"Yes, ma'am. This number." Into the confused whirl of Ravinia's mind, he added, "Are you anywhere close to Deception Bay, Oregon, to possibly identify the body?"

"Are you kidding?"

"No, ma'am."

She actually was not all that far from Deception Bay. She was heading to Seaside, for a funeral, and Deception Bay was only about forty minutes south. She said slowly, "You want me to come to Deception Bay to identify a body that was holding a note that said, 'next of kin' and included my cell phone number?"

"Yes, ma'am. If possible. The body has been transported to Ocean Park Hospital morgue. Are you in the area?"

If he called her "ma'am" once more, she was going to lose it.

"I'm really having trouble with this. A male body? And he had my number."

"Yes, ma'am."

She gritted her teeth. Who? How? She probably had enough time before the funeral, as she'd left Portland early, but did she even want to help him? She had a bad feeling about it already, and she avoided Deception Bay as a rule. She'd grown up there, lived most of her life with her sisters and aunt at Siren Song Lodge, not far from the town, but when she'd left five years ago, she'd pretty much left for good.

Still, her curiosity was growing.

She glanced at the clock on the phone. "I can be there in an hour, maybe an hour and a half. But I can't stay long. I'm heading to a funeral."

"Good." He sounded relieved. "Thank y—"

She clicked off.

A dead guy? Washed up on the *beach*? Which beach?

There were several beaches in the area. Nonetheless, her mind drew a picture of the small, secluded beach below the highway across from Siren Song. North of Deception Bay. It was no more than a spit of sand between two treacherous outcroppings of rock, the closest beach to Echo Island.

She felt a little niggle of dread. If the man's body was found there, was he trying to get to Echo?

Ravinia's fingers tightened around the wheel. Strange things seemed to be happening lately. It had been a long spell of quiet, but maybe that was ending. First Declan Bancroft Sr., the love of her Aunt Catherine's life, had died a suspicious death, though nobody but Ravinia seemed to think his death was anything other than an accident. The older man had fallen and hit his head, that was true, and then had succumbed to his injuries. That was also true. But it was the fall itself that Ravinia questioned. And now this unknown body with *her cell number* attached?

She shivered as she watched the wind blow the fir limbs that lined the road and swayed toward her Toyota Camry as if waving her onward. Something's coming, she thought. A shift in the wind that sent a thrumming through her body. Premonition.

She didn't like the feel of it, but her curiosity was aroused.

When she came to the junction at Highway 101, she drove past the turnoff that led north to Seaside and aimed the nose of her Toyota south for Deception Bay.

CHAPTER 2

Nev watched the woman walk off the elevator and into the brightly lit corridor outside the morgue, long strides eating up the ground between them. She glanced around, spotted him, and headed directly toward him along the brightly lit corridor outside the morgue. She wore billowy, loose-fitting black pants encircling a slim waist, a black blouse with a high neckline, and a black wool coat that moved around her like a cape. Small pearl earrings studded her ears and peeked from behind dark blond, chin-length hair. Wary sea-green eyes, slitted with suspicion, caught his as she approached.

So this was the tense voice on the phone. He'd been expecting someone older, the way she'd come back at him when he'd explained about finding the body on the beach. He'd lied about the note being in the dead man's grip because its true location invited more questions than he wanted to explain on the phone, and he wanted to make sure this "next of kin" showed up in person rather than just hung up on him. Less said the better on a call. He'd been curious about who would answer the number, and her abrupt, "I can be there in an hour, maybe hour and a half. Can't stay long. I'm heading to a funeral" had convinced him she would be much older. Somewhere in her thirties, at least. But she looked to be in her mid-twenties. She'd hung up before she'd given him her name, but here she was in the flesh. Drop-dead gorgeous . . . except for the tight frown on her face.

"Next of kin?" he greeted her.

· "Detective Rhodes?" she returned icily.

"Yes, ma'am."

She held up a finger, as if she were about to scold him, but seemed to think better of it. "This note you found. Clutched in the man's hand. Where is it?"

He produced the small missive from the pocket of his own coat, now in a small plastic bag. He held out the flimsy paper so she could read it for herself, but he didn't hand it to her. "Actually, it was pinned to his body," Rhodes admitted now. "There was a pen in his jacket pocket." Nev had rethought his motives about taking the note when he'd arrived at the hospital, wondering at himself a bit. He'd called in the information about finding the body to TCSD and had spoken to his partner, Detective Langdon Stone, who'd been with the Sheriff's Department more years than Nev had been in law enforcement as a whole, explaining that he'd taken the note because of its fragile nature, but that he was turning it over to the forensic team. What Lang thought of that Nev didn't really know yet.

She stared at the note in silence.

"It looks like he wrote it before he died," said Nev carefully.

"And pinned it to himself? Come on." She lifted her brows at him.

"That's my theory."

"Why?" She was baffled.

Because he knew he was dying . . . ?

"What was his cause of death?" she asked.

"Looks like drowning, but it's yet to be determined."

Her frown deepened, and her gaze, if possible, grew more intense. "I don't have a lot of time. Where's this body?"

"This way." He turned down the short hallway and strode to the morgue door. She was a half step behind him but kept up stride for stride, the hard soles of her shoes echoing against the tile floor. "Who are you?" he asked as he pushed the door in, inviting her to precede him. "You never said."

"You never asked."

"My mistake." But he hadn't really had time. "I'm asking now."

She hesitated briefly, then answered, "I'm Ravinia Rutledge."

"Rutledge . . ."

"Yes, I'm one of them," she said coolly, breezing past him and through the inner door, where the supine body lay beneath a sheet in a sterile room with white tile walls, dull silver drains in the floor, and illumination that glinted off stainless-steel counters and equipment.

The pathologist was inside. Dr. Sazlow, pushing sixty, with thinning gray hair, bushy white and gray brows, crisp lab coat, and thick glasses. He straightened a bit as Ravinia entered.

Nev made quick introductions, then nodded to Sazlow, who lowered the sheet from the man's face.

Ravinia's mouth tightened. Barely visible, but Nev noticed. Everything about her radiated tension.

The dead man was somewhere around thirty, not much older than Ravinia, Nev guessed. Stiff, salt-laden blond hair, a strong chin, grayish skin, but it was the eyes that drew attention. They were still wide open, that odd silvery shade. It looked, somehow, as if he were staring up at something far away.

Nev had planned to close the man's eyelids, but when he'd reached Ravinia on the telephone, he'd decided to wait.

Now, as she gazed down at the corpse for long moments, her jaw set, the wheels in her mind clearly turning, it seemed she couldn't believe what she was seeing. Nev half-expected her to pull out a pin and stab the John Doe to see if he was really dead.

"Do you recognize him?" asked Nev. When she didn't answer, he added, "Are you his next of kin?"

She half-turned toward him but couldn't quite tear her eyes from the dead man's face. He saw then that her skin had whitened. Despite that telltale sign, she stated emphatically, "No."

"No?"

"He's a stranger." She was shaking her head, dark blond hair shimmering under the harsh fluorescent lights. "It's a mistake."

Nev shot Sazlow a glance. The older man shrugged at him. People reacted in all kinds of ways to corpses.

She motioned to the ashen face of the dead man. "He was alone?"

Nev nodded. "No one else was around."

"You said he was washed up on a beach around Deception Bay?"

"The beach across from Echo Island. That stretch is difficult to reach."

She made a sound of sardonic agreement. "He drowned?" She glanced at Sazlow.

"We'll know more after the autopsy," said Nev, beating Sazlow to the punch. "You sure you don't know him?"

"No."

"We need to identify the body—"

"I said I don't know him," she stated firmly. "I'm positive about that." She took a deep breath. "Look, I'm sorry, I have to go. I don't want to be late."

Funerals . . .

Nev knew of only one funeral today being held in the Seaside area. One of the area's most prominent citizens, Declan Bancroft, was being laid to rest. There were likely others, he supposed, but seeing as she was apparently a Rutledge, one of the mysterious women who inhabited Siren Song Lodge, he made an educated guess: "You're going to the Bancroft funeral."

"I—yes." A pause. "Are you?" she asked in consternation.

"I didn't know him."

"Most of the people attending won't either. That won't stop them."

There was something about her tone that suggested she would gladly not attend herself, but maybe she had no choice. Nev, who'd made a point of disregarding anything he'd learned about the clan of the crazy woman who'd lived on the island—he wanted to erase as much as possible from his mind about Spence's tragedy—nevertheless knew a few things about Siren Song and its inhabitants, known collectively as the Colony, who resided there. You couldn't live in the area without some information trickling in about them, whether you wanted it to or not, so he said, "You're related to the Bancroft family?"

She gave him a hard look. "Not me." She then abruptly pushed back through the door and began striding quickly away.

Nev caught the closing door with his hand and had a heck of a time catching up with her because she was hauling ass.

"Miss Rutledge?" He almost jogged to keep her in sight. "Miss Rutledge?"

She was already at the elevator doors, her palm pounding the button. Over her shoulder, she said, "I told you I don't know him."

"Is that the truth?"

She half-turned. "You calling me a liar?"

"It seems like you know something, and it was your number pinned on his shirt. We really need an identification. He had no wallet. Nothing on him."

"I'm sorry, Detective. I can't help you." The elevator car doors opened, and she stepped inside, turning around to face him, her gaze intense. They stared at each other in silence as the elevator doors began to close.

Suddenly, Nev felt a strange heat sear through him.

He jerked in surprise.

What the hell was that?

He blinked.

The doors shut, and Ravinia Rutledge's visage disappeared.

Mouth dry, Nev rubbed his chest, alarmed, watching the numbers over the door illuminate in succession as the car rose from the basement to the ground floor of Ocean Park Hospital.

Did she do that?

The area surrounding his heart was still suffused with heat. Strange . . . spooky. Now his pulse began to race, but it was because he was certain she had somehow intentionally caused the rush of heat through his body.

He exhaled slowly.

There were those stories about the Siren Song women . . . purported extrasensory gifts . . . visions, an eye into the future, God knew what else.

Yes, I'm one of them, she'd said, and the words held new meaning.

He grimaced and let his hand drop, the heat dissipating to a soft warmth that was surprisingly pleasant, which he thought was even more dangerous. That was the word that came to mind.

He didn't believe the women of Siren Song were so gifted. A lot of smoke but no fire. Fortune-tellers making a buck, the family of the crazy lady on the island. Grifters, probably. Very attractive grifters, if Ravinia Rutledge was a sample of their clan.

The moment passed, and Nev took stock of himself. He felt, well . . . normal. Shaking his head, he warned himself not to make too much of it.

The last two days had been difficult, from Henry Wharton's death, to his trip down memory lane about Duncan and Spence, to the body washed up on the nearest beach to Echo Island. Nev had been drowning in unpleasant memories.

The elevator car stopped at the first floor, the number 1 remaining illuminated for long seconds as she departed. He thought about following her. He had more questions. Her number had been on that note, after all, but there was more to it than that. Ridiculously, the woman intrigued him.

He glanced at the elevator call-button panel, then turned to walk back to the morgue, where he looked down at the corpse one more time. No more answers there.

Sazlow was hovering, waiting for the word to slide the stretcher back into its steel drawer. Nev finally nodded at the older man, who pushed the body—still a John Doe—into the locker. The drawer closed with a soft but definitive click, and Nev walked into the hallway.

Even though he'd dismissed Ravinia as the cause for the heat in his chest, his hand strayed to the space over his heart one more time. She couldn't have caused the heat that had scorched through him. It wasn't possible.

Ignoring the gooseflesh and slight lifting of the hairs on his scalp, he strode to the elevator and pressed the call button. When the doors opened, he half-expected that Ravinia had returned, but he was disappointed. He stepped into the empty car.

Silas. It's Silas!
Oh, God. He's dead!
Silas is dead!
Her heart pounding, her mind in turmoil, Ravinia turned down the hall and walked blindly around a corner, skirting a nurse pushing a patient in a wheelchair toward the front doors, nearly colliding with a briskly walking woman in a lab coat heading in the opposite direction.

"Excuse me," the woman muttered, her glance anything but friendly as she swept by.

Lost in her own thoughts, Ravinia ended up at the hospital cafeteria, pushing through the doors and then looking around blankly. What was she doing here? She couldn't think beyond the shock of seeing Silas, his skin gray, his eyes open as he lay unmoving on the slab.

Her gaze fell on a vending machine with a display of snacks, candy bars, and small bags of chips. Beyond the glass, clutched in a metal spiral, lay a package of Hot Tamales. She stumbled forward, her head clearing a bit, and noted, gladly, that the machine still took money, though the prohibitive cost was on the level of highway robbery. Didn't matter. She plunked down her dollars and was rewarded with a box of the cinnamon candies. Years earlier, on her sojourn south to find her missing cousin, she'd practically lived on them.

Gathering herself, she threw a small handful of the candies in her mouth.

Pull yourself together.

She chewed and swallowed, then ate a second handful as well, after which she forced her thoughts back to the here and now. Despite the shock of seeing Silas in the morgue, she had things to do, a life to live.

Even if Silas did not.

She dropped the half-empty box of candies into a pocket and, with a slightly clearer head, retraced her steps to the hospital's sliding-glass doors at the front of the building. They opened automatically as she stepped outside and across the sidewalk.

Immediately, she was hit in the face by a slap of wind.

She staggered a bit, one boot slipping off the curb. Her foot smacked downward, and the jolt jarred her spine.

Shit. She moved toward her car, reaching into her pocket, finding the pack of candies, and tossing back some more Hot Tamales. By the time she was behind the wheel of her Camry, she was uncapping her water bottle and slugging down long gulps to quench the fire from the cinnamon candies.

She knew the body lying in the morgue was Silas. Though she'd only met him a few times and their last meeting was over five years ago, she was certain the corpse lying dead in the basement of the hospital, here, in Deception Bay, was him. Those eyes. Unforgettable.

She could remember him so clearly. Could see herself hurrying toward him that last meeting on the road outside Siren Song, the time when she'd turned toward the town of Deception Bay and he'd headed in the opposite direction, on a mission of his own. She smiled faintly at the memory.

"What are you doing?" she asked him.

"Waiting for you."

"Like you knew I'd be here," she said dryly.

He smiled as they walked to the side of the road together. He wore a dark blue Gore-Tex jacket, and his hair was covered by a hood. But she could see his blue eyes. Crystalline. Almost silvery. She realized that it was the week's growth of beard that darkened his jaw that made him seem different than the last time she'd seen him. Older. More sexy in some way that reached right down to Ravinia's toes.

"I have something for you," he said.

"Yeah?"

He slid the pack from his back. She had a sense it was all he owned, that he was a vagabond of sorts. Well, so would she be by the end of the day.

To her confusion and disappointment, it was a sheaf of papers, rolled up and rubber-banded together. "Take these to your aunt."

Startled, she asked, "How do you know who my aunt is?"

"The middle-aged woman who wears long dresses and puts her hair in a bun and runs the cult in that lodge where you live? Catherine Rutledge. She's more well-known than the mayor in Deception Bay."

"What is this?" Ravinia asked, looking down at the papers.

"Something she's been looking for."

"You were the one on Echo," she realized, looking toward the outline of the island far out in the water. "You set the fire. Why?"

"Sometimes you have to burn things" was his unsatisfying answer.

"Who are you? What do you want?"

"I'm a friend, Ravinia. Take Catherine the papers. She'll know."

She hadn't told him her name, and she didn't know his. "Where are you going?" she asked when he turned away as if their meeting was over.

"I've got some things to do, but I'll be around."

"Will I see you again?"

"You never know," he called over his shoulder. "Maybe it's our destiny."

Well, they had met again, but not until today. And only one of them was alive to remember it. She hadn't known his name then, but Aunt Catherine had filled her in. Silas, Ravinia's half brother, who'd been adopted out when he was an infant . . . like Charlie.

She shivered inwardly at the thought of her other half brother.

Tossing a few more Hot Tamales in her mouth, she pulled out the small black purse she'd wedged under the front seat of her silver Camry. Removing the remote vehicle key from the pocket of her coat, she placed it inside the purse again. Hands on the wheel, she stared straight ahead through the windshield, but didn't yet start the car. Instead of seeing the parking lot that meandered around the building, she saw Silas as she'd last seen him alive. That knowing smile. Those cryptic words. A sense that he was going to take care of all of them.

And yet he'd been the one who'd failed.

She felt like crying. She'd hardly known her half brother, but she'd known *of* him. That he'd been on their side, hers and her sisters' and Aunt Catherine's and Elizabeth's, the *side of good.* She and Silas had been two travelers who'd crossed paths just before she headed south to California and he headed in search of Declan Jr., better known to all of them now as Good Time Charlie.

"*Charlie,*" she spit out. If he was the cause of Silas's demise, she would find him and kill him herself.

Ravinia had never met Charlie, her other half brother, also known as Declan Jr., but if he was anything like her murderous, sick-minded, vengeful cousin, who'd done his damnedest to destroy them all a few years before she'd left for California—and Aunt Catherine certainly believed that to also be Charlie's mission—well, then, he needed to die. Plain and simple. He needed to be removed from this planet, once and for all. She'd felt Silas was the man to send Charlie back to the hell from which he'd risen, but that apparently hadn't happened. At least it didn't appear so, because Silas was dead, and Charlie . . . ?

What if he was still alive?

A chill ran through her, a whisper of fear that sparked into a quick, hot anger. She couldn't let it happen. Charlie couldn't be the one who survived, who prevailed!

Ravinia smacked the heel of her hand on the steering wheel. This wasn't the way it was supposed to happen!

What *had* happened?

That detective . . . Rhodes . . . said Silas had been found alone on the beach just across that dangerous stretch of water from the island. Her stomach twisted. Had Silas been back to Echo? If so, why? What was there on that forlorn rocky outcropping any longer? Ravinia knew Silas had been there at least once before, to set the fire and burn the bones of the man who'd sired Charlie. And he'd brought back a sheaf of papers with the addresses of their adoptive parents and handed them to Ravinia to give to Aunt Catherine, a task to which he'd been commissioned by her. Aunt Catherine had understood the threat Charlie posed before any of the rest of them, and she'd wanted Silas to find him and get rid of that threat once and for all. Had he? After five years, had Silas finally found Charlie? Was Silas's death the result?

Please, no . . .

Her heart ached at the thought.

Aunt Catherine had given Ravinia a task as well: to find Catherine's daughter, Elizabeth, Ravinia's cousin, a woman Ravinia hadn't known existed. Elizabeth had been in danger—grave danger from Charlie, it seemed—and Aunt Catherine had needed her help.

Charlie. Declan Jr. *Beelzebub.*

Ravinia's muscles clenched at the thought of him. How could he be her own flesh and blood?

Remembering the meeting when Aunt Catherine had ordered Ravinia up the stairs to her room, where she'd laid out her task, caused the hairs along Ravinia's arms to lift.

Catherine held out the piece of paper to her, and Ravinia had taken it reluctantly, not sure what was coming. "What's this?"

"It's what I'd like you to do for me," said Catherine. "It's comforting to know that Silas appears to be helping us, but I can't take the chance. Declan Jr.'s too strong, and if he senses that there's someone vulnerable out there . . ." She pressed her hand to her mouth and shook her head. "I couldn't keep her. Not with Mary so dead set on me giving up Declan. I did as she asked, but fertility is one of our—assets."

"You had a baby," Ravinia realized in surprise.

"Elizabeth. I gave her away at birth, but now I want you to find

her." Ravinia took the piece of paper and read the name: Elizabeth Gaines. "She could be married now. This is the last information I have on her."

"I'm not sure how I'll find her, but if I do . . . ?"

"Let me know she's all right. And keep her safe."

Ravinia came out of her reverie to start the Camry and put the silver car in gear. She had time, but she didn't want to wait outside the hospital any longer. If she was early, she would just pull into the lot and sit there until others arrived.

She was still so boggled by seeing Silas's corpse she didn't notice another vehicle pulling out of the parking lot behind her, a small SUV following at a distance, tucked behind a faded red pickup.

As Ravinia drove down the long, tree-lined drive that led from the hospital, the gnarled and tortured pines blowing in the wind were the only witnesses to the small, gray SUV that kept Ravinia's silver Camry in its driver's sights.

So, this is Ravinia.

Lucky's eyes narrowed as she stared through the bug-spattered windshield.

The jealousy that sprang into her breast surprised her, an unwelcome emotion that had no place in her heart.

She bit down on her lower lip as the pickup separating the two vehicles turned onto a side road leading to a low-lying building housing clinics, but she kept her eyes straight ahead, on Ravinia Rutledge's Camry.

This Ravinia was the youngest of Mary's daughters. The one whose doggedness could be both a blessing and a curse. That damned doggedness better not get in her way. Lucky wasn't going to let it. No way.

She followed Ravinia in her newly acquired SUV with the stolen license plates. She couldn't tell you whose car it was, a nondescript Subaru Outback that she'd "inherited" from the thief who'd wrangled it away from a fellow miscreant who lived barely under the line of legality, just as she mostly did. She was wanted. That was true. Hunted. To be sure.

But she herself was a huntress, so those who sought her out could just wait until she was ready to be caught.

She set aside her jealousy with a bit of an effort, but the weight pressing on her still felt like a ten-ton gorilla was sitting on her chest. Her emotions were deep and ragged. Not just jealousy, but anger and sorrow.

And she knew who had to really pay for her sorrow. She just needed to find him.

As she held the wheel in a death grip, she inhaled and exhaled, thinking hard. She was going to have to switch license plates again. Soon. Being near Deception Bay was dangerous. Too dangerous. Too soon. She had so recently left her mark. She couldn't be caught before this last deadly mission was completed.

A small mew of pain passed her lips. From the corner of her eye, she caught a glimpse of the ocean, wide and ever-moving, beneath a sky of billowing, dark silver clouds. Her own thoughts were a swirl of emotion, seething and grim.

With all the power she possessed, she clamped down hard on her emotions. Anytime she let them gain control, she got herself into trouble. Hadn't she learned that over the years? Emotions were for the weak, and she had no time for weakness.

She had to be strong to find and destroy him. No one was going to stop her. Not the law, and certainly not Ravinia Rutledge. A private investigator now? That *girl*? Hah. If anyone was going to find him and send him to his maker, it wasn't going to be Ravinia.

"I'm coming for you," she whispered. Thinking his name in her mind. Not Declan Jr., the name he'd been christened with by his birth mother, because it was a lie. Not Henry Charles Woodworth, the name he'd been given when christened by his adoptive family, because it didn't say who he really was.

No, the name they'd all learned later, the name that represented him: Good Time Charlie.

"Charlie," she whispered.

Charlie . . .

CHAPTER 3

Detective Savannah Dunbar, her swollen belly preceding her, headed inside the back door of the Tillamook County Sheriff's Department. She was taking off her coat as she glanced to the hallway leading to the front of the building.

May Johnson, the heavyset, Black receptionist who you could hardly scare a smile out of, was peering down the hall to see who'd entered. At the sight of Savannah, her expression lightened. "Well, there you are," she said.

Savvy could scarcely hide her surprise. Though May liked Savannah well enough, she rarely looked so . . . *delighted*? Not a word Savvy usually associated with the dour receptionist.

"What are you doing here?" May asked, frowning. "Aren't you late for a funeral? And aren't you supposed to be on leave?"

Now that was the expression May usually wore, and Savannah felt the world right itself again. May had been with the department long before Savannah came on board, and for all her glowering, suspicious nature, everyone who worked at the TCSD felt the department could not run efficiently without her.

"Not late to the funeral yet, but getting there," said Savannah. "Officially on leave at the end of next week. You know that."

May's eyebrows drew together. "And when's that baby due?"

Savvy, though distracted and tense, almost smiled at May's demanding tone. This was her second pregnancy. During the first, when she'd been a surrogate for her sister and her sister's husband, everyone at TCSD, especially the men, had been so solicitous of her they'd nearly driven her crazy. Five years later, they hardly seemed to notice. They all expected her to leave the job, and, well, this time she probably would. Neville Rhodes had already been hired, and though no one had said it was to take her place, it basically was. If she decided to stay on after this baby's birth, there would probably be a juggling of personnel, but they'd been shorthanded for a while now, so she doubted it would be difficult.

But . . . this time the baby was hers. Hers and Hale's. Hale's first son had been with his first wife, Savvy's sister, Kristina, though Savannah had been the surrogate who had carried baby Declan to term. The tragedy was that during the pregnancy Kristina had been murdered. Savvy's heart grew cold at the thought. Years after Kristina's death and a long courtship, Savannah and Hale had finally tied the knot. Fertile as she was, Savvy had gotten pregnant soon after they had wed, and so, here she was, about to give birth again.

"'That baby' is still a few weeks away," said Savvy, fully aware that's what she'd said the last time she'd been pregnant, and it hadn't turned out to be the case. Baby Declan had arrived earlier than expected. And yes, now, during this pregnancy, those nagging Braxton Hicks contractions had been bothering her for weeks, just like last time she'd been carrying a baby.

She was having another boy. Her own, this time. Baby Declan, Hale's son, who was now five years old and great-grandson to Declan Bancroft Sr., whose funeral was almost upon her, would soon have a baby brother.

Theirs was a complicated family, made all the more so when Hale had insisted on naming his first son after his grandfather.

"You tell that baby not to be born in a car this time!" May yelled as a phone started ringing.

"Oh, he won't," assured Savvy. "Not taking any chances. Is Detective Rhodes here?"

May pointed toward the hall to Savvy's right. "Think I saw him head toward the break room." The phone on May's desk was still ringing. "Yeah, yeah, hold your horses," she said, scowling as she picked up.

"Thanks," Savvy called, but May had already started talking to the caller.

She headed down the short hall and pushed open the door to the break room, swinging it away from herself as she stepped inside. *Not taking any chances.* Her thoughts naturally turned from the baby to her husband and then her sister. Kristina had been killed by a man very much the way Declan Bancroft had recently died, in a house, by a blow to the head. But Kristina had been purposely assassinated, while the elder Declan's death was likely an accident. He'd fallen down the stairs at his own home and hit his head on the stone floor at the base of the steps. His funeral was today, and she was pushing the time if she didn't get a move on, but she needed to talk to Rhodes about the John Doe he'd found on the beach this morning, and she hadn't wanted to wait until after the funeral.

She glanced around the room, where two round tables stood vacant and the aroma of coffee from a half-full glass carafe warming in the coffeemaker filled the small space. A discarded newspaper littered one of the tables, where a couple of paper cups had also been abandoned. Walking to the alcove located behind a row of vending machines, she spied Rhodes.

"There you are," she said in relief.

He was hanging his coat in his locker. Looking over, he said, "Oh, hi," clearly surprised to see her. She tried not to be irritated. The whole department knew her maternity leave wasn't scheduled for another week, that Rhodes was transitioning into her job, so why was it that everyone thought she wouldn't come into the office? Though most treated her normally, some of the old-timers acted as if she was suddenly a porcelain doll, that she might break. She was pregnant, for God's sake, not incapacitated!

She felt more than a little sense of déjà vu.

Five years earlier, she'd taken some time off to take care of baby Declan, and she'd been juggling motherhood ever since. She still wasn't sure she wanted to go through all that again after this child was born.

"The body you found on the beach," she said, coming back to the here and now as she dropped her coat onto the long bench running between the rows of lockers. "You told Lang it had a note attached to it with Ravinia Rutledge's phone number?"

He nodded. "Word travels fast. The lab's got the note now."

Before Nev, Detective Langdon Stone had been Savvy's partner and still kind of was—at least for one more week, and maybe longer if she decided to return to the department after her leave.

"Ravinia didn't recognize him?" asked Savvy.

"That's what she said."

"But you didn't believe her?" she asked, seeing his hesitation.

"Not sure what to believe," he admitted.

"What did she say about the note?"

"Nothing."

"You questioned her?"

Rhodes sent her a look. "It's in my report."

She held up a hand, realizing she'd pushed too hard. "Can you tell me what he looked like? The John Doe? Do you have a picture of him? Is it uploaded to the department?"

"Not yet, but soon." After a moment, he added, "He was young. Mid to late twenties. White. Appeared in good shape, a little beat-up, maybe from the tides . . . but no physical signs of a struggle, no obvious wounds. No gunshot. No knife wounds . . . don't know the cause of death yet. We'll learn more from the autopsy."

"Hmmm." She was impatient, her mind spinning, old fears resurfacing. "Maybe I should stop by the morgue, but I'll have to do it later; otherwise, I'll be late." She glanced at her watch. "I probably shouldn't have even come in today, but I just had to get out of the house for a while." She was talking more than usual, her nerves getting the better of her.

"Late for Declan Bancroft's funeral," he guessed.

"Well, yeah. I should be there already. I should have gone straight to the chapel, I guess, but it was just . . ." It was just that Hale's mother, Janet, was such a piece of work. Savannah had tried to like the woman, had really, really tried, but all she'd managed was bare toleration. And she didn't want to deal with her today—or probably ever. "Just let me know when there's a picture of the John Doe," she said.

"You think you might know him?" Rhodes was regarding her intently.

"I don't know. I hope not. But this is a small town. Anything's possible." She smiled and shrugged. "Listen, I'm sorry I'm in such a rush. Thanks for the info."

Savannah had not only been waylaid on her way to the funeral because she wanted to avoid Janet, Hale's mother, but she also had needed to grab a bite to eat, and her curiosity had pushed her here to find out what Rhodes had learned about the John Doe. She'd left home, grabbed a muffin and decaf coffee at the Sands of Thyme bakery before landing here, searching for Rhodes and information.

Are you purposely trying to be late for this funeral?

She pushed that thought aside. Nothing good would come from the answer. And she had just enough time to get to the funeral home in Seaside if she floored it.

"Funerals," she said.

"Funerals," parroted Rhodes, his tone ironic.

It was then that she remembered that he'd gone to his friend Spencer Wharton's father's funeral. She didn't know the Whartons personally, but she knew the story of Spencer's death. It was part of the lore surrounding the inhabitants of Siren Song—the Colony, as they were sometimes called—and Echo Island, and she knew they blamed Neville Rhodes for their son's death. The Whartons had cold-shouldered the Rhodes family as a whole. Neville's parents had moved away, south, to somewhere in Arizona, the last Savannah had heard, though that could be old information. Rhodes too had left the area, gone off to college at Oregon State, away from Deception Bay, where news of the tragedy always followed him. As she understood it, he'd lived in the Willamette Valley for years, worked in Portland, migrated to Seaside a few years back, and now he was here at the TCSD.

"You went to Henry Wharton's service." She regarded him seriously, watching his expression.

"Yes, ma'am." He slammed his locker door shut and twisted the knob.

She didn't need to ask how the service had gone. Obviously, Rhodes didn't want to talk about it, and she understood.

Lang had told her that Candy Wharton had slapped Rhodes hard after the service, and she could make out the faint bruising on his left cheek beneath his stubble. It was a shame the Whartons were fixated on blaming Rhodes, when he and their son and another boy had all been in the boat together when it had been swamped and sunk. Rhodes was lucky to have survived, but she suspected he had been, and probably still was, plagued by survivor's guilt.

But the three of them were by far not the only adventurers who'd tried their luck at getting to Echo Island and the "crazy witch" who lived there, also according to local lore. Many had tried and failed.

Savannah glanced out the window to the gray day beyond. The sky was unsettling and overcast.

The crazy "witch" who had lived on the island had been Mary Rutledge, sometimes called Mary Beeman, depending on who you talked to. Mary's relationships, marriages, and children were as much of a mystery now as they'd been five years earlier.

Savannah rubbed her arms against a sudden chill.

She thought of Catherine, the matriarch of Siren Song. Catherine, aunt to the brood who lived there—Mary's children—had asked Savannah for a favor. She had wanted a DNA test on the faint traces of dried blood on a knife that, according to her, was likely to be that of Henry Charles Woodworth . . . a psychopath, if there ever was one . . . *Charlie* . . .

Savannah's heart jolted painfully at the thought of the madman who'd nearly killed her. Back then, against her own better judgment, she'd had the knife tested, but the blood hadn't been Charlie's. The stains on the blade were from an unknown woman, presumably Mary Rutledge Beeman, though that had never been proven, despite the fact that Charlie, during his vicious attack on Savannah, had sworn he'd killed the old woman.

And then Catherine had done an about-face. "She could have cut herself," she'd said, and without evidence to the contrary, Mary's remains had never been exhumed.

But now a body had apparently washed up on the shore . . . from Echo Island, and Ravinia Rutledge's phone number was written on a note pinned to it.

"Was his face burned?" she asked, thinking now about how Charlie's face had been pressed into the hot coals during their fight. She could still almost smell the stench of burning flesh, and her stomach seized. She had to take several deep breaths.

"Didn't seem like it," Rhodes answered slowly, his blue eyes holding hers. "I told you, no marks—"

"I know, yes. Thank you." But she'd had to know, though she didn't want to answer any of his questions. "I'll check on it after the funeral, but for now I've got to go." She glanced up at the large plain clock on the wall above the refrigerator, one hand ticking down the seconds. "I'm probably going to be late."

"It'll take a while to get to Seaside," he agreed. The drive on Highway 101 snaked along the coastline and cut through several small towns rife with speed traps. "An hour."

"Yeah. . . . Maybe I'll have to turn on my lights and siren," she said, and when she saw his sideways look, added, "Kidding. I'm kidding!" A Braxton Hicks clenched her tissues, and she drew a breath. Pushing through the swinging door, she glanced back at him. "Try not to let the Whartons get to you. It's not your fault they died and you didn't."

"Thanks," he said, but she was pretty sure he'd dismissed the sentiment.

She glanced at the clock one more time and groaned. She'd left Hale in the lurch, with hardly a backward glance. His mother, in from Philadelphia for the funeral, was a handful at the best of times. Savannah was trying hard to sympathize, because not only had Janet just lost her father, Declan Sr., whom she didn't seem to either understand or care for all that much, but she'd lost her second husband to a heart attack a few months earlier. Savvy wished she could feel sorry for her mother-in-law, offer condolences, but Janet . . . well, Hale's mildly spoken words about her said it all, "She's just a bitch, that's all."

Snagging her coat from the bench, she slid her arms through the sleeves and headed for her vehicle, hurrying down the back steps as best she could, given her ungainly body shape. She'd forgotten what it was like to have your center of gravity seem to shift, with the extra weight out in front, but it had all come crashing back to her now as a gust of cold air clutched at her hair. Tillamook was a few miles inland and rarely smelled of the sea, but today she thought she caught the briny odor over the scent that drifted through the town from the surrounding fields of cattle. She tossed a look at the sky as she climbed into her hybrid SUV. At least it wasn't raining yet.

Backing out of the parking space, she eased onto the main street, heading north to Seaside. Half the town would be at Declan's service. Maybe more than half. She'd liked Hale's irascible grandfather, and she certainly missed him, but she wasn't looking forward to all the folderol.

"Funerals," she said, echoing Neville Rhodes's sardonic tone.

Nev stared at his computer screen, blind to anything on it. Savannah's words still rang in his ears, and he wondered about her question about whether or not the corpse's face had been burned. She clearly had someone in mind.

Even though she'd only been gone half an hour, he'd been busy, checking with missing persons and on Ravinia Rutledge. Through a little Internet digging, he'd discovered she lived in Portland and was a private detective. When he searched Rutledge in the database, he'd also discovered that there were several who lived in the area; most had previous addresses in Deception Bay, and most had lived at least parts of their lives at Siren Song.

Were they all related to the mystery man he'd discovered on the beach just across the treacherous waters of the bay to Echo Island? Leaning back in his chair, he rubbed the stubble on his chin, then winced slightly when he touched the bruise left there, compliments of Candy Wharton.

Savannah clearly knew something more than he did about the John Doe, and if it had to do with Siren Song, the Colony women, or Ravinia Rutledge, he only had himself to blame for blocking out anything to do with the "cult" of people who had lived in the lodge across from Echo Island for most of his adult life.

Above the top of his computer screen, he saw Langdon Stone return to the squad room. Lang had been at his desk earlier but had gotten a call from his wife, Claire, and had stepped out of the squad room for a while to take it. Lang had then entered Sheriff Sean O'Halloran's office for a few minutes. Nev wondered what that was all about, but it well could be about the position of sheriff itself. O'Halloran was considering retirement from the department by not running in the next election, and he'd made it known that he wanted Langdon Stone to run for the office.

So far, Lang wasn't jumping at the opportunity.

Stone, tall, lean, tough-minded, but with a streak of humor that kept him from being too much of a Sergeant Joe Friday, caught Nev watching him. "Something going on?" he asked as he slid into his desk chair. "You see Savvy?"

"We talked in the break room a little while ago."

"I noticed her beeline back there. I told her about the body with the number pinned to it and that the number was Ravinia Rutledge's."

"I know."

"Savannah had a tough time with one of Mary Rutledge's sons a few years back. He damn near killed her. You know about that, too, right?"

Nev nodded slowly, thinking of Mary Rutledge, aka Mary Beeman, aka the witch of Echo Island. He knew about the psycho who'd attacked Savvy and killed one of TCSD's own, Fred Clausen. That killer had somehow been connected to the Siren Song cult and then seemed to vanish. There was no escaping all of the information about the Colony, even if you tried to actively avoid it, as Nev had.

"If you find anything else on the John Doe, tell me or Savvy."

"I will," assured Nev.

"If that body connects any way back to Charlie, we all need to know." He was dead serious.

"You think it does?"

"Maybe. With Charlie, you never know."

"You call him Charlie?" Nev wasn't eager to expose how little he recalled about the particulars of the attack on Savannah and Clausen, but now he needed to know. For years, he'd avoided listening to anything that had to do with Siren Song, or Echo Island, or the woman who'd lived there because it had just been too damned painful. Now his lack of interest and information was hindering him.

Lang snorted. "That bastard has so many names it's hard to keep them straight. His adoptive name was Henry Charles Woodworth, but he goes by Charlie or sometimes Declan Jr."

"Declan—as in—?"

"Declan Bancroft Sr., Hale St. Cloud's grandfather. He's not really a senior, but everyone calls him that."

"The guy they're burying today."

"That's the one. Charlie sometimes refers to himself as Declan Jr." Lang's phone buzzed; he glanced down at it, but didn't pick up. "The way I understand it, Charlie was adopted out. His new parents re-named him, but he thinks he's Declan Bancroft's son, and, as I said, even calls himself Declan Jr., or at least he did. Savannah tried to rea-son with the son of a bitch—as if anyone could. She told him that it wasn't true, just a lie perpetrated by Charlie's mother, but he wasn't listening. Then he disappeared after attacking her and killing Clausen, so who knows what he thinks now. I'd sure like to get my hands on him."

"He vanished after the attack at Bancroft Bluffs." Nev tried to sound like he wasn't fishing, even though he was.

"Savvy nearly went over the cliff there, before that big chunk of it fell into the ocean, that is. And Fred Clausen . . ." Lang's face grew grim, and there was a long pause as he remembered the older detec-tive who'd been shot and killed by Charlie.

"Was he burned somehow?" Nev finally asked as Lang grew quiet. "Charlie?"

"So, you know," said Lang.

"Only because Savannah asked if the body on the beach had been burned. I just wondered."

"Ah, yes. She'd want to know if we'd learned Charlie was really dead. She said that part of his face was badly burned. But still, he somehow disappeared." Lang shook his head. "You'd think that if he'd survived, someone would have seen him, noticed he was disfig-ured, and the way gossip flows through Deception Bay, we would have heard about it, but it's been five years, and nothing."

"Maybe he is dead."

"One can only hope."

The back door opened, and a couple of cops in uniform walked in, heading straight toward the break room.

Nev said, "The new John Doe's face wasn't burned at all."

Lang exhaled. "Not Charlie, then. Too bad. None of us want to tan-gle with him again, but if that son of a bitch is still out there, we need to nail him. There's no chance he's improved over the last years. He isn't made that way. It would be nice to know he was six feet under, but his body hasn't shown up, and this guy in the morgue doesn't sound like him."

"We should have pictures of the John Doe soon," Nev said. "I don't know why we don't yet, but I just checked the computer. Nothing. Maybe a glitch in the system." He should've taken some with his phone when he had the chance.

Lang glanced at his watch. "Sometimes it takes a while."

"Maybe, but Savannah's not waiting. She said she was going to check on the body after Declan Bancroft's funeral."

Lang grunted an acknowledgment, then said, "Her . . . grandfather-in-law's funeral, if that's even a term." He glanced down at his computer. "What time was it supposed to start?"

"She didn't say. Just that she was probably going to be late."

"The Bancrofts will wait for her," Lang predicted. "She's the glue in that family, since she married Hale. Without Declan Sr., it's just Hale and Savannah, their son, Declan, and the new baby on the way. Well, there's Hale's mother, Janet, but she's pretty much out of the picture. Lives back east."

"Their son's named Declan too?"

"I know. Named after Declan Sr., Hale's grandfather, the kid's great-grandfather."

Nev processed that.

"A lot of Declans, I know. Although really only two, because there is no Declan Jr. according to Savvy and Catherine of the Gates. Catherine Rutledge," he explained. Lang ran his hands through his hair and sighed. "You should talk to Savannah. She knows the ins and outs of that family more than I do." He thought for a moment. "But here's something else you should probably know before that talk." He then sketched out the story that Savannah's sister, Kristina, had been Hale's first wife; she'd become one of Charlie's victims during his rampage in Deception Bay five years earlier. Savannah had been pregnant at the time, surrogate for Hale and Kristina's baby. Hale was working closely with his grandfather then, and he and Declan Sr. had put Bancroft Development on the map.

Nev's mind wandered a bit as he thought about where he'd been when Charlie was terrorizing Deception Bay. He'd just started with the Seaside Police and had been on the force when Kristina St. Cloud, Savvy's sister, was killed.

"Why does Charlie think he's Declan Jr.?"

"Because his mother, Mary Rutledge Beeman, told him he was."

The crazy woman on the island. The one who'd cut off a hank of her hair for Spence. The one he was certain had wanted to fuck him, or had that been all male bravado, Spencer's machismo talking? After all, no lock of the witch's hair had ever been found.

Had it been lost in that roiling sea?

Or had it all been a figment of Spence's imagination?

Or a flat-out lie.

They'd never know.

Lang was still trying to explain it all, and Nev had to shake back the memories of Spence and Duncan and Echo Island from his brain to keep up. ". . . Mary wanted her sister, Catherine, who was in love with Declan Sr., to think he'd been unfaithful to her. Mary apparently wanted to break up that affair, so she said she'd slept with Declan Sr. and Charlie was his son."

"Could that be true?"

"Catherine told Savannah it was a lie, so I'm going with that. Like I said, talk to Savannah. She knows the most about them."

May had left her desk and was standing next to the printer, which was noisily pushing out paper. The two men paused and glanced her way, and she, in turn, gave them a look, narrowing her eyes as if trying to discern if they were actually working.

Lang pretended to frantically type on his computer, and she sent him a faint smile before gathering up the papers spit out by the printer and returning to her desk. Lang then looked back at Nev. "Supposedly Mary could lure men to her by some unknown means. Don't know if that's true. What is true is that she had a number of lovers. But, again, according to Savvy, it was Catherine who had the affair with Bancroft, not Mary. Catherine had Bancroft's second daughter, Elizabeth, whom she gave up for adoption because Mary was descending into madness and Catherine was scared she would harm her baby. After Elizabeth was adopted out, Catherine stayed, taking care of all of Mary's offspring as she grew worse. Then five years ago, Charlie threatened everyone. Catherine wanted to find Elizabeth and make sure she was safe. It was Ravinia who went on a hunt for her and found her in southern California."

"Bancroft died from a fall?"

"Hematoma. Head injury after falling down some steps. He was in his eighties and apparently tried to go upstairs and slipped."

Nev had heard about Bancroft but wanted clarification. It killed him to realize how much he'd missed now that he felt compelled to know everything about Ravinia. She'd whetted his appetite to know everything, maybe with that hit to his heart? Damn, but his need now was almost like . . . desire.

What did she do to you?

"I'll try to catch up with Savannah later," he said.

"Yeah. She's got her hands full with the Bancroft funeral."

"She mentioned something about Hale's mother," said Nev.

"Janet Bancroft St. Cloud . . . can't remember her second husband's name—wait, Spurrier, I think. Lee Spurrier. That's it. He died recently, I understand."

A lot of deaths, Nev thought, as the image of the John Doe's face swam to his consciousness.

Lang's phone rang again, and this time he took the call, then, holding his phone to his ear, he headed for the break room, and Nev went back to his computer and email, looking for the pictures of the John Doe, which should have been uploaded. Was Ravinia the dead man's next of kin? Was he her brother? Cousin? Or . . . husband? He didn't like that particular thought and gave himself a swift mental kick. She said she didn't know him, so he should believe her.

You know better. She lied. Don't kid yourself.

More cops came and went, some hauling suspects, others alone.

May handled a couple of people who'd wandered in with questions, while catching all the non-emergency phone calls that came into the department, and Nev read a report on a drowning victim, the captain of a small fishing boat that had capsized while crossing the bar at Tillamook Bay. The Coast Guard had handled the rescue, but it had been too late, and the captain had died from hypothermia and a heart attack, compliments of the frigid ocean.

Still nothing new in the missing persons reports up and down the coast. Not one missing person that fit the John Doe's description.

When Lang returned to his desk with a cup of coffee, Nev asked, "How well do you know Ravinia Rutledge?"

"Not well. Like I said, most of my dealings have been with Catherine. Savannah knows Ravinia best." He smiled faintly as he sat in his chair. "You're the one who grew up around here, Rhodes. I'm the newbie, in a manner of speaking. You should know more than I do."

Langdon Stone had been with TCSD for years, but essentially he was right: he'd moved to Tillamook County for the job, while Neville had grown up here.

"Been gone a long time," said Nev. "Since my friends didn't make it back from Echo Island. Just thought it was best if I left."

Lang made a noise of understanding, then touched his own left cheek and said, "Heard what Candy Wharton did to you yesterday. You okay?"

"Putting it all behind me."

Lang looked skeptical but didn't offer anything further.

"I'm trying to catch up on the Colony," admitted Nev. "I'm late to the party because of my boat accident. Didn't want to know anything about any of them."

"But now you want to know about Ravinia." He phrased it more as a statement than a question, which irked Nev, even though it was the truth.

"She opened the door, in a way."

Lang smiled faintly. But he didn't press Nev further, just launched into more information about Siren Song, specifically Mary and her lovers, and how it seemed unlikely the girls, Mary's children, even knew who their fathers were, how Catherine had locked the gates after Mary grew mentally ill, and how just recently things were changing, in no small part due to Ravinia's influence.

He finished with, "Years ago, Catherine told everyone Mary was dead, but she apparently exiled her sister out on that godforsaken island. Maybe for good reason, maybe not. You never actually made it there, did you?"

Nev was saved from answering as the sheriff stuck his head out of his office and called Lang back into his office.

I did make it to the island, but it was Spence who encountered Mary Rutledge and then came racing back, sliding down the hillside into the boat, dislodging pebbles and small stones that rained down on us like artillery fire as we scrambled to get away from the island.

Once again, Nev saw Spence hanging onto the boat's hull with his diminishing strength. And he remembered waiting outside the hospital in those dark days afterward, even though Henry and Candy wanted him nowhere near their son, especially as Spence entered the arms of death.

CHAPTER 4

Ravinia parked in the north lot of Seaview Funeral Chapel and eyed the building, which neither had a sea view nor was much of a chapel. It was utilitarian, painted brown, a concrete building flanked by two large Douglas firs and with a wide wooden porch that wrapped around three sides. The chapel had been built to withstand the elements, Ravinia guessed, as she'd never been to it before. In actual fact, she and most of her sisters had led such extremely sheltered lives for most of their lives that this was her first funeral, and probably theirs as well. Aunt Catherine, fearing dangers from all sides, had locked the doors and kept them all inside. She'd forced an antiquated fashion on them straight out of the nineteenth century, which Ravinia had particularly resented. It wasn't until the events five years earlier that Ravinia had even owned a pair of pants, those first pairs sewn by Ophelia, who, like Ravinia, had escaped Siren Song Lodge's gates.

It was a testament to how much things had changed that they were attending Declan Bancroft's funeral, most of them anyway. Ravinia wasn't quite sure whom she would see when she walked inside, how many of her sisters. Aunt Catherine had reluctantly opened the gates five years earlier, when she'd confessed her fears for her own daughter's safety, and more freedoms were enjoyed by all her sisters, not just Ravinia.

She watched as people started gathering, walking along a pretty, curving flagstone path, a refreshing architectural touch leading to the porch and inviting people inside.

She stayed in her Camry, hunkering down in the driver's seat, needing a few minutes to herself. She'd been rushing all day and had been running on adrenaline and anxiety, first about the funeral in general and now about Silas. *Silas.* She couldn't get his face, his unseeing eyes, out of her mind.

He was the one who was supposed to find Charlie. He was the one who was supposed to stop him, neutralize him, *kill* him. Not that Silas had ever really said that was his aim. It had just been understood by Aunt Catherine and therefore all the rest of her sisters too. Silas had brought the papers back from the island, and he'd burned the bones of Charlie's father.

The devil who gave me D.

Ravinia grimaced. "D" as in Declan Jr., aka Charlie. Mary had written those words in her journal. Eventually, the book that had been hidden away at Siren Song had been found, and Ravinia had read a number of the private passages, taking note of the pages that gave tantalizing clues to the identity of her and her sisters' fathers, although there were still more questions than answers.

She still didn't know all the particulars, but she did know who Charlie's father was. Aunt Catherine had deigned to let that information out, as she also had the fact that Declan Bancroft Sr. was Elizabeth's father. Maybe Catherine knew who the rest of their fathers were; maybe she didn't. Maybe no one did.

Now, of course, there were heredity tests.

She saw the first drops of rain spatter against the windshield. Sometimes she wondered why she had the urge, the drive, to find out all she could about her family when so much of the truth was damaging. The worst she'd learned so far was that Charlie's father was not Declan Bancroft, the man being interred today. No, Charlie's biological sire was Thomas Durant, as evil a man as had ever walked the earth. Ravinia's skin prickled at what she'd heard of Durant, the monster who'd also been Mary's father, making Charlie's father also his grandfather.

Bile rose in her throat at the thought of the incest.

Mary, at first, hadn't realized Durant was her father, as he'd left when she was too young to remember him and had returned during her sexual heyday. Who knew who had seduced whom, but the result was that he'd fathered Charlie—a monster siring another monster—and the distillation of their particular genetic code seemed to have intensified Charlie's "gift," and not for the better.

Thankfully, Durant was long dead. Killed by Mary herself as he was attempting to rape Catherine. Mary had saved her sister and murdered her father/lover, and Silas—Oh, God, Silas . . . Her thoughts splintered for a moment, and she had to push aside her emotions . . . Silas had been given the task of taking Durant's bones to Echo Island and burning them. Aunt Catherine had insisted on this course of action, as she'd said it was the only way to insure that Durant, whom she was certain was pure evil, would not rise from the dead. She firmly believed burning Durant's bones was akin to the searing of the neck of the Hydra in ancient myth and would prevent the man from being resurrected.

Well . . . *maybe* . . .

Many people thought Catherine Rutledge was crazy, and Ravinia had to admit that burning Durant's bones to make sure he was really dead was out there. But her aunt was so often right about things that Ravinia knew better than to question her. She was well aware that she and her sisters had abilities that were more far-reaching than those of other people. Hadn't she used her own "gift" just this morning to look into the depths of Detective Neville Rhodes's soul? And she knew Charlie was the devil incarnate, an amoral monster who fed off the misery of others.

And Silas. What had happened to him? He'd done Catherine's bidding, taken the myth of the Hydra and performed it as a modern-day remedy, even though Durant was long dead and gone and only bones.

If Charlie had anything to do with Silas's death, I'll kill him myself.

She pressed her lips together with grim determination. Good Time Charlie. Her half brother. Someone she'd never met.

Yet.

Ravinia stirred in her seat, watching mourners begin to gather and walk up the steps of the funeral home. She had a moment of disbelief as she watched Aunt Catherine, relying heavily on the arms of Ravinia's sisters Ophelia and Cassandra, slowly working her way inside, other mourners stacking up behind her slow progress.

So old! Ravinia thought, taking in her aunt's gray and white hair, the bent body, the painfully careful steps. When was the last time she'd seen her? A few months ago was all, wasn't it?

More like a year . . . or longer, Ravinia!

Could that be?

But oh, how her aunt had aged since she'd last seen her, when-ever it was.

And Ophelia seemed much older too. There was something dif-ferent about her too, something Ravinia couldn't put her finger on. Ophelia's blond hair was swept into a chignon offering a view of her regal neck, all above a plain black dress that reached her knees.

Cassandra looked pretty much the same, though she too had grown older. Her lighter hair was pulled away from her face and clipped at her crown. In the past, Cassandra had always seemed younger than Ravinia, even though she was older, but now . . .

What had happened?

And where was Isadora, the sister who'd always fashioned herself after Catherine's schoolmarmish ways? Had she stayed at Siren Song with Lillibeth, the sister closest to Ravinia's age? Lillibeth had been wheelchair-bound most of her life and had rarely left the lodge. She too had always seemed immature for her chronological age, and being locked away at the lodge hadn't helped.

Ravinia felt a swelling in her chest of what? Longing? These were the women she'd grown up with. And yet . . . she was angry with them too. For living in a different time, for accepting Aunt Cather-ine's decree and, in Isadora's case, almost glorying in it.

"Well, hell," she muttered as she climbed out of the car. She was glad she'd gotten away from the cloistered walls.

The wind snatched at her hair, and she congratulated herself on scraping it into a bun, although there was a good chance it would come undone if she didn't get inside soon. Cold blasts seemed to hit her from all sides, raindrops still falling from the leaden sky. Bending her head and placing a hand over her hair, she hurried along the path and up the steps to the porch.

Once inside, she caught a glimpse of her family, clustered in a far corner of the wide anteroom. People were gathered outside the chapel in small groups, their conversations a hushed buzz that didn't quite drown out the soft music piped through hidden speakers.

Ravinia passed double doors flung wide to the chapel, where semicircular rows of chairs had been placed around a central dais, with a white lectern at its center. A velvet rope kept the mourners at bay until the service. Massive bouquets of white flowers were arranged in enormous white pots and lined either side of the outer walls, while a spray of lilies and roses draped the top of the polished mahogany coffin, nearly covering it. Thankfully, the coffin was closed. Though she'd never been to a funeral before, she'd heard tales of open coffins and seeing the dead person lying supposedly peacefully within. She'd seen one dead body today. She didn't feel like seeing another. And though she was pretty sure Declan Bancroft's corpse would behave, her fertile imagination touched on others she wasn't so sure would stay dead. Not Silas, she thought with a pang of remembrance. But if she ever saw Charlie in a coffin—and she fervently hoped that day would come soon—she wouldn't completely trust that he would remain dead. He seemed to be able to defy the laws of nature and life. Why not defy the laws governing death too?

Easing through the crowd, she caught up with Ophelia and Cassandra. There was no sign of her aunt. "Where's Aunt Catherine?" she asked Ophelia.

Ophelia was taller than Ravinia but had similar features, her eyes as blue, her hair paler than Ravinia's darker shade.

Cassandra spoke up. "She wanted to talk to Mr. St. Cloud alone. They're back there." She inclined her head toward the double doors at the back of the anteroom.

Ophelia fiddled with the sleeve of her dress and said, "Aunt Catherine's not doing well."

No kidding. "What happened?" Ravinia asked, glancing at the closed doors.

"She's just having a hard time adjusting to all of this." Ophelia motioned with a hand to include the funeral and mourners all collecting outside the chapel.

"He was the love of her life, and now he's gone." Cassandra sighed.

Declan Sr. . . . Elizabeth's father . . . Catherine's one love.

Cassandra, a romantic at heart like Lillibeth, was smack-dab in the middle of her lodge sisters' birth lineup: Isadora, Ophelia, Cassandra, Lillibeth, and Ravinia. She'd been christened Maggie at birth, but when it became clear she could sense the future, their mother had changed her name to Cassandra, the seer from Greek mythology, and instructed everyone to call her Cassandra from that day forward, which they had done. Ravinia, being younger, had never known her as anything but Cassandra, and when Cassandra had tried to get everyone to revert back to Maggie, having a love/hate relationship with her own "gift of sight," it hadn't taken. Ravinia had warned her in advance that she would never be able to switch names at this late date.

Now Cassandra looked at Ravinia through those wide blue eyes, with their slightly enlarged pupils. The effect made her seem younger, and it was hard to take her seriously sometimes, especially her predictions, which was exactly the nature of mythical Cassandra's curse: the ability to see the future but have no one ever believe you.

"It's Lillibeth's dreams too," reminded Cassandra.

Ophelia sighed, long-suffering. "It's not Lillibeth's dreams. Catherine knows they're not real."

"What dreams?" asked Ravinia.

She was looking toward the two doors, willing Aunt Catherine to appear. She wanted to tell her about Silas, but she needed to find a way to catch her alone. Ophelia had a way of sweeping in and usurping information that Ravinia sometimes wanted to keep between herself and her aunt. "What dreams?" repeated Ravinia.

"Lillibeth is having romantic dreams about some fictional guy, like a hero in one of those historical novels," said Cassandra, shooting Ophelia a dark look. "Seventeenth-century stuff."

"Really? Like the same guy?" asked Ravinia.

"She's been reading romantic novels," said Ophelia shortly.

"Well, good for her," said Ravinia, faintly amused. At least somebody in the lodge was living a life, even if it was vicariously.

"She woke up screaming again last night," Ophelia informed her smartly. "We all ran down the stairs, except Catherine, who's been sleeping downstairs in the main room. Which is another story. We need another bedroom on the first floor or a lift or something. She can't just lie on the couch. It's not good for her."

"She wakes up screaming from romantic dreams?" questioned Ravinia.

"She does it all the time," snapped Ophelia, clearly wanting a change of subject.

"Not all the time," Cassandra corrected. "Just sometimes. It's frightening to her, sometimes. But this man is real to her." Cassandra appealed to Ravinia. "It's a real romance, but something's gone wrong. It's a warning."

"Don't play into her fantasies, Cassandra. It's not good for her, or you, or any of us. Lillibeth retreats into fantasy as a means of coping with being trapped inside a cell of her own making, but we don't have to be part of it." Ophelia turned to Ravinia as well, looking for an ally. "It's not healthy. She should be here today with us, supporting Catherine and Elizabeth and Chloe, but she won't leave her room."

"She's waiting for another message," said Cassandra.

"Well, it's a not a *real* romance," Ravinia reminded them carefully, stepping closer to her sisters to allow an elderly woman who was leaning heavily on a cane to pass by.

"It is real. It's the past and the future. That's what she said," Cassandra insisted.

Ophelia made a sound of exasperation. "Lillibeth says a lot of things, but she's just covering up that she had a nightmare and got us all downstairs in a panic. That's why Aunt Catherine's on the couch. She was struggling to get up and slipped. She can barely walk because she wrenched her back."

"How would you know?" Cassandra asked pointedly. "You're not home all the time, are you? You don't really know what's going on. I'm telling you, Lillibeth is seeing something. Something *real*." She glanced at Ravinia, her color high. "I've seen a little of it too."

"Oh, please. You're just saying that." Ophelia glared at her.

"Maybe it's a little of both, like reality blended with fantasy," Ravinia intervened. It was odd that she was in the position of peacekeeper. Normally she was the one making waves. But life at Siren Song had apparently changed.

"*All* fantasy," Ophelia stressed. "We are not in Salem, Massachusetts, and this is not the damned witch trials!"

"Where did that come from?" asked Ravinia.

"Lillibeth thinks this all started there. Her lover and his other woman, the witch, and the fire and the baby, I don't know. It's always some version of that."

Cassandra shot Ophelia a hard glance, before turning to Ravinia. "You should talk to Lillibeth," Cassandra implored Ravinia.

"About her dreams?" Ravinia wasn't sure about that.

"Just see her." Cassandra said. "It's been a while. It might do her good. Come to the lodge after the funeral."

"Well, I do want to talk to Aunt Catherine . . ." she admitted. But this was just the kind of drama Ravinia sought to avoid. She looked around the room. More people had joined the throng and were milling around the anteroom, but Aunt Catherine was still behind a closed door.

"We'll all be at Siren Song later," Ophelia said in a half-hearted invitation.

People shuffled behind Ravinia, so she and her sisters moved toward a small alcove with a window that looked out to the grounds, where the flagstone path, now wet with serious rain, wound through a few trees. Mourners were continuing to enter the building, some with umbrellas, others shaking water from their coats, the hum of conversation now drowning out the soft music.

Ravinia said, "You mentioned Elizabeth and Chloe. Are they here?" Ravinia had bonded with Elizabeth's daughter, Chloe, five years earlier. Now Chloe was ten, possibly eleven. Ravinia wasn't sure when Chloe's birthday was, and mentally kicked herself. She and the girl had connected, but then Ravinia hadn't made any effort to keep in touch.

"They're here," Ophelia said with a hitch of her chin toward the far side of the room. "In a room with Hale and Janet, the whole family. I think there's a reading of the will later. Aunt Catherine's part of that too. Probably what they're talking about now." She slid a glance up and down Ravinia's body. "I see you're in pants."

"Always." Ravinia looked down at her palazzo pants; the billowy black fabric had been no proof against the wind, pressing hard against her legs but offering little heat.

"They're cool," said Cassandra. She, like Ophelia, was wearing a straight black dress that hit the middle of her knees. No long, printed cotton gowns anymore, thank God, though the dresses' style was a little out of date. "Isadora would have worn stiff, black satin with white lace around a high-necked collar and a cameo around her neck."

"Bullshit. She doesn't have a cameo," disagreed Ophelia.

"Oh, yes she does. Aunt Catherine gave it to her."

"She appropriated it from our mother's things," corrected Ophelia. "Catherine would like Isadora to join the world of today, but she did her job too well, and now Isadora doesn't like leaving the lodge, so she's happy to stay with Lillibeth." She glanced impatiently at her watch. "What's the holdup?"

"Got somewhere else you'd rather be?" asked Cassandra.

"Anywhere." Ophelia glanced to the doors leading to the chapel. Still roped off.

"Patience is a virtue," Cassandra said piously, and Ravinia decided to turn the conversation again, even though she too was thinking it was time to get the show on the road. "How is Lillibeth physically?"

The weakest of their clan, Lillibeth had always lived in her own world, where she clung to childhood rather than reach for adulthood.

"Pretty much the same," said Cassandra. "Isadora too. Ophelia, tell Ravinia what happened when you tried to take Isadora out to get her nails done."

Ravinia turned to Ophelia, really curious.

"It went about like you'd expect," Ophelia answered the unasked question. She looked down at her own pink-painted toenails peeking out from a pair of opened-toed black pumps. "She wouldn't even get in the car."

"Isadora's good to Lillibeth, though," Cassandra said loyally. "And Lillibeth needs her."

"Lillibeth needs to get out of her room and away from those dreams," Ophelia stated firmly. "Maybe away from Isadora and Catherine mother-henning her too. She'll never grow up if they don't let her." She glanced at Ravinia. "Maybe then she wouldn't have all these stupid dreams."

"I don't care what you say. Lillibeth's dreams have meaning."

Ophelia glanced out the window, scowled at the dark sky. "She probably just wants to get laid."

"Ophelia!" Cassandra gaped at her in astonishment.

Ravinia too was startled by her older sister's comment, so far removed from everything they'd learned growing up.

"Well, don't you think so?" Ophelia bristled. "She's been locked in that wheelchair all her life, like we've been locked in that lodge. It's not natural. It's time to get out and live the rest of our lives. Find people to love. To marry. Or just have an affair with. I don't care. It's past time, really. And Isadora should know that too. Sex is what keeps the species going, and we should all go out there and get some before it's too late!"

"Wow," said Ravinia. Now here was a new side to her sister.

Cassandra was staring at Ophelia in open-mouth disbelief. "You're having an affair," she declared.

Ophelia laughed. "Are you trying to look into my future?"

"I don't have to. It's pretty clear on its own."

Ravinia glanced from one sister to the other, slightly uneasy. She herself was still a virgin and kind of intended to stay that way. Not that she didn't find men attractive, but they just weren't trustworthy, in her opinion. Okay, there was Rex Kingston, Joel Rex Kingston, to be exact, the California PI who was now Elizabeth's fiancé, a trustworthy, good guy.

So there was one.

"You're seeing someone special," Cassandra accused Ophelia.

"I'm dating," Ophelia admitted. "That's all. Just dating. Nothing you have to see. It's just a fact that I have my own apartment now, and therefore a life."

Cassandra shook her head. "You're so militant these days, Phee."

"I just feel the waste of a lot of years, that's all."

Ophelia had used the last five years to become a nurse at Ocean Park Hospital. Ravinia wanted to tell her she'd just been to Ocean Park herself; it was on the tip of her tongue. But then she would have to explain about Silas, and she wasn't ready for that.

Now Cassandra turned from Ophelia to look at Ravinia, frowning. "What's wrong?"

"Nothing," Ravinia lied and hoped Cassandra wasn't trying to look deeper inside to possibly probe her psyche.

"You're worried about something," Cassandra accused.

"Aren't we all? And don't try using your powers on me," said

Ravinia, waving her hands in front of Cassandra's face as if to ward off a hex, smiling to let her know she was half-joking, emphasis on the *half*.

"It's something about the family. One of our sisters?"

Ravinia's smile dropped. She didn't want Cassandra learning about Silas before she was ready to tell all.

"It's one of our sisters, or maybe . . . brothers?"

Ravinia felt herself tingle all over at Cassandra's accuracy, but she was saved from a response when Detective Savannah Dunbar strode in from outside. Ravinia needed to talk to the detective, but she had a sketchy relationship with law enforcement officers of all stripes. Her meeting with Detective Rhodes was fresh in her mind, but here was the woman detective who'd nearly died at Charlie's hands five years earlier. Savannah knew Charlie as well as anyone, and better than most, but Ravinia was still leery about sharing information with anyone, least of all an officer of the law. She certainly probed for information herself, but was stingy about giving it out.

"It's a girl," said Cassandra into the suspended moment. She too had caught sight of the pregnant detective.

"It's a boy," corrected Savannah as she approached and gave a nod to Ravinia. She looked around at the knots of people with relief and said, "Good. No one's seated yet. I thought I'd be way late. Do you know where Hale is?"

"They're all in another room," said Ophelia, indicating the door in the back, still shut tight. "We're waiting for Catherine."

"I'll check it out." She met Ravinia's eyes before working her way through the crowd to the rear door, her auburn hair catching fire under the lights of the anteroom. Clearly, she had something she wanted to say to Ravinia, but now was not the moment. Immediately, Ravinia rethought seeking her out. She didn't want to talk to the detective about Silas yet, either, and she knew, without Cassandra's powers of prediction, that's what the detective would want to do.

CHAPTER 5

Once Savannah was through the back door and had shut it behind her, Ophelia muttered, "Let's get this over with."

Ravinia gave her older sister a sharp look. There was a restlessness about her that was new. "Do you have somewhere to be?"

"Not really. I just wonder what's keeping them all. We've been standing here a while."

As if hearing her, one of the back doors opened, and Savannah walked into Ravinia's sight line again. Now she was accompanied by a tall, dark-haired man whose head was cocked, listening to whatever she was saying. Hale St. Cloud. Savannah's husband. Ravinia had never actually met the man, but it was an educated guess.

Another woman was with them too. Someone closer to Aunt Catherine's age. She wore a black netted hat with a wide brim, perched at a jaunty angle on her head. Likely Hale's mother and the deceased man's daughter, Janet Bancroft St. Cloud Something-or-Other. Ravinia had never seen her before either, as she lived somewhere in the east—Philadelphia, she thought.

Janet's hair was slicked back into a tight bun, one that wasn't going to be decimated by any damn wind, like Ravinia's bun or Ophelia's chignon, thank you very much. Its flat black color absorbed light, seemed to swallow it up. Janet had been her mother's rival, back in the day. They'd gone after the same men, apparently, and Mary, with her special gifts, had won the day more often than not. Hale's father, Preston St. Cloud, had apparently been swept away by Mary, and Janet had divorced him in record speed when she found out. Janet had remarried soon afterward and moved away, and Preston had since died.

Elizabeth stepped through the back door. Ravinia spied the crown of her blond head above a white-haired, stooped gentleman who stood in front of her, undoubtedly a contemporary of Declan Sr.

Elizabeth was clearly waiting for someone, and Ravinia was wondering if it was Aunt Catherine, when Elizabeth's daughter, Chloe, who'd apparently zigged and zagged her way through the crowd, burst into view right in front of her.

"Ravinia!" the girl cried in delight, throwing herself into her arms, causing Ravinia to stagger back a step.

"Chloe, my God, you've gotten big!"

"You don't come see us anymore," the girl accused, slowly releasing her grip on Ravinia.

"I was down in Newport Beach last . . . year . . ."

"A *year*." Chloe gave her the evil eye.

It did come as a bit of a surprise that it had also been over a year since she'd been to southern California.

"You're coming to the wedding," Chloe said in a tone that brooked no argument.

"Your mom and Rex are getting married?"

"Well . . . someday . . ."

"Hi, Chloe," said Ophelia, and Cassandra echoed the same. Chloe looked around at Ravinia's sisters and tucked in her chin as she whispered a quick "Hi." They were basically strangers to her.

"Rex didn't come with you?" Ravinia asked.

"He was going to, but Mom said it was okay if he stayed. He's got lots to do. And we're only going to be here a little while anyway." Chloe's lips broke into a wide smile. "We came on an airplane!"

"You're one up on me," said Ophelia, and Cassandra murmured an agreement. Ravinia too had not been on a plane. Her work was centered around Portland, and she rarely drove out of state, even though the Washington border was just north of Oregon's biggest city, across the Interstate Bridge from Portland's northern limits.

Chloe tugged on Ravinia's hand, pulling her away from her sisters and into the crowd of milling mourners. Ravinia allowed herself to be led. She understood that Chloe felt like a fish out of water. She'd felt much the same way during all those years at Siren Song.

"What about the wolf?" Chloe whispered when she was convinced they were out of earshot of anyone they knew.

Ravinia felt a pang of regret. She tried not to think of the wolf that had tracked with her on her trip to California and back. The wolf was real to Chloe, and it was real to Ravinia, but it was an apparition to some, maybe to most, though it certainly had manifested itself enough times to be *something* even to the disbelievers. It had been Ravinia's companion throughout her trip to find Elizabeth. Ravinia had often thought it was her brother Silas in wolf form. *Silas* . . . she remembered again with another gut punch.

"What's wrong?" Chloe demanded, aware of Ravinia's mood shift.

"Nothing."

"*Something's* wrong," Chloe argued. She'd always been way too attuned to Ravinia's feelings and sometimes her inner thoughts, a connection Ravinia didn't share with anyone else.

"I haven't seen the wolf in years. I told you that."

"You *still* haven't seen it?"

Ravinia shook her head, and Chloe's shoulders slumped in dejection. Ravinia suggested, "Maybe it was here to help us when we needed it, but now it's moved on—"

"Don't say that!" Chloe declared in a harsh whisper that turned a few heads. "Don't ever say that!"

"I feel bad too, Chloe."

The girl regarded her through slitted eyes, her expression doubtful. But Ravinia was telling the truth. Whatever it was, ghost, shared wish with Chloe, actual wolf . . . it had been missing for years. Gone. And Ravinia had no means to bring it back.

She spied Elizabeth again, or at least her crown of blond hair, as she wove through the other mourners and headed toward the alcove where Ophelia and Cassandra were still in deep discussion.

"Let's talk to your mom," Ravinia said, wending her way past a table where people were picking up funeral pamphlets or signing the "celebration of life" guest book. She reached her sisters about the same time Elizabeth did. Elizabeth wasn't alone. She'd been helping someone along, and that someone was Aunt Catherine, bent over a cane.

Ravinia felt a distinct shock. What had happened to her so recently vibrant aunt? Catherine appeared twenty years older than she actually was. A contemporary of Janet St. Cloud, yet from appearances now, the two women could have been from different generations.

"Aunt Catherine." Ravinia stared at her aunt. This severe aging wasn't just from falling off the couch. She looked as old as Declan Sr. had been, even though she was at least twenty years younger.

Her aunt straightened as best she could, and Ophelia moved forward automatically to relieve Elizabeth of the burden of ushering her, but Elizabeth shook her head. Aunt Catherine was her mother, even if they'd spent most of their lives apart and rarely saw each other. For today, at least, she clearly wanted her mother to be her responsibility.

"What happened to you?" Ravinia demanded of Catherine. She didn't think her aunt was even sixty.

"I told you. With Lillibeth's screams, she fell off the couch," answered Ophelia.

You didn't say she was barely able to walk, though!

"I can speak for myself, Ophelia," Aunt Catherine said with asperity. Turning a sharp blue eye on Ravinia, she said, "I'm slowing down some."

"No kidding." Ravinia had never held back with her aunt.

Chloe squeezed Ravinia's hand extra hard, clearly uncomfortable.

A series of soft chimes sounded, and the funeral director moved the ropes keeping the crowd at bay, then invited everyone inside for the service.

En masse, the large group moved forward. Ravinia, still shaken by the deterioration of her aunt, kept with Chloe. It was strange and disturbing. Aunt Catherine had always been the stalwart bulwark against any and all unseen forces out to undermine and hurt and possibly destroy their sect. It just felt wrong that she seemed half the woman she'd always been. Ravinia felt a pang of guilt for leaving them in the lurch. She'd never been happy at the lodge, but she could have been more helpful.

And Silas . . . his dead body was imprinted on her mind. *Next of kin . . .*

"I'd really like to talk to you," Ravinia said, leaning toward her aunt as they moved into the chapel.

"She has a secret to share," whispered Cassandra to Aunt Catherine.

"Would you stop?" snapped Ravinia. This is what she remembered. How her sisters, the whole cloistered atmosphere of Siren Song, had gotten on her nerves.

"Come by the lodge. We'll talk after," Catherine said over her shoulder.

Well, okay. But there was the reception at the luxurious, cliffside Bancroft home, with its supposed panoramic view, directly after this service, and Ravinia was definitely going to that. She'd promised Elizabeth and Chloe, and well, she wanted to.

"After the reception," she clarified, but Aunt Catherine acted like she hadn't heard her as Elizabeth led her to one of the chairs at the end of an aisle.

Nev filed his report about finding the body of the John Doe this morning, asking for a rush on the autopsy, as Lang had suggested, then walked to the break room, as much to stretch his muscles as to grab the final cup of coffee from the carafe on the coffeemaker before returning to his desk. Whenever he'd had a free second, he'd searched for more information on Ravinia Rutledge and learned little more than he'd discovered earlier. He now knew that, aside from growing up at Siren Song, she'd left for southern California, it seemed, and after a short stint there, she'd returned to Oregon, got her PI license by working/apprenticing of a sort, at a private detective agency in Portland for a few years before branching off on her own. She hadn't related the "private detective . . . branching off on her own" information to him at the morgue, and it didn't appear that Savannah or Lang knew about it, either. He'd have to check with them and see what they had on Ravinia.

He'd just opened his email again when he spied Lang striding through the front doors of the building, not his usual entrance. Lang's expression was dark, his jaw clenched. As he reached Nev's desk he said, "We've got another body."

"Another one?"

"Not the John Doe in the morgue—in fact, not a JD at all. The wife called it in, and Deputy Rodriguez went to check it out, and then after I talked to Rodriguez, the wife called me directly. Swears the body is her husband, swears it's a homicide."

Nev had already closed down his computer and was shoving his chair back. Another body? Rare for them to have one in a day or even a week, but two in one morning? "What happened?"

"According to the missus, her husband went out last night and never came back. She thought he might be going to Carter's Bait Shop and then to get a drink nearby somewhere."

"In Sandbar?" Nev clarified.

"Right."

"Was that unusual?"

"Don't know for certain, but probably not. But he didn't come home that night or the next. The first night wasn't a big deal; I take it that it happens sometimes, but never for more than twenty-four hours, so after the second night, she started seriously worrying, and she went looking for him earlier this morning. Found him sprawled out on the dune near Sandbar."

"Jesus. No one else saw him?"

"If they did, they didn't call it in, but anyone who saw him might have thought he was just sleeping it off." Lang shrugged, but his expression was still dark. "It happens."

"Was it a robbery?"

"Possibly. She claims his wallet and phone are missing. Rodriguez confirmed. Also confirmed that it looks like a homicide—the victim stabbed, blood all over his clothes."

"Jesus," Nev whispered as they walked down the hallway to the break room and his locker. "You know I live near Carter's."

Lang nodded. "I'm hoping you know someone around there who might trust you more than they trust me. A lot of the locals don't have much faith in the cops."

Nev grabbed his coat from his locker and shrugged into it before following Lang out the back. They picked up one of the department's black-and-yellow SUVs. Lang took the wheel.

Once they connected to Highway 101 and were heading north, crossing the Wilson River Bridge, Lang said, "The wife sounded like an automaton. In fact, she delivered the news like she was making a report. Almost like nothing was wrong. It either hasn't hit her yet, or she's one cold-hearted killer. I suggested she stay home, but she wouldn't hear of it. Insisted on staying on site until I got there."

"I thought she didn't know you."

"She doesn't. Got my name from Rodriguez."

"Oh."

"Her name's Jenny Norman, and he's—"

"Shit. Stanford?"

"—Stanford Norman. You know them?" Lang looked over at him.

"Somewhat. They live down the street from me." Nev grimaced. "She must be in shock, because she's normally pretty vocal. Stanford spends a lot of time at the local bar or hanging out at Davy Jones's Locker. There are rumors about him."

"Drinking problem?"

"Maybe." Nev glanced out the passenger window to the wide pastures filled with dairy cows, the October sky spitting rain. "It's more like the way he looks at women . . . younger women . . . much younger."

"How young?"

"If he could hang around a school as often as he hangs around a bar, well, that's where he'd be."

"Ugh."

"Yeah, like that."

Nev recalled the man with the fleshy lips and sliding eyes. He was a guy who pretended he was happy to see you, but his eyes and thoughts were always elsewhere. Nev hadn't seen his predilection toward young females in action, but he believed the rumors, because everyone at Davy Jones's Locker felt the same way about him. "If he's gone past just looking, I don't know about it, but I've heard he's not interested in older women, and I mean anyone over nineteen."

"His wife know? I mean if you know, and the word around town is that he's on the prowl . . . ?"

"Sometimes a person hears and sees what they want to," said Nev.

Lang was pushing the speed limit, passing slower vehicles as they reached the bay, the steely water reflecting the dark sky. "So how young?"

"The way I heard it, the younger the woman, the less developed she is, the more he's on her like glue."

"Shit. Maybe someone felt he got what he deserved," muttered Lang, glowering as he switched the wipers to a higher speed.

"Yeah."

Ten minutes later, Lang pulled into Carter's cracked asphalt lot and parked next to a rusted truck, its bed filled with crab traps, orange plastic buckets, some fishing rods, and gray tarps. He switched off the engine and half-turned in his seat. Nev had reached for the door handle, but stopped.

"We all know the history. It had to be tough going to the Wharton funeral."

"We?"

"Everyone in the department."

Great, Nev thought. "I'm fine."

"Uh huh."

"Savannah already mentioned it, so if this is more empathy, thanks, but I'm good."

Stone, like just about everyone around the area, knew that Nev had been with Spence and Duncan in the rowboat the day of the accident that had killed both of Nev's friends.

"Candy Wharton's never been known for her reticence," said Lang.

"She's got some power behind her," admitted Nev with a faint smile. The burn of the slap was just a memory now. "She needed a target, and there I was."

"Okay. You let me know if something else crops up. It is assault."

"I'm fine," he said again, and opened the door of the SUV.

Stone dropped the subject.

Ravinia listened to the service with only half an ear. To his credit, the funeral director tried not to drone. He kept altering the timbre of his voice as he listed Declan Bancroft Sr.'s many accomplishments, most of them about his business, the housing tracts he'd developed, spearheading their construction along with his grandson, Hale. Ravinia knew for a fact that some of those developments had caused consternation and anger among the beach locals. There was a proposed new housing tract going up next to the Foothillers, the name the local Native Americans had accepted and adopted from years of being referred to as such in their unincorporated town not far from Deception Bay. The town was in the foothills of the Coast Range, hence the name. The Foothillers didn't want the gentrification, and Bancroft Development had backed off, although other companies were still going forward.

There were high windows above the minister's head, and Ravinia found herself watching clouds scuttle by, driven by the wind. As her gaze lifted upward, a column of light broke through, sending a shaft of illumination over the congregation, as if from heaven above. A murmur of appreciation rolled through the crowd. Most probably saw it as a positive sign for Declan Sr., but Ravinia was thinking of Silas.

Maybe we'll meet again.

Feeling dampness on her lashes, she blinked herself back to the present. Of course, Cassandra's dark pupils were fixated on her, which kind of pissed her off as she thought about how little she could get past her sisters. Since leaving Siren Song, she'd gotten used to working alone and not being questioned, but whenever she was in her family's presence, she was back to being the youngest of the flock. She turned away from Cassandra's stare.

The only real reason she was at Declan Sr.'s funeral now was because Elizabeth had requested she be here, and Ravinia had wanted to see both Elizabeth and Chloe. Ophelia had mentioned that Aunt Catherine wanted her to come as well, but that hadn't carried as much weight . . . until now, with the news of Silas.

Her gaze fell on Janet Bancroft St. Cloud's black hat. *Spurrier*. That was her current last name. Stiff-backed Janet was seated three rows in front of Ravinia and a little to one side of the chapel, along with the rest of Declan Bancroft's family: Elizabeth, Chloe, Hale, and Savannah. Hale's five-year-old son, Declan, was likely at home being babysat, and Ravinia didn't know why Janet's husband wasn't with her. Ravinia could just see a sliver of Janet's facial profile, her uplifted nose and pugnacious chin.

It was in high school, apparently, that Janet had first become Ravinia's mother's nemesis. From Janet's demeanor, Ravinia could well imagine the two women had experienced quite a blistering rivalry. Ravinia had never known her mother; Mary had been presumed dead, then was discovered to be exiled, then had actually died, so Ravinia had never had a chance to know her. Maybe that was for the best, because according to anyone, actually *everyone*, who had known her, Mary was a strange, clever, and crazy woman who was obsessive, vindictive, relentless, and possessed of a gift of alluring sexuality that caught men in its web and brought them to her almost unwillingly if, and when, she turned her red-hot interest their way. Aunt Catherine said she was gifted with pheromones, a unique gift she'd passed on to her son Charlie, the kind of external hormones that some butterflies emitted to catch a mate. Ravinia was willing to believe it, since Mary's ability to enslave men was a known fact.

She shifted in her seat. Thoughts of her mother always brought on conflicting emotions that she didn't want to deal with. Even so, Ravinia was bound and determined to get Aunt Catherine to tell her and her sisters who their fathers were, or who they could be, given the fact that many men had passed through Siren Song before Aunt Catherine, having wrested control from her sister, shut the gates for good. At that point, Catherine had taken Mary's daughters in hand, changing their attitudes, dress, and way of life to something more common to the nineteenth century, but she'd never revealed the answers to the basic questions they had about their fathers.

Such crap.

Only after her mother's journal was discovered and Aunt Catherine needed Ravinia's help to find her own daughter, Elizabeth, had Aunt Catherine deigned to tell Ravinia anything at all. From the journal, Ravinia had learned about Janet Bancroft, who was prettier, smarter, and wealthier than Mary Rutledge and therefore bore the brunt of Mary's ire and jealousy. When Mary discovered that Janet was engaged to Preston St. Cloud, who was by all accounts just as good-looking, smart, and wealthy as his bride-to-be, Mary went after him with a vengeance, just to take him away from Janet. At this point in her life, Mary had apparently lost what little touch with reality she'd once possessed, and no one could talk her out of her laser-like focus on Janet's fiancé, least of all her sister, Catherine. At first, Mary failed to turn his head. Preston went on to wed Janet and live fairly happily, maybe, those first few years of married life. Mary, meanwhile, had threatened Catherine, should she try to thwart her in her quest to steal Preston. Should her sister dare get in her way, Mary vowed, she would steal Declan Bancroft away from Catherine as a means of retribution. Ravinia had decoded that journal entry, and Aunt Catherine had reluctantly confirmed it:

C. I can take D. from you. Don't think I can't. Be smart about him, or I'll prove my power to you. Give him up now, before you make me do something I don't want to do. You can't keep him. I'll have him too. J's husband AND father.

Aunt Catherine had apparently done as Mary suggested rather than fight with her, though Ravinia didn't know for sure. She did know that her aunt had been overwhelmed by how many children Mary had, so she'd adopted out the more troublesome, youngest ones, the last two boys being Silas and Charlie. Charlie, whom Mary had erroneously named Declan Jr. as a coup de grâce against Catherine's dictatorship, though Aunt Catherine swore Mary had never actually slept with Declan Sr.

But when Janet, years later, learned that her husband *had* been ensnared by Mary, who'd then given birth to another child, a son, shortly after their affair, Janet accused Preston of being the father and divorced him for his infidelity. Mary loved it and crowed that she'd slept with both Declan Bancroft *and* Preston, *J's husband AND father*, and only later had Ravinia—and Aunt Catherine, who'd always feared it was true—learned that Declan Sr. had never been enthralled by Mary. He'd escaped her net through his love for Catherine, apparently. Mary had lied about him, and they'd all believed it because of her sexual prowess, because she was so good at getting any man she wanted. But Catherine had felt the only safe thing to do was give up her own child, Elizabeth, believing Elizabeth would fare better outside the sphere of Mary's influence.

Catherine also made sure that Mary's son—the one purported to be Preston St. Cloud's son, but who was actually Thomas Durant's—was also given up for adoption. Charlie . . . who would never believe he was sired by someone else . . . Mary's own father, the man of the bones on Echo Island that Silas had burned as a means to send the bastard back to hell. If—

"Ravinia . . ." Cassandra whispered softly, breaking into her thoughts.

Ravinia bent her head to her sister, then could feel Aunt Catherine's dampening gaze, even though she didn't look up.

"You need to come to the lodge."

"I know. I want to talk to Aunt Catherine and—"

"But you're not coming," Cassandra charged.

It was true. Ravinia had really had no intention of going to the lodge, no matter what impression she'd given her sisters. She planned to head back to Portland as soon as the reception at the Bancroft estate was over. She just needed to get Aunt Catherine alone for a few minutes before she left.

"I'm actually pretty busy with work," she said, which wasn't exactly true.

Cassandra wasn't about to be put off. She whispered, "Lillibeth needs to tell you about the dreams."

"Cassandra, I think you can handle it."

"Maggie. Remember? It's Maggie now."

"Maggie," Ravinia repeated, internally rolling her eyes. So they were back to that again. She'd hoped they were past it.

"If you won't help her, who will?"

"Shhh." Ophelia leaned forward to wave a finger at them.

In turn, Ravinia shot Phee a butt-out look.

Cassandra subsided into silence, but if possible, her pupils loomed even larger, nearly swallowing up every bit of blue in her irises.

Ravinia closed her own eyes and tried to concentrate on the minister's words. Sure, he tried with the up-and-down inflections, but it would help if he weren't so damn boring.

"Did you talk to Andrew Wharton at all?" Lang asked Nev as they trudged up the hill of the dune. The rain was slapping at them in fits and starts, herded off the ocean by the wind.

Nev shook his head. Spence's brother had stayed far away from him. Probably on purpose. Three years younger than Spence, he'd blamed Nev for the loss of his brother as well. Andrew might have pleaded with Candy to stop her attack on Nev yesterday, but that was as far as he would go. Andrew didn't want to get too close to the man his parents, and possibly he, hated so much.

Lang said, "Spencer's death was a long time ago."

"Not long enough for them."

"Or maybe you either?"

Nev had liked it better when everyone stayed away from what had happened to Spencer and Duncan, when the subject of the tragedy had been locked away by time. Henry Wharton's funeral had broken those gates wide open again.

Which reminded him . . . "I thought you'd be at the other funeral today."

"Declan Bancroft's?" asked Lang.

Nev nodded. "For Savannah."

"I didn't know the man. His personal property might be a little south of Seaside, but Bancroft Development is located there, and that's where Hale—and Savannah now—live. Bancroft never came this far south, at least all that much."

As they reached the crest of the dune, Nev noticed a small crowd gathered a hundred feet away, clustered around a strip of flapping yellow tape, their legs obscured by the tall beach grass. He and Lang bent their heads to the wind and trudged toward them as a slim deputy in uniform approached.

Nev recognized the dark-eyed deputy, Ed Rodriguez, and with him was Jenny Norman, a woman in her fifties with curly, graying hair clamped into a frizzy ponytail; a windbreaker and Spandex black pants stretched across a round body. She saw the detective approach and came running forward, kicking up sand. Though she knew Nev some, it was Lang she threw herself at; she started bawling her eyes out, her large breasts crushed into his chest. So much for being an automaton.

The deputy shook his head in a half apology. "Mrs. Norman—"

Lang lifted one hand in an it's-all-right gesture as Jenny sobbed against him.

Nev approached the body, which was lying faceup to the sky, eyes open, lips parted as if in a question. Splotches of blood stained Stanford's shirt. Stab wounds maybe, underneath the fabric. There was a utility knife with a five-inch blade, now covered in sand, beside the man's left hand, almost as if he'd dropped it himself. A hypodermic needle lay beside his right ear.

But still, the most remarkable thing about the corpse was that someone had taken the time to expose his genitals.

Nev looked up at the other people standing on the other side of the yellow tape. Two men and a woman. The smallish woman was standing far back from the corpse. She was young, in her twenties, barely over five feet. Her straight brown hair was also pulled back into a ponytail she'd threaded through the back of a pink baseball cap. In a gray jogging suit, her arms wrapped around her body, she looked pale and wan, her brown eyes round beneath the cap's visor. The thirtyish man was obviously with her, standing close; upon seeing "the law" arriving, he threw his arm around her for support.

"The Weatherbys," Rodriguez said, nodding in their direction. "Dennis and Corey. They found the body. The other guy is—"

"Leonard Eby," Nev said.

"You know him?"

"Yeah." Eby had lived in the area all his life, was a fixture on this part of the coast. "You get their initial statements?" He motioned to the group braced against the wind and huddled on the dune.

Rodriguez nodded. "Still a lot of unanswered questions, though."

Nev glanced down at the dead man. "You didn't mention that his pants were down."

"The wife was next to me when I called it in, and I wanted to get your reaction," Rodriguez said. "It's a little strange."

A lot strange. Nev glanced at his partner.

As Lang was still consoling Jenny Norman, Nev approached Eby. In his early seventies, with a craggy, lined face and hair that was more white than gray, Eby was a fisherman, had been all his life, if Nev remembered right.

He caught Nev's eye as he separated from the others to stand on a rise with a clear view of the body. He nodded at Nev. "Rhodes."

"Hi there, Leonard," greeted Nev. "What do you know about this?"

"Not much." Leonard hooked his thumb at Jenny. "Lady there came to the bait shop, looking for her husband. Said he hadn't been home for a couple of nights. About that time those people"—he indicated the couple—"were walking along and damn near stumbled over the body, the way they tell it. The woman there started screaming, and I hiked it over here. Lady followed after me," he added, nodding toward Jenny Norman again. "Says it's her husband."

"Stanford Norman," said Nev, eyeing the corpse.

Leonard frowned down at the body. "Never met him before. The wife, neither, until today. Maybe heard the name though . . ." His bushy eyebrows drew together as he stared out to sea, where storm clouds boiled in a pewter sky.

"He spends time at the Locker," said Nev, shortening the name of Davy Jones's Locker to what the locals called it.

"Don't go there much," Leonard explained, his eyes on the sky. He pulled a faded hat from his back pocket and forced it on his head. "Me and alcohol aren't friends anymore."

Leonard Eby was a fixture around the area. It had been years since he'd touched a drop of booze, Nev had heard, but before that there had been a lot of loud carousing, and he'd been kicked out of more than one bar along the coast. Nev had heard the tales and knew Leonard by sight, though they'd never interacted before.

Nev said, "So it was the couple who actually found the body and alerted Jenny?"

"Jenny and everyone from here to Japan." He nodded to the west to the Pacific Ocean, its gray expanse broken by riffles of white caps from the wind, the air brisk and briny. "That woman's screams will be reverberating through the Coast Range for years."

Jenny might have held it together on the phone, but since encountering Lang, she was a blubbering mess. It was almost comical seeing how Lang was trying to carefully extricate himself from her embrace.

"And the knife and hypodermic?" Nev asked, and Leonard just shook his head.

He scratched the gray beard stubble on his chin. "Was he shootin' up? Having a bad trip? Then stabbed himself?"

Unlikely, Nev thought.

Leonard observed, "It's weird, man."

Nev wouldn't argue the point. "We'll figure it out."

Now Leonard gave Nev a steely look from beneath white eyebrows. "You went to the Wharton funeral yesterday."

So, even Leonard Eby knew. There were small towns, and then there were even smaller towns. Sandbar was in the smaller category. "Yep."

"Don't mean to speak ill of the dead, but Henry Wharton was a right prick. Big on blaming others for his own problems. World might do just fine without him."

Nev didn't say anything to that. Gossip ran rampant along the coast, and Henry and Candy hadn't been quiet about their feelings. Nev's own parents had stood up for their son, but the Whartons had made bad-mouthing Nev a job. It had hurt, but Nev, who was grieving himself, had tried not to let it get to him too much. But the Whartons' ongoing broadcasting of their feelings and opinions was probably what had sent Nev's parents to Arizona and a new life. He'd done the same, escaping to Corvallis and Oregon State University, avoiding the coast for years. He'd eventually migrated back and until yesterday had loved it. He was back in the fishbowl again.

Lang finally freed himself from Jenny's strangling embrace just as the coroner's van pulled into the bait shop lot below the dune.

"Pecker's out," observed Leonard as he stared down at the corpse.

"Yep." Someone had made a point of placing Stanford's penis front and center. "Thanks, Leonard," Nev said. "I might have more questions."

"Okay, but I'm fresh outta answers. I'm gonna get out of the rain, if you don't mind. Could use a smoke."

"Sure."

As Leonard ambled off, down the dune, Nev approached the younger couple. She was shivering, her teeth chattering. Lang was still talking to Jenny Norman, who was sniveling and wiping her eyes with her sleeve.

"What happened here? I know Deputy Rodriguez took your initial statement, but why don't you walk me through it?" suggested Nev.

The Weatherbys exchanged glances, and Corey said, "We were just walking, and there he was," all the while shooting worried but penetrating looks to her husband, almost as if she were trying to telegraph him some hidden message, maybe to keep his mouth shut.

Dennis, in a camo jacket, matching cap, and jeans, did not appear to be getting the message, however. "We just came down to the beach for a few days. We're staying right over there." He hooked a thumb to a line of houses set back from the dune, closer to the road. Nev's rental was in the same area. "Kind of a second honeymoon. We got here Wednesday . . ."

"Wednesday afternoon," clarified Corey.

"Yeah, we're staying through the weekend, or we were," he said, glancing at his wife again. "I don't know now."

The two of them were looking at each other in a way that suggested both of them had something more to say but neither wanted to say it. Nev said, "Did you see something?"

"Not today. Well, not yesterday, either," said Dennis at a stricken look from Corey as Lang approached. Jenny Norman followed him over while Leonard Eby was smoking a cigarette under the bait shop's metal awning.

"You saw something, though," Lang said to the reticent couple.

Neither answered, so he continued as if they had. "When was that?"

"We didn't see anything last night. It was dark. We were just out for a walk," Dennis repeated.

"No, we didn't see anything," Corey said quickly.

Lang regarded them both tolerantly. Jenny Norman looked as if she might grab him for support again.

Nev thought about the night before. Nothing. But the previous night? He'd dropped into bed, exhausted, after getting back from the bar, his mind full of images of Spencer and Duncan and the Whartons and Echo Island. He'd been half dreaming and had woken with a start, his heart racing at the mental picture of a grinning witch rising out of the sea. She'd rushed straight at him, holding out a swatch of her black hair, the image burned on his retina.

A noise had awakened him. From the direction of the dune and the ocean. A shout, maybe. A voice. And as he'd blinked awake, he'd been thankful that the spell of the nightmare had been broken. He'd gotten up, walked barefoot to the window, and stared out at the darkness, then returned to bed and fallen back on his pillow.

He'd waited, thought he might hear something else.

But nothing.

Finally, he'd drifted off into a fitful sleep.

Now, he looked at the Weatherbys and said, "You heard something the night before last?"

He sensed Lang swiveling to look at him but kept his eyes on the couple. Dennis looked like he was going to say something, but his eyes flicked to Corey, maybe for permission.

She was the one who finally broke.

She turned her eyes to the sky, rain dampening her tense features. "Yeah. Right. Not last night. The night before. They were . . . they were doing it in the dune," she said in a rush, her tone tinged with disgust.

"*Doing* it?" Jenny suddenly straightened to her full height. "*They?*"

Corey lifted a shoulder and grimaced. "He was making a lot of noise."

"What? No! Stanford wasn't doing it with anyone!" From automaton to bawling griever to rage-filled wife, Jenny Norman suddenly looked ready to physically rip into Corey. Lang held out his arm, ready to hold her back, if necessary. Corey shrank into Dennis, and they both appeared a bit frightened.

Nev clarified, "He—Mr. Norman—was having sex with someone on the dune."

Jenny turned on him as if he'd attacked her personally, but before she could say anything, Dennis cut in, "He was with a girl."

Jenny made a noise in her throat, but Dennis went on, "I could see her pigtails when she got up and ran off. It was pretty dark. Couldn't see anything much more than her silhouette, but I saw that."

"How old?" Nev asked, his muscles taut.

"We told you, we don't know!" Corey insisted.

Dennis caught Nev's drift. "Couldn't really say, but maybe preteen or early teens—but I don't know. Just that she was at least five feet . . . well, I think. As I said, it was pretty damned dark."

"We left. Right away. Didn't want to hear any more," said Corey in a rush.

"And you didn't call anyone—"

"We didn't really see anything, it was so dark and—"

"Stanford does not cheat," said Jenny tautly, nearly spitting the words. "And not with . . . not with a *girl*! For Christ's sake, you people are sick!" Her face twisted in revulsion, but there was a flicker of something more in her eyes. Knowledge? Suspicion? Fear?

Leonard called from beneath the bait shop awning, "Here comes the cavalry." The crime scene team had joined the EMTs from the van, and they'd all hiked through the beach grass and just reached the crest of the dune.

"Rhodes," said Lang, hitching his chin to indicate he'd like a word alone.

They walked a short distance away as Deputy Rodriguez showed the techs the body and surrounding area. "They saw more than they're saying," Lang said.

"They don't want to get involved."

"A girl?" Lang met Nev's gaze.

"I'll check with them after work tonight, once I get home. See if they know anything else, or if anybody does. Maybe stop in at the Locker."

"Everyone here needs to make a formal statement," said Lang, then muttered, "Pigtails."

Nev nodded grimly. Could be an adult in pigtails, he reminded himself. No sense getting over his skis on this one. But he did remark, "Whoever she was, she survived. He didn't."

"A knife and a hypodermic needle?" Lang said, eyeing the crime scene. A photographer was taking digital shots of the deceased and the area surrounding him, while a tech was collecting anything of interest on the ground. Laying out a grid, sifting through the sand, and going over the dune with a metal detector wouldn't be easy in this weather. "Doesn't sound like a kid, at least," said Lang. "Someone stabbed Norman, possibly drugged him and got away. But we should check with the hospitals—she could have been injured. I don't think Norman stabbed himself, but he could have cut her. We'll need to search the area. If she was wounded, any blood trail would be erased by now, but these dunes could hide another body."

"Or," Nev said, sending his gaze toward the horizon and the vast, choppy Pacific Ocean, "she could be out there."

"Shit, then we'll never find her. Let's just hope she was lucky and got away unharmed." Lang shoved his hands into the pockets of his pants. "Either way, we still have to find her." He glanced up, looking toward the town.

Nev followed his gaze to catch sight of a big, white news van rolling down the street before pulling into a parking space in front of the bait shop.

"Here we go," said Lang as the passenger door of the van opened and a slim woman reporter stepped outside. "Looks like bad news travels fast."

"Never fails," said Nev.

From inside her SUV, Lucky waited, rain collecting on the windshield as she stared through the rivulets at the blocky, brown building that was Seaview Funeral Chapel. The service had seemed to take forever, but at least now the hearse was in position under a portico, and soon the funeral attendees who had gathered inside to pay their respects would be funneling out of the chapel, climbing into their cars, and following the long black vehicle to the cemetery.

Maybe she would go to that part of the service too. Stand toward the back, away from the grave site. Watch the coffin holding Declan Bancroft being lowered into its grave without anyone seeing her.

But she would see them.

The women of the Colony.

She knew a lot about them . . . a *lot*.

Lucky watched grimly as another dark thought crossed her mind. She remembered the man she'd stabbed and left on the dune. She hoped that he lay there undiscovered, his corpse rotting, the creatures of the sand and sea picking at dead flesh.

She hadn't wanted to get involved with him. She'd told herself that her time of seeking out the sick predators who preyed on children was long over. All of that—the hunting of the filth of humanity—was behind her now.

Or so she'd thought.

She'd spent years as an advocate for the innocents, a silent and invisible assassin, and her work hadn't gone unnoticed, of course. The bodies of the dead perverts had racked up notices at police departments all across the country while she fulfilled her mission, but each kill increased the likelihood that she would be found out.

For years, she'd avoided this stretch of Oregon beach, where her hunting had begun. Instinctively, she knew that, being here, she would be even more at risk because, for the most part, the few people who knew about her and her identity lived on this stretch of coastline.

But then she'd run across Stanford Norman, and her sixth sense of zeroing in on potential pedophiles kicked in.

And so she'd come across her latest victim. Norman had looked at all the younger women around him with lust. Lucky had immediately sensed him, and he'd sensed her back, apparently. She just couldn't let his sick perversion continue.

She'd caught wind of him by chance, sensing him at a soccer match that she was just driving by. She'd followed him to be sure and had deliberately crossed paths with him at a fast-food mart attached to a gas station, brushing against him. Yep. He was ripe and ready . . . She always marveled that others couldn't sense what she could.

As Norman pulled away from the gas station, she'd followed, and he'd driven straight to a school to park and watch the kids, some teens, walking to and from school. Lingering in his car. Sweating despite the cool October day.

At that moment, she'd known her work wasn't finished. She couldn't let it be. And so she'd gone to work, changing her appearance, making herself look younger than she was, much younger, and plotting the meeting. She'd learned his favorite watering holes, chief among them Davy Jones's Locker. She would let him know she had a fake I.D. He was so horny, he'd believe her. She would make him.

After strapping down her breasts so that she appeared board flat, she'd tied her blond hair into pigtails and purposefully avoided any makeup. She practiced changing her voice, making it sound breathy and girlish, and donned a pink dress that rode high on her slender thighs and a white jacket with lace.

Then she'd reeled him in.

It had been a risk. Dangerous.

She couldn't let anyone see her or recognize her features.

She was wanted in too many places, too many states, for ridding the world of evil scum like Stanford Norman. But neutralizing him had been a risk worth taking, even though it might jeopardize everything she'd worked so hard for: the semblance of a normal life for as long as she could have one.

That thought even now made her throat thick.

She'd caught his eye a time or two at Davy Jones's Locker. Spoken to him and named a local Sandbar dive, which he'd blurted was near where he lived. "Maybe I'll see you there tomorrow . . ." she'd murmured, running a hand over his arm and thigh. She'd designed the meeting, and when he came looking for her she walked right by him toward the beach. He saw her and couldn't resist. She allowed him to approach with his hungry smile and let him suggest they just keep walking to the beach, "to see the stars and the moonlight on the ocean," or some such crap.

Lucky had pretended to resist, muttering something about needing to be home when he took her hand in his. His fingers had been clammy, his breathing ragged and noisy, even over the pounding of the surf. And the scent of him—his eager, thrumming lust—had been cloying.

She'd let him lead her toward the sea.

At the top of the dune, when the ocean was visible, he turned to her and played his hand, jerking roughly on her arm and forcing her onto the dune with its sharp-bladed beach grass and rough sand. When he'd yanked down his pants, she'd spied his dick briefly before he'd pushed himself inside her, hard as granite. Words fell from his lips, "Baby" and "Sweetie" and "Little Sugar," while she lay beneath him, coldly calculating when to take him out.

Above her, the night stars had winked on and off behind scudding clouds as he rutted. Tamping down her revulsion, she waited for her chance to send him straight through the gates of hell.

His hands were all over her, his breath hot and sour.

His fingers brushed her back, sliding down her skin to stop suddenly when a finger encountered her scars.

His concentration broke for a second.

His "Little Sugar" shouldn't bear scars. Oh, no.

He'd pulled away from her, out of her, and stumbled a bit in the sand, his pants around his ankles.

"What happened to you?" he demanded, sounding repulsed, his breathing still ragged.

Lucky yanked the hypodermic from her jacket pocket. Unfortunately, it wasn't a lethal dose, she knew that, but she hadn't had time to prepare. Nonetheless, there was enough of the drug in it that it would knock him out, and then she could dispose of him. Maybe in the ocean. Drag him down the dune and throw him into the waves unconscious. Let him drown.

But he'd surprised her.

"My wife . . . my wife . . . can't know," he'd panted in alarm, his eyes round, whites showing in the night. He reached down to his boots, fumbling a bit before extracting a knife, its blade silvery sharp in the moonlight.

She'd sucked in her breath.

She'd been careless. Very unlike her. But she recovered and lunged, trying to jab her needle into his thick neck.

He feinted.

He slashed with the knife.

She rolled away but wasn't quick enough, felt a sting in her shoulder, a small nick she was lucky wasn't worse. "You little—" He leaped on her again, his feet tangled in his pants. She caught his wrist before he could cut her again, but he was heavy and determined.

She bit his neck, her teeth digging deep.

He howled in pain, and his grip on the knife loosened.

Still he was atop her.

With all her strength, she wrenched the blade from his fingers and gladly turned it on him. The first cut went deep in his arm. The second into his chest. He screamed and writhed, trying to get away, unable to kick free from his hobbling pants. When he collapsed on her, she was out of breath. She'd had to roll him off her with an effort. He was bleeding. Maybe mortally wounded. She didn't know. But she wasn't taking a chance.

She plunged the hypo into his neck, and he shrieked wildly, in terror and agony.

Then Lucky slid away from him, gasping for air, bleeding herself, naked, his blood on her skin. She fought the urge to throw up as she watched him, hoping he would die as he lay between the tufts of bending grass, his hands over his chest, blood staining his fat fingers. She waited, counting the seconds, tensely afraid someone had heard his scream. He asked in a rasping, desperate gasp, "Who are you?"

"Your conscience," she whispered flatly and watched in satisfaction as his muscles slackened and he was gone. Once assured that he was dead and would never again stalk the little ones, she searched for the hypodermic. Couldn't find it.

It was too dark, and she couldn't spend any more time, couldn't risk getting caught.

Hurriedly, she pulled up his pants and made sure his prick was displayed on the outside of his zipper before snatching up her clothes and shoes and running off naked toward the beach. She wanted the world to know what his crime was.

When she felt safe enough, Lucky quickly yanked on her clothes, then ran down the edge of the surf, feeling the cold, wet sand beneath her slapping feet. She was almost gleeful. It had been a while since she'd sent one of those bastards back to the hell from where he'd sprung. She couldn't wait to get back to the motel, full of her exploits, ready to tell Silas, looking forward to making love, *love,* not just sex.

Silas . . .

She came back to the present. The pain in her heart nearly overwhelmed her and she had to push it back and think clearly. Calmly. Coldly.

Silas was gone, but Ravinia Rutledge was alive.

She needed a face-to-face with her. Something. She hadn't quite figured it out yet.

But someone had to pay for what had happened to Silas.

CHAPTER 6

The service finally ended, and Ravinia expelled a sigh of relief as the piped-in music swelled again and people easing out of the chapel began to whisper among themselves. Her relief, though, was short-lived, as she belatedly learned that Aunt Catherine was not going directly to the Bancrofts from the chapel. The plan was that she would go to the cemetery to witness the interment, then to the gathering at the Bancroft home.

Great.

Ravinia's mood nose-dived.

She was already starting to feel antsy. Solemn rites, quiet attendances . . . these were not her specialty. It was amazing how well she could do with surveillance, watching a storefront or private home for hour upon hour, sometimes with nothing happening, but at least in those instances she was able to listen to music, make notes to herself, talk on the phone, or merely scroll through TikTok or some other app.

But this . . . ugh.

As she was filing out of the chapel along with the rest of the throng of Declan Bancroft's mourners, Chloe found Ravinia and clasped her hand. "I'm going to ride in the car with you."

Now Ravinia was doomed. She couldn't weasel out of it.

"All right, but I want to talk to Aunt Catherine first."

"Okay," said Chloe, and went in search of her mother.

With Elizabeth escorting her, Aunt Catherine was moving so slowly it was excruciating, and there wasn't a chance to tear her aunt away from the rest of those paying their respects to Declan Bancroft.

Ravinia was torn between concern and the heebie-jeebies as she waited on the porch, watching Elizabeth shepherd her mother down the few stairs to a side parking lot, all the while trying to protect the older woman from the steady rain by holding an umbrella over her head. The slow progression as they inched their way to the car sent Ravinia's nerves screaming. There was no way to separate her aunt from the herd.

So Ravinia would go to the cemetery.

With Chloe.

At least she'd have company.

Ravinia caught up with Chloe and Elizabeth and Catherine in the side lot. "You coming?" she said to the girl.

Elizabeth caught Ravinia's eye, then intervened. "Chloe," she said to her daughter, "would you mind sticking with me?" Elizabeth didn't say it, but Ravinia saw clearly that she felt she might need some help getting Aunt Catherine into her rental.

Ravinia almost offered to take Catherine herself, but held her tongue. Elizabeth seldom visited the Oregon coast, and Aunt Catherine, for all her debilitation, relished those infrequent times with her daughter. There had been so few of them.

Chloe's shoulders slumped at the change of plans, but she complied, marching back to her mother's car like a prisoner facing a death squad.

Okay, then. It was time to go on her own.

"I'll catch up with you later," she promised her aunt, then nearly sprinted along the winding path to the back lot where she'd parked. Once inside her Camry, she wove her way out of the lot and into the unbroken line of vehicles following the hearse as it drove through town and steadily into the rolling hills to the southeast. Arched gates stood open, and the line of cars pulled through, all parking along a narrow roadway that belted the stretch of green grass, a landscaped lawn stretching across undulating hills with a view of the far-off ocean.

Here we go again, Ravinia thought, climbing out of her Camry, locking it, and pocketing her keys as she made her way to the plot. The wind made it nearly impossible to brave the elements, and Ravinia saw Janet Spurrier desperately clutch the crown of her hat.

Hale had his hand on his wife's elbow, making sure Savannah didn't trip or twist an ankle as they walked toward the bier, held beneath a sheltering blue canopy supported by four white metallic poles.

Ravinia gripped the lapels of her coat close as the funeral director intoned a few words and murmured a prayer, and the silent crowd looked on as the coffin was slowly lowered into the grave. The spray of white lilies had been removed, and the sound of the first dirt tossed on the casket was surprisingly loud and final. With an eye toward the line of dark clouds approaching off the sea, the minister was a lot briefer than at the funeral chapel and ended the service with a final prayer. Soon everyone was hurrying back to their vehicles.

Once more, Ravinia sought a moment alone with her aunt, again reaching Elizabeth's rental car.

"Aunt Catherine, we need to talk," she said as Elizabeth again held her mother's umbrella and the older woman glanced over her shoulder to scowl.

"Not now," Catherine said and settled into the passenger seat.

"But—"

"Didn't I just say, 'Not now'?" From the interior of the car, she leveled her gaze at her niece. "Ravinia, this isn't the time nor the place. Show some respect." She hoisted her chin up and stared out the front window of the car. "We need to go."

"Okay," Elizabeth said and sent Ravinia a what-are-ya-gonna-do look.

"Can I please ride with Ravinia?" Chloe said, hovering near her aunt.

"Do you mind?" Elizabeth asked Ravinia.

"Of course not," Ravinia said and, with Chloe bounding at her side, made her way across the wet grass to her silver Camry. Once inside the car, Ravinia pulled the tangled tresses free of their bun, then quickly banded her hair into a new bun, while Chloe buckled into the back seat. She started the car, once again in line, but letting others pass, noting when Ophelia, driving her Nissan Pathfinder with Cassandra in the passenger seat, eased around them.

"Don't you want to go?" asked Chloe, as impatient now as Ravinia had been.

"Yeah. I'm just thinking . . ." How was she going to talk to Aunt Catherine alone with all of her sisters, and now Elizabeth and Chloe, gathering at Siren Song? Was there a way to walk outside the house, onto the grounds, and away from the porch? Possibly at the private graveyard? Or was her aunt too compromised? And did she really need to stand in another cemetery today?

"Do you think Grandma is really sad about Mr. Bancroft dying?" Chloe asked, breaking into her thoughts. "I think she's really sad."

"I suppose you're right." Ravinia started her car, letting more vehicles pass.

"Wouldn't you be sad if your boyfriend died?"

"If I had a boyfriend, and he died, yes, I'd be sad," said Ravinia.

"You don't want a boyfriend?" asked Chloe, picking up on Ravinia's careful tone.

She slid the Camry into gear and noted a man in a rain slicker standing near an excavator. He was smoking a cigarette with one hand and had a cell phone pressed to his ear with the other as the big machine idled, rumbling. "Boyfriends are a lot of work, so no, I don't want a boyfriend."

"How do you know they're a lot of work? Have you had one already?"

Ravinia was starting to rethink her desire to have Chloe with her. The girl was peppering her with questions, the kind she didn't want to contemplate. "I've been really busy starting a new business. You know I worked with Rex when I was living near you guys."

Ravinia caught a glimpse of the girl in the rearview mirror. Chloe was drawing on the condensation on the inside of the passenger window, but nodding. Listening. "Then I apprenticed with these two detectives, a husband-and-wife team. Now I'm on my own."

"Are we *ever* gonna leave?" Chloe asked.

"Yep, right now." Ravinia finally eased onto the road behind an older-model Plymouth, a white sedan in which the woman behind the wheel was barely visible. They were at the tail end of the procession, almost the last car to leave the dismal cemetery. Not *the* last to leave, however, because as she drove through, under the archway of the main gates, she noticed a gray SUV tuck in behind her, the driver obscured by the rain.

"Is it fun working on your own?" asked Chloe from the back seat.

"Well . . ." *Fun* wasn't exactly the word she would choose.

"Do you have to chase bad guys?" Chloe sounded worried.

"Mostly I just do background checks. That kind of thing. I spend a lot of time on my computer."

"My mom worries about Rex," Chloe said. "She saw an accident."

"She *saw* an accident?" Ravinia questioned sharply and glanced at the mirror again.

"No, not that kind." Chloe shook her head. "Not the kind we don't talk about."

Elizabeth's premonitions of danger. "Okay."

"It was a car accident. A real one. They ran into Rex's S-U-V." She said each initial distinctly, as if she were narrating for a legal case and making sure the court reporter got it down. "Mom said it was a fluke. She was worried about him, but not like if she'd seen it first, you know, like just before it happened."

"I know."

The Plymouth's brake lights glowed bright as the driver slowed at an amber light. Ravinia followed suit, her Camry idling, the Subaru behind her doing the same. She glanced again at Chloe. So young. So innocent. And living with a mother who wasn't like the other moms who belonged to the school's PTA.

Elizabeth's precognitive ability was both a blessing and a curse. Those split seconds of warning before a disaster saved lives but also caused questions. She'd been hounded by a reporter, among others, to explain how she knew in advance of a catastrophe what would happen, and of course, Elizabeth had no answer. There was none.

Recently, Elizabeth had told Ravinia in confidence on a phone call, while Chloe had been sleeping, that she thought her bouts of fore-telling disaster seemed to be disappearing. "They don't come so often. I'm relieved, but . . ."

"You don't want anyone to get hurt that you could have maybe helped," Ravinia finished.

Elizabeth sighed. "Gifts, huh?"

Yeah. Gifts. Ravinia's power to look into the heart of individuals wasn't necessarily fading, but it had become more capricious. Some-times she called on it and nothing happened, which was unfortunate because she relied on it more than she'd realized. Ravinia had looked into the hearts of the PIs she'd worked for in Portland, J. D. Bauer and his wife, Adela, of Bauer Investigations, when she'd first been hired, and that had worked fine. They hadn't put together that it was her who gave them the "searing" scan, which was helpful, especially since she'd learned that neither of them was a particularly good person. Adela's heart was hard, wounded, unable to feel like it should, but it was J. D.'s that had made Ravinia's own heart go cold. There were metaphorical dark corners inside his pump that held secrets she couldn't penetrate. Though he hadn't known it was she who had looked into his heart, he'd somehow divined the feeling had come because of her. Afterward, he'd regarded her with a kind of fear hidden by overbearing bonhomie, as if he were determined to convince her he was on the up and up, a "good guy."

Even though she knew better, Ravinia had stayed in the employ of Bauer Investigations as long as she needed to get experience and Oregon accreditation. Only once had J. D. made a move on her, and then it was to simply run his finger up her arm. When she'd jerked away, he'd said she should have that mole on her arm looked at, and that Adela had found one that looked like it and it had been precancerous. What mole? There wasn't one. And when the weather turned warm enough to go sleeveless, Ravinia had checked out Adela's arms.

There was no mole on her either. Nor any sign that one had been removed.

J. D. was a liar and acted like he neither liked or trusted Ravinia, except for those times when, chameleon-like, he'd been overly friendly. She knew he was completely aware of her. He didn't have to tell her he found her attractive. His eyes did that.

She was glad to be on her own.

I'm glad you're on your own too.

Ravinia glanced at Chloe in surprise. The girl hadn't spoken, yet the words were plain as day. She sought to send a message back. A simple "me too." But Chloe didn't seem to pick up on it. She just stared back at Ravinia with her big, blue eyes, clearly waiting for a response, one Ravinia was unable to give. Once upon a time, they'd shared a bit of precognition, but time and distance seemed to have caused those gifts to fade.

"I'm trying to answer you, but I can't," admitted Ravinia.

"I wish it still worked." Chloe let out a sigh, then added, "The light is green."

So it was, but the white car in front of her hadn't moved. Ravinia gave a quick tap on her horn, and the Plymouth bucked forward, tires chirping as the driver turned quickly onto 101 to head farther south. Ravinia pulled out behind it. In her side-view mirror she saw the Outback following her had made the turn as well. "Thanks," she said to Chloe. The girl was about to reach puberty, when, for most of them, their gifts had surfaced and been the strongest. "Can you talk to anyone else?" asked Ravinia.

"Not really. Well, Mom. Sometimes. Not too much." She hesitated, shooting Ravinia a sheepish glance in the mirror. "I tried it on this boy in class, and I think it worked. He sort of woke up and looked scared."

"Did he know it was you?" Ravinia couldn't decide if she was worried or amused. Maybe a little of both.

"I just glanced around the room and didn't really look at him. He was staring at me, kind of with a freaked-out expression, but I didn't act like I knew it."

"Be careful, Chloe."

"I know."

"Do you?" asked Ravinia.

"I know how much trouble Mom gets in by helping people. She's always telling me to be careful too, and I am."

"Good." They were completely out of the town now, driving along the highway, glimmers of the ocean visible through the branches of tall fir trees, the rain having finally abated, an October sun peeking through the clouds.

"If I had a boyfriend, I think I'd tell him." She shot Ravinia a quick look in the mirror, then glanced away.

"Do you have a boyfriend?"

"No . . ."

"Chloe, you're not filling me with confidence. Did you tell him about your ability?"

"He's just a boy."

"Chloe . . ."

"You sound just like Mom," Chloe said petulantly. "What good's having something special if you can't share it?"

"What's his name, this boy?" Again Ravinia was keeping one eye on the road as she glanced at the girl.

"I was just testing on him! It's . . . it's nothing."

"Don't bullshit me, Chloe. What's his name?"

She tucked her chin in. "Are you going to do something to him? Like in *Men In Black*?"

Ravinia frowned. "What men in black?"

"The *movie*? *Men In Black*? They're like government guys who catch aliens, and they have this flashy cool thing that erases people's memories, in case they see an alien."

Ravinia shook her head. For so much of her life, she'd never seen a film. Had barely been introduced to television. "I can't erase anybody's memory, so it's best if you keep that boy at arm's length, no matter how much you like him."

"I don't like him that much." She crossed her arms over her chest and stared through the side window.

Ravinia could just imagine the consequences if Chloe let others see her gift. Though she never thought she'd live to see the day, she was starting to understand Aunt Catherine's reasoning for locking the gates of Siren Song and damn near throwing away the key.

The rest of the ride was in relative silence, and twenty minutes later, Ravinia parked her car on the expansive apron in front of the Bancroft home. She could see around the side of the house to the rear of the property, where a sloping expanse of grass rolled toward the restless ocean, now diamond-sparkled with sunlight, its surface whipped into white caps by the wind. The sky was a layer of indigo eclipsed by scuttling, silver-frosted white clouds. The ocean itself was deep gray and restless.

Ravinia backed the Camry into a spot, nose out where no other car would block her in. She didn't like being trapped, and this appeared to be the kind of event where that could easily happen. Yes, she needed to talk to Aunt Catherine, and yes, that might entail a trip to Siren Song, but if she were lucky, she could manage a quick tête-à-tête here. She believed that, if Aunt Catherine knew about Silas, she might take matters into her own hands and initiate a lengthier, private talk.

"Come on, let's go," she said as Chloe climbed out of the back seat and they followed a few straggling guests toward the porch, but

Chloe hung back, her head swiveling back and forth, her eyes darting over the yard and exterior of the house.

"What's going on with you?" asked Ravinia, waiting before mounting the steps.

Chloe caught up with her. "I think the wolf is here," she said breathlessly, still surveying the shrubbery. "He just doesn't want to show himself."

Ravinia took this as an opinion rather than any "message" Chloe might be receiving. She didn't answer because she wished it were true herself, and she didn't want to crush Chloe's hopes any more than she already had.

But Chloe was too aware to let that pass. "You don't think so," she accused.

"I wish I knew why he was hiding," Ravinia answered, starting up the steps.

"You just don't need him right now. That's all."

Ravinia didn't answer Chloe's confident declaration. Deep in her heart, Ravinia felt the wolf was tied to Silas somehow, and now that Silas was dead . . . well . . . though there was no rule book about "apparitions," she believed the wolf had died with him. "Come on," she said, "we'd better get inside," as she made her way to the wide front door.

Refusing to be weighed down by melancholia, she took a breath and tried to shake off her sadness as she and Chloe walked across the expanse of polished hardwood in the foyer and past a long, narrow table covered with displayed pictures of Declan Bancroft as a much younger man. The framed photographs included his daughter Janet as a girl, and later Hale, after his grandson came along. Business awards and his college diploma were displayed, along with Declan in a black-and-white photo in which he was dressed in an army uniform—a man's long life, caught in snapshots, and capped by a stack of the same pamphlets that had been available at his funeral.

Conversation buzzed as they entered a grand room where wide windows commanded a one-hundred-eighty-degree view of the sea. Here the floor was gray slate cut into amorphous shapes that also covered one wall, which held a large, arched fireplace, the box capped by a rough-hewn mantel made from a thick block of rectangular wood.

Whatever furniture normally graced the room had been ex-changed for white plastic folding chairs. At the far wall of the room, a linen-covered table of hors d'oeuvres was overseen by the catering staff. Appetizers and canapés of every type, from pigs in a blanket to delicate, phyllo-cupped squares filled with kale and Parmesan and ar-tichoke hearts to bright pink, yellow, and red fruit cups and tiny tri-angular sandwiches. Nearby, a second table had been set up as the bar. Glasses of wine were already poured, and the bartender stood by, a young man in a black suit with a white towel over one arm, ready for orders.

Shedding her coat, Chloe beelined for the appetizers and came up with a tiny plate of pigs in a blanket.

Ravinia was held up, leaving both her coat and Chloe's with a woman who took them and disappeared into a downstairs bedroom.

Deciding she could use some food that hadn't come from a vend-ing machine, Ravinia stepped around an elderly couple deep in con-versation and tried one of the phyllo squares as she surveyed the milling crowd, some seated, others collected in small groups, still others standing at the windows and staring at the view. She picked up a small watercress sandwich next, her eyes still scanning the room. She didn't see Elizabeth or Aunt Catherine, but there were many rooms in Declan Bancroft's house, each one practically spilling with people, since no one wanted to venture to the covered patio outdoors, where the furniture was sliding around a bit, dancing in the teeth of the wind.

Ravinia squeezed past two couples involved in a deep conversa-tion about the housing market; they were speculating that Declan Bancroft's house would be put up for sale soon. She overheard a woman, someone called Sylvie, telling warm, anecdotal stories about Declan, and Ravinia realized Sylvie was a Bancroft Development company employee.

She headed out of the main room, with its view, in search of Eliza-beth and Aunt Catherine. Chloe, loaded with two more pigs in a blan-ket, traipsed after her. In the kitchen, she found her aunt flanked by Cassandra and Ophelia, all crowded around a small table, with Eliza-beth standing by, appearing as if she were a waitress ready to take their orders. There was no room for Ravinia, and frankly, she didn't feel like hovering around her family anyway. She loved them but always felt like a little bit of an outsider. Not from Elizabeth and Chloe so much, but definitely from the women who lived at Siren Song. And she certainly couldn't have that one-on-one with Catherine with her sisters hovering nearby.

Frustrated, Ravinia retraced her steps to the main room and the bar. She glanced at the wine, debating about having a glass. She wasn't much of a drinker. In fact, the only alcohol she had a taste for was champagne, but that celebratory drink wasn't in evidence here, which made a certain kind of sense. Honestly, though, she wouldn't mind a glass of champagne and some more Hot Tamales, a particular delicacy only she could appreciate, apparently.

She picked up a glass of white wine, more to have something to carry than because she wanted the drink, then wandered back down the way she'd entered, slowing her steps and pausing as she came to the stairs to the upper floor. Her gaze followed the dark green carpet runner as it ran to the upper landing, then on to the second floor.

This is where it had happened. Where Declan Sr. had died. At least according to Ophelia, who had called to convince Ravinia to attend Declan's funeral and relayed the events leading to his death.

As Ophelia told it, Declan Sr. had fallen down this very stairway, tumbling down the steps to the first floor, where he'd slammed his head on the stone floor. He'd lain at the base of the staircase for hours before someone—Ravinia believed it had been his grandson, Hale—had found the old man and immediately called for an ambulance.

By then, it had been too late.

She stared at the stairs and felt a prickling on her skin as she imagined him tumbling, hitting the railing, bouncing off the wall, flailing and grasping at nothing before slamming headlong to the floor.

She glanced upward to the second level and considered going upstairs. A certain nosiness went with her profession, and she was interested in seeing the rest of the house anyway. Would that be permitted? A tour of the second floor? She could always say she was searching for the restroom if someone found her and objected.

Before she could talk herself out of it, she took a swallow of wine and left her glass on a side table, then headed up the stairs. At the landing, she heard voices from above, muffled somewhat but raised in anger. She took the last steps slowly, listening. The voices were coming from a room at the end of the hall. One side of the pine double doors was closed, but the other was cracked open a bit, and a strident female voice drifted into the hallway.

"—didn't have to ask them here! Service and grave site weren't enough?"

A man's voice answered tiredly, "Stop hiding up here, and join the rest of us."

She guessed that the man was Hale St. Cloud.

"I'm surprised they even came. Really. And where are those hoary old dresses they wore for years? Now they're in black street length? My, how far we've come."

Janet, Ravinia guessed, though she hadn't ever heard her speak. Somehow she sounded just like Ravinia would have expected, especially since she was clearly talking about Ravinia's family.

Hale asked, "This is why you wanted a private conversation? To complain about Catherine and her nieces?"

"The *Colony*," Janet practically spat.

Ravinia made a face, pulling her shoulders in. The locals had dubbed them "the Colony" years ago, and it always came with a whiff of disdain. There was even an incomplete history written about them that Ravinia had yet to read, a slim volume penned by one of Mary Beeman's many lovers. That book was now located at the local historical society. Ravinia had always felt so-so about the "Colony" tag. Clearly, Janet was using it as an epithet.

Hale said, "I'm going downstairs. You can join me or not. Elizabeth is Declan's daughter too."

"Don't I know it," Janet complained bitterly. "That bitch-whore, Mary, screwed my husband *and* my father!"

"That's not true. You know that's not true."

"Which part? Mary slept with your father. That's a fact."

"Mary Beeman didn't sleep with my grandfather," he answered in a steely voice that was a warning.

It was a warning Janet ignored as she swept on, "Well, she slept with Preston! And then she had that bastard child he fathered!"

"Are you sure about that?"

"If you mean did I ever meet the child, no. Of course not. But a wife knows . . ."

Hale made a derisive sound.

"I should've divorced him sooner," snapped Janet.

"Dad's gone, Mom. He's been gone a long time. And you still want to believe any bad rumor about my father and anyone from Siren Song."

"I can't believe you defend them."

"Have you met Elizabeth? Go down there and really introduce yourself. She's great, and so is Chloe."

"She's your generation, not mine."

"She's *your* half sister."

"She's a bastard. Another one. That damned colony is littered with them!"

"My God . . ." Hale sounded practically speechless.

But Janet was undeterred. "After Mom died, Dad catted around. Maybe she's not the only one he got with child. Catherine was so hot for him, maybe Elizabeth isn't his only bastard. She could have had . . . twenty, herself!"

"What century are you living in?" he demanded in exasperation.

"The present one," Janet shot back. "Unlike *those women* at the Colony."

"Well, you're the one living in the past, not them. At least they're coming into the current world. Get over your grudges, Mom. Don't ruin the rest of your life."

Ravinia heard footsteps coming up the stairs behind her. She looked around for somewhere to hide. She didn't want to be caught eavesdropping. Spying a hallway bath, she slipped inside and quickly shut the door behind her. Then she ran the water in the sink and, after turning off the taps, gave herself a couple of seconds as the footsteps passed by the closed door and continued along the hallway.

When they receded, Ravinia peeked out and saw that the double doors had opened wider, and standing in the aperture was Detective Dunbar, her purse strapped over one shoulder.

Janet's voice had risen, and Savannah's appearance apparently hadn't slowed her down one bit. "My husband is dead. Do you hear me? Lee is dead! Dead! Just like your father. Just like your grandfather!"

"I'm sorry about Lee, Mom. His heart attack surprised us too. You know that—"

"You don't give a shit, Hale. None of you do!"

Savannah quickly stepped aside, the door opening farther. Ravinia didn't have time to shut herself back in the bathroom before Janet Bancroft St. Cloud Spurrier stormed into the hallway. Seeing Ravinia, she stopped short. "You," she said, quivering with rage. "You little bitch," she said distinctly. Her lips flattened, her eyes accused. "You're all just sneaky little bitches. I suppose I shouldn't blame you, with the mother you had. With all her"—she waved her hands frantically in the air—"woo-woo sexual enslavement. Bah. She was just an easy slut, and all the men she got were weak. Who was your father, huh? Do you even know? No, you don't. Of course you don't. Mary probably never knew which one it was!"

"*Mom*." Hale's voice rang down the hallway before he stood next to his wife in the doorway.

"Fuck it," said Janet, striding briskly past Ravinia toward the stairs. She didn't look back as she stormed away.

"I'm sorry." Hale, tall, dark, and handsome—all of the clichés—was shaking his head.

"Don't worry about it," said Ravinia as he and Savannah came toward her.

"I don't even know where to start," admitted Hale. "My mother . . . is not thinking clearly. Her husband died a few months ago, and now my grandfather's death on the heels of it . . . it's no excuse, but there it is."

Savannah put a hand on his arm and said, "Why don't you go down and make sure she's okay and all is well."

He uttered a strangled sound but nodded and headed for the stairs, where the sounds of conversation from the main floor drifted upward.

As soon as he made the lower landing and his head disappeared from view, Savannah said, "You weren't in the bathroom the whole time. You overheard everything."

Ravinia would have liked to lie, but what was the point? "My mother was jealous of Janet, and it looks like it goes both ways."

"For sure."

They walked together to the top of the staircase, then stopped and eyed the floor below, where people were still coming and going through the main doors and the sounds of the gathering reached them: footsteps and mingled conversation, clinking glassware, and soft bursts of laughter despite the solemn occasion.

Ravinia saw an opportunity to engage Savannah, who probably knew a hell of a lot about her family, maybe even more than she did, in some ways.

"Mary, my mother, threatened to sleep with Mr. Bancroft because she was mad at Aunt Catherine for falling in love with him, but I don't think it ever happened. And then she named her son Declan Jr., but it was just to twist the knife on both Janet and Aunt Catherine. Declan Sr. wasn't the baby's father."

"Oh, I know. I tried to tell—Charlie—that."

"When you fought with him."

Savannah nodded. "The night he killed Detective Fred Clausen and terrorized me. But, of course, he wouldn't listen to me. There was no talking to him, absolutely none, and the situation was . . . fast-moving."

Meaning that Savannah had been fighting for her life, Ravinia knew. "Aunt Catherine said Charlie's not Preston St. Cloud's son, either, though apparently Preston did get snared by my mother, which is why Janet hates us."

"Janet isn't the most forgiving soul on the planet," Savannah said wryly.

"No."

"Really knows how to hold a grudge."

"Amen." It wasn't easy to forget the hot anger in Janet's eyes as she'd glared at Ravinia just moments before.

"And she's still wounded and angry and can't see how wrong she is." Savannah gave Ravinia a studied look. "I've wanted to talk to you and your sisters and Catherine for a long time. It's just never felt like the right time. Maybe now isn't either, but here we are."

Ravinia wasn't so sure and braced herself, almost afraid of what was coming next.

"Your aunt told me that Charlie killed your mother on Echo Island. She gave me the knife that killed her, wanted a DNA test run, which I did, but the only DNA on it was your mother's. I think Catherine expected it to have Charlie's too, but when it didn't, she pretended it was all a misunderstanding, that your mother probably just nicked herself."

"I don't know about that. But Charlie's too smart to leave that kind of evidence."

"Is he? How do you know?"

"I've never met him but that's the impression I get."

"Do you know who his father is?"

Ravinia shook her head. She preferred to tell the truth, but sometimes lying was the only option. "I just know he's not Declan Bancroft." That, at least, was the truth.

"You know, once Charlie was gone, Declan Sr.'s memory improved. Hale said he'd been having problems and was sometimes confused, but as soon as Charlie was gone, he was as sharp as ever. Charlie admitted to me that he'd been gaslighting Declan. In his house. Making him feel like someone was there but never showing himself. And then recently, Declan started saying the same thing. He called Hale a few times to come and check the house."

Ravinia felt a shiver slide down her back. "I heard Mr. Bancroft died from a fall down the stairs."

"That's right."

They stared at each other for a moment, then Savannah said, "I confess that when Declan started hearing 'bumps in the night' again, my mind went straight to Charlie."

"You think he's back?" Ravinia asked, her mouth dry. It was one thing to flirt with that idea herself, another to hear it from the TCSD detective who'd faced off with him.

"I hope he's dead. I've hoped that for five years."

It sounded like she was saying she thought Charlie had returned. That he was "gaslighting" the man he thought was his father again.

Had Charlie killed Silas?

Ravinia suddenly wanted out of this conversation. She didn't like the itchy, uncomfortable way it made her feel. "What are you going to name your daughter?" she asked into the charged silence.

"We don't have a name for him yet," she answered somewhat distractedly. Her mind was clearly still on Charlie.

"Are you sure it's a boy?" asked Ravinia.

"Pretty sure. One of the technicians mentioned the baby's sex after an ultrasound. We were going to wait to find out, but that kind of gave it away. I have to assume he knew what he was doing."

Ravinia took a step toward the staircase. "Better buy some pink stuff. I'm putting my money on Cassandra. She definitely thinks you're having a girl."

"Wait."

Ravinia paused two steps down as the front door opened below them, and she watched as a couple she didn't recognize left.

"Can I ask you something?" Savannah was regarding her intently.

Here it comes, thought Ravinia, but she paused, one hand on the rail, and looked expectantly at the detective.

"You saw the body that Rhodes found on the beach this morning. Did you recognize him?"

And there it was. She shook her head and spread her hands. "I told him I didn't."

"Detective Rhodes thinks you might not have been telling the truth."

"Well, he can think what he wants."

"I'm stopping by the morgue when this is over to check on the John Doe. Tell me, Ravinia. Is it Charlie? I'd rather know the truth." Her voice dropped to a whisper, but she was intently focused.

Ravinia could read the hope in her eyes. She knew how Savannah felt. God, she understood. Ravinia wanted him dead too.

"It wasn't Charlie," she said regretfully.

Savannah exhaled a pent-up breath and asked, "Did you ever meet Charlie?"

"None of us has, really, except you . . . and your sister."

"Let me give you my cell number." Savannah said, reaching into her purse for a business card, and came to the top step, where Ravinia was still standing. She pressed the card into Ravinia's palm. "When you're ready to tell me or Rhodes who the body is, call."

"I said I don't know him."

"I'll believe I'm having a girl before I believe that." Savannah smiled faintly.

Ravinia was aware her lies were likely to come back and bite her in the ass. Still, she didn't want to say anything until she'd talked to her aunt.

Ravinia headed down the stairs. As she reached the landing, she looked back over her shoulder and found Savannah St. Cloud still watching. A moment later, she started down the steps herself, holding fast to the handrail against the gravitational pull on her ungainly pregnant body.

It was kind of crushing to be so easily read. Ravinia saw her glass of wine waiting on a side table, so she picked it up, walked back toward the bar, and dropped it with the bartender.

Savannah caught sight of her husband, who was caught in the middle of a group of Bancroft Development employees, each one balancing a small plate of food and a glass of some beverage.

"How're you doing?" Hale asked as Savannah made her way around another group of six or so people who had clustered near a coffee table, where they could rest their drinks.

"Okay," she replied.

"Just okay? Not 'fabulous' or 'sensational'?"

"Yeah, right. I forgot. I'm sensational. This is the kind of event I absolutely live for."

"You and me both," he said, laughing.

Savannah glanced at the bar, where Janet was standing with the back of her black hat facing her daughter-in-law. Savannah had overheard her mother-in-law ask the bartender for a glass of bourbon and soda, and he was handing it to her. She felt a twinge of empathy for the woman, who'd been widowed twice, first by Hale's father, Preston St. Cloud, second and most recently by Lee Spurrier. It was hard to go through one death of a spouse, and Janet now had been through it twice.

Didn't mean she wasn't a bitch, though.

"Hey." Hale interrupted her thoughts by sticking his elbow out, and Savannah slipped her arm through his. It felt good, safe to be with him, a port in a rocky storm. "Want anything to eat?"

"No, thanks. Shocking, I know, the way I put away food these days. I'd forgotten that, in the years between being pregnant. I can still really power it down, although I was much younger five years ago. Far younger than a mere five years."

"Math not your strong suit?" he asked.

"'It's not the years, it's the mileage'," she quoted.

"*Raiders of the Lost Ark*," said Sylvie Strahan promptly. She was Hale's right-hand woman and helped make the day-to-day operations of Bancroft Development go smoothly. It was, in part, thanks to her that they'd navigated the ins and outs of the lawsuits over Bancroft Bluffs, known facetiously around the area as Bankruptcy Bluffs.

"Indiana says it to Marion when they're alone together in the onboard cabin," Sylvie reminded them all.

"I'm definitely feeling the mileage," Savannah said with a smile.

"I don't think I've seen that one," said Ella Blessert. Ella, Bancroft Development's bookkeeper, was a stickler for protocol and a fussbudget of the first order. She was about thirty and acted like she was fifty. She was fiercely loyal to Hale and clucked over him like a mother hen sometimes, much to Hale's long-suffering annoyance and Savannah's amusement.

"Seriously? You haven't seen *Raiders of the Lost Ark*?" Sylvie stared at Ella.

"Is that the one with Harrison Ford?" asked Ella.

"Give me strength," said Sylvie.

Savannah looked out at the backyard of Declan's house, where storm clouds were gathering over the sea. This grand home was now Hale's house, as it had been left to him in his grandfather's will. Declan had given generous financial gifts to his two daughters, Janet and Elizabeth, but Hale had inherited the company and the house. Everyone seemed okay with their gifts, except that Janet had tried to freeze out Elizabeth, which wasn't a surprise. Janet was never going to accept her half sister, especially since that half sister was half Janet's age.

CHAPTER 7

"Rhodes!" Lang was striding down from the crest of the dune, leaving the forensics team still working in the sand as Nev watched the body bag holding Stanford Norman's corpse being loaded into the coroner's van.

It was the second time today he'd witnessed a body being hauled away. Odd and unlucky.

Nearby, Jenny Norman stood in shock and misery, her face ashen, her gaze too, locked on the van that held the remains of her husband.

Lang had let all the witnesses go, although Jenny Norman didn't seem to know which way was up, even though Dennis and Corey Weatherby had caught up with her and spoken softly to her. Now it seemed they were walking her to her car. She'd rejected any help from the police when Deputy Rodriguez had approached and had offered to have someone drive her.

It appeared she was listening to the Weatherbys, and Nev was a little surprised, not only that she was taking advice but that the Weatherbys were helping out. It was more goodwill on their part than he'd thought possible.

"Did you happen to see the vic's neck?" asked Lang as he caught up with Nev.

As if he could miss the unique bruising. "Bite marks."

"Human bite marks. Must've been some kind of struggle."

"A hypo, along with knife wounds."

"What the hell happened out here?"

"I guess that's what we have to figure out." They started walking down the rest of the dune to the street. Thankfully, the TV crew that had shown up earlier had left when the reporter and cameraman hadn't been allowed on the dune, none of the witnesses would speak to them, and Lang had referred the reporter to the public information officer.

They reached the department SUV and climbed in. As he started the engine, Lang said, "If we find the killer, the bite marks should be proof in a court of law. But a kid? A girl?"

Nev didn't respond.

"You seem to have checked out. What's up?"

"I keep thinking about the body on the beach by Echo." He exhaled heavily. "I wish she had come clean with me."

"Ravinia Rutledge."

Nev gave up trying to hide his interest. It wasn't working anyway. "What do you know about her?" he asked. All the while, he'd been figuring how to find the "girl" who'd been with Stanford Norman, maybe killed him. Nev had kept coming back to the man he'd found on the beach by Echo, and that, of course, would circle him back to Ravinia.

"Not much, really," admitted Lang. "Ravinia's been outside the lodge for years, but not the others. Catherine's methodology's strange, but she's fiercely devoted to Mary's daughters." He flipped on the wipers as he turned onto 101. "She tried to take them all back to a previous century, but she's loosened up some now, enough that Savvy said they were all going to Declan Bancroft's funeral." He shrugged. "Savvy said Catherine's one great love was Declan Bancroft, so the doors finally opened. There's a big age gap between Catherine and Declan, but I guess Cupid's arrow can strike anybody."

Nev recalled the heat he'd sensed envelop his heart when he was with Ravinia and felt a thrill of premonition, maybe fear. "Not if you don't want it to."

"Trust me, if a Colony woman wants you, you're had, man." Lang slowed for a logging truck piled high with the trunks of fir trees as it braked before turning off the main road. "Ravinia got to you, didn't she?"

"I had half an hour with her at the morgue," protested Nev.

"Long enough." Lang hit the gas again, as the truck rumbled up a side road. "If you're interested, there's a book about the Colony at the historical society. They won't let you check it out, but you can read it there. It goes into their history, and the guy who wrote it, Herman Smythe, lives at Seagull Pointe. Savvy interviewed him when Charlie was rampaging. Smythe claims he slept with Mary Rutledge, was one of her many 'studs.' Could be an empty boast, could be true. Like everything about the Colony, take it with a grain of salt. Or you could interview the man yourself, if he's still alive."

"I'm not interested in the Colony."

"Just Ravinia?"

Nev didn't respond, and Lang said, "You should probably put some pressure on Ravinia. Find out if she knows more about the body that washed up across from Echo Island. See if she had an idea who he is. Doesn't sound like it's Charlie. He's likely dead already. It's hard to disappear the way he has for five years."

That was certainly true. So who was their John Doe?

They drove in silence for a few miles before Lang added, "Charlie's not the only one with an axe to grind with members of the Colony. A few years before him, there was another psychopath bent on revenge against them. A male cousin who escaped from Halo Valley, the mental hospital that's halfway to Salem."

"I know it." And he also knew enough of this story to feel his chest tighten.

"He killed his doctor and went after his cousins. Managed to breach the walls of Siren Song. It was Ravinia who beat him back, but not before he stabbed her in the shoulder. He died falling from the old lighthouse. Broke his neck. Everything settled down after a while, but then a few years later . . . Charlie."

"Ravinia pretended she didn't know the body in the morgue."

"You're sure about that?" asked Lang.

"She's holding something back. I don't know what it is, but I'm going to find out."

Lang nodded. After a few more miles passed beneath their tires, he said, "They're all very pretty. The women of Siren Song."

"I just want Ravinia to come clean with me."

"Okay."

It was clear Lang didn't believe him, but Nev was through arguing, especially since Lang sensed Nev was trying to hide his interest in Ravinia. She knew who the dead man was, he was certain of it. So why was she keeping it a secret? He shoved his hair out of his eyes. He thought maybe Savannah would get the truth from Ravinia. They were both at the Bancroft funeral, and they knew each other, so maybe Ravinia would be able to confide in her.

But that idea didn't sit well with him. *He* wanted to know the truth. All of it. From Ravinia herself.

Hell, Lang was right. Ravinia had gotten to him a little. Despite his arguments to the contrary, Nev did want more information about the Colony. He was going to have to take a crash course on everything and anything to do with the women at the lodge, not just Catherine Rutledge and Ravinia Rutledge. He'd need to learn everything there was to know about Siren Song, which included Charlie and Echo Island. Maybe he would contact Herman Smythe, he mused, if the old man was still alive, and there was always, as Lang had said, the local historical society.

He didn't know exactly what Ravinia had done to him, but whatever it was, it had lit a fire under him.

Sylvie had moved on from her disbelief over Ella's ignorance about *Raiders of the Lost Ark* to funny little remembrances of Declan Bancroft. She was mimicking him, saying, "*Ack*, girl! You're a fine, fine worker, but you're not getting any younger!"

Savannah looked up at Hale, who was smiling, which was good because he'd been hit hard by his grandfather's death, harder than most of them. Declan's health had been on a slow decline, but he'd still been as sharp and irascible as ever.

"Then he had the nerve to tell me I was too skinny. He said, 'Nobody likes a bone but a dog.'" Sylvie threw up her hands in exasperation, and even Ella smiled.

"He was a relic," admitted Hale.

"He thought 'Me Too' meant another helping of ice cream," Ella joined in, which caused them all to stare at her in surprise, she so rarely joked about anything.

Savannah drifted out of the conversation, looking through the back windows to the sloping lawn and gray waters that melded into a horizon of equally gray sky. She and Hale had been married on that expanse of grass. A small ceremony in front of the ocean. Savannah had worn a short, white dress, and Hale had been in a black suit, and the skies had been blue, a rare, clear day in June at the beach. Hale's grandfather had sat on a chair in the front row, and Hale's then four-year-old son, Declan, had been the best man. Sylvie had stood up for Savannah, high over the ocean.

There was no fence separating the cliff from the yard, as the old man had insisted it would block his view. Hale had often argued about it, but there was still no barrier. As she looked at the spot where the lawn disappeared, she sensed her insides tighten, as they always did these days when she felt too close to a precipice. The eerie feeling, akin to acrophobia, was relatively new to her. She'd never had trouble with heights until she'd nearly fallen over the cliff at Bancroft Bluffs the night Charlie abducted her.

The day of the wedding, she'd been very conscious of the edge of the property, only a few yards past where the nuptials took place. Now, inwardly shivering, she turned her thoughts to the happier moments of the wedding. After their vows had been pledged, rings exchanged, and kiss shared, Hale and Savannah had hurried as man and wife into the house to dance the night away in this very room.

She smiled, remembering the maid of honor and best man dancing, toddler Declan giggling in glee while Sylvie twirled and dipped. Today, Hale's son was with the Carmichaels, friends of Hale and Savannah, who, years before, had the unfortunate circumstance of being the first to discover Kristina's body inside the house Bancroft Development had been building for them. She felt the familiar heartache she experienced whenever she thought of her sister, Hale's first wife and five-year-old Declan's mother.

So much tragedy . . .

The baby kicked hard, and Savvy inhaled a bit sharply. Hale looked at her, his eyes questioning, and she shook her head. Savannah had never told Hale how much the edge of the cliff bothered her. She hadn't wanted to put her oar in the water, so to speak, in the argument between her husband and his grandfather. Now, though, this property was Hale's, and though, since Declan Sr.'s death, he and Savannah had discussed moving to Declan's house, they had one of their own that was closer to Bancroft Development, so who knew what the next plan would be? If they did end up here, by God, there would be a fence on the property, one that couldn't be scaled, one that would keep the children safe.

Like the walls surrounding Siren Song? Built for the protection of the girls growing up in the lodge?

"Excuse me," she murmured now, moving away from Hale and his two employees. She didn't want him to feel her shudder and start asking questions.

She picked up a small cucumber sandwich and nibbled at it, then caught a glimpse of Ravinia Rutledge's blond head. The girl had been snooping when she'd been upstairs, no doubt about it. Savannah wondered about that. And she wondered about Ravinia's connection to the body Rhodes discovered on the beach—had it seriously just been this morning? The corpse wasn't Charlie, which was a real disappointment.

When Savannah had heard that Ravinia Rutledge's number was pinned to the corpse, she'd been sure that's who it was, and she'd been jubilant. Charlie was dead! Definitely dead! Finally!

Except he wasn't.

Finishing the sandwich, she rubbed the crumbs from her fingers. She'd actually thought—been convinced, almost, as if she'd had a premonition, like the women at Siren Song—that Charlie had been back a while, maybe here at the house once again, gaslighting Declan. The old man had complained about someone being in the house, just as he had before. Had Charlie been here again? Had he somehow been responsible for Declan Sr.'s death?

She still remembered Charlie's mocking tone when he'd held her captive, and it filled her with renewed rage.

I like you, Detective. I really do. It's too bad you couldn't hang around a while, but you're not the type to play along.

Kristina never played along, Savvy had fervently denied.

Oh, she did. She did. She helped me haunt the old man. She despised him.

"Liar," Savvy whispered now, as she blocked Charlie's image from her inner vision and moved to the bar.

"Can I get you something, Mrs. Bancroft?" the bartender asked.

"Umm. Soda water would be great."

He brought her a glass with ice and a slice of lime, and she took a tentative sip. Good. She had to stop being so imaginative. It wasn't her nature, as a rule, but this pregnancy, and thoughts, fears of Charlie's return, had made her feel vulnerable and uneasy.

But . . . Declan had hardly ever gone upstairs in recent months. He'd lived on the first floor and had been completely aware of how unsteady he'd been. So what had he been doing at the top of the stairs? What had caused him to attempt the steps? Why had he gone up there?

And then hearing about the body on the beach today, and Ravinia . . .

For a moment, she let herself remember more of that terrible night when she'd been under Charlie's control. The terrible, sick, snaky feeling of desire he'd sent by a means she didn't understand. The desire he'd ignited in her . . . for *him*. She'd known then what her sister had been victim to, what she'd suffered from those weeks before her death: Charlie's pheromones.

Do you believe in sorcery? Kristina had asked, almost pleaded with her, and Savannah had thought her sister was having some kind of breakdown. Even so, Savannah had dismissed the urgency in Kristina's voice. Until she too had been lassoed by that dark, sexual twine Charlie wrapped her up in. He'd planned to kill her, like he'd killed Kristina. He'd planned to look into her eyes as she was dying, like she'd seen him do to Fred Clausen, drinking in some evil elixir that caused him to shudder with ecstasy.

A cold frisson slid down Savannah's spine, and she shuddered herself. She'd been lucky to survive. One of only a handful Charlie had put under his spell.

"Hey, there."

Savannah felt hands encircle her waist from behind, and she reacted as if goosed in the half second before she realized it was her husband.

"Sorry," she murmured.

"You're jumpy," he said as she turned around in his arms, back to the present once again.

"Aren't you? A little? It's a difficult day."

"That's why I'm back for some anesthesia." He slid his arms away from Savannah and said to the bartender, "Dewars on the rocks."

"Hale, I want to find out the sex of our baby. I know we overheard that technician say it was a boy, so we've assumed he was right, but maybe he was wrong? Or talking about somebody else?"

"I thought you wanted the surprise."

"I did. You're right. But that was a dumb idea. I want to know what we're having once and for all."

"It's about ninety-nine percent accurate."

"I'll take my chances," she said dryly.

"Okay." Then, "How're you holding up so far?" he asked, as the bartender handed him his drink.

"Doing okay. Can't lie. Going to be glad when this is behind us."

He lifted his glass and looked to the ceiling. "To you, Granddad," he said, then after a long swallow muttered, "You and me both . . ."

"Time to leave," said Catherine, looking from one to the other of her nieces, who were flanking her. Cassandra slid out of her seat first, just as Elizabeth returned from a second trip to the appetizer table.

"Ready to go?" asked Elizabeth, setting the tray on the table. Chloe, who was hovering in the background, reached around her mother for another pig in a blanket.

"I've seen enough," said Catherine.

Ravinia was outside the nook area and stepped back when Aunt Catherine, leaning heavily on Elizabeth's arm, came through the aperture and started making her way to the front door.

"Should we say goodbye to the Bancrofts?" Elizabeth looked over her shoulder.

"Ophelia, come here," ordered Catherine.

Ophelia immediately obeyed, and Catherine transferred her hand to Ophelia's arm from Elizabeth's. To Elizabeth, she said, "Go say goodbye. They're your family."

Elizabeth was clearly torn. "Chloe and I are leaving tomorrow," she started to explain, but Catherine cut her off with, "We'll see you at the lodge."

Cassandra followed after them, leaving Ravinia with Elizabeth and Chloe. Elizabeth made a sound of amusement or sorrow. It was hard to tell.

"My mother," was all she said, and there was a wealth of meaning in those words that Ravinia could appreciate.

He stepped into the bar, looked around, and grinned. It was empty at this time of day, basically a converted warehouse for a distinctly low-brow clientele. The bartender was a skanky bitch with bleached-blond hair and dark roots who kept her eye on him as if he were going to steal the furniture. Ha. The chairs were broken and mended back together with black electrician's tape. The scarred wooden floorboards reeked of beer. The only pictures on the wall were faded, dusty scenes of tropical beaches, nothing like the Oregon coast, nothing like the gray October skies beyond those dusty windows filled with dried bug carcasses.

He didn't especially like beer, but this was the kind of place you'd better damned well order one if you wanted to blend in.

"PBR," he said to the woman, and she brought him a Pabst Blue Ribbon in a can and a glass still rimmed with some woman's lipstick that hadn't quite come out in the dishwasher. He imagined who that woman would be. Someone ripe and luscious with plump red, parted lips who was begging, just begging, for what Good Time Charlie could give her.

The thought sent hot desire shooting through his bloodstream. He would scarcely admit it to himself, but he was grateful, fucking *grateful*, for the feeling. Without sex he felt his powers diminish, and he'd been woefully abstinent for a long, long time. Too damn long, courtesy of that monster who'd imprisoned him.

He heard a pitiful mewl and realized belatedly that the sound had passed through his own lips. It was embarrassing. The skank shot him a sideways look. *She'd heard.*

Goddammit. Now he was going to have to take care of her too. No one, but no one, could feel sorry for him.

Once the idea took root, he couldn't let it go. From anger, he moved to interest to out-and-out desire. The bar was empty. Had been all morning because half the town was at dear old dad's funeral. He'd thought about going himself. Toyed with the idea, but there was no fun in that. The fun had been in killing the old goat. Too bad he'd died before Charlie could see that last light in his dimming eyes. He'd been gone too fast, his eyes closed, and when Charlie had pried them open, they were fixated. *Fuck.* He'd been in such a rage he could barely pull himself together to get out of the house and away, even as he'd heard the jangle of the keys. He'd had to run out the back and, taking a big chance, dropped down the sheer wall of rock. Hanging above the roaring sea had been a test, and he'd gritted his teeth and swung his body, hand over hand, holding onto exposed rocks and roots, steadfastly working his way over to a neighboring property, where a fir tree rose from a ledge below.

He'd been able to climb down to that precipice, and from there he'd worked his way along a stony path to the narrow beach below. He'd walked steadily northward. The beach had given out to a trail used by hikers, and from there, it had been easy to use the paths and service roads that wound for miles up and down the coast.

He'd left his old banger car in a Seaside parking lot and hitch-hiked down 101 to get to Declan's, then had camped in the brush around a property about a mile north of the house. That property was a dinky vacation home with a weed-choked lawn. Charlie had never seen anyone using it besides some teenagers drinking straight vodka from a bottle and smoking weed. He'd thought about joining them one night. The girl was kind of dead-eyed and passive, but he thought he might be able to get a rise out of her without too much effort. But the guys were big and stupid, and Charlie wasn't sure he could incapacitate all of them at once in his diminished state.

It hadn't always been like this, he thought angrily. The seedy bar where he was sitting fading from his consciousness as he remem-bered escaping with that nanny . . . man, what was her name? Victo-ria. Victoria Phelan. Jesus. It shook him how much he'd lost in the intervening years. But at that time, when Victoria had driven him into Canada, he'd been horridly wounded. He'd still been powerful, though. The fire had scarred him, but it hadn't killed him. He wouldn't let it kill him. Refused. He'd vowed to return to the States, deter-mined to head south. In the process, he'd sworn, he'd fuck them all.

But . . . *things happened.*

His muscles contracted, just thinking about it.

He couldn't go there. Not now.

Pushing thoughts of the last five years aside, he concentrated in-stead on his purpose. That detective bitch had been the reason he'd nearly lost his life, the reason his skin had burned and crinkled in that raging fire. He felt the melting of his flesh again as if it were hap-pening now and almost heard himself scream.

It was time for payback.

And now she was Hale St. Cloud's wife. Christ!

He had to fight to keep from sneering. She was family to him. His father's daughter-in-law . . . no . . . grand-daughter-in-law? Who the fuck cared? The point was that she was moving in on Charlie's domain.

Well, he wasn't going to let her.

To top things off, she was pregnant again.

He would kill them both. Her and her unborn child.

And then the others.

His jaw tightened so hard it ached.

The others—those freaks of Siren Song—were slowly taking baby steps forward, peeking their noses out of that lodge, the lodge that was rightfully his too.

All of them . . . *all of them* . . . conspiring against him all his life!

"You okay, mister?" the skank asked.

Charlie realized he'd crushed his can without drinking a drop, beer foaming over his hand and pooling onto the sticky bar.

"Just fine, darlin'. Why don't you come over here and help me lick this up?"

The look on her face was indescribable. She'd probably heard about everything there was to hear in a place like this, but he'd still surprised her. Inside, he was chortling.

"I'll get you a towel," she said.

She bent down and reached for something under the bar, and Charlie sent his pheromones her way.

C'mon, babe, he silently told her. *C'mon and suck my dick.*

She reacted so violently she hit her head beneath the bar. "Shit!"

Charlie laughed aloud.

She staggered backward and looked at him in horror . . . and desire.

He got off the bar stool and sauntered to the front door of the bar. Through the blinds, he could see the backside of a building on the edge of Seaside. A no-account area bordering on decrepit. He turned the deadbolt and looked back at her.

She was standing against the wall behind the bar, her arms spread wide as if she were keeping the wall from falling. "Who . . . who are you?"

"My mother named me Declan," he said, walking around the bar and moving in on her. "But I prefer Charlie."

She was squirming for him, and he hadn't even touched her yet. "Charlie?" she questioned shakily.

He pulled down her pants, amused to find she was going commando. Drew his own trousers down, gratified by the size of his woody. No erectile dysfunction today. He pulled her onto him and screwed her six ways to Sunday with her howling for more, while her eyes pleaded for him to stop.

"You're . . . a monster . . ." she moaned in anguish.

One flailing arm hit his face, and she touched the burned wreck of his ear. Fury blasted through him, and he closed his hands over her neck and squeezed and squeezed. Her eyes bugged out, and her face turned blue, and then she started to fade, and he stared deep into her soul, and he felt the glimmer of that delicious power, not much, but some, far better than what he'd gotten from dear old dad.

She gurgled something, and he said, "Love you too."

He then went through the cash register. Measly two hundred dollars. Fucking credit cards, fucking Venmo, fucking Zelle . . . and headed out the back door. His car was a block away, and there was no one around to notice the guy in a jean jacket, work boots, and shoulder-length brown hair. The hair was to cover his ear. The bastard who'd imprisoned him had done the work on his face, but the ear had been burned to a nub by the fire. Hadn't been able to restore it. Or maybe the bastard had kept that particular plastic surgery skill a secret? He'd wanted Charlie, and he'd kept him in his house, and it had taken years, *years*, for Charlie to rebuild his strength enough to send the fucker to hell and get on with his mission.

First Seaside, then Deception Bay, then to southern California to wipe the bitches from the planet.

And maybe a trip to Portland for the youngest one, who imagined herself to be a private investigator.

Silas was dead, so the boys/men were no longer a problem.

This time, it would be easy pickings.

He already had one on the hook . . .

CHAPTER 8

Ravinia watched while Elizabeth and Chloe said their goodbyes to Hale and Savannah, with promises to keep in touch. There was a warmth to Elizabeth's hugs that had been entirely missing in her nod to Janet, who refused to do more than appear bored and turn away. Chloe, once again in her coat, cocked her head and hugged Janet anyway, which made Janet's eyes open wide with dismay, but Chloe was smart enough to make it quick. Then the girl grabbed her mother's hand and jauntily skipped away toward the door.

Ravinia smiled inwardly, certain Chloe knew exactly what she was doing. She said her goodbyes as well, saved from even talking to Janet, who stalked to the bar after Chloe's hug and quickly ordered J&B on the rocks.

Savannah said, "I'll call you later" to Ravinia, as if they'd planned some kind of future date, which, if that's what Savannah had in mind, Ravinia was not going to make. Hale glanced from one of them to the other, but didn't say anything as Elizabeth and Chloe headed outside.

Ravinia shrugged into her coat and cast a final look around Declan's ocean-side home. As she made her way to the front door, she glanced up the stairs and imagined the old man tumbling down. Had he been that unsteady? Had he gotten up to the top and then stumbled? Why had he mounted the stairs in the first place? Savannah had said Charlie had gaslighted the old man. Was Charlie back? *Had he killed Silas somehow?*

No proof of that. None whatsoever.

With no more answers to her questions, Ravinia walked outside to the cold October day, where Elizabeth and Chloe were waiting for her.

The wind had died down to a kicky little breeze that nevertheless drew strands of blond hair across Elizabeth's lips, which she brushed away. She said, "We're heading to Siren Song. I didn't intend to. We have a motel in Seaside, and then we're leaving for the airport tomorrow. But before Catherine left, she asked me to stop by and . . . I don't think I can just leave without saying goodbye. Especially to Isadora and Lillibeth. I'm not sure when we'll be back."

"You're going to come too," said Chloe, as if there were no question.

"I am," Ravinia told her. But if the family reunion was continuing, it was going to be later and later before she had any chance to talk to her aunt alone.

"You can stay with us at the motel," said Chloe, as if she'd read her mind.

Ravinia gave the girl a sharp look. *Had* she read her mind? "Actually, I'm going to try to make it home tonight. To Portland. I need to get back. I kind of just up and left things."

Ravinia felt increasing dread the nearer she drew to Siren Song. She thought of Silas again, his inert body, and questions filled her mind that she'd ignored in the shock of the moment and the duty of the funeral. Had he drowned? How could he have had the presence of mind to write her number down if he was dying? That detective—Rhodes—had said the pen was in his pocket, so what did that mean, if anything?

She needed more information from the medical examiner, she thought, just as they reached the turnoff for the lodge. Elizabeth pulled in first and had enough space to turn around and park, facing out, in the grassy space in front of the lodge gates. Ravinia did the same.

For once, they didn't have to wait long outside the high, wrought-iron gates as Ophelia was Johnny-on-the-spot, letting them all in before locking the gates securely behind them. Chloe, thrilled to be in the forested expanse beyond the walls, took off at a run through the trees, only to catch up with them on the porch just as Isadora shepherded them through the door.

Inside, the great room, with its huge stone fireplace on one end, was divided from the kitchen by the large trestle table with its long benches.

Isadora, tall, blond hair pulled into a tight bun, chin lifted, wearing one of the full-length print dresses they'd all been forced to wear for years, greeted Elizabeth and Chloe with a courteous smile, while her eyes took in Ravinia's palazzo pants with a look of distaste. Well, hell. You couldn't please everyone. Ravinia felt a prickle of annoyance and was thrown back into a memory of all those years she'd railed against the restrictions. She wasn't the only one who had rebelled. One of her sisters had escaped the confines of the lodge years before. Unfortunately, she had perished outside the gates, and Aunt Catherine had doubled and redoubled her efforts to keep the rest of them safe, though, of course, with mixed results.

"Don't mind her," Ophelia whispered and took everyone's coat to hang in a nearby closet.

Catherine was on the couch. She was sitting upright, one hand on an overstuffed arm, but Ravinia got the sense that she would lie down for the night as soon as she had a chance.

"I've got some soup and bread," Isadora told them, indicating the seats around the table. Cassandra was already seated, and Elizabeth politely joined her, patting the seat next to her for Chloe. But her daughter hesitated, her eyes taking in everything within the lodge, and she actually took a few steps toward the curving wooden staircase, looking as if she wanted to explore.

"I'm not hungry, thanks," said Ravinia.

"You should join us," insisted Isadora.

"There was a lot of food at the reception." Ravinia moved toward her aunt as she heard the sound of Lillibeth's wheelchair working its way from her main floor bedroom.

Ravinia glanced to the hallway and saw her sister.

Lillibeth was wearing a nightgown with a thin blue robe over it, the color matching the shade of her eyes, making them more luminous. Even so, she looked tired and drawn.

There was space at the end of the table for her, and Isadora had already laid out a place setting. "I'm not hungry, either," said Lillibeth quietly.

"You said you'd eat your favorite soup," Isadora reminded her.

"I know, but I'm not hungry."

Ravinia sensed this was a long-running argument. She turned her attention to her aunt. For a split second, Catherine let down her guard, and her expression changed, momentarily displaying her consternation and fear before her mask slid smoothly into place.

What the hell was going on here?

Chloe settled into the chair next to her mother and said, "I like soup too." She'd turned into a natural peacemaker, Ravinia realized, recalling the somewhat recalcitrant child she'd once been.

Ravinia perched on the couch beside her aunt. Before she could say anything, Catherine lifted a hand, forestalling her. "I want to talk to you alone."

Well, hallelujah. "When?"

"Now. Help me upstairs to my room."

Ophelia, who had come to stand before the fire, sucked in a breath, but Catherine quelled her with a look.

Ravinia looked at the steps. "You sure?" she asked.

"Yes." Catherine forced herself to her feet and, using her cane, walked to the stairs.

Isadora shot Ophelia a glance. "Aunt Catherine, I don't know—"

Catherine interrupted, "Go on with the meal. See to our guests," then to Ravinia. "Now you," she said. "You help me." She grabbed the rail with a gnarled hand.

Ravinia felt her sisters' gazes but did as she was told. It took Catherine's fortitude and Ravinia's strength, but together they made the climb and the short distance down the hallway to Catherine's room. "Well, that wasn't so hard now, was it?" Aunt Catherine said and sat heavily on the bed, the mattress with its quilted coverlet sagging a bit beneath her weight.

"What happened to you?" asked Ravinia.

She waved a hand as if to dispel the question. "I've grown a little older. That's all. It happens to the best of us."

"Oh, really," Ravinia said dryly.

"Don't be impertinent. I know I've aged a lot since you last saw me. It doesn't matter. What matters is Lillibeth."

"Lillibeth? Well, okay. She looks . . . unwell. But there are a few other things happening as well." Ravinia closed the door. "I've been wanting to tell you all day that Silas is dead. I saw his body in the morgue this morning. I didn't identify him. I wanted to talk to you first. It's just . . . when I saw him I . . ." Tears were suddenly burning behind her eyes. The brother she hardly knew, but he *mattered*. "I couldn't believe it. He was supposed to kill Charlie."

Catherine had gone rigid. Gazing straight ahead, but unmoving, as if staring into some abyss only she could see.

"Aunt Catherine?"

The older woman blinked, then focused on Ravinia. "Are you certain it was Silas?"

Ravinia nodded. "I only met him a couple of times. But yes, it was the same man. You told me he was Silas."

"Who knows this?"

"Besides me, and now you, no one. At least I haven't told anyone, not even the police," assured Ravinia. "The detective who found him didn't believe me when I said I didn't know who he was. I get the feeling the police, and that detective—Rhodes—are going to come back to me."

"Oh dear God." Catherine clasped her hands together and squeezed.

Ravinia expected her aunt to ask how he'd died, and she was about to say that, at first appearance, it looked like Silas had drowned, but she'd forgotten that Aunt Catherine seemed to always be one step ahead.

Catherine said in a quiet but knowing way, "Declan Jr. killed him."

Ravinia felt a bolt of fear shoot through her. She'd been thinking the same thing about Charlie on and off all day, but just hadn't wanted to go there. Savannah had flat out asked her if the dead man was Charlie, but still, to have Catherine say Declan Jr. killed him—she'd never switched to calling him Charlie, even though she was the one who'd made it clear he was not Declan Bancroft's son—jolted her.

"On Echo?" Ravinia asked, turning to the window and the direction of the island.

Catherine got to her feet, swaying a bit, holding onto the bedpost for support. "He's here now. He won't quit until he's got what he wants."

"What are you going to do? Lock up the lodge again?"

Catherine ignored the question. "Lillibeth is having bad dreams. It's a sign."

Ravinia could feel the skepticism taking hold, the same skepticism she felt whenever she heard bald predictions, even though she knew they might prove to be true. "Ophelia said they're just romantic dreams."

"That's how it starts. Romance . . . sex . . . and then when he has you . . ." She left the thought unfinished.

Ravinia stared at her aunt. She knew Catherine was equating Charlie to his father, Thomas Durant, who'd attacked her, forcing her into a closet. Though Durant had been Mary's father, he was long gone before Mary and Aunt Catherine's mother, Grace, married John Rutledge and became pregnant with Catherine. At that time, Grace erased every memory of her first husband and used the last name of Rutledge for both of her daughters. But unbeknownst to Mary and Catherine, Durant returned years later, changed, disguised, never telling anyone who he was, and had sex with Mary himself. Maybe he'd "romanced" her first, or maybe her power to entrap, combined with his, just caused the explosion between them. Whatever the case, by the time he came after Mary's younger sister, she was wise to him. She found him atop Catherine, ripping at her clothes, and had slammed the butt of a shotgun against his head, killing him instantly and saving Catherine from being raped.

"Don't look at me that way," Catherine snapped, as if she'd read Ravinia's thoughts.

"I'm processing the 'romance' comment. You were talking as if you experienced the same thing."

"You know about Thomas from Mary's journal."

Ravinia nodded. Catherine had objected strenuously to her reading Mary's diary, but it hadn't stopped her. Ravinia knew Catherine had a journal as well, but to date she'd guarded its contents.

"Thomas had his ways," Catherine admitted. "I almost fell for them . . . for him. But then I met Declan, and things changed." Her voice softened for a moment, and then her jaw clenched and her words, again, were harsh. "Thomas couldn't stand that his spell over me was broken . . . and . . . if it hadn't been for Mary saving me . . ." She left the thought unfinished.

"Mary might have saved you then, but she threatened to take Declan Sr. from you. I read the journal," Ravinia reminded her aunt.

"Mary was difficult."

That was putting it mildly.

Aunt Catherine had solved the Mary problem by exiling her to Echo Island and telling anyone who asked that she'd died and was buried in the graveyard behind Siren Song. In truth, it was Thomas Durant who'd been buried in Mary's grave until Mary herself died. Catherine had then asked Earl to bring Mary's corpse back to the mainland, and he'd complied, burying her temporarily at the back of the graveyard as Catherine decided what to do about Thomas Durant's bones. Ravinia herself had helped Earl transfer Mary to her rightful place beneath the headstone with her name, but they'd had to dig up Durant's remains first to make room. They'd expected to find Durant's rotted skeleton in Mary's grave, but the bones hadn't been there. When Ravinia had related that news to her aunt, Catherine realized Silas had taken the bones to Echo Island and burned them. Burning the bones was more than symbolic for Catherine, though Ravinia didn't feel the same.

"I don't think romance is the problem and I don't care about the bones," Ravinia said now, crossing the room to stand by the window. "They're gone, and whether they ever had any power or not, or if my mother was just plain nuts and you've all made up these crazy stories, I just don't care. I care about Silas, and what happened to him. Do you think he was on Echo? Did he go there for some reason? *Is Charlie there?*"

"They're not crazy stories." Her aunt's face settled into that obdurate expression Ravinia knew so well.

"Okay. Something's happened, something I don't understand," Ravinia relented. "To make you age like this. I mean—" Ravinia searched for a reasonable answer. "Unless you're sick and you're hiding it from me."

"I'm not sick."

"Is Charlie—er, Declan Jr.—on Echo?" Ravinia repeated. "Did he and Silas have some kind of meeting, fight, whatever? What happened?"

"I don't know. But you—you need to find out how Silas died."

"Oh, I mean to," Ravinia said. This was so like her aunt. Decreeing what everyone should do. "But I might have to identify his body to get that information."

"Once you know how Silas died, you'll know if Declan Jr.—Charlie—is the reason he's dead."

"Okay." Ravinia felt a bit lighter. The onus of keeping Silas's identity secret had weighed on her. There would be lots of questions. Detective Rhodes would want to know how she knew Silas and the whole history of his relationship to her and Siren Song and Charlie and the nature of the adoptions. She wasn't sure at this point exactly how much she could or would tell. Just enough for him to learn about Silas, although she already sensed that Rhodes would pressure her for more details than she would be willing to reveal.

A board creaked in the hallway outside. There was a sharp rap on the door a bare second before Ophelia let herself into the room. "What's so secret you didn't want anyone else to know?" she asked Ravinia.

Ravinia regarded her stonily. Ophelia always tried to intervene in her relations with their aunt. That hadn't changed in five years.

"We were discussing Lillibeth's dreams," said Catherine. "Ravinia has agreed to spend the night."

Ravinia's mouth dropped open. Ophelia was looking at Catherine with consternation. "I don't think that's necessary, do you?"

Catherine looked past Ophelia to Ravinia and said firmly, "We both think it's a good idea."

When Ophelia turned to look at her, frowning, Ravinia gave up her plan to leave and said slowly, "I don't have to be back till tomorrow."

Ophelia looked from Ravinia to Catherine and just lifted her hands, as if surrendering, then returned to the hallway.

"Thanks," Ravinia said dryly, but Catherine just shrugged.

Catherine insisted on staying in her room for the rest of the afternoon and night, instead of sleeping on the sofa, and Ravinia left her and headed back downstairs where Ophelia pulled her through the anteroom off the kitchen and outside into the cloudy, cool afternoon. "I think it would be better if you went back today. There are still a few hours of daylight left. Your room hasn't been slept in since you were last here, and we've closed it off to save heat." She was staring into the trees. "You know Aunt Catherine just wants to protect all her missing chicks. Don't let her influence you."

Ravinia said, "Oh, it's no trouble." Having been coerced into staying now Ravinia was going to use the time to learn more about what was going on at the lodge. "Besides, I'd like to talk to Lillibeth. Cassandra said—"

"Cassandra—Maggie—is wrong more than she's right. She wants to make more of Lillibeth's nightmares than there is."

"Five years ago she said, 'He's coming,' meaning Charlie, and she was right."

Ophelia walked to the porch rail, then turned back to face her sister, "You and I have always gotten along. I made you your first pairs of pants. I don't want you to be upset. I'm just letting you know that it's not necessary for you to stay. You've got your own life. So do I, finally. Lillibeth is still recovering from a case of pneumonia. That's all."

"It's no big deal. My overnight bag's in the car. I'll just go get it." Ravinia headed back inside the lodge and crossed the dining and living areas to the front door and the trek down the walk to the gate and to her Camry. She wasn't exactly sure what Ophelia's objection was, but now that she'd made the decision to stay, she wasn't going to be dissuaded.

Lucky turned her gray Outback into the lookout above the beach nearest to Echo Island. She'd cruised past the road that led to the entrance to Siren Song Lodge and noted Ravinia's car was parked next to another. When Ravinia had taken a left, following after the car in front of her, Lucky had kept her Subaru heading south the short distance to the turnout and hoped she hadn't been noticed.

She couldn't stay here long. Her license plate would give her away if some enterprising cop decided to run it. She needed to stay in the shadows, but she needed these few minutes. She would have liked to go down to the beach and throw herself on the sandy ground of the last place he was alive. She'd been rescued off a nearby beach a number of years ago herself, and though she appreciated the symmetry, it didn't lift the sorrow in her heart or the rage boiling inside her.

She got out of the car and walked to the edge of the precipice. There was no time to fight her way down the cliffside and that forlorn, steep path.

Echo Island was a dark hump in the distance.

Silas had made the dangerous trip to the island, even though he'd said he wouldn't. He'd lied to her to keep her from learning exactly what he intended to do. And Echo had killed him. She knew that for a fact. Going to that island had been playing into the hands of a malevolent fate.

She drew a heavy breath and exhaled slowly. She had a final job to do. She knew it would be her last, and now she didn't care.

Vengeance was how she had lived. Vengeance was how she would die.

And she was going to take Charlie with her.

"Next of kin," Nev muttered. He'd called the coroner's office, twice at least, looking for a cause of death, even a preliminary cause, and he'd been brusquely told that the information would be forthcoming. "As soon as we know something more, we'll call."

Yeah, right.

Stone too was at his desk, following up on Stanford Norman. He'd also put a call into the coroner's office and gotten nowhere.

Now Nev twiddled a pen between his fingers and read what little he could find on Ravinia Rutledge and her fledgling detective agency in Portland. Not much. She'd been open less than a year and appeared to be handling background checks and some process serving.

His cell phone buzzed.

He answered and heard Sazlow's voice on the other end of the connection.

Finally!

"Doesn't look like your John Doe drowned," he started off and explained that there had been no water in the victim's lungs, but at the very least he had been drugged—the point of penetration from the hypodermic needle discovered beneath his left arm. "We don't know what was in the hypo, yet. The tox screen won't come back for a while, and we're trying to get what we can off the needle itself." Sazlow also explained that the victim had been in some kind of fight with persons unknown or maybe a battle with the sea itself, though again, he said there wasn't any water in his lungs, though he did have bruising down his arms and legs, along with possible strangulation marks on his neck, though that wasn't certain.

"But someone killed him using a hypodermic needle," clarified Nev, his gaze shooting across his desk to Lang, who was deep into a telephone call with Norman's employer, a software company out of

Portland for which he worked remotely, while Nev was following up on their John Doe.

"In some capacity, yes. We'll know for certain soon."

Nev waited for Lang to end his call, then told him what he'd heard from Sazlow.

Lang thought it over a minute, then said, "So both our bodies were found on a beach, just not the same one, and both had hypodermic needles at the scene. Stanford Norman was stabbed the previous night, and John Doe might have been in a fight." He leaned back in his chair. "And then there's the fact that Norman was bitten."

"And we have no idea who 'the girl' with him was," said Nev.

"The girl." Lang nodded.

"Where did he pick her up? Or where did she pick him up?"

"Good question. How young was she?"

Nev checked his watch. The afternoon was wearing on. He could feel how tired he was. Last night had been short, too few hours of sleep, and now it was catching up to him.

"Think she's old enough to bar hop?" asked Lang. "Norman hung out at bars. Older girls, even women, can wear pigtails."

"It's possible," Nev said slowly. "Before I recheck with Corey and Dennis, I'll stop by the Locker." Other than Sandbar's small establishment, Davy Jones's Locker was the closest and most popular watering hole around, and Norman was a known regular. "I'll see if anyone remembers a woman with pigtails." Not much to go on, but something.

"Good. I'm going to meet Savvy at the morgue." As he spoke, Lang reached for the jacket he'd tossed over his chair. Half the time, he didn't bother hanging it in his locker. Nev had tried to keep his personal items locked up, but he was getting the hang of things around TCSD and was beginning to loosen up on some of the rules, learning which ones were critical and which ones were generally ignored.

Nev wasn't sure how he felt about Lang meeting Savannah. He was feeling kind of competitive about the John Doe case. Would have rather had her be on Stanford Norman's. Sure, the detectives at TCSD worked as a team, but he wanted the one attached to Ravinia.

"Check in with me later," said Lang as he headed toward the back door.

"Okay." Glancing at the clock again, he decided to follow Lang out. There was something else he wanted to do as well.

Savvy watched the reception catering staff start to close up shop, and she found Hale at the front door, saying goodbye to an elderly couple who'd known Declan and driven from Portland for the funeral. Janet was beside him, but she was looking a little loose around the edges from alcohol consumption.

Savvy said, "I've got some work to do, so I think I'm going to head out. You're okay to oversee everything?"

"You don't . . . don't . . . have to mother him," said Janet, losing her balance slightly and stepping back.

Hale glanced at her, then turned back to Savvy, deadpan: "Darling, I know how much you love someone telling you what to do and asking how you feel over and over again, so I'll jump right in. Don't overdo yourself. Take it easy. It's been a long day."

"You're so right. I do love being told what to do and being asked over and over again how I feel," said Savvy, pressing her lips together to hide her smile.

Janet frowned at her. "You should take care of . . . you are having a Bancroft."

Hale's eyes were filled with suppressed mirth. If she hadn't been so pregnant, Savvy might have doubled over in laughter. Leaning forward, Savvy gave Hale a kiss. "I'll meet you at home in an hour or so."

Hale already knew she was going to the Ocean Park Hospital morgue. "I'll expect the 'or so,'" he said, then looked around and said, "I've got this."

"I put in a call to Dr. Evanson. I want to know the sex of our baby for sure," reminded Savannah.

Hale nodded.

"You are having a boy," said Janet deliberately. Now she had one hand pressed against the wall and was spending an inordinate amount of time focusing on Savannah.

"Yeah, maybe." She gave them both a wave and headed to her car.

As the afternoon waned, Nev drove toward Davy Jones's Locker. The place was a rambling, shingled building, leaning toward decrepit; once red, it was now a faded salmon color on its way to weathered gray from the continued lash of wind, rain, and salt water off the ocean. It had surprisingly good breakfasts, *huevos rancheros* being its signature dish, if you could use that term for a dive bar, but its main menu was a lavish assortment of fried seafood straight from the freezer to the fryer, accompanied by pretty damn good french fries or heavily dressed cole slaw, if you were taking the healthy route.

It was early for the serious drinkers, but there were always a number of regulars scattered around who didn't seem to much care if it was five o'clock or not.

He pulled onto the gravel drive that ran parallel to the Locker, ending at the bar's rear entrance. The front doors were mainly used by tourists, and as he drove by, he saw a nicely dressed man and a woman step onto the last of the broad, weathered front steps to peer through the porthole window in the arched entry door. They seemed reluctant to go inside, and he almost rolled down the window to suggest somewhere else. A cute name and a cute porthole did not a grade-A establishment make, but whatever. They could discover it for themselves. Longtime locals like Nev always used the back door.

When Nev pushed in, he saw the couple standing just inside the front door, conferring. They were clearly reluctant to take a seat at any of the wooden booths that rimmed three walls of the room, the red Naugahyde seats just starting to fade to pink as well.

There were a number of wooden tables and chairs scattered around, all vacant, as patrons chose the booths first. The place smelled of stale beer and cooking oil, and as Nev took a seat at the bar, his back to the front entrance to get a good view of the rear door, just as the man leaned in to hear something his lady friend was saying, and a moment later they turned around and left the way they'd come in.

Well, yeah. Nev smiled to himself. He was on duty for a while yet, but he ordered a beer anyway. The bartender and the patrons might not know he was a cop, or they might, but if they saw him with anything but alcohol, he would be suspicious. And if they recognized he was with law enforcement and adhered too closely to the rules, he would be treated like a leper.

He wanted to ask about Stanford Norman right away but was aware that would also be outside the understood rules of the lowbrow establishment, where silent TVs broadcast a variety of sports, while country music battled with the noise of pool balls clicking, the fryer sizzling in the tiny kitchen, and conversation humming throughout. Better to settle in a while and see who came in. He knew one of the bartenders by name, but that man wasn't working today. Instead, he was being served by a thin, silent man with a bald head, a long beard, and heavily tattooed forearms visible from beneath a black Davy Jones's Locker T-shirt, the white print art on its front displaying a school locker with a trident wedging open the door and a pair of evil-looking eyes peering out above a Cheshire grin.

"I might need one of those," said Nev, pointing to the shirt.

"Thirty bucks."

"You're kidding me."

The man shrugged and went to serve another customer.

Well, maybe not, then. Nev took a swallow of his beer, then pulled out his phone and scrolled through his call list until he found the number he wanted. He looked down the bar, the phone to his ear.

"Hey, man, what's up?" Rand Tillicum answered.

"I wanted to talk to you about the Colony."

A long, weighty pause. "Why?"

Nev debated about bringing up the dead body found on the beach to his good friend. But it was likely on this evening's news, so he probably wasn't giving anything away. Briefly, he went through the events of the morning, though he didn't mention the note that was pinned to John Doe's shirt. That was not for public consumption yet. But he did mention that TCSD thought there might be some connection to the women at Siren Song.

"Because of where the body was found?"

"It's closest to Echo. And you know the women at the lodge. I just thought you could give me some background," he said and noticed the barkeep hovering near the taps, possibly eavesdropping.

"My dad knows them," corrected Rand.

Rand was a Foothiller, the name given to the unincorporated "town" in the foothills of the Coast Range near Siren Song, populated mainly by Native Americans. Periodically, waves of activists tried to change the name of the area, but the Foothillers themselves dug their heels in and refused outside interference of any kind. Recently, there was a move to rip down older homes and build new ones, bigger ones, and turn the area into a true municipality, but again, the Foothillers resisted. Large housing development companies, like Bancroft Development, were treated as invaders. Nev could well imagine they wanted nothing to do with Detective Savannah Dunbar St. Cloud since she'd married into the Bancroft family. Nev, however, had been friends with Rand since they were kids, almost like an older brother at times, though in recent years they'd drifted their separate ways.

"What do you really want?" asked Rand.

"I want to know about Ravinia."

"Ravinia." That surprised the mixed-heritage man, whose father had basically worked for Catherine Rutledge and the women of the Colony for most of his adult life.

"I met her."

"In relation to this dead body?" questioned Rand.

"You told me that you and your dad helped her and the Colony out once." Again, Nev hadn't paid close enough attention.

"My dad helped them all the time. They don't like to be called the Colony. You want to get to know them, you've gotta give that up. And why do you want to know them? This is about the last thing I expected from you."

"I'm catching up." Nev took a breath. "I want to go to Echo."

Rand just started laughing. "C'mon, man."

"I'm serious. I want to know if something happened there that got this guy killed. I thought Earl could take me." Again he noticed the bartender shoot him a glance before delivering a beer to a customer three stools down.

"It's too late. Bad weather all around. And my dad's too old anyway. He hasn't gone there in several years. It's just a piece of rock anyway. You, of all people, should know better, Nev. *You.*"

Rand wasn't wrong. When Spence and Duncan died, and Spence's family made Nev's life hell, Rand had been about his only stalwart friend. "I know what Echo's like," the younger boy had commiserated at the time. "My dad's had a few really rough times. He's lucky to be alive."

"That island's cursed," Rand said now. Then, "How'd you meet Ravinia?"

"She's a PI in Portland" was Nev's less than straightforward answer.

"What?" Rand sounded like he was going to laugh again.

"She's here for Declan Bancroft's funeral."

Rand snorted. "Bankruptcy Bluffs. That old swindler."

Nev could have argued with Rand that the houses on Bancroft Bluffs that had fallen into the sea, or were still on the bluff but condemned, were not necessarily Declan Bancroft and Bancroft Development's fault. A lot of people had had a hand in allowing that piece of property, situated on an unstable dune, to be developed, not just Declan Bancroft.

"So what do you want with Ravinia?" Rand asked cautiously.

"Like I said, just some background." Rand's comments had made him realize something else. Though it might not give him more information on Ravinia per se, the police report on the death of Detective Clauson and the attack on Savannah at Bancroft Bluffs five years earlier would tell him more about Henry Charles Woodworth.

"You said you met Ravinia? You've seen her. Recently?"

Very recently. He thought of her striding into the hospital, black coat billowing, sea-green eyes regarding him suspiciously, wind-loosened hair curving under her chin.

"Have you met any of the others?" asked Rand carefully.

"Not really. You?"

"Not for a while. They have . . . they're different."

"So I've heard."

"I don't believe all the shit about them," Rand was quick to say. "I've just heard what my dad's said for years. He thinks they're special, but then he also thinks the old shaman of our tribe was too. The man's long dead, but my dad respected him and listened to his predictions. He believed in him. The women at Siren Song *are* different," he conceded, "but it's probably from being locked up all those years. There's no real hocus pocus there. People just love to make up stories."

Nev once again recalled the sudden warmth that had enveloped his heart and rubbed his chest instinctively.

"My ancestors mingled with theirs. That's true, but the stories . . . well, anyway. Get over Echo, man. There's nothing there."

Nev gave up trying to convince Rand that he should go out to the island, but he wasn't convinced there was nothing there. And he wanted to go without anyone else from the department tagging along. His relationship with Echo was personal. TCSD didn't have a police boat that could navigate the ocean. Of course, there was the Coast Guard. But he didn't want to get them involved, either.

What he really needed to do was talk to Ravinia Rutledge again. Get her to open up. She just needed to tell him what she knew and why the hell her phone number was left on the body.

Savvy's phone buzzed as she was parking in the hospital parking lot. She glanced down and saw it was Dr. Evanson's office. "Hi," she answered as she was working her way out of her seat belt. Everything seemed to take just a little more effort these days.

"Hi, Mrs. St. Cloud. This is Dani Summers with Dr. Evanson's office. You left a message for the doctor about the sex of your baby."

"Yeah, I know we had a whole different plan, but I—er, we changed our minds." She climbed out of the car and locked it remotely as she headed to the wide glass doors of the hospital. Thank God the rain had stopped, at least for the time being. "One of the techs at the ultrasound spilled that we were having a boy, and I just want to double-check, so that we know now for sure."

"Ahh . . . do you remember who gave you the ultrasound?"

"No . . . I . . . it must be in the file. He just offered it up."

"Could it have been Hansen?"

"That sounds right."

"Okay. Well, I think the doctor should call you and talk to you."

Savvy walked past the reception area to the elevators, only to stop short. "What do you mean?" she asked anxiously. "Why?"

"No, no, there's nothing wrong. Really. It's just . . . Dr. Evanson will call you." And she hung up.

To hell with that. Savvy wanted to call right back. Now. But the elevator doors opened in front of her, and she stepped around a hospital aide pushing a wheelchair with a woman in a leg cast, which extended in front of the chair. As the doors closed, Savvy pushed the button for the basement level, slid her phone into her coat pocket, and forced herself to wait, but it was difficult. The baby, as if feeling her tension, gave several sharp kicks.

It's a boy . . . Do you want to know your future?

She pressed her lips together, remembering "Mad Maddie" Turnbull's words the last time she was pregnant. Madeline Turnbull, Justice Turnbull's insane mother, who'd spoken from a near-catatonic state and made her prognostication five years earlier, correctly as it turned out, much like Cassandra was predicting that this time she would have a girl.

With an effort, Savannah pushed those memories aside. Mad Maddie was dead. Justice was dead. And if Cassandra had some insane insight into Savvy's current baby and future, well, bring it on.

Through the windows to the morgue, Savannah saw Lang standing near an attendant, who opened the drawer where the body had been placed after examination; an autopsy was scheduled for sometime in the next few days. She walked into the sterile room, with its gleaming tile and stainless-steel equipment, but even before she drew close, she saw that the dead man wasn't Charlie. She'd really known already, but hope springs eternal. She exhaled heavily. She hadn't realized she'd been holding her breath.

"We got some things going on here," said Lang, and then he showed her the hypodermic mark under the man's left arm and the bruises and scrapes over his extremities. "Ravinia looked at his face, not the damage. Maybe she should have seen it. Work on her emotions, so that she'll feel like coughing up the guy's name."

"Are we sure she was holding back?" asked Savvy. "Ravinia seemed pretty positive at the reception that she didn't know him."

"Rhodes is convinced. He's not the type to go on instinct, so if he believes it, I'm going with him."

"Okay."

She looked the body over. He was in good shape. Strong. If someone hadn't administered a drug, he might have survived, although Echo seemed to take victims like trophies. "He did get beat up."

"Yep."

"Those marks on his neck?"

Lang eyed the bruises. "Looks like someone attempted to strangle him."

Savvy agreed. "Definite homicide."

"That's the premise I'm working on."

"So who is he, and who killed him?" she mused, eyeing the corpse as if she could glean answers from his cold, inert body. "Who wanted him dead?"

"That's what we have to figure out."

They spent a few more minutes discussing the killer's modus operandi before they left the basement morgue together. When they reached street level, Savvy checked her phone and realized she'd missed a call, but she didn't recognize the number on her cell's display. She checked for a voice mail, and when she didn't find one, she said a quick, "See ya later," to Lang and started walking to her vehicle as she phoned the unidentified number.

When the call was answered, Savannah heard background noise, as if the call was being broadcast through speakers, as a woman's voice asked, "Hello, Savannah?"

"Dr. Evanston?" Savannah guessed, recognizing the doctor's voice.

"Yes, I'm sorry. I'm in the car. Taking my kid to dance class. You wanted to know about the ultrasound?"

"Actually, the sex of the baby." She started to go into her change of decision about learning the sex, but the doctor cut her off.

"Look, we've had a problem with Hansen, and he's no longer with us. He was indiscreet. I can't tell you how sorry I am that he said something to you before you were ready."

"It's fine," Savannah assured her as she unlocked her car and slid into the driver's seat. "I'm over it. I just want to know if I'm having a boy. He said I was having a boy. Really, all I want to do is just clarify."

"Well, that's just the thing. Hansen sometimes got it wrong, or lied . . . we don't know what he was doing. But it was unprofessional. And I apologize."

"Dr. Evanston, what am I having?" Savvy asked flatly as she stared through her windshield past the strip of greenery that separated one row of parking slots from another in the hospital lot.

"A girl. I hope you're not too disappointed. I know that he told you you're having a boy, and there's no excuse—"

"*What?*"

"I'm really very sorry. I don't know what to say."

"No, it's fine. It's truly fine. I'm happy to have a girl!" Savvy sank back against the car seat, taking it all in. Wow. "I just wanted to know."

"Oh. Good." The doctor sounded relieved.

"Thank you, Dr. Evanston."

"I'm so happy to hear you say that."

"No problem. Truly. It's good news."

After Savvy hung up, she dropped her cell into the cupholder of her console, then pulled the seat belt around her swollen belly, pausing a moment before switching on the ignition.

In truth, she was delighted. A boy and a girl. One of each. Wonderful! She almost felt the sting of tears behind her eyes.

She picked up the phone to call Hale and tell him, then put it back down and slid the car into gear. She would rather tell him when they were home, alone, maybe in bed together, anywhere where Janet *wasn't*, to tell him the news.

As she drove toward Seaside and home, the realization that Cassandra had been right, just like Mad Maddie had been five years earlier, sent a shivery sensation down her limbs. Damn, but those Colony women were almost always right.

CHAPTER 9

Nev glanced up from his beer as the back door to Davy Jones's Locker opened.

A couple entered to meld with the ever-gathering crowd of patrons who had stopped by for a drink, though, so far, the stools next to Nev were unoccupied.

He felt a jolt of awareness. Spence's ex, Lana, with Spence's brother, Andrew.

Flashing back to the scene at Henry Wharton's funeral, Nev steeled himself.

He'd just finished his own meal—a seafood platter that had arrived in a red, woven plastic basket lined with waxed paper. Three frozen shrimp and three frozen fish sticks, fried in oil to gourmet perfection, had been paired with a paper cup of coleslaw slathered in dressing to within an inch of its life. He'd washed it all down with his first beer, which had grown warm. Now that he was officially off the clock, he'd ordered a second.

"You got it, man." The bartender, a man whom Nev had learned, over the course of the past hour and a half, was named Marty, swept up the remains of his meal, then deposited a fresh, cold beer on the bar in front of him.

Just as Andrew and Lana stepped closer.

They didn't see Nev at first, and he silently cursed his luck. He couldn't move without being seen, but he ducked his head, thinking about how to remain unnoticed. He'd been just about to start quizzing Marty about what the barkeep knew about Stanford Norman, but now was stymied. He didn't want them—or anyone else, for that matter—overhearing the conversation.

Shit.

Nothing to do but face them head-on.

At the same moment he came to this conclusion, Andrew Wharton glanced over and met his eyes. His mouth opened in surprise, and Lana, who'd been facing Andrew, turned to see what had caught his attention.

She blinked, then a tentative smile crossed her lips, and she lifted a hand in greeting. Nev raised his own palm.

They didn't seem to know what to do.

Nev didn't need to be a member of the Colony to read their minds: they'd come to the Locker because it was not the place any of their friends and acquaintances were likely to be.

Forcing smiles, they wended their way to him.

"Twice in two days," said Andrew.

"How're you doing?" asked Lana. She was more circumspect in Andrew's presence than yesterday, but was nice enough to ask again.

"Well, I'm drinking beer at the Locker," said Nev in answer to her question, which brought out a big, fake laugh from Andrew and a titter from Lana.

Lana rushed in to fill the moment. "Andy and I've been talking a lot lately. We just thought we'd get together."

"Yeah, you know, go over stuff," agreed Andrew.

Nev thought of Lana sitting by him in the pew and Andrew at the front, beside his mother. Candy didn't like Nev, but she didn't like Lana, either. Nev flicked a glance at Andrew. "Your mom know?" he asked.

"That we've been talking?" He shrugged. "She's not in my business that much. Sorry about her . . . and yesterday. It was all . . . you know . . . ."

Yeah, he knew.

"You look a bit bruised," said Lana, reaching up a hand to his cheek and then dropping it, as if realizing her action was too intimate in front of "Andy."

"How long have you two been seeing each other?" asked Nev.

"Talking, you mean . . . ?" Lana looked to Andrew for help.

Andrew regarded Nev for a long moment before glancing around and gesturing toward an empty booth. He said to Lana, "Head on over there. I'll join you in a minute."

Lana reached out and squeezed Nev's arm in goodbye before doing as Andrew had directed.

"A year," he said, leaning on the bar. "Longer, actually. A year and a half. Wasn't going to tell my dad and kill him before his heart did. Figured I'd find a time to tell Mom later. She's kind of irrational now. Sorry," he said again.

"Don't think she's going to take it well," said Nev as he sipped his beer.

This time his bark of laughter was ironic. "She's unforgiving. They were both unforgiving. For what it's worth, I always knew what happened to Spence wasn't your fault. Sure, I blamed you at first. It was easier. Hurt less. But I always knew it wasn't your fault. If it was anyone's, it was Spencer's. He always had a hard-on for that island, like he was drawn to it. Well, you know better than me."

Nev thought about what Spence had said about the "witch" who'd lived there. *She wanted me to fuck her. Can you believe it? And I wanted to! I really wanted to!*

Mary Rutledge. Ravinia's mother. His hand clenched around his beer.

"I just wanted you to know you and I are okay. At least I am," said Andrew.

"We're okay," agreed Nev and took a swallow.

Andrew gave him a brief smile, then went to meet up with Lana at one of the Locker's two scarred wooden booths with hard benches. Nothing but the basics at the Locker.

Marty came over and examined Nev's beer, which was still three-quarters full, then turned back around to take an order from the single waitress on duty, a twenty-something redhead who wore one of the Locker's T-shirts and a tattoo of a rose, complete with leaves and thorns winding up one arm.

One of the TVs at the back of the bar had been tuned in to a football game and currently seemed to be solely for Marty's entertainment, because no one else was watching. Nev glanced at it and called to the bartender, "Hey!" which brought Marty slouching to his end of the bar. "Think we could get the news on?" Marty looked disinclined to agree, but before he could turn him down, Nev asked, "You know a guy named Stanford Norman? Comes in here a lot, I understand."

Nev felt a change in attitude in Marty. A definite chill. "Yep."

"He's dead," Nev told him. "Should be on the news tonight."

"Dead? Seriously? Jesus!" Marty's brown eyes blinked in surprise, then he went to the other end of the bar, bent down, and grabbed a remote, switching the channel to a Portland news station. He happened to hit it just as the newscasters were discussing the possible homicide at Sandbar. When he returned to Nev's end of the bar, Marty said, "Norman was just in here . . . I mean, oh, God. Someone killed him?"

"Looks that way. He came in here a lot?"

"Sometimes . . . yeah." Marty nodded, bald head bobbing.

"You've served him?"

"Who wants to know?" Marty asked mildly, his eyes suddenly suspicious.

"Tillamook County Sheriff's Department."

"Ah. That why you're taking so long to finish a beer?"

"One of the reasons."

"I can't help you much. Sorry." He paused, then added, "You know Jeff Padilla? Tends here a lot."

"We've met," Nev said. Jeff was the one bartender he'd struck up conversations with.

"Talk to him." Marty grabbed a towel and swiped at the bar. "He's had a few run-ins with Norman." He squinted at his watch. "He'll be coming on about seven."

"Okay, I will. Thanks. Do you know what the run-ins were about?"

"Bothering other customers, mostly. Hang on." He stepped to the end of the bar, where he collected a credit card from a man in his sixties, swiped it, and had the guy sign before he returned.

"You said Norman bothered some of the customers," prompted Nev as soon as he had the man's attention again.

"That's right."

"Like maybe women? *Young* women?"

Marty stroked his beard thoughtfully. "Yep."

"Do you know who they were?"

"Nope. Like I said, you need to talk to Jeff. He was there. I wasn't."

Three burly men in their early twenties grabbed seats at the bar, laughing and joking and calling out for service. Marty took off to deal with them. Conversation over.

Nev checked the time on his phone. He'd hoped to connect with Dennis and Corey Weatherby again. See if he could shake loose anything else in their recital of discovering Norman's body. But he felt there might be more to learn about Norman's assassin from Jeff Padilla.

He looked over the menu once again, which hadn't magically changed in the interim, ordered french fries and another beer, and settled in to wait.

At Siren Song, Ravinia sat down at the trestle table with Cassandra, as Isadora ladled soup into bowls Ravinia remembered from her youth. Everything about the lodge reminded Ravinia of growing up here and her need to break free, to escape the old timbers and high walls and the cloying feeling of being suffocated and imprisoned.

And now she was back. Ironic, she thought, as she sampled the soup, with its tantalizing aroma spiced with oregano and rosemary. It was really good, and she dipped her spoon in eagerly.

She'd changed into a pair of worn jeans, a black sweater, and Doc Martens. Isadora assessed her shoes, but didn't comment. Chloe, who'd finished her meal, along with her mother, said Ravinia looked "biker-chick hot," to which Elizabeth had exclaimed, "Where do you get that stuff?"

"TikTok," had been Chloe's sanguine answer.

Ravinia thought: *I've got to get on that app.* To date, she'd pretty much used her phone as a phone, or for GPS, or for recording or checking the Internet for her PI work, but she'd been delving into different apps and discovered there was a whole world of learning ahead of her.

Lillibeth and Ophelia had already eaten and had moved into the living room near the fire. Ophelia added a chunk of dry oak to the embers, while Isadora, ever in charge, was preparing a tray for Aunt Catherine.

"I'll take it up to her," said Elizabeth, as Isadora added a napkin, wrapping it over the flatware. "Chloe and I have got to get going back to our motel soon as our flight's early and I'd like one last goodbye."

"Your flight isn't too early, I hope," said Isadora. "It's a drive to the Portland airport from here."

"We're okay. It's not till late morning." Elizabeth took the tray from Isadora's unwilling hands and headed up the stairs before she could protest.

"We all need to talk to Lillibeth about her dreams," said Cassandra from the other side of the table. As Lillibeth was in the living room, she couldn't fail to overhear her.

"You can talk about it later," said Isadora.

"You don't ever want to talk about it, Isadora," accused Cassandra.

"That's true," agreed Lillibeth, with a lift of her chin. Pale as she was, she still had some spunk.

Chloe looked from Cassandra to Lillibeth to Isadora and suddenly broke into song, *"We don't talk about Bruno. No, no, no . . . We don't talk about Bruno!"*

"Chloe!" Elizabeth shushed from somewhere up the stairs.

"What is that?" Isadora demanded.

Elizabeth's voice wafted downstairs. "A song from a Disney movie."

"What movie?" Isadora demanded.

Chloe said, *"Encanto.* Bruno can predict the future, but they don't like hearing what he says. They don't want to believe him."

Cassandra turned from Chloe to glare at Isadora and then Ophelia, who had been sitting in the living room and staring out the front windows, her restless fingers tapping on her knee. "Oh, really?" she said pointedly. "They don't want to believe him?"

"No. They have gifts like us, but they don't talk about Bruno!" Chloe nodded sagely.

"I believe you, Maggie," said Lillibeth. "I believe you do see things that will happen."

"Oh, for the love of—We *all* listen to you, Cassandra," Isadora snapped.

"But you don't believe her," Chloe singsonged, pointing out the obvious.

"Exactly!" Cassandra kept her eyes on Isadora.

Ravinia intervened, "I guess I'll have to see that movie."

Chloe started to sing again, but Ravinia shook her head in warning, and the girl's voice trailed off.

Cassandra pushed her bowl away as Ravinia was finishing hers. She might've started out the day with Hot Tamales, but she was ending with vegetables. A step up from her usual diet.

"Thank you for calling me by my name," Cassandra said to Lillibeth. To the room at large, she said, "Lillibeth's dreams are real. She needs our help." She seemed to want to say something else, but just shook her head as she stood and tossed her napkin onto the table. Then Cassandra/Maggie clomped up the stairs, making her displeasure known with each step.

Chloe whispered, "Uh oh."

Amen, Ravinia thought. For a few seconds, the rooms were quiet, only the fire crackling and a wall clock ticking, and Ravinia remembered other times in this very room when the sisters had argued. She picked up both her bowl and Cassandra/Maggie's and was about to carry them into the kitchen when Elizabeth's voice, coming from a distance, caught her attention.

"Chloe? Could you please come up here?" Ravinia pictured Elizabeth sticking her head out of Aunt Catherine's room.

As Chloe trudged up the stairs, Ravinia hauled the dishes to the kitchen sink. When she turned back to the great room, Ophelia was at her elbow, pulling her hair away from her face. She headed to the anteroom and came back pushing her arms through her black wool coat. "I've gotta go." When she saw the unspoken questions in Ravinia's eyes, she added, "To my apartment. This has been fun— loads of fun," she mocked. "But I'm done." She walked to the bottom of the steps and must've caught sight of the little girl on the floor above because she called up the stairs, "Bye, Chloe. Tell your mom it was good to see her again."

"Okay," Chloe said, her footsteps hurrying along the hallway overhead.

"You're not going to wait till Elizabeth and Chloe come back down?" asked Ravinia. She understood wanting to get the hell out. She'd certainly felt that way more than a few times over the years. But Ophelia? This new version of her sister kept surprising Ravinia.

"Who knows how long Catherine will keep them there." Ophelia pulled the collar of her coat close. "I'll talk to Elizabeth on the phone soon." She crossed to the front door, opened it, and stepped through.

A swirl of chilly air swept inside, and the fire glowed bright for a second before Ophelia yanked the door shut behind her.

"She's dancing with the devil," Cassandra said from the stairway.

Ravinia looked up in surprise. Cassandra may have clomped up the stairs in a fit of pique, but she'd tiptoed back within earshot.

"Cassandra," Isadora muttered.

"I don't care what you say, you never listen." She then turned back around and raced up the stairs again. *Slam!* The sound was muffled on the lower floor, but they all got the message.

Lillibeth said, "I think I'm going to go to bed," and began wheeling her chair toward her bedroom.

"I guess someone had to take over for your insubordination. Didn't think it'd be Cassandra," Isadora said to Ravinia.

"What did I do?" demanded Ravinia.

"Set an example," Isadora said. "A bad one."

"Oh, come on. I wasn't the first to leave. You know that." Ravinia wasn't the only girl who had escaped Catherine's lockdown, whether by being adopted out or literally going over the wall, as she had. They *all* knew the stories.

Isadora didn't respond, and she and Ravinia stayed in the main room in cold silence. Ravinia was wishing she could leave, like Ophelia had, but she'd promised Aunt Catherine she would stay and . . . well . . . hell. It was one night. One lousy night. What could happen?

Jeff Padilla came into the bar a few minutes before seven and went directly through the swinging door at the end of the bar to the Locker's kitchen.

Marty, who'd warmed enough to ask Nev whether he was really going to chance going to Echo Island, as he'd eavesdropped on Nev's conversation with Rand earlier, hooked a thumb as Jeff cruised by.

"Here ya go. This is the guy you need to talk to about Norman."

"Yeah, I know."

Marty might have overheard his phone conversation, but he didn't know Nev and therefore didn't understand his history with the island. But Jeff Padilla did. He'd been a fixture at the Locker since before Nev was legal.

Nev chanced a look toward Andrew and Lana's booth. They'd

shifted toward the inner wall, and from Nev's angle, all he could see was her right arm and leg and his left. But their arms were reaching across the table to each other, hands touching and rubbing as if they couldn't bear to not be in contact.

Marty slapped hands with Jeff as he ceded control of the bar to his replacement.

Jeff was lean, handsome, and swarthy-skinned, a mixture of Hispanic and Native American ethnicity. Like Rand, he was a Foothiller, but he had a much sunnier disposition. A wide, white smile split his face as he recognized Nev.

"Why, hello, Deputy."

"Detective."

"Oh, God, that's right. Don't let it go to your head. You on duty?" He pointed to the beer. "I'm going to rat you out."

Nev chuckled. Hearing himself, he was brought up short. He couldn't remember the last time he'd laughed or found anything remotely funny. He'd lost himself in work and ignored his mother's admonishment during their last phone call to take a deep breath and put the past behind him. The trouble was, she was always saying things like that, a broken record.

"I'm not on duty, but I do want a little information."

"Man, you're always on duty, even when you're not. Be with you in a minute." Jeff threw a white terrycloth towel over his shoulder and took several orders from the waitress who had cruised through the scattered tables.

Jeff was a good ten years older than Nev. When all the shit had come down after that ill-fated trip to Echo, Jeff was one of those guys, even though Nev hadn't known him that well, that told the younger man that he had to put it behind him.

"Tragedy is tragedy. Can't blame anyone. Doesn't do any good. You gotta move on. Put one foot in front of the other, and ignore all the noise from other people who are dealing with their own grief. Got that?"

Younger Nev had nodded, but no, he hadn't gotten it. Not then. Not for a long time.

Now he looked at Jeff and saw someone who'd been hugely instrumental in putting Nev on the right path, even though the bartender had only said a few words to him. Those words had been consequential, as it turned out. Jeff would probably never know it. Would shrug it off even if Nev told him. It was just his nature. A bartender at a dive bar who really knew what it was to live a good life and share the wealth with others.

"What do you want to know?" Jeff asked, returning to Nev, his eyes watching the rest of the room, making sure the customers were satisfied.

"There was a homicide in Sandbar. The news touched on it."

Jeff's dark eyes focused on Nev. "Sandbar?"

"Dead body in the dunes. Guy was stabbed with a knife and a hypodermic needle. Tox screen hasn't come out yet, but the knife wounds alone look like they killed him." Nev hesitated, then said, "Stanford Norman. He lives in the area."

"*Shit,*" Jeff whispered.

"Heard he spent a lot of time here."

"That's a fact." The bartender was rubbing the back of his neck, taking it in.

"Heard he . . . hit on younger women."

Jeff had been staring blankly off in space since hearing about Norman's death, but now once again he turned Nev's way. "That is also a fact," he said grimly.

"Well, this is a bar. Unless some family's bringing their kids in for *huevos* at breakfast time, they couldn't be that young."

"We get groups of women in from time to time. Bridal showers, baby showers, wine weekends, book groups, you name it. They like the idea of slumming at the Locker. Hoot and holler and have a good time. Norman seemed to know when they were here. Maybe cruised the place and saw them come in. The bigger the group, the more you could be assured he would be sitting at the other end of the bar, watching the door. Would try to pick one or two off. Sometimes he was successful. Most times he wasn't. They had to look young. Flatter the chest, the better. He could be really insistent, and we had to show him the door a few times when his attentions were rebuffed and he wouldn't take the message."

"He's married. I wonder what he told the wife."

Jeff shrugged. "Sometimes it doesn't matter what they say. The wife has to believe them rather than rip the lid off the truth and have to deal with it."

"Was he in here recently?"

"Oh, yeah. He ran across this one gal who showed up alone a few times and drank club soda at the bar. Norman sidled right up to her and practically climbed onto her at the bar. Man, it was embarrassing. The gal kept pushing him away, but not enough, y'know? Maybe she was keeping him from getting all infuriated and chasing her down. Women have to walk a fine line. I've seen it a lot. The losers who hound them have to be treated nicely or they feel rejected and angry, and that can be dangerous. This gal pushed him off, but gently. I was surprised when he said, 'Let's go,' and she left some change on the counter and followed him through the back door. Last I saw of either of them."

"What did she look like?"

"Blond. Real attractive. You know, it was like she was trying to look younger. A lot of women do, but it's more subtle. This one had her hair in pigtails."

Pigtails. Nev's pulse sped up. "She was here earlier this week?"

"Nah . . . last week maybe. He came in a couple times afterward, looking around for her, I'd bet. Sniffing the air. Man, he was hooked."

"But he never found her."

"Not here. Maybe out there." He hooked a thumb in the direction of the coast highway, which ran in front of the Locker.

"Jeff, can you get over here?" one of the waitresses said after a huge sigh from the other end of the bar, where she placed orders.

"On it, babes."

"And don't call me babes," she said. "Ugh. You're such a Neanderthal."

"I call everyone babes."

"Only those with vaginas. Pretend I don't have one," she said, rapidly giving him the order for drinks from a crowd that had taken over two booths near Andrew and Lana's. Jeff tried to jolly her out of her mood, and it sort of worked. She gave him the finger, but she flipped him off while wearing a smile.

A few minutes later, Andrew and Lana got up from their booth, and Lana headed immediately for the back door. Andrew settled their bill with the waitress and then headed Nev's way. As he reached the bar, he asked, "You got a cell number I can have?"

Nev hid his surprise. "Sure." They exchanged numbers, and Andrew took one step toward the door, but hesitated, as if he were deep in thought.

"Something I can help you with?" asked Nev.

He shook his head. "Nah, but it was good seeing you." Then, "I mean it."

"Same," said Nev, watching the younger man walk away and through the back door.

Huh.

Nev dropped a few bills onto the bar—enough to pay for his tab and tip Jeff—then he too headed out the back way, skirting the waitress balancing a tray of drinks, before he stepped outside, where night had fallen and there was relative silence after the din of the bar. He glanced around the gravel lot and noticed a skinny cat slinking along the backside of the dumpsters near the rear fence.

Had Stanford Norman stood here?

Had he been waiting for the girl/woman?

Who the hell was she, and what really happened out on that lonely dune?

So far, he didn't have any answers. No more than he had about the John Doe he'd discovered on the beach.

With thoughts of dead men, the women of Siren Song, and especially Ravinia Rutledge, he drove home and parked outside his house. An owl hooted from somewhere in the surrounding trees as he let himself inside.

He went straight to the refrigerator, grabbing a last beer and cracking it open before settling into the one easy chair in his small living room. Sipping the beer, he considered making a fire in the brick fireplace with the meager pile of wood he'd purchased at a nearby grocery store and reminded himself to order a cord of firewood for the coming winter. There was room enough at the side of the house to stack it, but he hadn't done anything so permanent yet.

He started the fire, then took a trip to the bathroom to stare at his reflection in the mirror above the sink as he washed his hands. Beneath the day's grow-out he could see the faint, slightly green cast to his cheek. Candy had really walloped him. The bruising would fade and disappear in a few days, but for now the whiskers stayed.

In the living room again, he sat down in front of the blank television screen, listening to the spit and hiss of the catching flames. He thought about the body he'd found on the beach outside Echo, then he thought about Ravinia. He cast his mind to Stanford Norman, and then he came back to Ravinia again . . . those eyes, those legs, that mouth . . .

He closed his eyes. He could feel himself growing hard and immediately straightened in his chair. Jesus.

Annoyed, he checked his watch, then flipped on the TV and waded through a couple of inane sitcoms while he waited for the ten o'clock news.

At ten, he flipped to local news—local meaning Portland primarily and Oregon and southwest Washington in general. Even so, during the first segment, there was a brief mention of the body found in the dunes at Sandbar and a drowning victim in Deception Bay. The facts weren't completely accurate. Technically, the John Doe wasn't a drowning victim. The TCSD wasn't putting out much information on either victim until the final coroner's report came in, and even then some of the information would be held back from the public.

However, those weren't the only suspicious deaths along the Oregon coast, as a news team reported a surprising crime out of Seaside: a woman bartender who had apparently been strangled to death in her establishment, a place called the Smuggler's Den. Nev had never heard of the bar, but then there were tons of little dive bars that went in and out of business on this stretch of coastline.

A body strangled . . . like the John Doe on the beach this morning?

Was there a connection there?

Seaside was only about thirty minutes north of Deception Bay, so it was possible it could be the same perp. What had happened at that bar?

He picked up the phone to call Officer John Mills with the Seaside Police. They'd worked together, and though Nev's rise to detective had been one of the reasons he'd moved to the Sheriff's Department, leaving Mills had been the main drawback to switching jobs.

Mills was a good man and an empathetic, thoughtful officer. Though, in the end, Nev had chosen to take the promotion, he'd regretted losing Mills as a partner.

But then he looked at the clock. Closing in on eleven. Mills and his wife had a new baby, and he and Nev hadn't talked in months. Time enough tomorrow to learn about the third homicide in the past few day on the Oregon coast.

Ravinia stared at the shadows on her ceiling in the lodge. Leaves of the hedge outside her window were in constant motion, moving, waving in some kind of wild rhythm in the moonlight from outside, blown by the wind, which was making a constant, low moaning sound.

She lay on her old bed, aware of how hard it was. Her elbows actually hurt when she turned over. *Austerity be thy middle name*, she thought darkly, thinking of her aunt. She understood Catherine. She really did. She got where she was coming from, or had been, all these years, but that didn't make it right.

She flopped onto her side. She could get a damn rug burn from the sheets. Massaging her elbow, she then punched her pillow a few times.

Why did you pack your overnight bag? she asked herself.

Then answered: *Because you knew this was coming. You let yourself get roped in.*

She rolled onto her back once again, watching the dancing shadows, listening to the undulating keening of the wind and the more distant sound of the surf. She'd once thought it was a strange language she could understand if she just tried a little harder, but now she just felt annoyed and angry. Annoyed that she was in Siren Song once again, even if it was for just one night. Angry—in a full-blown rage, actually—that Silas was dead.

She pulled her pillow from beneath her head and buried her face in it. If she was going to cry, she wanted the tears absorbed before they ran down her cheeks. But she didn't cry. And with all the willpower she possessed, she held the sob inside her chest, a hard bubble that wanted to explode, but she willed it down.

Finally, she placed the pillow back under her head and thought about the day. She needed answers about Silas. Aunt Catherine's anemic response, a kind of "wait and see, but don't tell" attitude, wasn't enough.

What about Detective Rhodes?

She dismissed the thought immediately. He wasn't going to help her. He wanted her to give him a name, that was all. He was too . . . rigid. Actually called her *ma'am*. It was a blow to her identity to hear that term. Sure, he meant it as a sign of respect, but *ma'am*? She was barely twenty-five years old. Wasn't there something else? Some other way to address her?

She couldn't really think of one, and that kind of pissed her off too.

But I was the one who climbed over the fence. I was the one who went for help. I was the one who found Elizabeth and Chloe.

Thinking of them made her feel sad, and she closed her eyes to the dancing orgy of leaves on her ceiling.

Elizabeth and her daughter had left Siren Song after returning downstairs from Aunt Catherine's room not long after Ophelia had left. They had shared hugs all around. Even Cassandra had come downstairs to join in, but Lillibeth had remained in her room with the door tightly shut, though it hadn't been that late. And now the lodge seemed strangely quiet. Empty, almost.

"Call the wolf back," Chloe had whispered into Ravinia's ear before she had tripped toward the door.

If only that was in my power, Ravinia thought now, slightly depressed. She already felt the ache from missing them, and it had only been a few hours. Elizabeth and Chloe felt closer to her family than any of her sisters or Aunt Catherine.

CHAPTER 10

EEEEEEEAAAHHHH!!!

Ravinia sat bolt upright in bed. The terrified shriek rose to the rafters from the first floor, jerking her awake, causing the hairs on her arms to stand at attention.

Lillibeth . . .

Ravinia tossed off the bedclothes and, wearing the T-shirt she'd slept in, was up and struggling into her jeans in a heartbeat.

Doors banged against walls, and footsteps clattered on the upper hallway. She ran blindly out of her room.

"Help!"

She heard the strangled cry coming from her aunt's room and stumbled a bit in her headlong dash for the stairs on the heels of Isadora and Cassandra.

"Lillibeth's had another dream!" Cassandra cried breathlessly.

"Help Aunt Catherine, Ravinia," snapped Isadora, the drill sergeant.

"I—" Ravinia realized this scenario was well-rehearsed. Maybe not Aunt Catherine's call for help, but the swift response to Lillibeth's scream. She wanted to follow her sisters. She really did. She took two steps farther away from Aunt Catherine, but then heard another, weaker "Help" and turned back.

She threw open the door to Catherine's room to find her aunt trying to free herself from the sheets and coverlet that had wrapped around her thin legs. Clutching the bedpost, she was wobbling unsteadily.

"Stop! Wait." Ravinia rushed forward, grabbing her aunt by her shoulders, gently pushing her back down on the mattress, aware how fragile her bones felt. "Let me get these blankets and sheets off you."

It took a few precious moments to unravel her aunt, and by then, Catherine's imperiousness had resurfaced. "I'm fine. Let me get dressed, and I'll be right down."

"Really?" Ravinia said. "How?"

Catherine waved Ravinia off. "I can get dressed myself, Just give me a few minutes."

"I can't—"

"You can and you will," Catherine insisted, her color high.

After a long, silent moment, Ravinia acquiesced. "I'll be just outside the door."

"Fine."

In the hallway, she waited in a kind of suspended animation.

Voices floated from downstairs to the second level.

Isadora: "It's okay. You're in your own bed at Siren Song. We're all here." Lillibeth: "If she dies, I die."

"Well, that's just not true." Again, Isadora.

"It is true. You know it's true. Don't you, Maggie?" Lillibeth implored.

Cassandra, slowly: "Your romance is real."

"Oh, for the love of God." Isadora again.

"I'm . . . afraid we all die," Lillibeth quavered.

Ravinia had heard enough. She practically flew down the stairs.

"Where's Catherine?" Isadora snapped at her as Ravinia half ran, half slid into Lillibeth's bedroom. No one had turned the light on, and moonlight striped the bed, the hedge leaf shadows still dancing like maniacal imps. If anything, the wind had risen during the hours Ravinia was asleep.

"Aunt Catherine's getting dressed," said Ravinia.

"On her own?" Isadora asked on a rising note of outrage.

"Yes, on her own," Ravinia shot back at her. "You go up there and tell her she can't do it."

"Go upstairs and help her!" Isadora was practically shaking.

"Stop telling me what to do!"

"She needs help getting downstairs." Isadora glared at Ravinia in the dim light.

The argument was getting them nowhere. "Well, fine," Ravinia finally agreed. "I'll go back in a minute." She turned to Lillibeth. "What's the deal with this romance?"

Lillibeth bent her head. "She loves him . . . I . . . love him—"

"Who? Who is it you love?" Isadora demanded.

Lillibeth whispered, "But we've made mistakes."

Isadora leaned her head back and stared at the ceiling. "She'll never say who he is. This always happens."

"Maggie knows," said Lillibeth.

Ravinia looked at Cassandra. "What mistakes? What do you know?"

"The girl loves him, and he loves her, but there's a lot of darkness."

"Yeah, well, that doesn't really help. Who is this guy?"

"I'm not sure," Cassandra replied.

Isadora snorted. "See what I have to deal with?"

Ravinia tore her gaze from Cassandra to look back at Lillibeth and tried to control her exasperation, to be matter-of-fact and not judge. Her sister was obviously suffering from the nightmares, whatever they were. "Lillibeth, they're just dreams, and whatever happened, it's in the past. And you're not involved with any man here in Deception Bay, Oregon."

"It's the future and the past," said Cassandra.

"Yeah, and a warning," said Ravinia. "I know."

"What did I tell you?" Isadora said, flatly.

Silence fell across the room, punctuated only by Lillibeth's scared, stuttered breaths.

"It's not Charlie, is it?" Ravinia asked. The question popped out before she really thought it through.

They all stared at her in varying stages of horror, even Isadora.

"Ravinia . . ." Catherine's voice warbled faintly from upstairs, and Ravinia looked at all her sisters, one at a time, then headed for the staircase.

Lucky came to, suddenly wide awake and alert, like the hunted animal she was.

Moonlight filtered through the flimsy motel curtains, casting the small room in shadows.

Fully dressed, she climbed out of bed and glanced at the chair where she'd left her backpack, her meager belongings tucked snugly inside. It was just as she'd left it, and she felt a sense of relief. She'd driven to this place because it was out of the way, off the beaten track, so to speak, off the highway south of Seaside.

Satisfied that everything was safe and secure, she went to the bathroom and looked at herself in the mirror. She'd unplaited her hair from its twin braids, and it lay in wrinkled curls. She examined her reflection critically. It would be hard for anyone to tell her true age because, apart from her back, all of the scars of her life were on the inside.

She took a shower and washed her hair, wondering idly if it would be the last time she shampooed her tresses, the final time hot water would rinse her skin and cleanse her.

Did it matter?

Not really.

Fifteen minutes later, she left the motel room, stepping out into a cold, windy night, the air thick with the promise of rain.

Her heart ached. *Ached.* She threw her bags into the back of the Outback, all except the smaller one with her hypodermic needles and various tools and weapons. She stowed the smaller bag beneath the passenger seat and was already searching her mind for a way to get another vehicle. Too many people may have already seen this car and taken note.

Once upon a time, she'd been able to lift cars from Carl's Automotive and Car Rentals outside Seaside. Hunk O'Junks, Carl called them, and he left the keys to the older-model, sometimes nearly ancient, rentals under the floor mats. It had been a simple matter for her to take any one she wanted, and she had, though she always brought them back. But those days were long gone now. She'd lived several lifetimes since then and had graduated to grand theft auto instead of merely borrowing old clunkers.

Now she climbed behind the wheel, started the Subaru, and headed south, away from Seaside. She'd told herself she would never come back to this stretch of coastline and had kept that promise for a long, long time.

Until now.

As she passed the gates of Siren Song, the lodge where her

cousins lived, she thought of Catherine Rutledge, who had years before somehow found her half-dead, washed up on the shore. Or so
she'd been told. She couldn't remember how she'd ended up waking up in Siren Song, though she did recall oh-so-vividly opening her
eyes to an unfamiliar room, with Catherine lifting a lamp from the
bedside table and saying, *"You're with us now. You can stay here
until you have your strength back, but then you'll have to leave."*

"How long do I have?" she'd asked with an effort as the room had
swum in her vision.

*"As soon as you're better, you'll have to leave. You're not finished
with your work yet."* And then Catherine had spelled out just what
she wanted done. Needed done.

It had taken years to complete the task she'd set for her, and it still
wasn't finished.

But it was upon her now.

She drove several miles farther before she realized she couldn't
just run without a plan. Turning around, she drove back toward the
lane that was the entrance to Siren Song. There was a new dirt and
gravel access road a quarter of a mile farther north that led into the
unincorporated "town" of the Foothillers, more a loose grid of residences with a few commercial buildings tacked on. She hadn't
known much about it, but Silas had. He'd educated her on the Foothillers, and now she felt like she knew them, like they had a kinship.

Pulling into the access road, she turned the Outback around,
parking nose out, so she could see the highway and the vehicles that
would pass. Screened by piled brush from the bulldozers and plows
that had built the road for the developers, she waited. Some of the
Foothillers had objected to all the building, but new development
hadn't been stopped.

She didn't much care one way or the other.

She didn't much care about anything now that Silas was gone.
Killed. Slain . . .

Her blood pounded in her ears, and she ground her teeth together at the thought of his death.

Catherine Rutledge had been right. Her work wasn't done. The
old biddy had saved her life, and she owed her a favor, the favor of
completing her assignment: to kill Henry Charles Woodworth.

* * *

"I'm not going to believe in dreams," Catherine told Ravinia. Sitting on the edge of her bed, she felt a little stronger than she had earlier. Some of her spunk had returned, though it had taken inordinately long for her to slip out of her nightshirt and into her clothes. It had been embarrassing, but she'd gotten over it, and she hated this accelerated aging. Of course, she wasn't old by today's standards, but because a curse had been laid upon her head, her bones had brittled, and her muscles ached. All because of her sister.

They're my children, Mary had hissed. *Take them from me, and you will die before your time.*

Catherine had dismissed the curse at the time as just more of Mary's spewing and ranting. But now she believed.

Or is your infirmity just the product of a guilty mind?

Whatever the case, the truth was that she was dying. And she had so much more that needed to be taken care of.

"I don't believe in dreams, either," said Ravinia. Especially about imagined lovers and the witch trials, but then there was that history in the family, an ancestral link to those unenlightened times.

"I need to get downstairs and see to Lillibeth."

"Just take a second. She's okay."

"She's *not* okay."

"Isadora and Cassandra are with her. Listen, we can't hear her, they've calmed her down. Please, just give yourself a little time."

That was the problem, Catherine thought. So little time was left. So very little.

Ravinia was frowning at her in the dim light of Catherine's bedside lamp. How much of her life had been seen from behind that scowl? Catherine would never tell her, but Ravinia held a special place in her heart. Isadora might emulate her, a learned act that made her feel safe, apparently, but Ravinia was the most like her in mind and spirit, though she would be affronted that anyone could even think it.

Catherine threw a glance out the window toward Echo Island, where, five years earlier, she'd hoped to end the horror that had hovered over them from that miserable hunk of flesh that was Mary's father. Silas had burned Durant's bones in an effort to send the man back to the hell from which he'd risen. Had it been successful? She didn't entirely know. She had hoped so. Had prayed that they would all be safe. And for a while, it seemed so. They'd had five years of relative peace.

But now Lillibeth's dreams . . .

And Declan Jr. . . . Charlie . . . had returned and killed Silas. She knew it as if Silas, in dying, had whispered the truth into her ears.

She inhaled sharply.

"What is it?" Ravinia asked immediately. The girl was as alert as a fox.

"Nothing."

"Silas?"

"I said it was nothing."

"You always say it's nothing. And it's always something."

The girl would not let it go. Would never let it go. Catherine smiled to herself, careful not to let her feelings show because Ravinia would never let go when she had hold of something. Again, so like herself.

In that moment, Catherine made a decision. "There is a key inside the ewer on the top shelf of my closet."

"The ewer you used to use to wash with?"

"Yes."

There had been no indoor plumbing in the beginning, when Siren Song was first constructed. The lodge had been built from ancient timbers, old-growth fir. Only recently, the second floor had been fitted with electricity and a working bathroom.

Ravinia went to the closet. The ewer was too high for her to reach, for any of them to reach. The girl solved the issue by dragging a chair over, grabbing the pitcher, jumping down from the chair, and tipping it into her outstretched hand. A small key dropped into her palm, and Ravinia wrapped her fingers around it tightly.

"I used to keep it in the heel of my boot," Catherine said, almost wistfully. So many things had changed.

"What does it go to?" asked Ravinia.

"You know."

She sent Catherine a look. Then went unerringly to the drawer that held the box that protected Catherine's journal. Years before, her charges had hunted down Mary's matching journal, and Ravinia had read it, cover to cover, against Catherine's wishes. But, in a sense, the truth had armed Ravinia, and Catherine had encroached upon her to do her bidding and find Elizabeth, which she had.

Ravinia unlocked the box and pulled out Catherine's journal.

"Leave it, please. I want you to have what's at the bottom of the box."

Ravinia reluctantly set the journal aside and pulled out the sheaf of yellowing papers. "The addresses of Silas and Charlie's adoptive families. The ones Silas brought back from Echo."

"Ophelia was going to do the research on them, but Declan Jr.— Charlie—was gone, and so was Silas and I . . . let it go."

"You want me to follow up now," she guessed.

"Take the pages. Find out what you can about both of them."

"You can call him Declan Jr. still. We all know who you mean."

"That was Mary's name for him, to hurt me. I can relearn," she told Ravinia stubbornly.

"I don't entirely think that's true, Aunt Catherine," she responded dryly.

Catherine fought back her irritation. She might love Ravinia best, but she detested having her own faults thrown back in her face. "Come on, help me downstairs. We need to calm Lillibeth down."

"I already told you, she's not screaming, and Isadora and—"

"Just because we can't hear her, doesn't mean she's settled down. Now let's go."

Ravinia offered her arm to her aunt. "You really don't give any credence to her dreams? You said earlier we needed to help her."

Catherine pinched her lips together. She shared the thread of precognition that ran through their family, though it was undependable. Cassandra was the only one who seemed to be consistent. Catherine reluctantly took Ravinia's arm and couldn't decide whether to tell the truth or lie. The problem was that the truth had worked against her more often than falsehoods.

She chose to lie. "I think it's a harmless dream romance. I just worry that Lillibeth is letting it affect her physically."

"But it's deeper than a simple fantasy romance, isn't it? These dreams scare her, terrify her. Nightmares involving the witch trials."

"Those women were innocents; history has exonerated them."

Unlike Mary, Catherine thought, not for the first time.

Ravinia stared at her, and Catherine stared back, putting up a mental wall.

So far, Catherine had been able to keep Mary's daughters from seeing inside her thoughts, delving into her mind, but she wondered how long that would last.

"Okay," was all Ravinia said, and Catherine, hating every second of it, accepted her niece's help getting down the stairs. For years, she'd been able to march up and down the steps all day, hauling laundry, carrying trays, sweeping and cleaning or whatever and now . . . now, damn it, she was leaning heavily against Ravinia. But that was just the way it was. The way it had to be.

They met with the others in Lillibeth's room, where the pale girl was lying in her bed, propped by pillows, her wheelchair and sisters crammed around the old four-poster.

"Tell Aunt Catherine about your dreams," urged Cassandra as Catherine stepped close to the bed.

"I've told her and told her," Lillibeth said in a small voice. Her fingers were worrying the edge of the bedsheets, and her hair was a tangled mess. There was a fine sheen of perspiration along her upper lip.

"You haven't told me," said Ravinia. But her mind was already moving toward the quest her aunt had set for her. But was it safe for her to leave? As much as she'd resisted coming to Siren Song, it felt like Charlie was close. He'd killed Silas. Catherine had said it aloud, and Ravinia believed it. What if he began his mission again to kill them all and was somewhere just waiting for her, or Ophelia, or someone to leave so he could finish what he'd started so long ago?

"He loves me, but there's something wrong," Lillibeth said tearily. "I've done something bad, I think, I don't know what. Not yet. But really, really bad." She looked absolutely guilt-riddled for a sin she couldn't or wouldn't name.

"The girl in the dream," Ravinia cut in, refusing to get taken in by the melodrama. "Where is she, and what is she doing?"

"She's running away. She's running to the river, to a ship maybe—I don't really know, but she's trying to escape, and she can't get to the water. She's on a cliff and the river . . . or the ocean? It's far away."

"This is the same dream, over and over again?" asked Ravinia. She felt Aunt Catherine stir beside her and lower herself onto the edge of Lillibeth's bed, holding onto her cane, folding one hand over the other on its top. She said softly to Lillibeth, "Okay, I see that this is real to you. I don't want to hurt your feelings," she added quickly, sensing Lillibeth was about to protest, "but this seems . . ." *Like a fantasy.*

Ravinia heard the words as if they'd been spoken aloud.

"But it's real!" Lillibeth protested vehemently, one curled fist smashing against the mattress. "It's—they're going to kill her. The men on horseback who are chasing her. They're going to kill her and the baby!"

"What baby?" asked Ravinia. Despite herself, she felt a trace of fear, tiny caterpillar feet stealing up her spine.

"My baby."

"The witch's baby," Cassandra reminded softly.

Lillibeth reached for Ravinia's hand, squeezing it with surprising strength. "You're going to help us."

Isadora was shaking her head and glanced over at Ravinia. "See?" she whispered.

Lillibeth released Ravinia's hand and sank back on the pillows, but she held Ravinia's eyes. "I see us burning."

Ravinia had heard enough. "Maybe you're confusing history and romance with real life, Lillibeth. I don't want whatever you think is happening to you in your dreams to take you over . . . or consume you. You need to get out of this bed. Get some sunshine. Get out of the lodge."

"Ravinia . . ." admonished Catherine.

"We've got real problems," Ravinia said firmly. "Let's not make any more up, okay?"

"I'm not!" Lillibeth insisted.

"What problems?" asked Cassandra.

Ravinia threw her a look. "What? You can't see them, but you can see Lillibeth with some man and a baby and men on horseback chasing her down?"

"Why can't you believe me?" Lillibeth said in a small voice, scrunching down in the bed as if to hide from Ravinia.

"Because I can't believe in fairy tales or visions or warnings." Ravinia tried to hide her growing exasperation but failed. She turned to Cassandra. "Why can't you see something helpful?"

"Ravinia!" Catherine bit out.

"You're the one in trouble!" Cassandra blurted.

"All of us!" corrected Lillibeth. "All of us are in trouble."

Ravinia held up her hands. "I'm sorry. This isn't getting us anywhere. Lillibeth, dreams are dreams. " She turned to face her aunt. "I'll stay tonight but I'm leaving in the morning. I'm going to do as you asked. And I'm going to find out what happened to Silas too."

"What did you ask?" Cassandra queried Catherine.

"Silas?" Lillibeth quavered.

"Our brother." Ravinia looked pointedly from Lillibeth to Cassandra to Catherine. Her aunt's lips were pressed tightly over her teeth. "Tell them everything, Aunt Catherine. They all deserve the truth. Everybody needs to know that Charlie, Declan Jr., could be targeting us again."

Cassandra drew in a quick breath. "Is that true?"

"Yes. So we all need to get real and face what's really coming. Set the nightmares aside. We need to live in the now." She started for the door.

"Ravinia?" Lillibeth's voice was small.

She stopped, half in the hallway, and cocked her head but didn't turn around. She felt on the verge of screaming, or maybe crying.

"I love you," said Lillibeth. "I just want you to know that before everything happens."

"I love you too, Lillibeth," Ravinia said tightly.

"I don't want you to die."

"I don't want you to die, either," she replied, exasperated.

"I'll make sure the witch is dead," Lillibeth added, but Ravinia was already walking rapidly to the stairs, wanting to race up the steps and lock herself in her room, throw herself onto the bed, and drag a pillow over her head.

CHAPTER 11

Ravinia took off the next morning while it was still dark. She had to wake Isadora to get the key to unlock the gates, and her eldest sister performed the task in almost utter silence. But Isadora, in her bathrobe and hair plaited down her back, wasn't just holding her tongue. She was seething as well. Ravinia could feel the waves of muted condemnation emanating from her as they made their way along the path to the gate.

As Isadora turned the key in the lock, it made a grinding sound of protest in the cold, damp air.

Ravinia couldn't stand Isadora's superior disapproval a second longer. "What's your problem?" she demanded as the gate swung open.

Isadora's features were indistinct in the darkness, her eyes dark pools, but her voice was clear and sharp. "You haven't changed a bit. You always just bully your way through and don't care what misery you leave behind. I've picked up the pieces so many times. I wish you would never come back."

"Wow." Ravinia felt the rebuke like a slap. "Usually it's Aunt Catherine who tells me how bad I am."

"You've got her wrapped around your finger. She listens to you more than any of us. And it always comes back to harm us."

"You think Lillibeth is going to save all of us?" Ravinia snorted. "You don't believe in her dreams, either."

"No, I don't."

"Then let's move on. I thought her dreams were supposed to be about romance, but they're nightmares."

Isadora inclined her head in agreement. "You've got the papers from Aunt Catherine, right? The ones with the names and addresses of the adoptive parents of the boys. Our damned brothers. That's what she told us. So now what? You're going to *investigate*?"

"You're starting to hurt me where I live, Isadora," she warned as a car, headlights glowing in the dark, engine purring, drove past, tail-lights winking as it headed toward the Foothillers' town.

"It's a fool's mission. Ophelia looked into those adoptions five years ago, and it was a dead end. No information about Declan Jr., if that's what you're expecting. And Silas lived an unremarkable life. That's all that Ophelia learned."

Ravinia wished she could read Isadora's face better. An unremarkable life? Silas? Ravinia didn't believe that for a second. Who was lying, Ophelia or Isadora or Aunt Catherine? *Ophelia, because she didn't want to alarm Isadora, or Catherine, especially since she'd known Silas was going after Charlie.*

"You're way behind the curve on information," said Ravinia.

"Okay, let's call him *Charlie*, then. Not Declan Jr."

"That's not what I meant. Goodbye, Isadora. I know you'd like to hear me say this is the last you'll see of me, but I doubt that's true."

"Oh, I know you're working for Catherine, so you'll be back. Go ahead, go do your thing, whatever it is, while she and I keep everyone safe here."

"You should get out of the lodge more too. You're stuck in it as much as Lillibeth, maybe more so. Get your driver's license. Get a job in the real world."

"Find a romance outside of dreams?" she suggested bitterly.

"Yes!"

"When you've taken that advice yourself, maybe I'll listen." She swung the gate slowly back, edging Ravinia outside.

Ravinia drove away from Siren Song feeling completely out of sorts. She couldn't wait to get back to Portland and her own life. Could. Not. Wait.

Except . . . except . . . Silas was dead, and Charlie had killed him. She might not believe that Lillibeth was in some time warp with her dreams, but, from the bottom of her soul, she believed that Charlie was responsible for Silas's death.

*   *   *

From her hiding spot near the Foothillers' ongoing housing development, Lucky watched as Ravinia's Camry pulled out of the entrance to Siren Song, where it had been parked overnight.

Lucky followed, starting her car and hitting the gas, remaining at a distance to settle in behind the blurry red dots of the Camry's taillights.

So far, she'd been under the radar. As least she thought so. Ravinia appeared too wrapped up in Silas's death and yesterday's funeral to recognize she was being followed. But that could instantly change between heartbeats.

Lucky kept her distance and allowed a truck to pull in between them as they headed steadily north. At the junction to Highway 26, Ravinia's Camry slid into the exit lane, heading east to Portland, while the truck continued to lumber north.

Ravinia's going home . . .

Lucky slowed her Outback, thinking.

Silas's killer is here.

But . . . Ravinia wanted him as much as she did.

So what was this trip away from the coast all about?

Deciding to tail Ravinia to Portland, she followed along the sweeping curve, all the while keeping the Camry in sight. If Ravinia continued to Portland, she would pass right by what had been Carl's Automotive's Hunk O'Junks. The area now looked like an abandoned junkyard, with vehicles rusting in place. Maybe Carl had died and left the place to molder.

Lucky eased up on the gas, letting Ravinia's car get out of sight, knowing where she lived. Something Silas had confided when they'd been alone. In bed.

She'd been lying beneath him, her eyes closed, straining to pull him closer, closer yet. She loved him fiercely, and he seemed to love her. Maybe he'd just needed her to help him. She didn't completely know. She honestly didn't care. He was the one man who'd been completely honest with her, understanding her special strengths, never judging her. It had been a strange twist of fate that she'd spent all her life on the wrong side of the law, doing what she knew was the right thing, while he'd spent most of his life on the right side of the law, doing what he knew was wrong. Silas had told her about those years of complacency when they met . . . and how he'd broken free and become a vigilante. They had that in common.

She'd wrapped her legs around him and arched her back at the moment of climax, fighting back a scream of pleasure as he'd come inside her. She'd reveled in his deep moans and ragged breaths, loving the power, loving him.

"Lucky," he'd panted in her ear. "Lucky . . ."

It wasn't her name. It was her handle. But she'd used it for so many years that she only pulled out her given name, Ani, when she absolutely had to, to identify herself. More often than not, she wanted to be forgotten.

But not with Silas.

After lovemaking, she'd stared into his silvery eyes, and he'd gazed into her blue ones, each of them breathing hard, each of them half-smiling, knowing each other.

Their paths had crossed by chance, or maybe it had been destiny. She'd been traveling the road to redemption, as her past was checkered at best, criminal at worst, and he'd been on the opposite trajectory. Silas Rutledge, the model citizen, the good son, the excellent student who never had given his family any reason to worry.

But he'd told her he'd always known he had a mission to kill. He'd bided his time until adulthood and then had struck out on his own.

They'd run across each other at a beachside bar. For most of their adult lives, they had both shied away from the Pacific coast and any and all of the little towns that dotted its shoreline. They'd each kept their footprints around the area very small, invisible, in order to do what they needed to do.

But when they had met that day, it had been electric.

She'd walked into the local dive and felt him immediately. Not in the way she could feel her prey, the pedophiles she could sense with ease, the men she'd made it her life's mission to root out and bring to justice, wherever and whenever she could. In recent years, though, she'd mostly led the law to them and let the justice system do its worst . . . mostly, she thought, thinking of the bastard she'd left on the beach with his dick out. If she'd left that monster alone . . . if she'd stayed with Silas . . .

Sadness threatened to envelop her just as the fog was settling over the mountains.

She'd come to the beach to find Charlie, her ultimate quarry, and had settled in Seaside because being in Deception Bay was too dangerous. She had a feeling that he was on his way to finish what he'd started. Seaside wasn't a much better town to hide in, but she needed to stick around the area to set a plan in action. And that's when she'd encountered Silas. She sensed him right away, not like she could a pedophile, but there was something there. She'd stopped short on the spot. Arrested. Certain she *knew* him somehow.

There had been an empty bar stool beside him.

"Were you waiting for me?" she asked as she slipped in beside him.

"Yes," he'd answered. "I'm Silas," sticking out his hand.

She'd hesitated a moment, then clasped his fingers, feeling something pass between them. His silvery blue eyes bored into hers, and hers bored right back. "I'm Lucky," she'd finally responded.

And that was it. A partnership decided by unseen forces.

Lucky had been traversing the country, looking for the endless supply of sick pedophiles and taking them out one by one, never staying long anywhere, as her DNA was everywhere and it was only a matter of time before she was found. She'd always felt she would come back and maybe meet up with Catherine Rutledge again and tell her what she'd accomplished, the work she'd gotten done, how many she'd caught and killed before she was found out, eighteen and counting . . . along with the occasional person who got in her way.

She had sensed she would be working with Silas before he'd even said so. She hadn't had to hear that it would be the end of her; she'd known it already. And it would be the end of him too, he'd said.

A quote had filled her mind that she'd heard somewhere, but it was the credo she lived by: *Someone has to die in order for the rest to live.*

His brows had lifted in surprise when she'd said it. It was exactly what he'd been thinking, he'd told her when they were in bed together an hour later. She'd been faintly embarrassed at the scars on her back from the funeral pyre she was once lashed to, but he hadn't been repelled by her battle scars. If anything, they had fueled his ardor, along with the scar on her left hip that he'd lovingly kissed; he'd made her clutch the bedsheets and writhe, his tongue moving lower and lower as she'd melted inside. She'd never believed she could enjoy sex like she enjoyed it with him. She loved the feel of him sliding deep inside her, their studied coupling, staring into each other's eyes, thinking, always thinking. Were they distantly related? Yes. Had to be. But in the beginning, she hadn't known the particulars of how his family intersected with hers, and even when she learned, she hadn't cared.

They didn't talk a lot. Didn't have to. They both knew who they were after, who they were hunting: Henry Charles Woodworth . . . Declan Jr. . . . Good Time Charlie . . . The bastard had many names, wore many hats, and had always been a scourge to the world at large and the women of Siren Song in particular. Charlie had been missing for years . . . hibernating . . . keeping his whereabouts a secret. But recently the beast had woken and stretched, and he'd been sensed by both of them.

And he'd come back to Deception Bay.

The night before Silas's death, they'd shared a bottle of wine in their motel room as she'd told him of her exploits, of finally taking care of Stanford Norman, whom she'd stumbled upon on her quest to find Charlie. She'd been high on adrenaline these last few weeks. She hadn't intended to kill Norman, but she wasn't sorry she had, and it had gotten her blood pumping.

"I jabbed him, but he had a knife, and I turned it on him," she admitted. "I couldn't find the needle in the dark."

"They've got your DNA." Silas's voice had been grim.

"They've got it anyway," she'd answered. She didn't want to spell out that she'd had sex with the man and bitten him. It wasn't anything close to making love with Silas. "I'm ready to get Charlie now," she'd said instead, the mission they were on together.

He'd half smiled and taken her glass from her hand, setting it beside his own untouched one. She hadn't realized until that moment that he hadn't been drinking.

"You can't come with me when I face Charlie," he told her as the world had begun spinning.

"Of course I can. I am. It's my ultimate goal too. You know that."

He said regretfully, "I'm sorry." And his voice came as if from a distance.

For what? she'd wondered, feeling oddly unsteady as she jumped to her feet, knocking over the bottle, spilling red wine onto the stained shag carpet, watching the wine spread like blood . . . and that's the last she knew for what seemed like hours—or had it been minutes? Reeling, the world out of sync, she stumbled outside to see that her car was no longer in the lot. Where was Silas? She called for him and was suddenly standing above the beach near Echo Island and saw her Outback parked and waiting in the gray mist of early morning. She stared through the film and saw the outline of Echo seeming to grow as she stared at it. Had he taken a boat across the dangerous waters?

And then the body caught her eye.

Far below on the beach. And suddenly she was standing on that beach herself, the ocean roaring, her head pounding. She ran to the inert form, screaming, her legs leaden, and then *he* was there— Good Time Charlie—stepping between her and Silas, grinning like the devil he was.

"Who are you?" he demanded, but he connected her to Siren Song as he stood over Silas's still form. "Which one are you?"

"Get away from him!" she screamed at him, but Charlie had just laughed and laughed, and she kept screaming, shrieking, putting everything she had into it—

And had woken up with a start.

It had all been a dream. Except, no—it wasn't. She'd pushed herself up in the bed, leaning against the headboard, realizing that she was still in the motel and, yes, she had the crashing headache that said she'd been drugged, but she was sure she'd experienced something more tangible. She stumbled to the door and was relieved to see the Outback was parked outside the motel, still there. Afraid for Silas, she immediately climbed into the car and aimed for that lookout above the beach.

There were emergency vehicles and rescue EMTs on scene, so she drove on by, frightened and angry. She didn't have to be told Silas was dead . . . and she didn't have to be told who'd done it. She followed the rescue vehicles to the hospital and waited, and out stepped Ravinia Rutledge. Lucky had never actually laid eyes on the woman before, but she certainly knew of her because Silas had told her many things about this particular half sister. His association with Ravinia had caused Lucky pangs of jealousy she couldn't quite suppress, even though she knew Ravinia was family, his sister.

She reminded herself that they—she and Silas—had really made love, hadn't they? Before she'd been under the influence of the knock-out drugs she'd carried with her for years. She remembered him licking her ear while making love, a move of his she found a particular turn-on . . . didn't she? Or was that part of the vision/ dream as well?

It didn't matter now, she thought, still driving through the mountains, following Ravinia. She slowed to take in what was left of the Hunk O'Junks. There was one car, she saw, that was newer than the rest.

Maybe . . . ?

She cut her lights and pulled off the road, parking on the wide gravel shoulder. The house attached to the back of the decrepit building was mostly dark, just the hint of illumination in one window. Somebody living there?

After retrieving her small tool kit from beneath the passenger seat, she slid out of the Outback, then checked the license plates on the newer car. Still quite a bit of time on them; they wouldn't expire for another couple of months. Good. Using a screwdriver from her kit, she deftly unscrewed the plates and then slipped back into her car with them and the screwdriver, shoving everything beneath the seat as she eased back out on the road and headed east, switching on her headlights when she was out of sight of the scene of her theft. Dawn was just breaking when she pulled over about five miles farther on and switched her plates with the new ones.

Then she headed onward toward Portland and Ravinia Rutledge's home address, all the while remembering Silas.

I will kill him for you, she pledged to the ribbon of highway that led through the mountains.

For us.

Nev made it to work before seven. He grabbed a cup of coffee from the break room, fired up his computer, and researched everything he could find on the women of Siren Song via the Internet. There were lots of anecdotes, but little in the way of hard facts. As soon as he had a free moment, he was going to chase down *A Short History of the Colony* or maybe interview Herman Smythe himself.

He put in a call to Mills at seven-thirty but was told the officer wasn't in yet, so he left his name and cell number. He tried catching anything further about the body found at the Smuggler's Den on the news, but it was just more of the same. A woman. Found by a patron who'd come in the back way after being confounded by the locked front door. Looked like a homicide. No mention of strangulation today. That may have been news that had been leaked inadvertently, as no one was mentioning it any longer.

As soon as Lang appeared, Nev was going to head to the historical society. He checked the time on his phone, then consulted his contact list and entered Ravinia Rutledge's number. It rang on and on and then went to voice mail. He left a message, identifying himself and asking her to call.

If she didn't phone back, he was going to leave her another message. He didn't know what leverage he had to get her to talk to him, but he was going to use whatever he could think of. He was, after all, the law.

If he didn't hear from her ASAP, he'd talk to Catherine Rutledge or one of the other women at Siren Song. It wasn't the way Nev wanted to play it, but somebody from that cult knew something. And he was determined to find out what it was.

Savannah awakened from a sharp kick from the baby, a kick strong enough to make her sweep in a sharp breath. "Wow," she whispered, glancing across the empty bed and touching the cold sheets. Obviously, Hale had been up for a while.

At that moment, the bedroom door pushed open so hard it banged against the wall. Savvy immediately pretended like she was asleep, but couldn't quite hide the smile that touched her lips.

"Mommy!" Five-year-old Declan declared. "Get *up*!"

She didn't open her eyes. "Mommy's tired. I don't have to go to work today."

"Get *up*!"

"You come here." She tried to grab him as he came to her side of the bed, but he wriggled free and ran around to the other side of the bed, his blue eyes sparkling with mischief.

"Get up! You should go to work."

"Nah . . ." She leaned on her elbow and smiled at him. "Daddy's taking you to kindergarten."

"We need to carve pumpkins!"

Everything with Declan was at full decibel. The world was full of holidays that had to be enjoyed at full throttle, from the leprechaun trap they'd made back in March, to the Easter basket with the enormous chocolate bunny *and* the chocolate dinosaur, to the Fourth of July sparklers and back-to-school (it was Declan's first year, so technically not back to school, but don't tell him that) autumn-leaf collage, and now on to Halloween.

Savvy put her pillow over her head and made a muffled, "Noooooo!" which sent Declan shooting back around the bed to yank the pillow away from her face.

"You get up!" He threw the pillow onto the floor. "You can't stay in bed, you lazy lizard!"

She started laughing because that's what they said to him when he didn't feel like rolling out of bed.

"What's going on?" Hale stuck his head inside the doorway as Savvy heard the clink of glassware in the kitchen.

And that's when she remembered that Janet had stayed over. She could picture her mother-in-law dressed and ready and making herself a cup of coffee.

"Declan thinks I need to get going. He's right," she said, working her way out of the bed and onto her feet.

"I am?" Declan's little brows shot upward.

"You are." Her lower back hurt. Sleeping wrong, or another sign that their baby girl was imminent?

Baby girl.

Hale said, "Coffee's ready—but it's got caffeine. Sorry. Mom forgot. And now she's going out to get some pastries."

"Pastries?" asked Declan.

"Like donuts, or bear claws or something."

"Bear claws!" He knew what those were and dashed gleefully out of the room.

Savvy said, "I'm heading to the shower. I'll meet you in a bit. Is he going to be late for school?"

"It's Saturday."

"Jesus Christ," she muttered. "I'm so off these days, it's scary." She rubbed her back.

"What's going on? Anything?"

"No baby yet."

"You said that last time," he reminded, "and as I recall, I helped you have the little monster we now live with in the back of my SUV."

"Well, I'm not driving through the mountains this time until our daughter is born."

Hale gave her a look. "Thought we're having a boy."

Savvy hadn't been able to tell him what Dr. Evanston had revealed because Janet had been everywhere and there was no chance to get Hale alone, and then because she was exhausted, Savvy had gone to bed early, even before Declan.

Now she quickly brought him up to date. Finishing with, "I'm kind of excited to have one of each."

"You're sure?"

"Well, yeah." She shrugged. "That's what the doctor said. And both pregnancies have been called by the Colony women. Mad Maddie might not have lived at the lodge, but she's one of their clan, and now Cassandra . . . she was just so certain yesterday, so that's why I called the doctor."

Hale smiled. "You can decorate the nursery now."

"I think I was waiting because I wasn't completely sure."

"Hale? Savannah?"

Janet's voice brought them both up short. Savannah rolled her eyes. "I'll be quick," she whispered and headed to the shower.

Twenty minutes later, she entered the kitchen to find Hale putting his cell phone to his ear and walking away from Janet, whose strident voice was following after him, "—you'd better get a better nanny than the one you had for Declan. That Victoria person couldn't do anything but her nails."

"I'm not sure we're getting a nanny," Hale threw over his shoulder, as he headed out the slider to the deck, closing it behind him.

Savvy pictured the nanny who'd taken off with Charlie right after he was burned. Victoria Phelan. Young, disinterested in taking care of baby Declan even though it was her job, susceptible to Charlie, who'd coerced her into helping him escape. Her thoughts touching on Charlie almost hurt her brain.

Nearby, Declan was playing with his toy dinosaurs. Janet had brought back a pink box of baked goods that Declan hadn't seen yet, and neither Janet nor Savvy wanted to interrupt him just yet.

"How are you today?" Janet asked Savvy stiffly.

"Doing okay."

Janet nodded and, after an awkward moment between them, headed down the hall toward the guest room.

Savvy's cell rang as she was pouring herself a glass of orange juice. Lang's name and number appeared on the phone's screen. She answered with a smile in her voice, "Good morning. Now that I know it's Saturday, I'm going to assume this is a social call."

"Yeah, about that."

"Uh oh. What's up?" She cradled the phone against her shoulder as she tightened the lid on the OJ carton.

"Did you see on the news about the bartender from the Smuggler's Den?"

"No . . ." She immediately braced herself.

"Strangled. Raped, maybe. Broad daylight. The perp locked the front door and took her behind the bar. Went out the back."

"Strangled?"

"Like the body found on the beach. That bit of information hit the airwaves last night before it was locked down."

"The Smuggler's Den . . . it's that place that took over warehouse space in Seaside?" She found a pod of decaf coffee for the Keurig coffeemaker, then added water by rote and set her cup under the spigot.

"Yeah, it's Seaside PD's case."

"And you think it might be linked to ours?" she asked.

"Possibly."

Savannah felt a sharp pain in her lower back, one stronger than her usual Braxton Hicks contractions. "We need Ravinia to tell us what she knows."

"I just got to work. Rhodes is on it." He lowered his voice. "I don't know if it's a good thing, or a bad thing, but Ravinia somehow lit a fire under him. He's been careful since he came on board, maybe too careful, but he seems to really be putting his teeth into this case."

"He's been careful because he doesn't know whether I'm staying or leaving." She grimaced and rubbed her back. Something was definitely happening. But it was too early for the birth.

You said that last time, and Declan was born in the back of Hale's Trailblazer.

"Well, it's a fair question: Are you staying or leaving?" asked Lang.

"I'm supposed to start maternity leave in two weeks, you know that, but I might move that up. If you're asking if I'm quitting the department for good . . . ? I can't make that decision until after she's here."

"She?" Lang asked.

"I know." She watched as a slim stream of coffee flowed into her waiting cup. "It keeps changing, but I talked to my doctor yesterday, and we're all pretty sure it's a girl now."

He grunted acknowledgment. "Rhodes has a call into Seaside's Detective John Mills."

Savannah reacted to the name. "Mills was first on the scene of Kristina's accident. He talked to Hale."

"I remember," Lang said quietly to Savannah's sober tone.

"He wasn't a detective then," she said.

"Well, he's in charge of the investigation now. Rhodes wants to get Ravinia to spill what she knows before he exchanges information. Failing that, we could talk to Catherine Rutledge."

"Who do you mean by 'we'?"

"You and I, Savvy. Especially you."

"Oh, no. You know her better than I do," she argued as the Keurig sputtered to a finish. "You've known her longer."

"She gave you the lesson on genetics."

"But that was years ago."

"Mommy?" Declan said.

"Look, I can go with you, but don't think Catherine and I are such good buddies, 'cause we're not."

"I didn't say you were."

"You implied it."

"Mommy!" Declan was more insistent.

"I've gotta go," she told Lang. "Let me know if you need my help, but I'm just about out. Later." She clicked off, thinking of the case, and of Declan Sr.'s recent death, as she turned to Declan, who'd put together one of his dinosaurs, a T-rex in a noxious lavender color, and was proudly holding it up for her to see.

"It's lovely," she said absently.

Janet walked back into the kitchen just as Declan looked up and spied the pink box.

"Bear claws!" Declan cried.

"That's right," said Janet, picking up the box and opening it. She was smiling, the nicest demeanor she'd presented to date, and Declan ran to her, dinosaur in hand. "I got the best ones just for you and—"

Savvy gasped, stopping Janet short. The images of Declan Sr. and his unlikely fateful tumble down the stairs filled her head. Down and down and down he fell, each step jarring his old bones. The image filled her brain, and as it did she suddenly felt a sickening, snaking, *familiar* sense of sexual thrill that nearly knocked her over.

Oh. God. Oh. No!

Charlie!

She had to grab for support on the refrigerator handle while she dropped to her knees, her legs giving out.

"My God!" whispered Janet.

"Mommy?" Declan's worried little voice was nearly drowned out by the buzzing in her ears, desire running suddenly hot through her veins.

Charlie . . . pheromones . . . she'd been here before . . . and Savannah had combated his sexual trap before with thoughts of Hale.

Hale! Her love for him, her husband.

She squeezed her eyes closed, shutting out everything but the wall of resistance she mentally sent back to him. Charlie. God . . . *Charlie*. He was here! It was real! All the worry and doubt and fear hadn't been in vain.

Mooommmmyyyyy . . . Declan's watery wail was far away.

She felt hands pulling her to her feet. "Hale," she whispered, wavering, still unsteady.

When the sexual shackles receded, she dared to open an eye and drew in a long, unsteady breath. Janet's hands were holding her. Not Hale's. And her mother-in-law, after helping her up, was now staring at her with alarm. "What was that, Savannah?" she asked. "What the hell was that?"

Savannah leaned heavily against the counter. The pink box from the bakery was on the floor, the top flap open, donuts and bear claws visible.

Hale's mother took a step back, as if Savannah's behavior were not only inexplicable, but off-putting. Little Declan was staring at her, having dropped his T-rex on the floor. "Mommy?" he whispered, his chin wobbling, his eyes bright with tears.

"It's all right, honey," she whispered. "Mommy's all right."

Janet bent down and picked up the box of jumbled pastries. "You certainly are not all right."

Savannah shot her mother-in-law a look and put a hand out to Declan, not trusting herself to leave the support of the counter.

At that moment, Hale slid open the slider door. "What's wrong?" he demanded, taking in the tableau in a glance. He stepped forward and scooped up his crying son. "Savvy?" he asked, concerned.

"She had some kind of attack!" said Janet.

Savannah felt a gush of warm fluid run down her legs. "My water just broke," she said, grateful that she had an explanation for her behavior, even if it was a lie.

CHAPTER 12

Ravinia drove to her Portland apartment, located in an older building on the west side of the Willamette River. The exterior bricks had been painted so many times they seemed a half-inch thicker than when the hundred-year-old structure had first been erected, and some of the window casings were cracking, but still, this was home.

She parked in the tiny back lot with room enough for one car per unit. Rents had skyrocketed, and she was lucky her one-bedroom place was so small that she could afford it. Her "office" was a desk in an alcove next to the original brick fireplace, which had now been converted to gas. She'd hoped to have an office that was not her living space but wouldn't be able to afford one until her business grew. The same could be said about needing someone to work for her. It would happen when she could afford it. So, for the moment, she was operating from home, which was not ideal in any way, especially since she didn't want clients or anyone she had contact with through her work efforts to know where she lived. It was just currently financially prudent. The only way to be out on her own.

Once inside, she walked through the back door and tiny kitchen, then down the short hallway to her bedroom, dropping her overnight bag and coat onto her bed. After a stop at the bathroom, she moved to her desk with its landline phone, picked up the receiver, and pressed the numbers to access her voice mail. In her mind, she was still replaying her last conversation with Isadora and was already ruing her harsh stance about Lillibeth. In truth, Ravinia had been happy to hear Lillibeth was involved in a romance, albeit a fantasy one, when she'd heard about it at the funeral, and then she'd just turned a one-eighty, blasting Lillibeth's dreams, mainly because she was mad at Isadora and all the stupid restrictions at Siren Song. And because she was scared for Lillibeth, who seemed to be losing touch with reality more and more. She had been genuinely terrified.

Now, Ravinia cringed a little, thinking about how Isadora might relate the conversation to Lillibeth. Sigh. Too often Ravinia still lived out loud, something a good investigator did not do.

Ah, well. Next time she was in Deception Bay, she would make it right with Lillibeth. It wasn't the girl's fault she was in a wheelchair and therefore under more of Catherine's control.

There were a number of messages on her landline, which was her office phone. She listened to the first two and discovered she could have someone check out her vents for an amazingly reasonable price and that she should really check her vehicle warranty. There was one hang-up and another call from the man who'd wanted her to find his missing wife, letting her know her services were no longer needed as the wife had returned renewed from an extended stay at a spa. Ah. So much for that job. There was also a call from J. D. Bauer, her old boss, and lastly an inquiry for a possible divorce/surveillance job. She wasn't fond of divorce work. Sometimes angry spouses threw items at her: pots, pans, even a rolling pin once from a baker who'd turned her ire on Ravinia when she learned her partner was cheating, as if it were somehow Ravinia's fault. But beggars could not be choosers, and she phoned the caller, Jolene Fursberg, and made an appointment to meet her the next day at Laurelton Park in Laurelton, about twenty minutes west of Portland, a town she'd passed through on her way inland from the coast. Neither Ravinia nor Jolene wanted to meet at their place of residence, so the park it was.

The call from J. D. gave her pause. What did he want? He hadn't said in his message, which was typical of the cryptic and somewhat secretive man. He was a decent investigator; she would give him that. But she'd never completely trusted him.

Taking a moment to think, she opened one of the living room windows to dispel the dead and dusty air that had accumulated while she was away. She had been gone only one night, and the place felt as neglected as an ancient crypt.

As she considered making herself an egg and toast, her landline rang, surprising her. She realized it was the number of two of the hang-ups. Picking up, she answered, all business, "Rutledge Investigations."

"Ms. Rutledge?"

She recognized Detective Rhodes's voice immediately. Obviously, he'd given up trying to reach her on her cell phone when she wouldn't answer, so he'd located the number of her business line. "Yes, what can I help you with?"

"This is Detective Rhodes. Is it possible for you to come into the Sheriff's Department and meet with Detective Stone and myself?"

"No, actually, it's not possible. I'm back in Portland now, and working." A bit of a fib, but close enough to the truth to count. "I already told you everything I know." A bigger fib.

"I thought you'd want to know that Detective Stone is planning to go to Siren Song and meet with Catherine Rutledge. He's going to ask her about the body that washed up on the beach, and he believes she'll tell him who it is."

"Well, that's . . . good." No, it wasn't good at all. She didn't want Catherine undermining her. They were supposed to keep Silas's identity to themselves, weren't they? Aunt Catherine was keeping that information quiet, wasn't she? Now that she thought about it, Ravinia wasn't completely sure. If Aunt Catherine did just blurt out the truth, that would make Ravinia seem pretty damn churlish for hiding it.

The lodge still didn't have a landline, but Catherine had a cell phone now . . . one gathering cobwebs in the charger, but it would ring, and maybe someone—Isadora, probably—would answer it if one called.

"You want to say anything first? You know, like, maybe your memory's been jogged?"

She could hear the challenge in his voice and immediately rose to it, ready to tell him what he could do with his insinuations. She had to pull back, tamp down her reaction, act like a professional. "Sounds like you've got it handled, Detective."

"Okay, look, I get the feeling we got off on the wrong foot."

"Really?"

"Maybe we could start over," he said, ignoring her sarcasm, "and you could tell me why you think John Doe had your phone number."

"I wish I knew," she responded, meaning it. There were any number of ways Silas could have gotten her number, but why he wrote it down for, obviously, others to find . . .

He wants you to find his killer.

She suddenly wanted to tell Rhodes that John Doe was Silas. She wanted the help. Catherine already knew, and the Sheriff's Department wasn't going to give up until they learned who he was. Eventually, it was all going to come out, and then her reluctance to identify him would raise more questions than necessary about her own motives. Ridiculous. "Let me call you back," she heard herself say. "At this number on my caller ID?"

"Here's my cell." He gave her a different phone number, which she plugged into the contact list of her own cell.

"Okay," she said and hung up. Leaning against the wall, she took a moment to gather herself. The man put her on edge, that was for sure. She then used her cell to dial Aunt Catherine's, but the phone on the other end of the connection just rang on and on and on. No voice mail.

Well, shit. Some things never changed. So much for Isadora or someone else picking up.

She tried Ophelia next, but her sister's cell connected straight to voice mail. Ophelia was probably at Ocean Park, working a ten-hour shift. At least that was the schedule "Nurse O." had been on, the last time Ravinia had checked.

Giving it up for the moment, Ravinia went to her refrigerator and hung on the appliance door, peering inside. Surprise, surprise. It looked the same as yesterday: basically nothing inside.

Great. She slammed the refrigerator door shut and figured she'd have to opt for plan B, so she hung up her coat, snagged a jacket from her closet and slipped into it, then picked up her purse.

Slinging the strap over her shoulder, she headed outside and around the block to the nearest coffee shop, six blocks away. The weather was nicer in the valley, less wind and therefore less biting. Good. She could use the walk.

From the driver's seat of her SUV, Lucky watched Ravinia leave her apartment and head down the street on foot. The silver Outback was located across the street and about a block and a half down. Lucky had been thinking about what her next step might be. Sitting in a car all day was an invitation for some nosy neighbor to call the cops and find out who she was and what her intentions were.

No thanks.

She got out of her car and followed her quarry on foot.

Ravinia did not know who Lucky was, so she had the advantage of camouflage while in plain sight. Nonetheless, Lucky kept at least one full block behind her and was debating whether or not to approach her and talk to her about Silas. He'd trusted Ravinia, but Lucky did not feel the same. Of course, she never trusted anyone. It was one of the reasons she was still alive and out of jail.

He'd finally gotten through!

Nev was relieved and somewhat elated that Ravinia had actually picked up her phone. He'd suspected she was in Portland by virtue of the fact that she'd answered her office phone, which was likely a landline, in person. Nevertheless, he'd still asked her to come down to the station. Stupid move, he now knew. He'd just stayed on script.

But, hey, she's going to call you back.

He did a quick assessment of himself, a little baffled at how he felt.

What did she hit you with? Love Potion #9?

No . . . she was pretty and unique, and he was just . . . interested. That was all. Just interested.

Lang had dropped the idea of trying to meet with Catherine Rutledge on him as he'd headed for the break room. Nev had looked after him in consternation. Feeling ridiculously competitive, he'd decided to try Ravinia one more time, and lo and behold, she'd finally answered. Now he heard Lang's footsteps returning from the short hallway that led to the break room and back door. Nev pretended concentration on his computer screen as Lang, who was on the phone and saying something about Savannah, came back to his desk. When he didn't sit down, Nev looked at him over the top of his computer, just as Lang clicked off and said, "That was Savvy. She's at Ocean Park. Looks like Baby St. Cloud is coming early, which is Savvy's MO. I'm heading to the hospital now."

"You are?" Nev was kind of surprised.

"She wants to see me. Don't know why, but it must be important." He stuffed his cell into his pocket and grabbed his keys.

Nev clarified, "You're still planning to meet with Catherine Rutledge?"

"I'm sure gonna try. She has a phone she never answers, but I can call Ophelia. Or maybe I'll just drop by. That works so well," he said sardonically.

"Ravinia's calling me back."

"Oh, yeah?" He was heading toward the back door and looking down the hall toward the front desk, saluting May Johnson on his way out, some sort of thing he had going with her. If Nev tried that, she'd scowl and ask him what the hell he thought he was doing, but the dour receptionist had a soft spot for Stone. "Let me know if you learn anything."

"Will do."

Nev looked at the clock. Not even ten o'clock yet. Mills had texted him that he would call later, though he warned he didn't have much further on the female bartender's death than what had already been reported.

Knowing it was probably an exercise in futility, he nevertheless called the lab, looking for information on John Doe and Stanford Norman, and was told that nothing would be ready until the following Monday when the autopsy was scheduled.

Call back, he willed Ravinia Rutledge. He was counting on her to give him something more to work on, otherwise, he would basically be sitting on his hands, waiting for the rest of the weekend to pass.

Lang drove his Explorer down Highway 101, past the lane that led to both the Colony lodge and the Foothillers' community. He glanced over to catch a glimpse of Siren Song's front windows, high above his head and facing toward the sea. Blank eyes, ever watchful. He thought the same thing every time he happened to catch sight of them.

He'd known Catherine Rutledge since he first started with TCSD seven, no, eight years ago now. His daughter, Bea, was almost eight.

His daughter . . . he was tired of waiting for Catherine to wave her magic wand and allow Claire and him to adopt Beatrice. Ironically, if not for him, Catherine might not even know that Bea existed. He was the one who'd told her that one of Mary's daughters, a lodge escapee who'd probably given Ravinia the idea to keep scaling those high walls, no matter what the punishment, had delivered a baby before her death, a girl that he and Claire were still trying to adopt. To this day, Catherine was ambivalent, and so the adoption was stalled in a kind of purgatory.

Lang shook his head. Catherine still knew more than he and Claire did about Bea's birth mother, but Catherine was careful not to talk about any of the women of Siren Song, whether they grew up inside the lodge or not. She was a damn sphinx when it came to her charges, no doubt about it. She would let out just enough information to get whatever she wanted, without giving anything in return. And Lang was sick of it.

The truth was he wanted to have it out with Catherine. He'd always given her a lot of leeway; everyone in Deception Bay had. She was part of the landscape, and people generally treated her with respect, even if they didn't understand her kooky ways. He did too, and he and Claire and Savvy, come to that, had applauded her easing of restrictions over the past five years, ever since she'd reconnected with her own daughter, Elizabeth. She'd allowed Ophelia, who was a nurse now at Ocean Park Hospital, to move into her own place, and he knew Ravinia had permanently moved out, which left only a few women at the lodge, the ones he knew the least about. He still struggled with their names, except for the one who could sometimes predict the future, Cassandra . . . although Savvy said she had another name, one he couldn't remember.

The point was, however, as he drove on north to the turnoff to Ocean Park Hospital, that Catherine, for all her new and modern changes, still hadn't okayed the adoption. Just this morning, Bea had looked at him with solemn blue eyes and said, "I'm never going to be yours, am I?"

"You're already mine," he'd answered back, and Claire, her own luminous, brown eyes wide with concern, had turned around in surprise from the griddle, where she was making Bea her favorite cinnamon and coconut pancakes, and said, "Oh, honey, what brought that on?"

Bea had lifted her shoulders up and down several times. After breakfast, Claire had pulled the girl's hair into a ponytail. While she had clipped back the errant strands that framed Bea's face and curled under her chin with pink, tan, and white ice cream cone clips,

Claire had tried to ask her daughter about what she was feeling, but Bea had clammed up. That was all they'd gotten out of her before Lang left for work.

As it was Saturday, he wasn't really on duty today, but with two dead bodies under suspicious circumstances, he'd decided to check in. Sheriff O'Halloran would probably take it that Lang was giving in to his suggestion to run for office next year, working on his brownie points, but Lang was still undecided on that one. Last week he'd seen one of the TV life coaches saying on some infomercial, "Visualize yourself in the job!" and Lang had given it a shot, seeing himself in charge of Rhodes and Savannah, if she returned, and May Johnson and the other deputies and officers, though Warren Burghsmith, who'd been with TCSD about as long as Lang, had recently left the department entirely. Burghsmith had never really gotten over Fred Clausen's death at the hands of Henry Charles Woodworth.

"Charlie," Lang said aloud now. He hadn't encountered the man himself. It was Savannah who'd faced off with him, but Lang and the rest of the department felt angry, repulsed, and vengeful that Charlie had attacked one of their own. It had been difficult to put thoughts of him aside, which they'd all slowly managed over the years, although always with one ear eager to hear that the psycho had been caught. But that hadn't happened. The John Doe on the beach wasn't Charlie, either, though Savvy had initially thought it might be. Who was he? And how was he "next of kin" to the women of Siren Song?

At the hospital, once he found his way to the maternity wing and was let inside, Lang knocked on the wall outside the half-opened door.

"Come on in," Savvy's voice invited, and he entered to find her alone. She'd shooed everyone out of her room except Lang, she told him. That included Hale, who'd said he would be downstairs, while his mother, Janet, babysat little Declan at their home.

"I wanted to talk to you alone," she said. "And I didn't want to talk on the phone."

"Okay."

She was hooked up to all kinds of monitors. At least it seemed that way. Screens of numbers and lines and messages running by flanked her on one side. An IV stand, with fluid draining down a tube attached to the back of her wrist, stood on the other.

Seeing him eyeing the screens, she said, "Looked like we were going full bore for a while, but things have slowed down a bit, which gives us time."

"Time for what?"

"Take a chair, Lang. Sit down." She glanced at the window, then back at him.

"Uh oh." He did as he was directed, but he was getting a very bad feeling about this.

"Charlie reached out to me," she admitted, her face tense.

He realized, then, that she'd been putting on a good front, but she was what? Stunned? Frightened? Sickened? "When did he reach out?" he demanded. "This morning? He *called* your cell?" Lang was abruptly back on his feet. "Jesus, I gotta admit, I thought you were seeing ghosts."

"He didn't call my cell. I wish he had! He got into my head, Lang. Into my psyche." She swallowed, and he could see she was holding onto her composure with an effort. "Right before my water broke. Just . . . I can't explain it, and I don't want to. It's . . ."

"You don't have to explain." He didn't know what he believed about Charlie, but he knew Savvy. She was level-headed and smart and rarely undone, but she was definitely undone now.

"He sends out pheromones," she said unsteadily.

He nodded. "I know." She'd said as much before. It was hard to believe, but there it was.

"I don't understand how he does it, but he does. He enslaved my sister and killed her, and he's back. I know he's back. *I felt it!*"

"We need to find him," said Lang. "Is he close? Can you tell? Is that how this works?" he finished diffidently, trying not to feel like an idiot for asking the questions.

"I don't know. I think he has to be pretty close, which means he's in Seaside, or was this morning. I don't really know, but Lang . . . it's goddamn embarrassing, but the messages he sends are . . ." She lifted a hand to cover her jaw as she shook her head. "*Sexual.*"

"It's not your fault. Whatever it is, it's not your fault."

"I didn't want to alarm Hale. Our son was upset as it was when he

saw my reaction to Charlie's message and then my water breaking—"
As if realizing she was talking too fast, spinning out of control, she
caught herself, took another breath, then looked Lang steadily in the
eye. "Declan didn't want to stay with Janet, and I get that, I do, but
there was nothing else to do." Her small laugh was full of misery.

"Do you think you're safe here? Do you want a guard?"

"No, no. Hale's here, and I'll tell him, I just needed you to know.
Charlie's dangerous. When I felt that . . . I'd forgotten how sickening
it made me feel, but it came right back."

"You think he's after you." It was a statement, not a question.

"I don't know. But he wanted me to know he was here. Beyond
that . . ." She shook her head. "He isn't our John Doe, but I swear
there's some connection between the two. You, or maybe Rhodes,
need to get Ravinia to talk about that, but in the meantime—" She
suddenly sucked air between her teeth. "Oh, shit. I wish this wasn't
happening now!" she said as another contraction was obviously
building, her muscles tensing.

"Maybe I should get Hale." Lang took a step toward the door.

"No . . . it's okay . . . just wait a sec . . ." She closed her eyes and
bent forward slightly, bearing down. "Oh—Lord!"

Lang felt helpless. He and Claire had never had children. They'd
never tried to *not* have children, it just hadn't happened in all their
years together. Watching Savannah struggle through a contraction
made him want to do something, but he didn't know what.

She came back fairly quickly, exhaling loudly, then offering up a
crooked smile. "It's not that bad," she said on another short laugh,
looking at his face.

"I'd hate to see what you call bad."

"It's just labor. I can handle it."

"All right," he said dubiously.

"Really, I'm fine. It's childbirth. Happens every day, every minute."
She made a little shooing motion with her hand. "Go." She managed
a smile. "I'm good."

"Okay. I'll check in later. Right now, I'm going to stop by Siren
Song to talk to Catherine."

"Good. Warn her," said Savvy. Then she thought about that and
asked, "Can you call her?"

"You'd think so, but no one's picking up. I'll go make noise at the gate."

"Or throw notes through the bars?" she suggested.

Lang smiled faintly at Savvy's reference to his first attempt to reach Catherine. "It got her attention, didn't it?"

"She likes you. Much better than she likes me," she said.

"Not sure about that."

At that moment, Hale rapped his fingers on the open door and stuck them around the jamb. "How're we doing?"

"I'm outta here," said Lang, shaking hands with Savannah's husband as he prepared to take his leave.

"Be careful with Catherine," said Savvy quickly before Lang could disappear into the hallway.

"Always."

"She's aged a lot, Lang. I don't know when you last saw her."

Lang considered. "Not for a while."

"She's kind of fragile, I think."

"I'll keep that in mind," he said, finally taking his leave.

Catherine Rutledge? Fragile? He wanted to laugh out loud as he drove south again. Imperious. Rigid. Unyielding. Unemotional . . . those were all adjectives he would use to describe the matron of Siren Song, but fragile? Had she really deteriorated that far?

"Catherine of the Gates," he muttered, pulling up his own long-ago name for her.

What had happened to her?

Ravinia finished her bagel and coffee and then bought some blueberry muffins to take back to her apartment. Now, she was at her desk, looking into her iPad, which was propped up on its stand like a laptop, sipping at another cup of coffee she'd made for herself from the small, four-cup coffeemaker on her kitchen counter.

She had the old addresses for both Silas's and Charlie's adoptive parents, but she was scrolling through names in both of the cities where they had lived, hoping to locate their current residences. Hopefully, neither set of parents had moved, but what were the chances of that? Silas's family had lived in Cottage Grove, Oregon, and it looked as if they might still be there.

"Fingers crossed," she said to the empty rooms.

Charlie's family had taken up residence in Brookings, an Oregon coastal town just north of the California border, and also appeared to still be there.

Could she really get that lucky?

She'd attempted calling phone numbers she'd managed to dig up, but the landlines had been disconnected. They'd probably all moved to cell phones, of course. It would be a long drive to Brookings, but only a few hours down I-5 to Cottage Grove. She could plan an overnight trip and hit them both. Maybe tomorrow? A Sunday might find them at home, or if they'd moved, maybe the neighbors would know where they'd gone.

And what about Detective Rhodes? Had he learned anything more about Silas yet?

You should just tell him.

She glanced at her landline phone, then at her cell, sitting on her desk to the right side of her iPad. She started to dial Detective Rhodes, then stopped herself. She hadn't talked to Catherine, or Ophelia, or anyone associated with Siren Song yet.

The reason you're not calling Rhodes has nothing to do with Silas. You're just afraid to talk to him.

"Afraid?" she said aloud. No. Her own conscience was wrong. He was nothing to her. Just another cop to avoid.

Growling under her breath, she instead phoned her old boss, J. D. Bauer. When he answered, she almost led with, "What do you want?" but decided that might be counterproductive, so she faked some enthusiasm and said, "Hi, J. D. Got your message to call."

"Ah, Ravinia . . ."

This is what he always said, and she had a momentary thought, as ever, of how he singsonged her name so that it sounded a lot like "Nants ingonyama," the beginning of "Circle of Life" from *The Lion King.* She didn't know if this was purposeful on his part or if he had just picked up the inflection and didn't even know where it came from. She'd looked it up and knew the phrase was Zulu for "Here comes a lion . . ." She doubted he would like that ascribed to her, but that's how she took it.

"Was there something specific?"

"I wanted to go over an old case with you. I think you may have screwed up some things."

"Screwed up some things," she repeated, affronted.

"Little details I want to straighten out. You want to come to the office?"

"What things?" she demanded, her temper rising. "What case? When was this?" Her mind spiraled backward to the period she'd been Bauer's employee, and at no time that she remembered could she have screwed up so badly as to warrant this conversation.

"Come by around five, and I'll show you."

"No, I—"

And he disconnected.

"Aaaaarggghhhh . . ." she said, annoyed way out of proportion to the circumstances.

Her cell rang again, and she glared at it, expecting Bauer to have called back, but it was Ophelia. She slid her thumb across the screen to switch on the cell. "Ophelia," she said on a note of surprise.

"You called me? I'm on a break. I don't have tons of time, especially after taking off for the funeral yesterday. What do you need?"

"Hey, great to hear from you too. Let's get together again soon," said Ravinia.

"Very funny. I just saw you yesterday. Forgive me for wondering what the hell's going on."

"Okay. Aunt Catherine told you about Silas. Don't bother lying to somehow defend her, I really don't care. What I want to know is what you found out from the addresses for Silas's adoptive parents."

"What I found out?"

"Yes, Ophelia. What you found out. You called them, right? Silas's adoptive family? And Charlie's?"

"You have the addresses now. Look them up yourself. I've got to go, Ravinia."

"Thanks for being so damn helpful."

"Oh, my God." Ophelia exhaled in disgust.

"Just tell me what you learned," said Ravinia, ignoring her pique.

"I didn't follow up on them. Catherine didn't want me to, so I didn't. It hasn't really mattered till now. Whatever you need is probably on the Internet now anyway, so look it up."

"I tried, but I didn't really find anything."

188 Lisa Jackson and Nancy Bush

"Well, I'm sorry, but I can't help you."

Ravinia had hoped Ophelia would be more forthcoming, but that apparently was not to be. Pulling out the papers from the top drawer of her desk, she examined them again. The addresses were written in pencil, barely discernible after all this time. Had her mother written them down?

She folded up the papers and stuffed them into her messenger-bag purse. She could still feel how annoyed she was. Did Ophelia have to be so damn abrupt? Ravinia got that Ophelia had a new life outside the lodge gates, but so did she, and she wasn't that rude.

But weren't you? In the past, maybe?

"Not as bad as she is," she grumbled aloud, digging into one of the blueberry muffins. She had a momentary flick of remembrance as she slid the muffin onto a plate and plucked a paper towel from its holder. Earlier this morning . . . at the coffee shop/café that was called the Bakery Et Al. She'd been ordering the muffins at the counter and had felt eyes on her. She'd turned around abruptly, heart racing, expecting to find Charlie or some other perv staring at her, but the only people in the shop were women, except for one guy with his girlfriend, she had assumed, from the way they were holding hands across the tabletop and staring into each other's eyes. One woman in a baseball cap and sunglasses was just turning away from the line in front of the counter and taking a seat; otherwise, everyone else just flicked their eyes to her when she abruptly turned around.

Nerves. She'd felt on edge from the moment she'd taken off for the coast. Everything felt a bit off.

"Get over it," she muttered, biting into her muffin. She then set it back on the plate and carried it and a napkin to her desk. As she was making one more search for phone numbers for Silas's and Charlie's adoptive parents, her cell rang, and she saw it was Elizabeth.

"We're back home. Rex picked us up. I tried calling my mother, but you know how that goes. Would you let her know we're safe and sound?"

"Will do," assured Ravinia. "I'll let Ophelia know if I can't get through." It was still a little strange hearing Elizabeth refer to Aunt Catherine as "my mother," even though it shouldn't be.

"Chloe is desperate to talk to you. Here she is."

Ravinia heard a scramble on the other end of the phone, and then Chloe's voice came on. "I fell asleep on the plane, but I saw you talk to the wolf!"

"That must've been just a dream. I haven't talked to the wolf, Chloe."

"He told you where to go."

"Well, that's just not true. Believe me, if I see him, I'll let you know."

It took a few more minutes to convince Chloe that Ravinia had not seen hide nor hair of the beast before she could get off the phone and back to her plans. She wondered if Silas' and Charlie's adoptive parents would even be able to tell her anything helpful if she succeeded in reaching them? That was the curse of investigative work. A lot of dead ends before a road ever opened up.

But without sudden inspiration or a conversation with the wolf, Ravinia thought dryly, it was her best course of action.

CHAPTER 13

Lang stood outside the gates of Siren Song in a cool wind, remembering how he'd done much the same thing years before, the first time he'd attempted to meet Catherine and her charges. She'd ignored all his attempts. All of them had. Only when he'd shown up with Claire—Dr. Claire Norris, at the time—had Catherine deigned to let Claire, not Lang, past the iron bars.

Since then, things had changed, sort of, but he was pretty sure he still wasn't welcome. No man was, except for Earl, a Foothiller who'd been Catherine's go-to general handyman for years. Lang wondered how Earl felt about the creeping gentrification heading into the Foothillers' village, with builders like Bancroft Development buying up property from the locals and taking down the small tract houses, replacing them with sprawling, two-story structures. Okay, Savvy had said Bancroft wasn't one of the companies moving in, but Lang figured it was just a matter of time. He felt a pang of loss for what hadn't even happened yet.

His cell rang, and he saw it was from Rhodes. He answered, "No baby yet. She's still in labor."

"Uh . . . yeah . . . I want to talk to you about something." He sounded serious.

Lang pictured Neville Rhodes. Tall, lean, serious, a handsome guy with a gravity far beyond his years. Rhodes needed to lighten up a little, in Lang's biased opinion, but the tragedies he'd lived through had probably made that an iffy proposition.

"I think we need to go to Echo Island."

Lang's brows lifted. Although he agreed with the assessment, had been letting a similar idea germinate, it was a surprise, given his history, that Rhodes had been the one to bring it up first.

"All right," said Lang. The body could have been dropped from a boat and floated in, but it could have just as easily come from Echo. "You want to go?" he questioned.

"I told Earl's son, Rand, that I wanted Earl to take me, unless we could get the Marine Patrol."

"Echo's far enough in the ocean to be out of range for the Marine Patrol." And no one at TCSD wanted to go to Echo, including Lang.

"I figured. Rand said it's too late in the year, and Earl's too old."

"Probably both true . . ."

"I'm not asking you to go with me," said Nev. "You can if you want, but I'm going to check with Earl anyway. He knows that godforsaken piece of rock better than any of us."

"Okay." He tried not to sound relieved. "But are you sure you want to be the one to go, Rhodes?"

He expelled a heavy breath. "Sure. Why not. If Earl can't or won't do it, I'll come up with something else."

"This some kind of pilgrimage for you?" guessed Lang.

"It's just police work."

Bullshit to that. But Lang sensed Rhodes was determined, so who was he to talk him out of it? "Let me know what Earl says." He glanced down the flagstone path that led to Siren Song's front door. "And before you go, we should follow up with Ravinia and/or Catherine. See if we're really on the right track."

"Ravinia said she'd call me."

"Did she? Good." He almost told Rhodes he was standing outside the gates of the lodge right then, but until he saw the whites of one of Siren Song's inhabitants' eyes, he wasn't ready to admit he'd failed at making contact. To Nev, he said, "I'll talk to O'Halloran. See if there's any chance with Marine Patrol."

"Thanks."

"What about the Norman case?" he asked. Rhodes had told him what the bartender at the Locker had said about Norman being hot and bothered over a girl in pigtails who, if the Locker source was reliable about checking IDs, would have to have been over twenty-one. "Have you followed up on the girl in pigtails?"

"I plan to go back to the Locker, maybe tonight. See if anyone else remembers her. The place doesn't have any security cameras, but maybe someone will recall seeing her and how she got there. It's not a great place to walk to, so I'm guessing a vehicle of some sort. Also, I want to check with Jenny Norman again. She doesn't want to admit her husband could have been with someone else, but maybe she knows more about that than she wants to admit."

"He was a regular at the Locker. She probably suspects something," said Lang. "Mills ever call you back?"

"Briefly. Didn't have much more to say other than what we already knew. Told him I wanted to talk about one of our cases, and he said he'd check back later. Tech team was going over the Smuggler's Den, which is closed today."

Lang grunted an assent. SOP, standard operating procedure. He'd never worked directly with Rhodes before these two cases; the man was too new on the job. He'd kind of wondered how they would get along, but Rhodes had really dug in.

"Are you coming back in today?" the younger man asked Lang.

"Yeah, I'll pop in this afternoon. See ya then."

As Lang clicked off, he thought he discerned a flash of white behind some of the overgrown laurels near the front door of the lodge. Someone coming?

A stiff-backed woman in a long dress in a white and blue print suddenly came into view. He had a moment of blankness. Couldn't remember her name or much about her. Which one was this? Cassandra? The one who'd named the sex of Savvy's baby? No, this was *Isadora*. She'd been the one who'd first opened the gate to him and allowed Claire to enter.

"Detective Stone," she said, looking at him through the bars.

Well, she clearly remembered him. He put on a smile. "Hi, Isadora. I wanted to talk to Catherine. Is she here?"

"She's resting."

It was the middle of the day. She could be resting, he supposed, but he had a feeling he was being shined on. "Would you tell her I'm here?"

"What do you want to see her about?"

A touch of imperiousness here too, he thought. A younger Catherine. "Well, I'd like to talk to *her* about that."

"We don't have any secrets here."

He laughed out loud. He couldn't help himself. He knew some of their worst secrets. Like the fact that their "dark gifts" or psychic abilities weren't always used for good, even among the women, not just the few men who were related to the women of Siren Song. "Okay, well, tell her that Ravinia said she knows who the John Doe is who washed up on the beach," he lied. "She's talking to Detective Rhodes about him right now."

Isadora suddenly stiffened, as if hit by a freeze ray.

Aha, he thought, adding, "And I just came from a meeting with Savannah Dunbar, er, St. Cloud, and she told me that Charlie's back. He's already gotten inside her head, and it sickened her." Truth mixed in with a lie. An age-old method to get someone to open up.

Isadora had paled. "I don't think that's possible."

"Well, neither do I, actually, but Savvy doesn't lie or exaggerate or seriously believe in woo-woo, so I guess I'm going to have to accept that she's telling the truth." He stared at her through the bars. "So you go ahead, tell Catherine I was here and that I want to talk to her."

She blinked several times, then drew her composure around her like a cloak. "Good day, Detective."

"Good day," he said back, instinctively copying her dismissive tone. He hadn't expected to be let in, because that never happened, but he'd hoped Catherine would come out. Still, he'd delivered the message without having to throw notes through the bars. Maybe his words to Isadora would scare them enough to shake them out of complacency, but man, they were a rigid bunch.

Nev rolled his shoulders a couple of times, easing the tension. Desk work was his least favorite part of the job, but there was no escaping it. He glanced at his cell phone, willing Ravinia to call him back. She wanted to. She really wanted to talk to him. He could almost feel it.

"You're getting as bad as they are," he muttered to himself, thinking of the women in the cult.

It was too early to head over to Davy Jones's Locker and nose around some more because he wanted to connect with the nighttime regulars, but it wasn't too early to talk to Jenny Norman. He didn't relish the idea of interviewing the deceased's widow, but it needed to be done now that she'd had a little time to absorb the shock.

There was no other detective on site today, so he let May Johnson, who seemed to never take a day off, know what his plans were and that he would be available on his cell.

The receptionist frowned at him and said, "My nephew's here in case someone needs a real policeman." She didn't actually say *real* policeman, but that's what Nev heard in her tone.

May's nephew, Deputy DeShawn Wilson, one of the new hires, a young Black man who was as welcoming and optimistic as May was austere.

"DeShawn's my sister's boy," she said now, as if he'd asked.

Since this was more social interaction than May had ever shown him, Nev said, "DeShawn's good at what he does," which seemed to surprise her as she rolled her chair back to stare more harshly, her frown deepening as he headed out the back door.

He drove to Sandbar, stopping at his own place for a drink of water and to drop off his jacket in favor of a windbreaker. The weather wasn't exactly warm, but it wasn't cold either—well, except for the occasional burst of arctic wind.

The Norman house was about a quarter mile from his place, closer to Carter's Bait Shop. Apparently Stanford Norman had walked from his house to his rendezvous with the girl in pigtails. How had she gotten to the site? He reminded himself to ask old man Carter about any vehicles he hadn't recognized, though no one had been able to raise the curmudgeon the night before when they'd pounded on his door. With Carter's suspicion of police in general, this was no surprise.

Rhodes walked up a weed-choked path to a narrow front porch and knocked on the door. Heard shuffling footsteps inside. "Who is it?" Jenny Norman called through the panels.

"Detective Rhodes with the Sheriff's Department," he called back.

She took a moment before slowly opening the door a crack. She looked worse for wear, her hair uncombed and her makeup smudged and running. He felt a stab of empathy for her. He knew what the aftermath of tragedy felt like. The shock. The disbelief. The pain that settled in your heart.

"You were there last night," she accused before Nev could say anything.

"Yes, I was. We're searching for your husband's killer, and if you're up to it, I'd like to talk to you about him."

"You live around here?"

Nev nodded.

"He wasn't a cheater," she stated flatly, but her lips were quivering, and she pushed the door open.

"May I come in?"

Sighing, she stepped away from the door and nodded. "Yeah. Fine."

Nev entered the small, dark house. She led him down a narrow hallway to a room that faced west, though the ocean was obscured by the height of the grassy dune and curtains covered the lower halves of the windows.

Apparently, Jenny had been eating some crackers and summer sausage from what appeared to be a gift pack of meat and cheese and wine. A bottle of cabernet was still unopened, but crumpled foil packages and cracker crumbs lay on the counter, testament to her noshing.

"Mind if I record this?" he asked, pulling out his cell phone.

"Why not?" she whispered, slowly shaking her head as if the fates had conspired against her. "What do you want to know?" she asked, staring at his phone while pushing the plate of crackers and sliced bits of sausage his way.

"Can you give me a brief rundown of what happened when your husband disappeared?"

"I already told you guys everything." She inhaled on a slight hiccup.

"If it's all right, I'd like to hear it again."

She clasped her hands together in a tight grip, shaking her head, fighting tears. Then she let out a few sobs and turned from the counter to the small room with the huge television, the family room off the kitchen, and plunked down on a scarred, square leather ottoman.

"He got a phone call and just left. Didn't tell me where. Just said he was going out, and I thought he was going to the Locker, because that's what he did."

"He took his car?"

"Yep, but he brought it back, I guess. Sometime. I, uh, don't know when. I didn't hear him pull into the garage, but then I sleep soundly." Her eyes traveled to the bottle of wine, and Nev thought he might know why that was. She finished with, "So then he must have walked out to the dune to get some air, or something. Maybe sober up more, I don't know."

"That was after he came back from the Locker?"

"He goes to the Locker all the time . . . *went* to the Locker . . . Usually, he comes home before midnight, but I don't know. I was asleep, like I said. When I woke up in the morning, he wasn't here, so I went out to the garage, saw his car was there. But that still wasn't a big deal. He sometimes goes fishing with buddies all day, sometimes into the night if they stop for dinner or a few drinks. I thought someone came and picked him up and they spent the day on the ocean or in the bay—whatever. Then later, when he didn't show up, I was more worried. Thought it was a little odd."

"You tried his cell?"

"We share one. I had it. I know, it's weird, but it saves some money and . . ." She let her voice trail off.

"Then what?"

"Well, then, when he didn't show up again . . . I started calling around, to his fishing buddies, y'know, and I was getting worried, and I thought, hell, maybe he went out to the ocean, y'know, just to walk around. Sometimes . . . sometimes he goes down to the beach. It wasn't his usual, but I figured it was worth a shot. So I headed for the water, thought maybe he'd be on the beach or something. I musta walked right by him, but I didn't see him on the dune. He wasn't on the beach, so I went to Carter's. I asked old man Carter if he'd seen him, but that guy's half blind. And then I saw Leonard, and I was just going to ask him if he'd seen Stanford when that woman started screaming." Jenny pulled her shoulders in tight and shivered. "I knew something was wrong. I just knew it. But I didn't think he was dead. I didn't think someone had killed him." Tears started dropping in earnest. "He wasn't a cheater."

Rhodes kept his expression neutral. "Had anything changed over the last few weeks, or days?"

She shook her head.

"Do you know anything about the phone call? About who it was?"

"Yeah, it was Gary. He said it was Gary. Didn't I already tell you this?"

"Gary?" Nev asked, surprised. He'd gotten the impression Norman had received the call, no one had known from whom, then mysteriously disappeared. The cops were still checking the phone records of the Normans' landline.

She sighed. "Okay, I told Detective Stone I didn't know who the caller was. So sue me. I just wanted him to come right away. But it was Gary. They hunt and fish and camp and play pool and watch sports together. Stanford kind of put him off."

"Didn't you think it was important to let us know?" he asked the woman, who had seemed so distraught.

"I just didn't really think about it, okay? I was a little upset," she reminded him, but he wondered. "I called Gary back, a couple of times, and he wasn't with Stanford. I don't know who he was with. Stanford took the phone and walked away, and he was ready to go. He takes tourists out fishing, you know." She motioned toward the counter and the remains of the gift basket. "That's where that came from. He came back from a successful trip that day—before he, before he went missing—and he brought back this arrangement. The couple he took out fishing limited out with salmon, so they gave this to Stan as a gift." She looked over at the wine and packets of fancy cheeses and crackers. Nev realized there had been two bottles of wine in the package, as the other one, a bottle of chardonnay, had been dropped in a bag of recycling by the sink.

"Do you know the tourists' names?"

"No," she shook her head. "But Stanford works through . . . worked through that company in Deception Bay, Tillicum Fishing? You could find out through them."

Nev nodded, feeling a shimmer of surprise run through him. Earl and Rand owned Tillicum Fishing. During spring, summer, and fall, they operated the fishing business, while also running a local landscaping company. Once upon a time, Earl had been an exclusive handyman to Catherine Rutledge, but Rand had bigger ideas, and they'd branched out. Nev hadn't known Stanford Norman had been one of their employees.

"You're going to find who did it, aren't you? You're going to lock them up and throw away the key?" she asked anxiously.

"I'm working on it."

She relaxed a little after that. "He wasn't a cheater, but he was a man, you know."

"Ma'am?"

"I mean, he liked to look. All men like to look, so when one of those skinny models shook their little fanny his way, he would look." She shrugged. "I didn't begrudge him that."

"Skinny models?"

She waved him away and reached for a cracker, shoved it in her mouth. She then couldn't speak over the crumbs for a while. It gave Nev a chance to form another question. "Did he meet these models at the Locker?"

"The Locker? As if!" She laughed without humor. "Come on. No, they were in Seaside. We were walking along, and there was this shoot going on the beach for an upcoming festival or something, I think, and all these half-dressed girls were shivering like dogs, but they had to keep filming."

The memory brought on more melancholy, and her eyes filled with tears. She looked like she might fall off the ottoman, and Nev automatically moved to help her, which sent her into full-blown sobs as she clung to his hand and got to her feet. He awkwardly patted her on the shoulder. They stood that way a while before Nev could extricate himself.

"You saw these models yourself?" he asked. At her nod, he asked, "Were any of them in pigtails?"

That brought her up straight. "No." She was positive. "They were all drenched, with slicked-back hair and bikinis, and were bursting out of their bras. Fake boobs everywhere." Her lips pursed into a moue of disgust.

Nev filed that away. Didn't sound like Stanford Norman's cup of tea after all.

He asked a few more questions that got him nowhere, then clicked off his recorder and thanked Jenny before glancing at his watch and leaving.

Come on, Ravinia. Call me.

He climbed into his truck and dropped the cell phone in one of the drink holders. As if she'd heard his pleas, his cell suddenly rang, and he snapped it up, even as he registered that her name had not popped up on caller ID, though he'd added it to his call list. Instead, another name was running across the screen of his phone: Andrew Wharton.

"Nev Rhodes," he answered, snapping the phone into its holder as it connected to his Bluetooth.

"Hi, Neville . . . it's Andrew. Wharton."

"I see that. How're you doing? Surprised to hear from you so soon."

"Well, I overheard you last night at the Locker, when you were talking to the bartender . . . Padilla."

Nev aimed the truck north, heading to Davy Jones's Locker himself. "I'm about to talk to him again, maybe. I'm on my way there now."

"Are you?" He'd sounded careful and cautious, but now he perked up.

"Yep."

"Mind if I meet you there? Maybe I can help you find her."

Nev's brows lifted. "You heard me talking about . . ."

"The girl in pigtails. The one you want to find and ask about the guy who was killed. I saw them both at the Locker. So did Lana. It's been our hideaway, sort of."

"You saw Stanford Norman and the girl in pigtails?"

"Yeah. A few nights ago. Maybe a week," Andrew admitted, his voice low.

"I'll meet you there in fifteen," said Nev.

"I'll be there in ten."

Her cell phone rang as Ravinia was staring into space, debating whether or not to ignore J. D.'s damn near ultimatum that she come to his office and look over her supposed mistakes. But she was pissed that he even thought she'd made mistakes. Sure, she kind of ran by the seat of her pants sometimes, but she got results, which is more than she could say for J. D.'s wife, Adela, who pretty much rode her chair, chewed Nicorette gum, and waited for someone else to do the legwork. And who would that be? J. D.? Hell, no. It had always been Ravinia, which, to be fair, had been fine by her, except that she had pulled most of the weight around the agency, even while she was apprenticing.

She checked her phone and was shocked to see it was Catherine calling her. "Hey, there," Ravinia answered. "Did Ophelia tell you I wanted to talk to you?"

"Isadora met with Detective Stone at the gate. You told him that Silas was your brother. He wants to talk to me."

Ravinia was momentarily speechless at this accusation. "I haven't told him anything!" denied Ravinia hotly.

"Are you saying he lied?"

"That's exactly what I'm saying. Somebody's lying, at any rate. Are you meeting with him?"

"No." Her voice was a little shaky, Ravinia realized, as her aunt cleared her throat. "Isadora met him and heard what he had to say. If he's lying, there's no need to meet with him again."

"Actually, I want to talk to you about that . . ."

"You did tell him," accused Catherine.

"No, but that Detective Rhodes keeps calling. He knows I was lying to him about not knowing who Silas was. He's not going to give up, and that's probably why Detective Stone came to Siren Song. They're going to keep pushing until they learn Silas's identity. Maybe they can use DNA to figure out who he is, but they already know I've been holding back. I think I'd better clear that up. If Charlie's back, if he killed Silas, we need the police on our side."

"Charlie is back," Catherine stated. "He's already *contacted* Detective Dunbar."

"*What?*"

"Apparently she's at Ocean Park Hospital, having her baby. That's what Detective Stone said to Isadora. Detective Dunbar told him that Charlie had contacted her, unless she's lying about that too." Her aunt sounded perturbed.

"I don't think Detective Dunbar would lie about it." Ravinia's mind was whirling with the news, the proof of what she'd most feared. But she'd known. All along, she'd suspected, but now she knew Charlie had returned.

Catherine said, "You just said Detective Stone lied about you telling him Silas was your brother."

"Well, he's not Detective Dunbar, is he?" Ravinia pointed out. "Charlie killed Silas. We all know it, and now with corroboration that he's back from Detective Dunbar, there's no question. Charlie killed my brother, and I want him to pay," she added hotly.

"Well, don't tell that detective that," Catherine rejoined. "That won't help any of us."

"I disagree completely. Let's tell everybody. *Charlie's a killer.* People need to be warned!"

"Well, I don't want the Tillamook County Sheriff's Department bursting in to Siren Song and pretending they're going to save us, because that's what they'll say they can do, and we all know they can't!"

"You don't know that," argued Ravinia.

"Don't I?" Catherine asked, her imperious tone in place again. "You don't trust the police, either, Ravinia. You and I both know it. Why the sudden change of heart?"

"Because of what you just told me about Charlie. That he's *here*," Ravinia shot back. "He means to harm us and maybe Detective Dunbar too!"

"Ravinia, let's not argue. I—"

"I'm telling Rhodes about Silas, and about Charlie, if he doesn't know already. And no, I don't trust Rhodes or Detective Stone or any of them. But we need more than just us to fight Charlie. You know that. We need the police." She heard the pleading tone that had crept into her voice and immediately quashed it. That never worked with Aunt Catherine.

"I don't agree with you."

"Well, you should," Ravinia said. "If you want us to survive."

"Oh, fine. Do whatever you want, Ravinia," her aunt snapped. "You always do anyway." With that, she clicked off.

Thanks for the go-ahead, Aunt Catherine.

Ravinia found Neville Rhodes's number and placed the call.

Nev pulled into Davy Jones's Locker's back parking lot, doing his best to avoid the potholes that seemed to have grown bigger in the day since he'd been here. He parked his truck and skirted the water-filled traps as he strode toward the Locker's rear entrance. Still a little early for the regulars, but if Andrew Wharton had information, he wanted to hear it. His cell rang as he entered, but he didn't look at it, as he was pushing through the back door at the exact same moment. His eyes scanned the Locker's scarred wooden floors and rustic booths, looking for Wharton. It turned out the man was seated at the bar.

Wharton noticed Nev at the same moment and slid off his stool. He hitched his chin toward one of the empty booths, the same one he'd shared with Lana earlier. Nev nodded and wove through the scattered tables, glancing down at his cell as he reached the booth, and slid onto one of the benches. Ravinia Rutledge's name flashed onto the small screen. He hit the CONNECT button at the same moment his phone stopped ringing.

Crap!

Andrew scooted in across from him.

"I just got a call I need to return," said Nev apologetically.

Andrew lifted a hand in acknowledgment, and Nev headed back out the rear door, stepping onto the landing outside and quickly punching RETURN CALL for Ravinia's number. But the phone rang and rang before voice mail picked up. *Damn.* He'd missed her. Leaving a quick message, he headed back inside, frustrated with himself.

"That was fast," said Andrew.

"Yeah, I'll have to follow up later."

"You want a beer?" Andrew had brought his mug over from the bar.

"I think I'll take a Coke." He didn't add that since the waitress wasn't the speediest, he would be lucky to even get a drink at all. "You said you might be able to help me with the woman in pigtails."

Andrew nodded. He was thin to the point of gauntness, but he'd always been built that way. Spencer had been the brother with defined muscles and a strong physique.

He began, "Lana and me . . . we ran into each other here one night and just started talking and talking, about Spencer and all kinds of stuff. It was good, and it . . . well, I never expected to fall for Spencer's girl, you know?" He looked at Nev carefully, checking to see how he was taking that news.

"I get that," said Nev. He really didn't need a postmortem on Andrew and Lana's romance and how it related to Spencer, but he understood Andrew felt the need to explain.

"My parents will never understand. I mean my mother—now, I guess, she might be able to, but I'm not going to put it to the test. When Dad was alive, you couldn't mention anything about what happened. You know, how Spence died. He never got over it. Never. And he thought Lana was part of it, Spencer's 'woman,' if you know what I mean, even though she wasn't involved in what happened that night, you know?" At Nev's nod, he looked away, lost in his own thoughts, remembering the pain in their house.

Nev's gut tightened. His forever companion, survivor's guilt, sat heavy on his shoulder.

Andrew met his eyes again. "Mom actually hasn't gotten over it, either. I guess you know that better than most."

Oh, I know, thought Nev, forcing himself not to rub his jaw as more people came into the bar, scooting back chairs, laughing and huddling together in booths or at tables.

Andrew went on, "With Mom, you know what she's feeling at all times, even if it's inappropriate. With Dad, it was different. He kept it all bottled in . . . until he exploded. And then, watch out." Andrew took a long swallow of his beer, then wiped the back of his hand over his lips.

Nev really wanted to get past all this. "So, about the girl . . . ?" he asked.

"I saw her twice. I think. First time, she wasn't in pigtails. Just hanging out at the bar, but she had a hat on. I couldn't really see her hair. Second time, she was at a table alone, in pigtails. I looked over at her, thinking she was the same gal, and she turned her face away, as if she caught me staring, you know?" He took another drink from his near-empty mug. "Pretty sure it was her, though."

"Can you describe her?"

"Slim, but not weak. I mean, she didn't look like she'd fall over in a good wind. Hair looked light brownish, but it was swept up into the cap, so I only saw a little bit of it the first time. Blonder in the pigtails. Both times she was dressed for the weather. Jeans, I think, a jacket . . . sneakers . . ." He shrugged. "Mostly I saw her in profile."

"Was she with anyone?"

"Don't think so."

"You think she came in the front?"

"Maybe. You want me to try and flag down the waitress? You never got your Coke."

"I'm okay." Nev wanted to keep the conversation on track. "When you saw her the second time?"

"She was sitting alone when Lana and me came in. We sat down in this booth, so I had a view of her, like you do now." He leaned forward and turned his gaze toward the front of the building, then indicated one of two tables flanking the door. "See?"

From Nev's point of view, she would have been seated close to the end of the bar. "That time, I'm pretty sure she was waiting for someone. I mean, it seemed like it, the way she kept to herself. The bartender could probably tell you."

"Jeff Padilla?" he asked, as the waitress swept by with a loaded tray of beer mugs, not even glancing his way.

"Nah. Even though Padilla was still around, he was just getting off work, and the other guy was taking over. And then Norman came in and sat right down by her, like he was there for her. I don't know if he just moved on her right then, or what. I could be wrong," he admitted, rubbing a hand around his neck, "but I think she had her hand on his leg."

"What day was this?" Nev demanded.

"A couple of days before she killed him, maybe?"

"We don't know that's what happened," Nev reminded. All he would need is for Andrew to spout untested information as truth.

"Sure, sure."

"I'm just looking for information. That's all."

"Okay." Andrew shrugged.

"Would you know her again?"

"Oh, yeah."

"I'm going to tell Detective Stone what you just told me. He may want to interview you."

"Okay, but I'd like to keep Lana out of it, if I can."

"Well, he may want to talk to her too," Nev said. "See if she can add anything."

Andrew grimaced and finished his beer. "I guess. If he has to."

Nev asked a few more questions, but it seemed Andrew was tapped out of information.

Andrew glanced at his watch. "I'd better get going." He threw down some bills for his beer. "Was good talking to you, man."

"Same," said Nev.

Andrew took a couple steps toward the back door as Nev got up from the booth. Then Andrew snapped his fingers and did an about-face. "Just thought of something," he said, stepping closer to Nev again. "I couldn't hear much of what she was saying to Norman, but I walked past them, and I think I overheard her telling him she was lucky."

"Lucky to run into him, maybe?"

"Maybe." Again, he didn't sound too sure as he eyed the bar where a group of men in their early twenties had gathered, as if in staring at the spot where she'd been sitting, he could remember better. Finally, he shook his head. "Don't know." His cell phone buzzed, and he turned again, jamming his phone to his ear as he walked out the back.

"Okay. Thanks," Nev said, but Andrew was out of earshot.

When Nev followed after him out the back door and crossed to his truck, he got splashed by a newcomer bouncing his SUV through the potholes. Great. But he was due for a trip to the laundromat anyway, so whatever.

Lang had sent out the girl's description—what they had of it—so maybe someone, somewhere would come up with something.

CHAPTER 14

Ravinia listened to Nev's voice mail on the drive over to the Bauer Investigations office. She'd phoned him on a whim, ready to spill all about Silas, partly because she was pissed off at Catherine and Ophelia, though she did think he needed to know.

However, when he didn't answer, she began to second-guess her desire to tell all. Hearing the clear frustration in his voice about missing her call had made her smile a bit. She would tell him who Silas was, but she didn't want him getting in the way of her own background investigations into her two brothers. Not yet, anyway. He likely already knew, thanks to Detective Dunbar, about the threat from Charlie, so she needed to be circumspect about what else she told him.

In any case, she would call him back after she straightened out whatever error J. D. believed she'd committed. She knew Bauer had moved his office. After grumbling about the escalating rental rates in downtown Portland for years, he'd relocated to Milwaukie, a Portland suburb on the east side of the Willamette River.

Ravinia inched her Camry across the Sellwood Bridge, one of many bridges spanning the Willamette River connecting the east and west sides of the greater Portland area. The trip was slow, as rush hour was in full force, and the streets through Sellwood were narrow and clogged with traffic, pedestrians in the crossings and bicyclists zipping around the slow-moving vehicles.

Eventually, she wound her way into the city of Milwaukie and reached the offices of J. D. Bauer, Private Investigations, which was located in a two-story brick building that could have been retro-chic if there'd been any attempt to improve it over the years. As it was, the structure screamed deferred maintenance, which likely kept the rents down, which would definitely be the only issue important to J. D. Bauer. His offices were on the first floor.

At least he has an office.

It was nearing six o'clock when she parked on the street, locked her Camry, and, steeling herself for whatever confrontation lay ahead, walked past the parking apron that led to a fenced backyard. A smattering of rain hit her just as she ducked under the metal overhang that served as protection over the front door, and as she passed by a small window, she caught a glimpse of J. D. inside, his back to her and fiddling with something on his desk. She had the uneasy feeling that it had to do with her, and she immediately regretted agreeing to meet him here.

She rang the bell, tucking her arms around herself. On the next block, someone had already put out Halloween pumpkins. Way too early, she thought; you could count on them rotting before the holiday even came close.

The front door opened. "Hi, Ravinia. Come on in," J. D. said, stepping aside for her to enter.

She tried to gauge his mood. He'd sounded almost annoyed on the phone, as if he'd caught her screwing up again, *tsk, tsk,* though that wasn't her MO. Now he seemed . . . giddy? She didn't like that at all, but she walked down the short entry hall to his office.

Instantly, she saw what he'd been doing at his desk: setting up a tray with a crystal decanter of wine and some stemmed glasses. Now, though, the blinds on the window had been partially closed.

"Before we get down to it, let's have a drink," he said, pouring her an exceptionally healthy glass, the dark red liquid splashing up the sides.

"I don't drink wine," she lied. What was this all about?

He laughed. "Yes, you do."

"Well, I don't want any tonight. Tell me what I did wrong. Lay it on me, J. D."

He motioned her to a chair in a corner near the window,

and Ravinia perched on the edge of it. She would search his heart if she thought it necessary, but she already knew what a piece of shit he was.

"You worked for us just long enough to get your PI license, and then you left us high and dry."

"I apprenticed with you," she reminded him. "It's not like you were making me rich."

"We gave you a chance, and you left without even a thank-you."

"I don't know what you're talking about." Ravinia frowned at him. "That's not how it was."

"Adela and I felt we'd been used. So I did a little research on you. You've got quite the interesting family."

"I told you about them," Ravinia reminded him cautiously.

He waved a finger in front of her face. "Not even half of it. Let me remind you. I'm a good investigator. You may be out there thinking you're competition for me, but I can run circles around you, sweetheart."

Sweetheart? What was going on here? She'd always thought J. D. was a putz, but he'd never openly come on to her before, if that was even what this was.

"J. D., what are you talking about?"

"Oh, don't use that cold voice on me. I've got the goods on you. I've read your history. You're one of a bunch of freaks out there on the coast, aren't you? Killers too, the way I understand it."

"The way you—"

"How many people have you killed, Ravinia?" he asked bluntly.

"What?"

"You don't have a number?" he mocked.

"None . . . yet," she said meaningfully and started to rise.

"Don't get up," he warned. "Better sit right there and listen to what I have to say, and then maybe we can strike a deal."

"A deal?" she repeated, disbelieving. "Where's Adela?"

"Home. You think she doesn't know what you are?"

Adela had never been Ravinia's friend. Ravinia had always known that. "What am I, J. D.?" Ravinia asked flatly. She hadn't risen yet, but her muscles were tense, ready. She was calculating what she might have to do to get out of this situation. Throw the wine in his face? Grab the lamp from his desk and clobber him? Elbow him in the eye?

"I thought you wanted to discuss my work, or the fact that I some-how messed up, but that's not it, is it?"

"You're a goddamn witch," he went on, ignoring her question. "Casting spells. Burying people in that graveyard behind your lodge."

"Are you crazy?" she asked.

"I've talked to the townies in Deception Bay. They know what you're capable of, and they hate you all. I'd be doing a favor by taking one of you down."

"Taking me down?" Ravinia kept her gaze steady on his avid eyes. He looked unhinged, she thought, with a spurt of fear. Feverish. Maybe reasoning with him wasn't going to work. And he'd been dig-ging into her family, had enough information that meant he'd been at this, whatever it was, for a while.

"Someone said you use external hormones to sexually call your prey. Is that what you did to me? Sent me your love when you wanted a job? Warmed my heart?"

He'd never mentioned he'd been affected by her search of his heart. She'd thought he'd missed it, forgotten it. Most people didn't connect it with her. "You're not the first one who's listened to exag-gerated tales. My family's been dealing with this stuff for years."

"You're saying it's not true?" He'd moved closer to her and bal-anced a hip on a corner of his desk. His goblet of wine was held loose in his hand.

"I'm saying it's mostly fantasy."

"Mostly? Yeah, right. You're a liar, aren't you?" The grin on his face echoed the jack-o'-lanterns on the street, and her skin crawled.

"What do you want from me?" she questioned flatly, though it was obvious. He'd always had trouble disguising his lust, pretending it was just normal friendship, though she'd doubted Adela was fooled. She'd seen, and she'd blamed Ravinia, not her husband.

"Your mother had a string of lovers . . ."

Oh. God. There it was. "Well, I haven't, and you're not going to be the first."

"Come on, sweetheart." He pushed away from the desk, coming closer, blocking her path to the door.

"Chase me around the desk, J. D., and I will kill you," she warned.

His eyes widened a bit, a little bit of fear, a new excitement. "How're you gonna do that?" he challenged softly.

For an answer, Ravinia leapt from her chair and shoved him as hard as she could.

"Wha—wha—?" The glass of wine went flying, a ribbon of red floating in the air a moment before splashing in his face. He slipped. Staggered backward. Plowed into the desk, falling backward onto the wooden top. "Shit!"

In that split second before he scrambled to his feet, she decided to run rather than heed the boiling in her blood that urged her to kick him in the balls and inflict as much pain as possible.

As she ran out the door, J. D. bellowed and hurled his glass.

It shattered against the hallway wall as she moved swiftly through the front door.

"I'll sue you, you bitch!" he yelled after her as the door slammed shut behind her, but he wasn't following.

With trembling fingers, she found her keys and unlocked her car remotely.

As she passed by the window of the offices, she caught a glimpse of his shadow, behind the partially closed blinds.

In an instant, the blinds snapped open. J. D.'s flushed face, with his hard, hate-filled eyes, stared out.

Ravinia race-walked to her car, all the while telling herself not to run. *Don't bring more attention to yourself.* The light was fading, but nightfall was still over an hour away, and there were enough vehicles and pedestrians on the street to remember a girl running out of his building should J. D. manufacture a complaint.

Loser. Bastard. Fucker.

Heart racing, blood on fire, she slid into the Camry and drove off, her tires chirping as she hit the gas a little too hard. At the end of the street, she slowed for a stop sign, rolled through, and was determined to shove that loser J. D. Bauer out of her mind and get back on track with her mission.

"Ugh," she said aloud, driving through the center of Milwaukie, where lights glowed in storefronts, pedestrians were walking down streets, and damp leaves were scattered between the parked cars. Night was falling swiftly, she noted, squinting into oncoming headlights.

In a crystalline moment, she thought of Charlie and his pheromones, his means of sexually seducing his prey, and she felt sickened at the idea that anyone would be at the mercy of someone like J. D., unable to fight back, desire smothering fear, subverting the mind's natural defense mechanism.

She needed, they all needed, to finish what Silas had failed to complete: Charlie's complete annihilation. She steered her car back through the clog of traffic and, once more, across the river to her apartment, where, much calmer, she went inside, closed all the blinds, and picked up her phone.

Nev's cell buzzed a little after seven. The phone was lying on his kitchen counter, and he reached over and picked it up. Ravinia. Finally. He clicked on and answered, "Nev Rhodes."

"Ravinia Rutledge, here," she said, responding in kind.

"Glad you called back. Ready to talk about the body in the morgue?"

"Yes and no."

"Okay," he said cautiously.

"You want to know his name?" she challenged.

"Yes, ma'am."

"If you want to know anything from me . . . just *anything* . . . don't ever call me ma'am again. You got that?"

"Loud and clear." He found himself smiling at her rebuke for no good reason.

"Okay, then." She sounded somewhat mollified. "I got the go-ahead from my Aunt Catherine, so I'm not going rogue on this. His name is Silas, and he's my half brother. And I think he was murdered, killed by my other half brother, who my mother named Declan Jr. We call him Charlie. So go ahead and fire away. Throw the questions at me. I have some things to say too."

"Okay . . . Ravinia," he said and hurriedly searched the area for a notepad. He found one on the kitchen counter, along with a pen in the cupholder nearby.

"You're getting there."

He'd actually done it on purpose, and he had to fight a grin that was inappropriate for the issue they were discussing. A part of him was marveling at his own teasing. It wasn't like him. Maybe the women of Siren Song did have special abilities, because Ravinia sure as hell had done something to him.

"Something funny?" she asked coolly.

"No. I already know about Charlie. I've been talking to Lang, Detective Langdon Stone, about him."

A beat. Then, "I know who he is."

"Charlie attacked one of our own, about five years ago, and then disappeared."

"Detective Dunbar," she said, her tone wary. "Yes."

"Detective St. Cloud now. We want to get him as much as you do."

"Nobody wants him as much as I do." She was deadly serious.

"Okay. Let's get back to Silas. Why do you think Charlie is the one who killed him?"

"I don't have proof, so don't ask me for it. It's something I just know. That doesn't help you, I know. But if you want to find Silas's murderer, find Charlie."

"We don't know it's a homicide," he reminded her. "The autopsy's scheduled for Monday afternoon, though we may get a preliminary report earlier. I'm hoping."

"It's a homicide," she said clearly.

"I've been given some background on Charlie . . . and your family. No one's talked to us about Silas, so thank you for finally admitting you know who he is."

"Okay . . . you're welcome."

His lips twitched again at her cautious tone, but then he sobered. He'd had a talk with Lang, who, after seeing Savannah and attempting to meet with Catherine at Siren Song with no success, had brought him up to speed. Nev wasn't sure how much he wanted to tell Ravinia at this point. She clearly hadn't talked with members of her clan or she would know what Savannah had said about Charlie "contacting" her.

"What can you tell me about Silas?" he asked.

"Not a lot. I only met him a few times."

"Last name?"

"Well . . . Rutledge, before he was adopted out. He was supposed to be the one to take Charlie out, but did that happen before he died? I'd like to think so, but it doesn't feel like it."

"Take him out in what way?" asked Nev.

"Kill him. Neutralize him. Remove him from the planet. Whatever." She paused, as if thinking. "I suppose Charlie could be gone . . . maybe Silas lost his life in a battle with him."

"You think Charlie's gone?"

"Probably not."

"But you believe they fought."

"Yes . . . maybe . . ." She drew a breath. "Maybe Charlie's still on Echo."

Nev felt a chill ripple across the back of his neck, but said, "Coast Guard didn't see any activity."

"Did they actually go on the island?"

"No, but there was no boat anywhere, no means for him to have gotten there unless he swam, and that's a very long shot."

"Then he got away," she said simply.

Nev tried another tack. "Has he tried to contact you?"

"Charlie? No. What do you mean?" She paused, clearly examining his words. "Contact me, how?"

"In any way."

"No. I've never even met him, which is lucky, because he's killed people around Deception Bay, and I'm sure a lot of other places too. He killed Detective Dunbar . . . er . . . St. Cloud's *sister* and that other detective . . . Clausen. He's a killer. He hates all of us at Siren Song, and his aim is to destroy us."

Nev considered telling her about the woman bartender murdered at the Smuggler's Den but didn't want to get ahead of himself. He was still figuring out how much of the bogeyman tale surrounding Charlie was fact and what was fiction. He'd come a long way in a couple days from the skeptic he'd been, but it still seemed like there was a hysterical edge to what they were all saying.

"What do you people think happened to him—to Silas?" she challenged.

"No decision yet. Still doing the forensics, looking for evidence at the scene, and as I said, the autopsy's not in."

"I think Silas met up with Charlie and they had a fight and Charlie came out the winner. I would've put my money on Silas. He just . . . seemed so capable, but that didn't happen."

"From the few times you met him," Nev pointed out a bit dryly.

"He gave me confidence. He was like that. I felt, we all felt, that it was just a matter of time before we heard that Charlie was dead, and then we could go on with our lives without having to worry so much. But now Silas is dead . . . washed up on the beach . . ." She drew a breath. "If they weren't on Echo, they were on that beach. They had some kind of showdown. I just wish it had ended differently."

"Why do you think they picked that spot?" asked Nev, running with her theory to keep her talking and frantically scratching notes.

"It's all about the island, and that's the nearest beach to Echo on the mainland. You know about my mother?" she questioned, then didn't wait for an answer. "She lived on Echo. Charlie went there, and he's the one who killed her."

"Charlie killed your mother on Echo Island," Nev repeated.

"Yes," she stressed in reaction to the unconscious skepticism in his voice.

Nev said, "I heard she was buried in the graveyard at Siren Song."

"But she *died* on Echo, and we had to bring her bones back. Charlie *admitted* he killed Mary on the island to Detective Dunbar . . . St. Cloud. *Whatever*."

"All right. I'm just coming up to speed on your family," Nev said, though he wondered if that were even possible.

There was a long pause while they both gathered their thoughts. Then Ravinia said, "Look, Detective, he's coming for us. I'd like to believe, like the rest of them, that we can handle it ourselves, but I don't think we can."

"Okay. Tell me everything you know that would help us protect you."

"Are you just humoring me?" she questioned suddenly. "Don't you think we're a bunch of crackpots who should get with the real world once and for all?" That was so close to the truth that Nev was momentarily speechless. "Of course you do," she answered herself, faintly bitter.

"I'm going out to Echo," said Nev. Even as the words hung in the air, he marveled at himself. Always so careful, always so needing to not reveal his plans, always so eager to leave the rumors and lore and everything to do with the Colony far, far away from him.

"When?" she asked without hesitation.

"It's not set yet."

"Well, you're running out of time before it's too late in the year. You know it's nearly impossible to get out there."

Oh, he knew, he thought, his thoughts circling back to that treacherous, fateful trip through the ocean to the island.

"Did you contact Earl?"

Her question brought him back to the present. "Yeah . . . I was planning to."

"He's your best bet to take you there." She paused. "How do you know him?"

"I'm friends with Rand, his son."

"Really." She was clearly surprised. "Well, I suppose you know that Earl and my aunt have been thick as thieves forever. He's the only man she's allowed inside the gates for years. And, if you're going to Echo, you need to contact him," she reiterated. "He was always the one who took Catherine out there when she visited Mary on the island."

"Have you been to Echo?" asked Nev.

"No. It's always too dangerous to go. Even if I'd wanted to, Catherine wouldn't have allowed it." She paused, then added, "Be careful. People have died trying to get to the island. You need to know what you're doing."

Again Nev felt the age-old pain of Spencer and Duncan's deaths. He could almost taste the salt of the sea in the back of his throat, feel the desperation of that black, dark night.

Most likely, Ravinia didn't know he was the lone survivor of one of those ill-fated attempts, and he didn't feel like telling her.

"Your family's going to claim the body after the autopsy," he said, deliberately changing the subject.

"Well . . . yes."

"You said he was adopted, so there's another family," he explained. "His legal family."

"I'm his next of kin," she reminded, sharply. "My phone number was with him."

"Next of kin biologically, but not legally."

"I'll let them know, of course," she said, her voice clipped. "But yes, we'll claim the body."

"You know how to get in touch with them?"

"Yes."

"Okay. The county won't just give the body to—"

"I'll make sure everything's in order!" she snapped.

He let it go, but just for the moment. The lawyers could wrangle that one out.

"I'd better go," she blurted, as if she suddenly couldn't wait to get off the phone. "Let me know what you find out on Echo. And be careful. Charlie could be there, and he's killed two people around here that I know of."

"I'll be careful," Nev assured her.

"Good . . . Okay. Goodbye, Detective."

"It's Neville, or Nev, or Rhodes, if you prefer."

"Rhodes," she repeated, as if trying it out.

"Goodbye, Ravinia."

CHAPTER 15

LACEY'S, the name spelled out in huge, electric-blue neon letters and affixed to the building's roof, was as upscale a bar as could be found on this section of the beach. Several dozen small tables, each crowned by a votive candle, were scattered around the space, which was broken up by floor-to-ceiling black panels set around the open room. A U-shaped bar sat in the center, above which was a wood-framed glass cabinet hung from the ceiling, laid out above the bar, exactly matching its shape. Glassware of all types, wedged martini glasses, champagne flutes, beer tumblers, and shot glasses were in handy reach for the two bartenders, one male, one female, who were serving the customers.

Charlie had steered clear of Lacey's since he'd returned to the northern Oregon coast. The place was at the northernmost edge of Deception Bay, a new enterprise that had taken over a rundown shit-kicker bar and diner that had been renovated until it was unrecognizable from what it had once been. In his previous life, Charlie had worked construction and could already tell that the wealthy millennials who'd transformed the place were going to lose their Versace shirts on it. Too much money spent for a beach crowd used to burgers, hotdogs, and beer.

But currently the Ocean Park Hospital staff found Lacey's to be the place to be, and so Charlie had parked himself at a table near the door, better able to watch who was coming and going. Luckily, the customers didn't much dress for their surroundings. They still wore their beach gear, so Charlie didn't stick out so much in his jeans, black T-shirt, and black windbreaker. To be invisible to the crowd was his goal. His looks had been altered enough to keep him unrecognizable to anyone who might notice him.

He was waiting for one woman. His date. His lover. His latest conquest. She was putty in his hands. Wax to be molded. A means to an end.

She'd invited him to her place, but he made excuses to steer clear of it as much as possible. Didn't want to be seen coming and going, though he had used the key she'd given him to enter the apartment a time or two when she wasn't around to go through her things. He'd been chagrined to learn she'd known he'd been there, although she hadn't seemed to mind.

No, it was better for them to see each other at the no-tell motel that he'd paid cash for in Seaside, though after his abrupt killing of the female bartender (he'd never learned her name), he'd had to skedaddle out of the area and head south to his old stomping grounds, Deception Bay, which is where he'd made his current lover's acquaintance. He hadn't heard that the police were onto him over the bartender's death, so he was reasonably sure he could go back to the motel again. That was his plan for tonight.

He'd met his current woman at Lacey's. It was a dalliance, a risk, this delay, but what was life without risks? He exalted in the freedom, the power, after damn near five years literally shackled and waiting for a chance to escape and resume his mission, and he wanted to draw it out a little. Dr. Shithead—Dr. Gilbert Lendel—was the one who'd put him back together, but the price he'd exacted from Charlie had been way too steep. If he'd known at the beginning that Dr. Shithead was going to lock him up just when he was starting to get his mojo back after that *bitch* detective had caused him so much pain, he would have made a different choice.

Now he touched a hand to his face. No feeling there . . . and his ear . . . the prosthetic device was gone. Lost. Rage boiled inside him at that. His fists clenched, and he slid his hands into his pockets to hide his fury. Closing his eyes, he thought of his two recent kills, and that helped him start to unwind. When he was in control again, he sipped his scotch and soda. Alcohol was not high on his list of recreational activities. He much preferred to be sharp and alert. His powers worked best when unaffected. But if you didn't drink at a bar, bartenders remembered you, and Charlie, above all else, wanted to blend in.

His woman came in alone a few minutes later. *Ahh*, he thought in satisfaction. Should he send her a little Charlie love? He hardly needed to, she was so willing. Already a slave to it. But she would know what it was and look for him. He wanted to see that desperate desire written on her face.

He sent her a hot message, waiting, smiling. Anticipation was part of the game. She'd been focused on the bar, but now she looked around. She was tall and lithe, with a regal tilt to her head. Mr. Happy stirred in his pants at the look in her eyes. She was already melting. He positioned himself so she could see him lay one hand on his crotch and lazily stroke himself. Her lips parted but she turned away from him and took a seat at the bar.

His interest notched up. Good. She'd learned the game and was willing to play. No easy conquest. That didn't do it for him. When she resisted, that's when he was the most powerful. He remembered the fear in that female bartender's eyes as he'd slid inside her even while she was gripping his buttocks and begging for him, pleading for the ecstasy only he could provide; these were memories he could feed on. He loved it when they couldn't help themselves. He could feel their internal fight to keep from succumbing, but they couldn't resist. He'd seen it time and time again. Their bodies overrode their minds whenever Good Time Charlie was there.

Thinking about it, he wanted to crow with delight, but he kept his thoughts under wraps, his eyes on the pretty woman at the bar. He'd had her before and would have her again. Tonight. And he was glad to see she was pretending to ignore him because she'd never really resisted him. She'd been easy, too easy, really, which negatively affected both his sexual abilities and his powers, although staring into a dying person's eyes and feeling their departing soul refueled him faster than anything.

His mind switched to Silas. Dear old bro. Dead now. At his hands. He wished he could kill the fucker a second time. *And he hadn't given up his soul.* Bastard. Goddamn fucker. He'd somehow shut Charlie out in the end. Oh, Silas had been powerful. No denying it.

But he'd lost. *Lost.* Silas had played his own games with him, had sent him mental messages, pretending to be a woman, and had laughed at Charlie's attempts to seduce him. Well, who was laughing now, dear old *dead* bro? Who was laughing now?

Charlie smiled to himself. It had been a tough fight, but Charlie had won. They'd grabbed at each other in a raw, do-or-die conflict, seeing who could bash the other's brains in first on the shore of Echo Island, a fight that had moved from the burned-out house on the crest of the island, down the rocky tor, and into the boat and then when the boat had capsized, they had swam and struggled in the frigid ocean itself. Silas had nearly drowned him, which had only made it sweeter when Charlie got the upper hand. When dear old bro had staggered up the beach and lain down on his back, spent, Charlie, also weakened by the long siege of a fight, had gathered the last of his strength to get atop his brother and wrap his hands around his neck. In those heated moments when Charlie squeezed his neck, Silas had merely looked at him. In fact, they'd stared at each other and sent messages of hate back and forth. But then Charlie worried that someone would see them from up above on the road, and he'd squeezed and squeezed and finally managed to snuff the life out of his brother . . . or so he'd thought. As he'd worked his way up that godawful trail, he'd looked down and swore Silas's hand was inside his coat, not on the sand where he'd left it. But he'd had to snap his attention back to the goddamn trail, so steep in places you practically needed a rope to climb up. It took the remainder of his strength to reach the crest, and then he flopped down in the bushes at the trailhead, gasping for breath.

He hid there as long as he dared. He had to get far away from Silas. As soon as he was able, he staggered to his feet, glanced back once more to the beach, thought in confusion, *Is that a wolf?* Then, at a break in traffic, he loped across the road and headed down the lane that led past Siren Song and to the Foothillers' community, beyond where Silas had left his vehicle, the one he'd driven with him and Charlie in it, the one they'd stolen in Portland. Oh, Silas was no saint, though he knew those women at Siren Song thought he was something special. Yin and yang. Silas was good, and Charlie was bad. *Well, hey, you fucking whores. Guess what? We're both bad.*

Chortling to himself, he moved up to the woman at the bar. Though there weren't a lot of patrons inside the main area of Lacey's so far, there wasn't a stool left at the bar. With no place for him to sit, he just moved up behind her and put his hands on her buttocks. A guy on the stool next to her looked at his bold move and raised his brows.

Wanna say something? Do something? Go ahead and play the hero, asshole. See what that gets you.

But then Charlie's woman leaned back against him. Her eyes were closed, and she rubbed her head against his chest.

See? Charlie stared the man down, and the would-be hero finally turned away.

As soon as he did, Charlie whispered, "Come with me," and he pushed her away from him, then left the bar into a cool night, the wind having died down. He walked straight to his car, a cheap used Fiesta bought with cash recently. She came out a few moments later and slid into the passenger seat.

Neither of them said a word as he drove them back to Seaside and the motel, which was reasonably clean, which was about all he could say about it, and it had a bed. The first time he'd brought her here, she'd been filled with trepidation, shaking like the proverbial leaf even as she was flushed and eager and ready, so receptive to his sexual pheromones he'd believed he was back to full strength again. Alas, she was just a bitch in heat looking for any stud. But he hadn't known it then, and he'd ridden her until they were both sore, thinking Good Time Charlie still has it, oh, yes, he does! Which was a relief because he'd tried sending his love to other women since the fire melted his face, with mixed results. That damn detective, burning him . . . He still seethed about it and felt his skin charring, his hair sizzling, the pain screaming through his body. And there was more to it, something altered within. Being scorched and nearly killed had done something powerful to him that interfered with his gift, riddling him with doubt. So he'd crowed with jubilation when he'd recently driven by the house where she lived with that usurper, Hale St. Cloud, his goddamned nephew, who had everything his father should have given to him, and sent her a snaking vine of desire that he could feel got through.

Hah, bitch.

With thoughts of the detective in mind, Charlie pulled into the motel parking lot, dark emotions swirling. He didn't waste time. Damn near before the door shut behind her, he shoved his woman onto the bed. He wanted some fight from her, but she regarded him with sleepy blue eyes, simmering with desire, which was *not* the way the game was played. Instantly, he was in a foul mood. In frustration, he sent her a heavy blast of pheromones, hoping to scare her with his power. Her eyes flew open wide in surprise . . . and there was a flicker of fear.

Good.

"No," she whispered, and that was all it took. Charlie ripped off her clothes and his own. When she reached for him, he slapped her hands away. Only when she scooted across the bed did he grab her, and then they got down to the business of sex.

Well . . .

It wasn't as good as it could be. She was still too willing. He sometimes had to reach in his memory for the way Kristina St. Cloud had fought him, though she'd been no match for him, either. Sometimes he regretted killing her, but he was still angry at the way she'd managed to hide from him, like Silas, making him unable to look into her eyes and suck out her essence before she died. If only he'd gotten inside that bitch of a detective, Savannah Dunbar *St. Cloud*, but she'd managed to mentally fight him off too. This time wouldn't be the same. No way. His first message was just the beginning. He was coming for her too.

"I want you to meet some of my family," his lover said now, breaking into his thoughts, softly nibbling his good ear in the afterglow of her satisfaction.

Charlie damn near swatted her away. Postcoital snuggling? Nothing interested him less. Maybe he needed to stop this dillydallying. He had a sensation of sand sifting through his fingers, so maybe he should stop wasting one more second on someone who was too willing.

She was curled up next to him, her head on his chest. He knew she lived for these moments. How did other men stand it?

Her soft breath grew rhythmic, and he realized she'd actually fallen asleep! He grimaced and touched his face again. That brilliant, loony surgeon, Dr. Shithead, had been a true mad scientist. Charlie had needed the help, but he'd been unaware that Lendel had fallen desperately in love with him. Without any experience with male attention, other than Silas's messages, Charlie had made a costly mistake. He'd feigned loving the mad doctor back in order to get his face and body normal again, but it had then taken years—*years*—for him to finally break free.

Now he could see himself in the fly-spotted mirror at the end of the bed, his lover curled around him. He tried on a Good Time Charlie smile. He'd been afraid he would never look the same . . . and in that he'd been right. He was totally different. The scars were only visible upon close inspection, the patched skin a faintly different shade, but his ear was the dead giveaway, especially without the goddamn missing prosthetic. Dr. Shithead had regretted that he couldn't do much for the ear, so he'd given Charlie the prosthetic as a gift. Charlie had grown his hair out to cover the malformation, and Lendel had told him he looked like a natural born "surfer dude." His new, more hawkish nose was better, actually. He looked less prep-boy handsome, more cowboy rugged, which suited him just fine. The transformation made it possible for him to move unrecognized among the good people of Deception Bay.

However, his smile appeared fake, he realized, dropping it and staring at his angry reflection. Five years of captivity had ruined his Good Time Charlie natural insouciance, but it was coming back, little by little. When the immediate swelling and bruising of the surgeries had dissipated, Charlie had instantly wanted to try his new look, see if his charms were still in working order, but that's when things really went sideways. He'd thought he had the upper hand with Dr. Shithead during surgery and recovery. Hadn't dreamed the man would go all Dr. Moreau on him, hiding his newly created creature in a basement room. None of Charlie's wiles worked on the man. The bastard had fallen in love with him without any help from Charlie's gift. Lendel was as dedicated and nutso as any stalker . . . *and* he was wealthy and paranoid and able to enslave his masterpiece, and there was nothing Charlie could do . . . for a long time.

But finally . . . *finally* . . . this last Minnesota summer, Charlie had managed to convince Dr. Shithead that he'd grown to love him as well. Ever so slowly, Lendel began entertaining Charlie upstairs, though he kept his prize's legs shackled. No running away from the good doctor, no way. Charlie had already learned that if he tried sending out pheromones, it did no good, though Lendel apparently could feel something, because whenever Charlie tried, his privileges would be taken away.

But by the end of the past summer, Lendel had finally believed Charlie was tamed. Charlie had almost believed it himself, he'd felt so broken and defeated.

Until Silas contacted him. The first time his brother had gotten through since Charlie's capture.

That next life is beginning . . . Silas had messaged.

How had he managed to get through? Charlie had marveled. Silas's last communiqué had been when Charlie was running away with the St. Clouds' nanny . . . what was her fucking name again? Didn't matter.

But he recalled implicitly the message Silas had sent him back then when Charlie had tried his wiles on him: *Not a woman, big brother. See you in the next life.*

And Charlie had been stunned that the missives he'd been receiving, ones that fired him up, were from *his half brother*. When he got over that shock, he'd been primed and eager, ready to take on Silas and all the rest of them. No matter that he was still severely injured. He would get them all.

In the next life, then, he'd sent back, and he and Silas had played mental hide-and-seek for a while until Charlie cut it off. He'd been struggling, his powers weakening, and he'd had to find a way to come back from the brink without being bedeviled by Silas. When he'd been first injured in the fire, his strength sapped to the point of near death, Charlie had let that nanny take care of him, but eventually even she'd left him. Then the doctor—his savior, he'd thought at the time—had found him in northern Washington and driven Charlie back to his home in Minnesota. Lendel had convinced Charlie he could help him, and the doctor had done just that, working his plastic surgery miracles on his face, restoring his features—most of them. But somewhere in the process or because of Charlie's weakened powers, Lendel had also gotten past Charlie's radar for danger, something few had. Maybe the guy had some kind of power himself. Maybe he was some distant relative, blessed with the same kind of abilities as Charlie, Silas, and those whores at Siren Song. Who knew? Whatever the case, Charlie had been unable to free himself until that last, hot summer night.

His Good Time Charlie smile split his face naturally as he savored the memory of how he'd turned the tables on Dr. Shithead.

"Wine?" Lendel had asked him, even though he knew Charlie didn't appreciate alcohol.

They had been seated on Lendel's back deck, high above the lake, looking through the glass railing to the green waters far below. It had been early enough that the damn bugs, bigger and meaner than anything he'd encountered on the West Coast, hadn't emerged in full force yet, so it had been a fairly pleasant evening. And Lendel wanted to show off to his captive.

"What 'cha got?" Charlie had responded, disinterested. Lendel felt he was a wine connoisseur, and he wanted to teach Charlie the finer things of life, but Charlie didn't give a rat's ass. Didn't keep Lendel from trying and retrying, though.

The doctor had laughed. "Well, I'm not going to waste Chateau Lafite Rothschild on your palate, but I've got something good," he said. Charlie had chuckled too. Ha, ha, ha. Needed to keep the guy jollied up. Couldn't afford to piss him off and end up back in his cellar room.

Lendel then served some kind of white wine that was apparently good enough for Charlie, but not spectacular. Whatever the case, while Charlie sipped and plotted his escape, Lendel kept lifting his own glass, holding it up to catch the dying rays of sunlight, enjoying the sparkle through the pale amber fluid.

Charlie had silently urged Lendel to keep drinking, and for once, he seemed to have listened, because he proceeded to get shit-faced while Charlie poured his own glasses of wine over the edge of the railing whenever the doctor wasn't looking. Seeing Charlie's empty glass, the doctor would fill it to the brim again, remarking on how Charlie had better be careful how much he drank or he was going to get drunk.

"Can't have that," Shithead singsonged, waving a tsk-tsking finger at Charlie while he tried to maintain his own balance.

Get stinking drunk, you fucking asshole, thought Charlie, waiting and watching.

"What? We . . . at the bottom again?" Lendel asked, holding up the third bottle of wine and squinting at it, as he swirled the bottle, sloshing the liquid around inside. This time, he stumbled a bit as he moved toward Charlie, ready to replenish his mysteriously empty glass once more.

Quick as an adder, Charlie leapt up, snatched the bottle out of his hand, and smashed it over his head. Lendel cried out and went down, trying to cover his head with his hands as Charlie pounded his crown, temple, and face until the man was a bloody mess and lay still as a stone. He quickly searched Lendel's clothes for the keys to the locks of the chains binding him. Nothing.

He ended up spending the next three hours shuffling through the house, searching for the keys or some implement to remove the shackles. Filled with rage, he went back to Lendel and grabbed the bloodied bottle once more, prepared to hit Lendel out of pure frustration, when the doctor moved his fingers and beseeched, "Stop . . . please . . ."

"Tell me where the key is and I'll let you live," said Charlie.

"I can't . . . I can't . . ." he moaned through broken teeth.

"Tell me!"

Eventually he did, though Charlie had to threaten him with one of the knives he kept in a locked kitchen drawer, which Charlie had pried open with a screwdriver. Lendel finally spewed the combination to a small safe at the back of his closet, and when Charlie opened it, he found the keys to his shackles, a hefty envelope of fifty-dollar bills, and a booklet with pictures of Charlie he'd taken over the years, most with Charlie scowling at the camera. It was a relief to find the photos. Charlie wanted to leave no trace of what he looked like, then and especially now, so he burned Shithead's treasures in the fireplace, his gut tight at the hungrily licking flames, almost able to smell the meaty scent of his own burning flesh again. He'd had to snap himself out of a near-coma of misery to find the doctor's cell phone, which was still sitting on one of the outside tables. Charlie couldn't open it, but Lendel's face was available. Except the fucking thing couldn't recognize the swollen, pulpy mass that was left. In a fury, he'd stomped on the blasted thing, smashing the remaining bits with a hammer.

When he was finished destroying the phone, he realized Lendel had passed out again. Was dead to the world. Maybe completely dead. Charlie rolled him over and checked to see if he was breathing, which he was not. No pulse.

Goodbye, Dr. Shithead.

Charlie checked the garage and discovered the keys to his BMW waiting for him in the console. Before taking off, he hauled Dr. Shithead's body and shoved it over the railing. It tumbled down the bank and nearly into the lake, one foot missing its deck shoe and half dangling into the water. Then, with a mixture of hatred and glee, he threw the pieces of the broken phone after him.

The police would know Lendel had been murdered. There was no use trying to cover up the scene. But no one was aware that Lendel had a captive, as far as Charlie knew. The doctor was just like those wackos who kidnapped women and held them in cages or cells for years and years, while they lived their outside lives like they were totally normal. Lendel worked at a private hospital and never brought friends or family or anyone home. They probably all thought he was just one of those eccentric weirdos with money who chose to live like a hermit. The police would find the downstairs room and collect Charlie's DNA. Again, there was nothing to do about it. No hiding it. At least they didn't have a record of his new face. He still had time to take those women of Siren Song to hell with him.

At one AM that night, he drove the silver BMW away from the lake and south, dropping it at a rest stop near a freeway exit, then walking toward the still-open nearby mini-mart at the top of the ramp. He'd thrown his shackles out the window along the way, far from Lendel's home. It was so freeing to walk again, to run, if he wanted to, but he needed wheels to get him far away from Lendel's house. He hoped to get lucky and find a woman out alone, one he could send his special Charlie love hormones to, one he could get to do his bidding. That had not come to pass, however, so he had to come up with another plan.

He stayed in the shadows at the side of the mini-mart. No one was about. He had time to look down at his clothes, determined to buy new ones as soon as he could.

His opportunity to leave arose as dawn was breaking. A trucker, a big, burly guy with a smile as wide as the great outdoors, offered him a ride. Burke Franklin was an independent trucker whom Charlie effortlessly befriended. The guy was just happy to have someone along for the ride to Portland and then south to California. Charlie had already tried his pheromones on Lendel with mixed results, so he hadn't expected Burke to be drawn to him, but the man was easy to ensnare. He was looking for a buddy, not a lover, Charlie realized, so that's what he became. Burke Franklin's best buddy. They drove on out toward the West Coast. Charlie read him like a book and became what Burke wanted. He even lied about his affinity for country music, Burke's favorite, though music in general kind of scraped against Charlie's brain. Clear thoughts. No distractions. That's what he needed.

It took three days for them to make the trip because Burke started purposely slowing the truck down. He seemed to know, as well or even better than Charlie, that their time together was fleeting, so he was prolonging the trip some, clearly thinking Charlie wouldn't notice or care. But as they crossed into Washington State, Charlie began to feel tense, and the need to finish what he'd begun was growing, a raging bull inside him, snorting and pawing the ground.

Outside Spokane, Burke met a terrible fate. One moment he was driving along, chatting away to his buddy and bromance crush, Good Time Charlie; the next he was gurgling with a knife through his neck, and Charlie was manhandling the rig toward the ravine on the opposite side of the road, steering it close to the edge but not over. He practically climbed atop Burke to pull the rig to a stop, then he opened the driver's door, relieving the man of his wallet and phone before shifting the semi into gear and half jumping, half rolling out as the rig slowly wheeled forward, its cab dipping down first, toward the sea of Douglas fir trees at the bottom. Then, like the head of some gigantic, broken beast, it lopped forward, dragging the rest of the body crashing down behind it into the canyon far below. The sad truth was Charlie just couldn't afford buddies, so bye-bye, Burke

Franklin. With any luck, no one would find the vehicle for days. If he was lucky, weeks.

And then he was free, really free, for the first time in years! His luck held when the next car that came along belonged to a woman who saw Charlie about two miles from where he'd wrecked the semi and, once enthralled by him, drove him all the way to Portland. They had sex in the back of her Suburban in a high-rise car park. He never asked her name, and she didn't ask his, either, although he memorized her license plate. He didn't want to have to kill her, but he planned to keep tabs on her, just in case she heard about Burke's unfortunate accident and remembered it was near where she'd picked up Charlie. He used her for a few hours. They even went shopping together. At a downtown store, he bought some new pants, a shirt, a baseball cap, and black sneakers with the cash he'd taken off Lendel.

Initially, she was like a puppy dog, following in his wake, saying yes to whatever he wanted. But as time wore on, she started to worry. What had come over her? She was married, for Christ's sake! Her husband would be home tonight in *Spokane*! Hours away! She didn't know how she would explain about all her purchases. She had to go!

He got her to have sex with him one more time, even as she was screaming with fear and concern about the returning husband. Charlie held onto her with his sexual embrace, and she couldn't make herself leave. "Please. He can't know," she begged. She seemed to understand his power. Reluctantly, Charlie let her go. She couldn't tell on him without giving herself away, so he let her live. And too many deaths along the way could become suspicious to some nosy, overly ambitious cop and point to his path and the direction he was taking.

He opted to hitchhike the final leg to the coast. If he'd tried harder, he supposed he could have gotten her to take him. She was just like the nanny who'd helped him escape from the bitch detective and other authorities five years earlier, the kind of woman who would do anything for him. Lie, cheat, steal, drive him wherever he wanted to go, engage in whatever sexual fantasy he could . . .

Victoria. *That* was the nanny's name. For some reason he had a hell of a time remembering it. She'd been the one who'd hauled him to Canada after his face had been so viciously burned. She'd even stuck with him a while until his powers faded and he couldn't control her. She'd left before he really started to recover, and it still pissed him off when he thought about it.

She was another one he could locate, if need be. She'd blabbed enough about her family when he'd held her in thrall. He decided that, as soon as he was done with his unfinished business in Deception Bay, he might look for her. For the time being, he had Burke's driver's license for identification, and though the photo wasn't a great likeness by a long stretch, it'd done the job so far. Soon he would get better ID *and* a new prosthetic ear. Lendel's money was holding up and there was always an underground ready to service people like him, those who were living on the fringes, maybe seeking revenge themselves, and he certainly could manipulate people, women especially, better than most. In fact—

His lover suddenly lifted her blond head and looked at him cautiously. Now that her ardor had cooled, she examined him so deeply it gave him a bit of the willies. Immediately, he tossed out a sexual rope to entangle her, and though he could tell she felt it, she didn't immediately succumb. What was this?

"Meet my family," she said, sliding away from him to search for her clothes.

She'd been saying this a lot lately. "You really want me to?"

"Yes, I do."

Charlie laughed. "You think I'm the guy to take home to Mama?"

"Well, you're my guy . . ." She looked back at him, unconsciously sexy, her blond hair hanging down her bare back, lips still swollen from his punishing kisses.

Mr. Happy stirred again.

"Come here," he ordered, but she shook her head and picked up her bra.

He grabbed her arm, and she yanked it back. Now her eyes flashed fire . . . and an invitation . . .

"God damn you, Burke," she muttered as he came across the bed and pushed her up against the wall.

He slid into her so fast she gasped. Then they were wrestling. His hands in her hair, hers in his. She brushed his mangled ear, and he slammed her against the wall. She'd never gotten so close to it before. Fuck. He needed that new prosthetic!

"Okay, I'll meet them," he breathed in her hair, still gripping her hard.

Her heart was beating like a captured bird. "Okay."

He released her, and she collapsed in his arms. "That hurt," she told him.

"You get me going, and I lose all control."

"Sure." She slipped away from him and finished redressing.

He narrowed his eyes at her. She had no idea that he did, in fact, plan to meet her family. All of them. He'd targeted Ophelia Rutledge on purpose, and she'd fallen for him as if she'd been waiting for him.

But he didn't like this new mood one bit.

"Take those clothes back off," he ordered.

Was that a flash of resentment in her blue eyes? A millisecond of rebellion?

"I have to go see my family now. You won't go with me, so I'll go alone. Lillibeth is struggling, and we don't know what's wrong. She's just consumed by these dreams, a story that she completely believes, and—"

Charlie leapt forward and smashed his mouth against hers to get her to stop talking. He knew all about Lillibeth's dreams, and Cassandra's visions, and that hag Catherine's stiff rigidity. Ophelia couldn't stop going on and on about them. Charlie was her first boyfriend, and she apparently hadn't learned the art of shutting the fuck up. He didn't need to know any more about them. When the time came, she would get him inside the lodge, and he would kill them, one by one. He could just imagine how powerful he would become after looking into their dark souls. His half sisters. Mother Mary's twisted brood.

Her hands pushed at him. "Burke, for God's sake, I've got to *go.*"

"Not yet."

"If you don't drive me to my car, I'll Uber."

"I'll drive you back . . . when I'm good and ready."

"Well, I'm going now." To his surprise, she pushed him away with sudden strength. "I'll call you," she said determinedly, then headed out, shutting the door firmly behind her.

He liked her to fight back, but he didn't like the rebellion she'd gotten away with. That wasn't supposed to happen. He didn't like her knowing the number of his burner phone. And he sure as hell didn't like her shoving him aside.

He started to chase after her, but stopped himself. Let her pay for a ride. He had better things to do.

She knows who you are.

The thought came unbidden. With its own secret terror.

She does not, he told himself. She wouldn't ask him back to meet her family if she knew.

Unless she's trying to trap you.

Charlie flopped back on the bed, churning inside. Maybe he should take another cruise around her apartment. She'd as much as said she was heading for Siren Song, so maybe he could find something that would explain this new attitude.

He shot to his feet. Quick enough that when he reached the door and stepped onto the minuscule porch, she was just getting into a black Toyota and being whisked away. He watched the car disappear out of the crumbling asphalt of the motel's parking lot, felt drizzle against his face, and decided he couldn't trust her.

Of course he couldn't.

Within minutes, he was headed for Ophelia's apartment in Deception Bay.

He would have to make sure she was telling the truth and going directly to Siren Song. His thoughts turned to that damnable jailer, Catherine Rutledge. As much as he planned to kill them all for throwing him away, it was Catherine who'd locked them all up. Locked them up almost as much as Dr. Shithead had locked him up. He, Charlie, was going to free them from her.

Catherine, you whore. I've taken one, and I'll take all the rest soon. And that bitch of a detective. And anyone else you think you can hide from me. And then I'm coming for you.

"What is it?" Isadora asked her aunt as Catherine suddenly gave a full-body shudder. They were seated side by side on the couch in Siren Song's living room, the fire crackling, the lights burning low.

Catherine smiled that tight, controlled curve of her lips that spoke of her strength and that Isadora hadn't seen in a while, a smile that gave her hope Catherine was going to be just fine.

"Just someone walking on my grave," the older woman said.

"Is there anything I can get you? A cup of hot tea?"

Her aunt just patted her arm. "No, thank you."

"Is something wrong?"

"No, dear."

Isadora sensed her aunt was lying, but, unlike most of her sisters, she didn't possess any particular extrasensory gifts and had to content herself with believing Catherine knew what she was doing.

CHAPTER 16

Lucky stood in the shadows outside Ravinia's apartment complex. Downtown Portland felt far away from this older home that had been converted to apartments sometime in the distant past. Somewhere there was the pungent scent of ripe pumpkins. She turned her nose to it and looked up at the sky. The birds were going to sleep. Their trills fading off. Their fluttering disappearing, to be replaced by the swoop of bat wings as night fell and a mist filled the air.

She felt a strange melancholy, a brief longing for a life she could never have. She thought of her sister, her twin, who'd found a way to have those things, settling down, marrying, shoving her gift of prediction to some back corner, pretending to be normal. They'd met only once as adults, and Lucky had done her damnedest to steal the man her sister loved and ruin her life, kill her, if necessary. She'd felt much like her sick and twisted brother, Justice, had. Wanting revenge. Wanting to make them pay, the others whose lives had been so charmed, while her own had been full of neglect, abuse, and despair. However, her twin had managed to survive and thrive, and Lucky had been the one to barely escape with her life.

The last few years, she'd used her own gift to remove sick pervs from the planet, seeking out pedophiles, luring them to her, killing them. Sometimes they hadn't committed a crime yet, except in their minds, but she knew they would, if left to their own devices. She was their prophylactic, keeping them from their victims. If asked, she would not be able to tell how many people she'd killed.

Ravinia appeared tucked in for the night, her car parked and locked, the windows of her apartment, like so many in the building, glowing softly. The sound of traffic was a hum, the city still awake, despite nightfall.

Lucky felt the rain—a soft drizzle now—and adjusted the hood of her jacket as she eyed the building, then ducked behind a tree as a car passed, beams of headlights washing along the wet pavement. She knew it was counterproductive, but she felt protective of the girl, though given half a chance Ravinia would turn her in to the authorities. Lucky had some insight of her own. Call it a gift, or precognition, or just plain awareness, but she understood that Ravinia, for all her belief in herself that she was a rebel of sorts, would follow the straight and narrow path. If and when she learned of Lucky's string of kills, she would call the cops and send her straight to prison for life. That, above all else, could not happen. Lucky would kill herself first, and she wasn't averse to taking others with her, if that was what it required. Ravinia Rutledge might think of herself as practical and level-headed, but Lucky had her beat, hands down. She could do whatever it took to meet her needs, where Ravinia would hesitate before taking a life, a hesitation that might cost her by ending her own.

Still . . . Ravinia was Silas's sister, and he'd let it be known she was off-limits. Lucky would never go out of her way to hurt her, but Silas knew she would hurt Ravinia if she got in Lucky's way, so he'd laid down the law. Ravinia was to be left alone, as were all the Siren Song women. They weren't Lucky's sisters, but they were her blood.

And since following Ravinia, getting a sense of her, Lucky had a grudging respect for her. Ravinia was devastated about Silas's death and blamed Charlie. Lucky felt the same way and knew the blame was deserved.

Which was why, after waiting a few minutes, making sure Ravinia was apparently safely in for the night, Lucky melted back into the shadows and found her way to her Outback. She retraced the route across the river and back to the offices where Ravinia had met with her old boss. Good. He was still there, visible inside the window, watching something on a small TV mounted above the desk, still covered in red-wine stains. Lucky had seen Ravinia shove him after an unwanted advance. She'd then run out, the prick glaring through the blinds after her. Lucky had silently applauded her.

After a few minutes, Lucky realized the guy appeared to be

236 Lisa Jackson and Nancy Bush

stroking himself. Well, of course. Ravinia had thwarted his attempts at seduction, so now he was frustrated and watching porn.

Time to do something about him. She knew without a doubt that his interest in Ravinia would only intensify. Ravinia was in his sights, and thwarting him had only fueled his need. He was already a man teetering on the knife's edge between normal attraction and obsession. He was going to lose that battle and go after Ravinia like the rabid, crazed fan that he was. Ravinia had unfortunately stepped into his life at the exact moment he was drifting from gazing longingly at beautiful, unapproachable women to focusing on just one. Lucky hadn't been there when Ravinia started at Bauer's agency, but she could well imagine the gulp of reaction he'd swallowed when she'd walked in, the surreptitious glances her way that increased over time, the ideas crystallizing in his lizard brain as he convinced himself she was the one for him and that he deserved to have her.

So Lucky was going to do Ravinia a favor.

Pulling out another hypodermic, her current, favorite modus operandi, one she'd shared with Silas, she had a brief shiver of fear when she considered that the authorities probably now had her fingerprints from her last kill. They still didn't know who she was, but they had to have pages and pages of those fingerprints on file. Maybe they even had a name for her, like *the Girl Who Kills Molesters.* No, something shorter . . . *Man Hater* . . . no, *Man-eater.* Wasn't quite accurate, but the police didn't have a clue what really motivated her.

She hugged the side of the building, her black clothes disappearing into the overall darkness. Beneath his window, she tapped lightly. He jumped up as if goosed and peered out, separating the blinds with his fingers. She was a little below the window, so she simply lifted a hand in front of the pane, crooking her finger and slowly inviting him outside.

In an instant, the blinds rolled upward, and his face was framed in the window, his startled gaze finding hers. "Who the fuck are you?" he demanded as he threw open the sash.

She lifted her face to the square of illumination, and she whispered, "Your girl."

"What?" Confusion darkened his gaze. "I don't know what the hell your game is, but get the fuck off my property!"

"Oh, come on, J. D., don't you remember me?"

He squinted. "No," he said succinctly.

She stepped just outside of the light, still visible to him but not so much to the surrounding area. "I'll be in the backyard," she whispered. She deliberately took off her jacket, then started on the buttons down the front of her blouse, letting it flap open so he could see her black lace bra and otherwise naked torso.

"Go away," he said, but his voice said something else.

"If you won't come out, you could invite me in."

"Who are you? What do you want?" But curiosity was replacing his fury and annoyance.

"I'm your nightmare . . . and your dream girl. If you send me away, I won't come back. Better make a good choice."

"Yeah? I don't know what this is, but I don't want any part of it."

She exhaled on a sigh of regret and bent down to pick up her blouse and jacket. When he didn't move from the window, she unzipped her jeans and slid her hand inside, throwing her head back and moaning, looking at him from beneath her lashes.

"Just a minute . . . just a minute . . ." He ducked back inside, and she could see he was heading for the front door. She hurried to the back and through the low gate. There were buildings on all sides, but they were all dark, and the property was rimmed by a thick laurel hedge.

It didn't take long for him to meet her. He was hurrying, a bit out of breath, and she knew he'd been afraid she would leave. He stopped short. "How do I know you?"

"We've met before."

"Nuh uh. I woulda remembered." He came a few steps closer, carefully, as if afraid she would bolt. She stayed put, but the needle was hidden behind her right palm. "What are you doing here now?"

He was only a few paces away, but he was cautious, lifting his head as if scenting the air like a wary deer. She moved toward him slowly. "I'm here for you." With her left hand, she took his right and guided it down to her crotch.

He inhaled on a gasp and grabbed her fully.

Her right hand came up, and she jabbed the hypodermic into his neck. He screamed and backed away. "Fuck! Oh, fuck, oh, fuck. What did you do? *What the fuck did you do?*"

Lucky quickly threw on her blouse, forcing her arms down the sleeves, then did the same with her jacket before zipping up her pants.

"I killed you," she said matter-of-factly. This time the needle was filled with belladonna, deadly nightshade. No mere sleeping potion. "Consider it a gift from Ravinia."

"Whad . . . wha . . ." he burbled. He was down on his knees.

She waited just long enough to watch him topple over onto his back, making sure he wouldn't be getting up and doing something stupid like picking up his cell phone and calling 911. She then bent down and picked up the needle, as she should have done at her last killing, although it was really a moot point, as she was going to make it easy for the police to make a connection.

As J. D. Bauer, Ravinia's ex-boss and the owner of Bauer Investigations, breathed his last breath, she yanked down his pants and pulled out his penis.

The call from John Mills came in long hours after Nev was back at his apartment and standing by the back window, leaning a shoulder against the wall and gazing out at the dune while slowly drinking a beer. He'd spent the afternoon trying to find a way to get to Echo, but the department wasn't interested in sending the Marine Patrol outside their waterways into the ocean. As Lang had said, that was for the Coast Guard. And Rand hadn't gotten back to him with Earl's number, so Nev was planning a trip to the Foothillers' town tomorrow, to look up the older man himself.

"Rhodes, sorry, man, today was out-of-control busy," Mills greeted him. In the background, Nev heard the wail of a crying baby. "What do you want to know?"

"Whatever you can tell me."

"Why the special interest?" he asked curiously.

"Well, we had a homicide down here that bears a marked resemblance to one of yours. I'm not saying they're connected. Not yet. I'm just gathering info. I'll let you know what I learn."

"Okay. Good enough." Mills then related that the woman's body had been found on the floor behind the bar. Petechial hemorrhages in the eyes suggested strangulation. Marks on her neck said the same. "She was alone at that time. Probably just opened the bar. Whoever he was, he just waltzed in and killed her. No working cameras, which I'm guessing he knew. A woman pedestrian noticed a vehicle down the street behind the bar about that same time. Black. Small SUV, maybe. The witness wasn't good with makes, or cars in general, so we don't know what we're looking for. We're checking into the bartender's background. Her name's Delores Thorburn, but nothing out of the ordinary has turned up so far. Pays her bills on time. Lives fairly simply. Had a boyfriend, but he moved on last year and is in Vancouver, Washington, back with his wife, though they're still divorced. Still checking on him. It looks like Delores had recent sex, but no signs of rape."

"Was that usual for her, do you know? Sex with a customer or someone right at the bar?" asked Nev.

"Not even close. She made a remark to another employee just like a week ago about how long it'd been since she had sex. Said she wasn't all that worried if she ever had it again, so it wasn't like she was on the make."

"But she had recent consensual sex?"

"Unprotected, so we're doing a DNA test. The sexual activity might have been with the guy who killed her," said Mills. As Nev rolled that over in his mind, Mills asked, "Who's the body you've got?"

Nev hesitated. He'd called Lang and told him that Ravinia had named their John Doe as Silas Rutledge and that she wanted help from TCSD to keep her and her sisters safe from Charlie, who she was convinced had killed Silas. They'd decided to keep that information to themselves until after the autopsy. So far, the newspapers and television people hadn't descended on them, but next week, as the tale leaked out, it was bound to be a different story.

With all that in mind, Nev merely told Mills that a John Doe had washed up on the beach and they were still in the process of trying to learn who he was. "I'll let you know what I know as soon as I can," Nev promised, but Mills was a seasoned investigator.

"You're keeping something from me," he said.

"Give me till Monday. I'll call you first."

"Okay." He didn't sound too happy that Nev hadn't offered tit for tat, but he accepted it.

Nev almost called Lang again, but decided there really wasn't much new to warrant a Saturday evening call. He spent the rest of the night brooding about Ravinia and Echo Island and what he was going to do next. The rushed toxicology report on Stanford Norman had come in and indicated he had enough Rohypnol, the date-rape drug, in his system to incapacitate him, or possibly kill him.

The jury was still out on that point, though. Once the full autopsy report came in, then maybe they would have some answers.

"Push, push, push!" Dr. Evanson commanded, and Savvy bore down, counting in her head. "Good, good."

Savannah collapsed back on the bed in a full-blown sweat. The last time she'd delivered, the baby had come fast, too fast, really, but this little girl was taking her time.

Hale held a washcloth to put on her forehead, but he didn't make a move to actually place it on her. She'd practically bitten his head off when he'd tried to apply it earlier, which she'd since apologized for. He'd literally been her savior when Declan was born.

Between contractions, she'd told him what she'd told Lang about Charlie. He'd reacted with concern, but she knew he was questioning if it was what she'd really felt or was something to do with being in labor. She didn't blame him. Well, she sort of did. She'd known he wouldn't want to believe Charlie was back and targeting her. She certainly didn't want to believe it herself, but she wanted Hale to believe it! Was that convoluted thinking? Yes. But she didn't care, and, oh, oh, *here we go again* . . .

"*Push*," Dr. Evanson ordered, and Savvy closed her eyes and bore down with all her might.

EEEEEEEOOOOOOOOWWWWWW!

Catherine's eyes flew open at the blood-curdling scream from Lillibeth's room. She struggled to her feet from the couch, swaying slightly. It didn't take long for Isadora and Cassandra to clatter down the stairs and meet up with her, nearly bowling her over in their haste to get to their sister. As best she could, Catherine hurried after them. The three of them huddled in her room.

Lillibeth was writhing on the bed, holding her stomach. "Help me . . . help me . . . *The baby's coming!*"

"Stop that," Catherine commanded harshly. She wanted to slap Lillibeth.

"No. Shhhh. She has to come out of it by herself," whispered Cassandra.

"Help me to my knees," mewed Lillibeth.

"What?" Isadora asked. "She can't get to her knees. *And there's no baby!*"

"Shhhh," Cassandra admonished again.

"She has to stop this," stated Catherine. She looked to Isadora for support, and Isadora went up to Lillibeth and grabbed her by the shoulders. "Wait!" Catherine cried. As much as she wanted to dispel any notion that the nightmares had any merit, she knew Cassandra was right at some level. It would be worse to shake Lillibeth out of the terrifying dream world than to let her come out of it naturally.

"It's foolish nonsense, and it's escalating," said Isadora, her tone so perfectly mimicking Catherine's that even Catherine heard it.

Lillibeth collapsed onto her back, her hands moving feebly but the rest of her in repose.

"The nightmare appears to have passed," said Catherine. "Let her wake on her own."

Isadora pressed her lips together, but Cassandra nodded vigorously.

Minutes passed . . . long minutes, while Lillibeth lay silent and still, except for rapid movement of her eyes beneath her lids and the occasional overall twitch.

Cassandra eventually squeezed past Isadora to take her place next to Lillibeth. Catherine heard Isadora suck air through her teeth and cringed a little, knowing she made the same sound herself when her authority was thwarted.

Lillibeth slowly wakened, blinking a bit, as if she didn't know where she was. As she looked around, tears formed in her eyes, and she reached out blindly. "Ravinia," she said on a sob.

"She's not here," said Cassandra.

"I want Ravinia," she rasped. "Please, please . . ."

"Oh, for God's sakes," muttered Isadora, leaving the room. Catherine turned to follow her, but Isadora returned moments later with Catherine's cell phone in hand.

Lillibeth reached a trembling hand for the phone.

* * *

Ravinia woke up on a scream and sat bolt upright in bed. Shocked. Heart racing.

She scrabbled for the switch to her bedside lamp. As the room flooded with light, she glanced fearfully around the room, staring into its still-dark corners. There was danger. Blood. Death. *She could see it!*

But no . . . there was no peril here . . . not in her apartment . . . not in her own bed.

It had been Neville Rhodes in the forefront of her dream. Climbing Echo's harsh, rocky shore and sliding back into the sea, struggling upward, dragging himself ashore, only to fall back down in a cascade of scattered stones, never surfacing a second time.

Ravinia flopped back onto the bed. Only a nightmare . . . a goddamned very, *very* real nightmare, but just a nightmare.

What time was it?

She struggled upward again to check the time on the clock on her nightstand. One-thirty.

Her cell blasted in the silent room, sending Ravinia's pulse flying again.

Catherine's cell?

Shit.

"Catherine?" she answered tensely.

"It's Lillibeth, Ravinia," her sister said in a tear-choked voice. "I'm dying, but my baby can be saved."

Ravinia's mouth formed to ask "What?" but before she could speak, there was a rustling and sounds of protest.

The voice on the other end of the phone was now Cassandra's. "Don't come back yet," she ordered in an urgent whisper. "You need to find Charlie. Concentrate on that. Do what you do to find him." She exhaled. "I guess you can tell that Lillibeth had another dream."

Ravinia shook the cobwebs from her mind. "Look, Cassandra, I know you think they're real, or partially real, but I wouldn't put too much stock in them."

"I don't think they're literally real, but they have a real message. Do you know anything about Charlie? Did he fight with Silas on Echo?"

"I don't know. I'm going to try to find his adoptive parents, and Silas's. See what they can tell me. That's what Aunt Catherine asked me to do."

"You'll find him, or he'll find you. Don't let him fool you. He has charms. But do it as fast as you can. We need to know where he is."

Ravinia's breathing had returned to normal after her own nightmare about Nev, but Cassandra was making her uneasy. "What do you think the dreams mean?"

"Ravinia!" Lillibeth was on the phone once more, and Ravinia could hear her clearly. "When I get all of the message, I'm going to die."

"Lillibeth, that's not true!"

"No, it's all right. Really. I understand now, and I'm not going to be scared anymore." Her voice was growing in strength. "You just have to save the baby."

"These dreams aren't messages, they're just dreams," she finished a bit lamely. Her sister's sudden turnabout was almost creepier than her screams.

"The dreams tell the story of our past and future. I'm preparing myself."

"Okay, let's be clear. It's not your past. It's not anyone's past. It's a . . . a manifestation of your worries. That's what dreams are."

"Ravinia . . ." Lillibeth said, her voice almost a whisper.

"Yes?"

"Come back soon. And be careful. It's me in the dreams, but sometimes it's you."

More rustling, and then Catherine's voice, calm and cold. "We're all sorry we woke you. We'll let you get back to sleep now."

"Fat chance of that. What does Lillibeth mean about messages? What's going on? And why am I in them?"

"We look forward to seeing you next time you come." And she clicked off.

"Oh, for the love of God!" Ravinia dropped the cell from her ear and lay back in the bed. Like, sure, she was going to go back to sleep after that. And no, she didn't believe in Lillibeth's dreams. But, man, this had given her a jolt.

After a few minutes, she got up, threw on a robe, and went into her kitchen to make some herbal tea. If she'd had any whiskey, she would have thrown that in too, but alas, all that she had was some vanilla extract, and she wasn't that desperate. Instead, she searched inside her laptop case for the aged, lined notebook pages that held the names of the adoptive parents of both Silas and Charlie. She had addresses but no phone numbers, though she'd earlier found a land-line number for Silas's parents, Kurt and Diane Blavek, which she'd tried twice, but it just rang and rang and rang, no person or answering device ever picking up.

A search now on her laptop left her with the same landline number. In the back of her mind, she'd always figured she would try to interview both Silas's and Charlie's parents in person. Even if she could discover a number, telephone interviews just weren't the same. She already knew where she hoped to find them. She could throw her belongings in an overnight bag and head down I-5 to Cottage Grove and, after attempting contact with Silas's parents, keep heading south and cut over to the coast and possibly interview Charlie's adoptive parents in Brookings as well. It would be a long day, but she would effectively kill two birds with one stone, if she could actually locate them all. In any case, she needed to rest up, so she took her cup of tea back with her to bed.

Savannah cradled her baby girl in her arms, exhausted, but her face was creased in a huge smile. She'd allowed Hale to put the wash-cloth on her head toward the end of the birth, and they'd both laughed. He was now just outside the door to her room, talking softly on the phone to Janet, who'd insisted they call her, no matter what time it was, as soon as their little girl was born.

What's your name? Savvy silently asked the baby. She was swaddled in a white blanket, and her head was protected by a wee, pink stocking cap that covered the wisps of dark hair that were faintly touched with red.

Mary, came the name sliding into her consciousness, and her heart galumphed in fear. Was that Charlie talking to her, or her own fevered brain still processing the slimy rope of sexual awareness she'd felt?

Hale clicked off the phone and came back to her bedside. "You look beautiful," he said.

"Ha, ha. Did you get that from some handbook on what to say when your wife gives birth?"

"How'd you know?"

"Oh, I'm pretty clear on what I look like right now."

They both smiled and gazed down at the sleeping baby, whose rosy lips were gently moving.

"She's perfect," he said.

"She is."

"They're going to kick us out tomorrow, so we have to name her," added Hale.

This had been an ongoing discussion, and because they couldn't decide, Savvy had made a list of their top ten choices. Had Charlie sent her Mary's name? Savannah had a full-body shiver, just thinking of it, but before Hale could ask about it, she said, "How about Annabel?"

It was the top name on Savvy's list, but Hale wasn't as sure. They'd both considered naming her after Kristina but hadn't quite been able to pull the trigger on that one.

"Sure you don't want Janet?"

Savvy chuckled and shook her head. Not Janet. Not Catherine . . . and not Mary.

He held up his hands like he was a photographer, sighting a picture, zeroing in on the baby.

"You know, she does kind of look like an Annabel," he said, then reached out to gently touch her swaddled body.

Savvy felt her eyes suddenly flood with tears. She was so lucky . . . so very lucky.

"Hey," he said, his brow furrowed with concern.

"I love you, Mr. St. Cloud."

"I love you too, Mrs. St. Cloud."

"If . . . if something happened to me, like because of Charlie, and—"

"Stop it. Nothing's going to happen to you. Because of Charlie or anything else." He was suddenly dead serious. "Stop worrying. You said Lang is on the case. He'll take care of him. I'll make sure of it."

"I know, I know." She nodded vigorously. "You think maybe this is the beginning of postpartum? It's just life is so good, you know? I just don't want anything bad to happen." She couldn't help her mind flicking to Declan's fall down the stairs. She still wasn't ready to mention her fears about the nature of his death to Hale, even though she now knew Charlie was out there, maybe nearby.

"Nothing bad is going to happen," Hale assured her, and Savvy gave him a smile through her tears.

She didn't know how to tell him she just didn't believe him.

CHAPTER 17

It was late morning by the time Ravinia roused herself from bed and stumbled through a shower. So much for an early getaway. After last night's phone call, a part of her felt an urgency to get back to Siren Song and check with Lillibeth and Catherine and all of them again, but she'd just been there. If she ended up in Brookings tonight, she could stay over and wend her way up the coast, but it was a long, long drive up Highway 101 from Brookings to Deception Bay. Hours longer than the freeway, although, no matter what, you had to cut over from the valley somewhere to get from the freeway to 101, so that took extra time . . .

Whatever. She would just hit the road and see what happened.

Ohhh . . . Ravinia swore beneath her breath. She was supposed to meet that new client, Jolene Fursberg, at Laurelton Park today, and that was going to take time too. She debated about calling Jolene and rescheduling, seesawing back and forth. The truth was, she could really use the business. Snatching her cell, she checked in her app for notes to see what time she'd agreed to meet her. Noon. Hmm. Well, okay, it would put her behind schedule some, but she could make the meeting before she took off and headed south.

Once dressed and ready, she headed to the coffee shop again for another muffin and coffee, returning within the half hour. There were a number of pedestrians walking by on her street, many with leashed dogs. Normally, there were hardly any people in her neighborhood, but it was Sunday, and the weather was decent, a few degrees warmer than it had been, and the wind had died down some, though a check on the weather app said not to expect the sunshine to last. Glancing at the vehicles parked along the street, she saw a woman putting on lipstick, looking at herself in the rearview, sunglasses covering her eyes, and a man and a woman and their enormous dog, something with tight, black, curly fur, squeezing into a black Camry. "You need a bigger car for that animal," she said aloud, but she was already across the street and knew they wouldn't hear her.

She climbed up the front porch steps and then into her apartment, snagged her repacked overnight bag, took a last look around, then at eleven-thirty hit the road for Laurelton Park. She'd reheated her coffee and had it in the paper cup from the coffee shop, sipping at it very slowly as she wanted to minimize bathroom stops on her trip south.

Checking her rearview as she pulled out from the back lot, her thoughts touched on the call from Lillibeth, which left her feeling unsettled, then flipped back to her fight with J. D. Asshole. Had he really believed he could blackmail her into sex? Sure, there were things about her family she didn't want dug up, and yeah, it bothered her that the Deception Bay locals thought they were a bunch of kooks, maybe even a cult, but that wasn't really news. There'd always been a certain amount of friction between the two factions. Nothing she could really do about it, but it pissed her off that J. D. had assumed she would make some kind of deal with him if he what? *Didn't tell anyone?* The information about her family, true and false, was readily available.

Her mind then tripped back to Lillibeth and her dreams. What had she meant about Ravinia being part of her dreams? That was creepy, even if she didn't believe the dreams were "messages from beyond." Cassandra was giving them too much weight, wasn't she? She thought of Cassandra desperately urging her to find Charlie. They all seemed to think their safety rested on her, and yeah, she'd told Catherine she would find Charlie, but what if she couldn't? Just because she'd succeeded in finding Elizabeth five years earlier didn't mean she would locate Charlie.

"You made investigation your profession," she reminded herself.

Again, no guarantee of success. Charlie's a different animal.

As she entered the Laurelton city limits, she mentally switched to her conversation with Detective Rhodes. She'd purposely omitted telling him she was doing background on both Silas and Charlie. Yes, she wanted help. Protection. At least an awareness by TCSD that they were vulnerable, but she didn't trust Rhodes to really understand the threat Charlie posed and do what was necessary to stop him.

You should really talk to Detective St. Cloud.

She turned onto Mason Street, which ran on the east side of Laurelton Park. There was parking on the far side of the street from the park, but Ravinia turned left onto the entry road, past the rustic LAU-RELTON PARK sign, which was six feet by six feet and carved into a rectangular block of wood, and found a parking space.

The park itself consisted of a grassy, fenced swath of ground used as a makeshift dog park and a separate area down an incline and nearer the street with picnic tables set amid a copse of alders. Ravinia nosed into a spot beside the industrial gray cinder-block restroom.

As she stepped out of her car, Ravinia assessed the area. She seemed to be alone, although there was another vehicle in the lot, a blue Ford Escape and several other cars and trucks parked on the street. She saw, then, that there was a woman inside the fenced area about a football field length away, playing with a small dog, possibly a terrier, who was dancing around beside her. The woman threw a small ball in Ravinia's direction, and the dog wheeled around and ran after it like a maniac, feet flying so fast it was almost a comic book whir.

Was that Jolene? Unlikely, with the dog.

After a moment, Ravinia strolled down to the picnic tables. The area was defined by a floor of wood chips that separated it from the grass. The dog enclosure was on one side of it, Mason Street on the other. She sat with her back to the street, so she could face the restrooms, parking lot, and fenced enclosure, her eye on the woman with the dog.

A door to the bathroom suddenly opened, and a woman stepped out. She glanced around and, spying Ravinia, hurried down the hill to her table.

"Ms. Rutledge?" she asked somewhat breathlessly. She was somewhere in her mid-forties, Ravinia guessed. Pretty, with dark brown hair that had some natural wave and big brown eyes peeking behind long bangs and capped by winged brows. She wore a black jogging suit, the jacket zipped all the way up to her neck, and a pair of white Nike sneakers.

"Jolene?"

"Yes," she answered with relief. She took a seat opposite Ravinia, crossing her arms on the table's painted boards. "You sounded older on the phone."

Ravinia nodded. She got that a lot.

Jolene gazed around restlessly. "I don't have a lot of time. My husband's with a friend, helping him out, ostensibly. It's really just a drinking opportunity for them on Sunday morning, but at least it gives me some time. I told him I was going for a run. He doesn't let me out of his sight. It's like being a prisoner."

"What exactly do you want me to do?" asked Ravinia.

"Follow him. Find out where he goes. I know he's seeing someone. I want to know who the bitch is."

"Okay," Ravinia said carefully. "You feel like a prisoner and want a divorce . . ."

"Yes."

"So you're looking for ammunition for the divorce." Ravinia had detected a hint of jealousy in Jolene's words, so she wanted to make sure she understood the assignment.

"Of course. He always goes for the trashy types. Or he has since we got married." She rubbed her arms as if at a sudden chill. "It's just who he is."

"He's done this before?"

"Oh. Many times."

"Okay, give me the particulars about where he works and what his routine is, and I'll see what I can do, although I won't be able to start till next week."

Her face clouded. "Like, what day? Not tomorrow?"

Ravinia shook her head. "I'll call you before I do anything."

"I'm not sure that's good enough," she said, sitting back. "I need information, and I mean *dirt*, on that man, and I need it now. I've got things to do. You're making me wonder if you can really do the job."

Ravinia fought her annoyance. This was twice in two days that her ability had been questioned, first by J. D., although that had been a ruse, and now by Jolene Fursberg. "If you don't want to hire me, I'm—"

"Oh, fuck," Jolene expelled, her eyes bugging as she zeroed in on something happening behind Ravinia.

Ravinia quickly turned around. A black Tesla was just reversing into a parking space on Mason Street, squeezing in between two silver SUVs, doing a damn good job of it, actually.

Jolene's arm shot out, and she grabbed Ravinia's hand, squeezing it hard. "That's him! Oh, my God, *that's him!* He parked behind my car! Oh, fuck, oh, fuck, he *tracked* me!"

Ravinia felt a spurt of fear as she eased her hand free. A man stepped out of the Tesla and crossed the road directly opposite them in several ground-eating strides. Jolene scrambled out of her seat, and Ravinia did as well. They both turned to face him. *Rick*, Jolene had told her on the phone. Tall, muscular, with a fixed smile on his face that boded ill will. Uh oh. This did not look good. Ravinia braced herself.

"You're supposed to be with Tim and Carl," Jolene declared in a high voice.

"What the fuck are you doing, woman?" he demanded, circling the table like a panther. He lunged, trying to grab her.

She jerked back, just in time. "I told you I was going for a run!"

"Who's this?" He snapped his head in Ravinia's direction but didn't take his eyes off Jolene.

"A friend."

Now he did slide a glance Ravinia's way, his disbelief palpable. "Okay, *friend*, what's she been telling you?"

"All right! She's a private investigator!" Jolene cried suddenly. "She's going to nail your ass!" And then she bolted for the road.

Rick roared, a primal sound that brought the hairs on the back of Ravinia's neck to attention.

Rick was already racing after his wife. Ravinia hesitated for half a beat, deciding on the best course of action. She could chase after them both on foot, but they were heading to their cars. She bolted up the hill for her Camry, yanking her cell phone from her pocket, ready to call 911, if necessary.

As she reached her car, she saw that the woman with the dog was now standing beside the blue Escape. "What happened?" the woman asked, her expression worried and curious as she stared toward Mason Street.

Ravinia glanced behind her and saw Jolene was revving up her Mercedes SUV. Rick was reaching for the Tesla's door, jaw set, glaring at his wife.

Looked like Jolene was safe for the moment, so Ravinia eased her phone back into her pocket. "Marital problems," she said, unlocking her car.

The little dog jumped at the woman, its muddy paws leaving marks on her jeans. She absently petted its head but kept her gaze on Mason Street. "Oh, sweet Jesus!" She sucked in a breath, her hand flying to her chest. "She almost ran over him with her Outback."

What? Outback? Ravinia had opened her door but shot a glance at the woman. She then looked back at the street. The Tesla was islanded on the street. Both the silver Mercedes and silver Subaru Outback were gone. Rick was just dropping into the driver's seat. Ravinia didn't have the time or energy to explain to the woman that the wife was the one in the Mercedes, not the Outback.

Sliding behind the wheel of her Camry, she thought about that—a silver Outback. Hadn't she seen that car somewhere before? Or was she just imagining things? Either way, she had no time to think about it now.

She drove out of the park, cautiously turning onto Mason as she headed back to the main highway, all the while keeping an eye on the Tesla. Rick was sitting behind the wheel, but he wasn't moving. She half expected him to suddenly whip out behind her, but by the time she turned off Mason, he still hadn't pulled out. Good.

She called Jolene from her cell, but the woman didn't pick up. No surprise. Ravinia hadn't given Jolene her mobile number. "Jolene, it's Ravinia Rutledge," she said, leaving a message in the woman's voice mail. "Don't go home. Go somewhere safe. This is my cell number. Call me as soon as you can."

She clicked off. Nothing more to do until Jolene called her, *if* she called her. They'd never actually signed a contract.

Divorce cases.

Shaking off the heebie-jeebies as best she could, she aimed for I-5 south and Cottage Grove. She would call Jolene again in half an hour if she hadn't heard from her.

* * *

The goddess of opportunity occasionally smiled on Lucky, and today was one of those days.

She'd followed Ravinia to Laurelton and slid her vehicle into a parking spot on the street when she'd realized Ravinia was pulling into the park. Lucky had been debating what to do with her appearance. Sunglasses and lipstick had been her disguise outside Ravinia's apartment, but to get close to her now in Laurelton, she opted for the baseball cap, smashing it onto her head and hiding most of her hair.

Ravinia had walked down to the picnic tables, which were directly opposite her car, so Lucky had merely rolled down her window to see what would happen next. Within minutes, a woman had come out of the gray building and joined her. Who was she? Did she have anything to do with Silas or Charlie?

Lucky had just about concluded that this woman wasn't connected to anyone associated with Siren Song and had been starting to wonder if Ravinia was the best conduit for her search for Charlie when a black Tesla had parallel-parked in front of her. She was pissed. She'd purposely left enough room between her Outback and the silver Mercedes to allow space for her to charge out of the spot if she needed to move fast.

But the Tesla squeezed right in.

Lucky had just switched on the ignition and started to reverse, to give herself some room, when this ape got out of the Tesla and marched across the street and into the park. He accosted the woman meeting Ravinia. He'd grabbed at her, and she'd stumbled backward. Then the woman had made a mad dash, running wildly for the Mercedes. He'd chased her down, but at a slower, yet menacing pace.

He might kill her, Lucky thought.

At his car, he glared at the Mercedes the woman had jumped into. Then he glanced back at Ravinia, watching her hurry up the hill to her Camry through cold, snake eyes.

He will kill her, she concluded. "Hey, asshole," Lucky called softly, just loud enough for him to hear.

His head swiveled her way.

"Yeah, you."

Her hand crept across the seat to her pack of syringes. Only a few left. She shouldn't waste them. But would this really be a waste? Her fingers curled around the hypo.

He stalked to her open window, sticking his head inside. "Fuck you want, bitch?" he snarled.

Her gaze held his. "Just this." Quick as lightning, she struck, plunging the needle deep into his neck and thumbing the plunger, shooting poison deep into his throat.

"Wha—" He jerked upward in surprise, his head banging the window frame. His eyes were wide, his mouth open. For a second, he looked as if he might try to pull her from the car. His hands lifted, then fell. "What'd you do?" he asked, stumbling backward.

She had to bump the car behind her, wrenching the steering wheel. She hit the accelerator and clipped the Tesla's rear end as she tore out of the spot. He managed to just stagger out of the way before she flattened him as well. As she was driving in the opposite direction from the main road, she had to whip into a narrow drive to get turned around. She then drove back the way she'd come, just in time to sight the tail end of Ravinia's car turn off Mason and onto the main highway.

Lucky punched it, her Outback speeding forward. The asshole had apparently somehow grappled his way back into his vehicle. And there he sat. As Lucky drove by, she saw that he was slack-jawed and stupefied.

That's two, she thought with satisfaction, following a good distance behind the Camry. She'd thought she was the kind of person who unconsciously drew thugs, scums, and murderers her way, but Ravinia took the cake, racking them up at the rate of at least one a day.

Lucky was beginning to really like her.

Sunday afternoon.

Nev normally liked the peace and quiet and general nothingness he had to do on Sundays, but today he was a caged lion, pacing back and forth across the room. The television was on, tuned to a golf match that didn't interest him, and he took a look out the window, noting that the rain had eased a bit, the day still dark, the clouds still threatening. There was little to do while he waited for the autopsy and more lab results on Silas Rutledge and Stanford Norman, both scheduled for tomorrow. He'd talked with Lang again this morning and told him what John Mills had said about the Smuggler's Den's bartender. Lang had informed him that Savannah had delivered her baby and had named her Annabel. That, at least, was some good news on this bleak day.

He thought about driving up to Seaside and checking out the Smuggler's Den himself, but it was still a crime scene, and he was up to date there as well. Mills would tell him of any future developments.

He wondered if the historical society was open. He could look at *A Short History of the Colony.*

Or he could go to Seagull Pointe and interview the author, Herman Smythe, in person, assuming the older man was still alive.

Or he could go to the Foothillers' community and see if he could find Earl.

Or . . . he could drive to Portland and find Ravinia and . . .

What?

Ask her on a date? Pretend he was just in the area? Find a way to end up in bed with her?

He raked his hands through his hair and laughed at himself.

Oh, sure, Rhodes. That's how it works.

Growling under his breath, he grabbed his keys from the coffee table where he'd dropped them and headed for his truck. He wasn't sure where he was going, but he was going to do something.

"Ms. Rutledge?" the tear-filled voice asked. Jolene Fursberg's name had appeared on the screen of Ravinia's cell phone, and she'd accepted the call as she drove steadily south on I-5.

"Jolene. Hi. I'm driving. Are you okay? Where are you?" Ravinia glanced down at her phone, which was sitting in her cupholder.

"I'm at a friend's, but I have to go home. I just have to."

"I don't think that's a good idea."

"Listen, Rick, he's never been this scary before," she said, sniffing. "I think he just lost it for a minute. But I love him . . ."

Oh. God. "Don't go home. It's not safe," Ravinia warned her. "Call him, if you must, but stay away."

"I've tried calling him. He won't answer." More sniffling through the speakers of the car.

"If you go home, he could be waiting for you. Don't do it."

"You don't understand," she said, stronger. "I'm not paying you. I don't even know why I called you."

"Just don't go home, Jolene."

"Mind your own business," she snapped, then clicked off.

Well.

She thought about it for about five seconds, then phoned Detective Rhodes.

"Ravinia?" he answered, sounding surprised.

"Hi . . . Rhodes."

She was surprised how much it warmed her heart to hear his voice. At that moment, she realized she'd never tried to see into either Jolene's or Rick's heart. Then again, she hadn't really gotten a chance before all hell broke loose.

"What's up?" he asked.

"Well, this incident happened," she said, then proceeded to explain about the string of events at Laurelton Park, giving him the makes and models of the Fursbergs' cars and Jolene's cell number. "I know it's not your jurisdiction, but I don't know anyone with the Laurelton police, and I wasn't sure they'd listen to me. I warned her not to go home, but I think she will anyway."

"And you think she's in danger."

"Yes." Ravinia didn't hesitate.

Rhodes said, "I'll inform the Laurelton police."

She could picture him making a note, his hair falling over his forehead, his eyes dark with concern. "Good. Thanks."

"Where are you now?" he asked.

"I'm driving south on I-5 . . ." Should she tell him what her plans were? She'd asked for his help but hadn't been completely forthright about hopefully checking with Silas's and Charlie's adoptive parents. Instinct told her to keep those plans to herself . . . instinct, or years of training from Aunt Catherine.

"Are you coming back to Deception Bay?" he asked, though they both knew the freeway was far from the coast.

"That's the plan. Maybe tomorrow? I've got some things to do first, but I need to see my sisters and check in." That sounded lame, but it was the truth, she thought, as she passed a slow-moving minivan covered in bumper stickers.

"Call me. We should have information on your brother's lab work and autopsy by then."

"I'll do that."

"Okay."

They both hung on the phone a few seconds longer than necessary. Feeling weird, Ravinia said abruptly, "Talk to you tomorrow," and hung up. What was it about that man? She kept wanting to contact him, and she wasn't even sure she liked him.

Liar.

Okay, she liked him . . . a little, she admitted to herself as she noticed the sun breaking through the clouds.

He just wants information from you.

Well, okay, sure. That's what she wanted from him too.

Shaking her head at herself, she pressed her toe to the accelerator, pushing the speed limit, needing to get her tasks done ASAP so she could return to Deception Bay.

CHAPTER 18

Tires bumping over potholes, Nev drove his truck along the narrow road that ran by Siren Song on his way to the Foothillers' community. He'd done as Ravinia requested and called the Laurelton police, who'd taken down Jolene Fursberg's name and number and promised to check on her. Then, with time inching by, he'd gotten into his truck and taken off, needing to push forward on the investigation, or at least feel like he was. Sunday or not. Sitting around and waiting until tomorrow for further answers from the lab wasn't cutting it.

A bulldozer was working to the north of the Foothillers' community, digging up what had been an open field between the Foothillers and a house on the edge of the clearing that separated the community from the surrounding area, a house that had once belonged to a woman, long dead, who'd been labeled a witch.

"A lot of that going around out here," he muttered to himself.

He passed the gates to Siren Song and gave the closed gates and the lodge beyond a long look as he drove by. Since finding the body on the beach and meeting Ravinia, he definitely had more interest in the woo-woo elements surrounding the Colony women than he'd had a few days earlier, though he still didn't believe most of it. Maybe Ravinia's relatives were more perceptive than most people. He'd give them that. And maybe there was really something to all the lore surrounding them. He'd certainly felt something from Ravinia . . . possibly. Or it could be that he'd just imagined that sudden flash of heat to his heart.

He reached the Foothhillers' community, which was laid out in uneven blocks surrounded by newly blacktopped streets. Most of the houses had been 1950s ramblers, though a number of them had been modified and added onto; second stories were now a common sight. He drove to Earl and Rand Tillicum's place. Father and son still lived together in a home in its original condition. Rand's mother had left when he was young. Now Rand and Earl worked together, and neither seemed eager to change his lifestyle.

Nev parked near the front of the house, then strode up the gravel walk to the wooden steps that led to the front door. He knocked loudly and waited, then knocked again, but there was no answer. He hadn't really expected there to be, since Rand hadn't returned any of his calls. He'd hoped Earl might be home on a Sunday, but if he was, he wasn't answering the door.

"Great." Nev glanced around the yard and drive, noticed no vehicles, and decided he was out of luck. He gave up, then drove to the Foothillers' general store, where he parked his truck beside a scattering of other trucks, motorcycles, and SUVs, all of which were parked nose-in to an old-fashioned hitching post, which was part of the establishment's overall western decor.

The store had been around as long as Nev could remember, though it currently looked as if it had recently seen an overhaul of new paint and siding, along with a few new, light-colored patches on the composition roof. Nev had been to the store more times than he could count with Rand, but this time he was on his own. It was probably just as well, really, as Rand had already expressed how he felt about Nev engaging his father for another attempt to reach Echo Island.

He stepped inside.

The front of the general store was a mercantile space, with everything from groceries to dry goods to animal feed supply. Nev walked through it, garnering a few glances from the employees, who were used to only seeing their neighbors and friends. Though he was in jeans, sneakers, and a navy windbreaker, basic Oregon beach garb, he wasn't a regular, and most folks who did know him also knew he was a cop. That fact tended to make some of them skittish.

He passed through the café at the back of the mercantile section and into the bar at the far end of the store. The mirror behind the oak bar was currently adorned with orange, green, and yellow decorative lights in the shape of jalapeño peppers. Several older men in Stetsons were either standing at the bar, one foot on the brass rail, or seated on scarred wooden chairs and overturned barrels, a tableau straight out of a western movie. Of the men grouped at one table, a trio of Native American faces turned his way and regarded him with careful consideration. One of the men tipped his hat back and said, "You're that friend of Rand's."

"That's right." Nev was glad he remembered.

"Where's Rand?" a second one asked.

"I'm not sure. I'm actually looking for Earl."

"Earl." The first man frowned.

"Rand's father," explained Nev.

"I know who Earl is," he said patiently. "What d'ya want him for? You know where he lives?"

"I just went by there. No one answered."

The third man lifted a bottle of beer, murmuring just before it reached his lips, "Mebbe he doesn't wanna see you."

"What d'ya want him for?" the first man asked again. He took off his hat and ran his hand through his stiff, gray hair.

"I'm trying to get out to Echo."

All three of them regarded him silently for a moment, and the first man turned his hat around in his fingers a few times. He finally asked, "You still police?"

"That's right. With the Sheriff's Department."

"Can ya get those thievin' rats away from our town?" the third one questioned, hooking a thumb in the direction of the adjacent field with the construction equipment.

"That's where Rand is. With the lawyers." The second man also took off his hat. His hair was still black, currently marked with a hat ring, and his face was less weathered than those of his two friends. He wore jeans, a jean jacket, and cowboy boots. "Tryin' to get them to stop tryin' to gentree-fy us," he said, purposely drawing out the word.

They all made sounds of disparagement, as a fourth guy showed up and kicked out a chair. Red-haired and bearded, wearing black motorcycle leathers, he sat down. "Am I missin' somethin'?"

"Nah, Jim. Just talkin' to a friend of Rand's," the first man answered, then to Nev. "We'll make sure Earl knows you stopped by."

Nev nodded. "Appreciate it."

"Ain't you the one whose friends got killed tryin' to get out there?" The third man's dark eyes glittered. Nev nodded again, and he added, as if Nev were a little dense, "It's just a piece o'rock."

"Billy's right," the first man said. "Why do'ya want to go there?"

"Follow up, I guess," said Nev honestly. He explained briefly about the body found on the beach, keeping Silas's name to himself until the department was ready to release it to the public. "Maybe I'll learn something about what happened to him."

"You wanna beer?" Billy asked.

"Thanks, but I've got another stop."

"Siren Song?"

"They let men in there now?" Nev countered.

All three of them broke into smiles. "Nobody but Earl," said the first man, who then reached out to shake Nev's hand and introduced himself as Frank Ames. The second man followed suit, saying he was called Martin. They'd heard about Stanford Norman's death and asked him more particulars about the case, but Nev told them the same thing he'd said to Ravinia, that they were waiting for lab results.

After some more conversation, Frank said, "Like I said, let Earl know you're looking for him."

Nev thanked them and headed for home. At the last minute, he swerved into the parking lot of the Deception Bay Historical Society, wondering if it was open on Sunday. He got out of his car, looking at the sky. The sun was playing tag with some fast-moving clouds, better weather than they'd had, at least for the moment.

He headed up the wide steps of the white clapboard building and peered inside. He couldn't see anyone. He checked that the front door was locked, and it was. There was a BE BACK SOON notice on the door, which said they would be gone until three.

Checking the time on his phone, he saw he had about an hour to kill, so he got back into his truck and headed for Seagull Pointe and Herman Smythe, the author of *A Short History of the Colony*. If the man was still alive, he'd likely still be at the assisted-living community. Nev figured he might as well go to the source.

Seagull Pointe was located on the north end of Deception Bay. Nev headed inside, and when he explained he was there to see Smythe, the receptionist told him how to find his room. "His daughter's with him," she added, as Nev turned toward the hall she'd indicated.

His daughter?

Nev walked down the corridor, stopping at the room with a white card in a slot on the door that read: MR. HERMAN SMYTHE. The door was slightly ajar, and Nev tapped on it lightly. A woman in her early forties answered. She was blond, blue-eyed, and statuesque, and her smile was careful. "Yes?"

"Hi, I'm Detective Rhodes with the Tillamook County Sheriff's Department. I was hoping to talk to Mr. Smythe about the Rutledge family who live at Siren Song Lodge. I work with Detective Stone and Detective Savannah St. Cloud." He flipped open his wallet, displaying his badge and I.D.

An elderly male voice quavered from within. "Who is it, Dinah?"

She opened the door wider. "Hi, I'm Dinah." She held out her hand and gave Nev a firm handshake. "I'm sure my father would like nothing more than to talk to you about his favorite subject."

Dinah looked a lot like the Siren Song women. Before he could ask, she smiled and shook her head. "I look like my mother, but I'm not related to any of them. Dad just went for a type."

"Come in, come in." Herman Smythe waved him forward as Nev stepped into the room.

He was seated in a wheelchair and peered at Nev from beneath bushy white brows. His hair was a white horseshoe atop a shiny pate. He wore dark gray pants and a tan shirt, coupled with a pair of bright green suspenders, and his feet were encased in thick-soled, black Nikes.

"Who are you?" he asked.

Nev repeated his introduction, a bit louder this time, right in front of the man.

"Take a seat." He indicated a folding chair that Dinah had obviously occupied before he entered. As he sat, he noticed the seat was still warm.

"I didn't mean to take your seat," he apologized.

"Don't worry about it. I was just leaving." She walked over to Herman, pointed a finger at him, and said sternly, "Do what the doctor says."

He tried to look past her, scooching one way and then the other to see Nev. "Go," he said, flapping a hand at her.

She turned to Nev, who was ready for an admonishment about not tiring the older man out, but she surprised him by saying, "Don't be afraid to just get up and leave when you're ready to go, or he'll keep you here forever."

"Okay." Nev grinned.

"I'm serious," she warned, then she ducked out the door, closing it softly behind her.

The older man lifted a shaggy brow, his eyes sparkling. "You want to hear about the ladies? That right?"

"That's right. I'm interested in background on the Siren Song clan, and I heard you wrote *A Short History of the Colony*."

"Have you read it?" he queried.

"Not yet. I stopped by the historical society just before I came here, but they're closed till three."

"So you decided to get it from the horse's mouth."

"Something like that." Nev said. "And if you don't mind, I'll need to record this."

Smythe waved a hand. "Go ahead. It's all in the book anyway. Go ahead. Record all ya want to." He leaned in closer as Nev set his phone to record the conversation. "Well," Smythe said, "whad'ya want to know? Who the girls' mother was? Mary Rutledge Beeman, or so she said when she was alive. But, you know, was she ever married to Richard Beeman?" He lifted his right hand and seesawed it back and forth. "Maybe yes, maybe no. Mary liked to make things up. And rightly, her name should have been Mary Durant, not Rutledge. Her mother, Grace, was married to Durant before she married John Rutledge, so Mary's *real* father was Thomas Durant. Catherine's was John Rutledge."

"Do you know all the girls' fathers?" Nev asked curiously.

"Oh, no. Nary a one, sir." He shook his head. "For all I know, some of those girls could be mine. Been meaning to get a DNA test. See if I match up." Again his eyes twinkled, and Nev couldn't tell if he was serious or just shining him on. "One of these days Catherine'll unlock the doors, and maybe then we'll all know."

"She's loosened up some."

"Don't believe it. She shut that door and threw away the key. But then Mary was something else in her day. Never knew another woman with such a sexual appetite."

Nev nodded. He'd been getting that impression.

Warmed up, Smythe got right down to talking about Siren Song, Mary, Catherine, and the revolving door of men Mary had taken as lovers. He repeated much of what Nev had already gleaned, but there were some new bits too. He said there'd been a bunkhouse behind Siren Song for many years, before Mary and Catherine were born, and, according to Smythe, the rough and rowdy crowd of men who lived there off and on over the years were most likely the girls' fathers. He rambled on and had a tendency to repeat himself, but Nev just let him go until suddenly he stopped himself and held up his right hand, lifting an index finger into the air. "It appears I lied about not knowing all the fathers. Mary had a boy with Preston St. Cloud," he said. "St. Cloud's gone, now, rest his soul, but he was married to Janet Bancroft until Mary got hold of him and turned up pregnant right after." He smiled a knowing grim. "She had a boy with St. Cloud. Named him Silas."

Nev stared at him. He'd just heard Silas's name for the first time from Ravinia recently. "You sure about that?"

"Why? Somebody say it's not true? I told that girl detective the same thing."

"Ravinia?"

"Who?" He frowned hard at Nev. "Thought you said you were from TCSD." He rubbed a hand over his grizzled jaw. "That red-headed one. That's the one I'm talking about."

"Oh, Detective Dunbar," he said, using Savannah's maiden name in order not to confuse Smythe.

"That's the one. I told her the same thing when she came to visit me. How's she doing? Someone said she married a Bancroft."

Well, so much for trying to keep things simple. Herman Smythe was still damn sharp. "She married Hale St. Cloud, Janet Bancroft's son with Preston St. Cloud." Which would mean that Silas Rutledge was Hale St. Cloud's half brother, if Smythe was to be believed, Nev realized. Could this community be more incestuous?

"Ah, Janet," said Smythe on a long-suffering sigh. He rubbed his nose and looked up at Nev from the tops of his eyes. "I thought that woman was gonna kill Mary after St. Cloud warmed her bed." Smythe chuckled at the thought of it. "Janet divorced St. Cloud quicker than you can say lickety-split. Bad blood between those two women for years. They hated each other since school days."

"You know for a fact that Silas was Mary Rutledge's and Preston St. Cloud's son?"

"Well . . ." He shrugged. "Timing's right. I was kicked out by then. Mary didn't like her lovers sticking around, and she'd slowed down some by then too. She died soon after that boy's birth, I believe. Umm, no, wasn't there another . . . ?" He rubbed his jaw and bent his head in thought.

"Henry Charles Woodworth," said Nev. Smythe either didn't know, or had forgotten, Charlie's murderous rampage along the coast five years earlier.

"Another boy? She had mostly girls, but then at the end, two boys . . . ? There was that last girl."

"Ravinia?"

"Ah, yes. There was a Virginia, wasn't there?"

Before Nev could correct him, he jumped back to talking about Mary and her many lovers again, so Nev listened with half an ear, as he was repeating himself once more. His attention was grabbed again when Smythe added, ". . . –therine burned the bunkhouse down to get rid of 'em. They were supposed to be working the grounds, but they were there for Mary and—"

"Did you say *Catherine* burned the bunkhouse down?" interrupted Nev.

"—that's how she got them to leave," he finished. He then fixed Nev with a bright, birdlike look and responded, "Yes, sir. That's what I said. Now, there's no proof, so don't be thinking you're going to go after her. Catherine'll deny it anyway. We just all know it's true."

"How?"

"Well, it only makes sense now, doesn't it?" Smythe queried.

"So no evidence."

"None that I know of."

"Was anyone injured in the fire?"

"Nah. Never heard that."

Nev tried to turn the conversation to focus on the girls, now women, who were still living at Siren Song, but Smythe didn't have much to say about them, so he thanked Smythe for talking with him, then took his leave. He thought about Catherine Rutledge as he drove south and was just passing Siren Song again, glancing up at the lodge roof and windows crowning the high hedges surrounding the property, when his cell phone rang.

He checked the number but didn't recognize it. "Rhodes," he answered.

"Earl Tillicum here."

Even driving, Nev straightened in his seat. Rand's father was a man of few words, with a stoic demeanor and an expressionless face. He didn't waste time with small talk, or any talk, for that matter, most of the time.

"Hi, Mr. Tillicum."

"Earl," he responded. "Heard you want to go to Echo."

Nev tried to read his tone but found it impossible. "That's right. Rand said it might be too late in the year, but I was hoping you would be interested in taking me there."

"Today?"

"Well . . ."

Today?

Nev glanced at the time. Nearly four. He had a sudden sick feeling in his gut. It had been late afternoon, getting toward evening, the last time he'd rowed to the island.

Swallowing, he said, "Today would work."

"Weather's good," Earl said. "I'm at the marina now."

Already? "I can be there in fifteen minutes."

"Good. I'll be waiting." And he hung up.

Nev drew a breath and exhaled.

The marina Earl meant was really just a bare-bones boat-launching area, but it was the closest one to the island. If he and Earl were really ready to go—and it looked like they were—they would have to row out around the point that took them to the private beach where Silas Rutledge's body had washed up, while fighting the crosscurrents that sought to throw watercraft off course, slamming them into the rocks and cliffs.

Yet it was still the best option.

Nev didn't have time to go home and change, even though his jeans and windbreaker would be more hindrance than help if he got thrown into the water again.

The marina was coming up on his right.

He was nuts to go to Echo. He thought about calling Earl back. He needed more time. He thought too of calling Lang and saying . . . what? That he'd changed his mind? That they didn't need to go to Echo? Nev had been the one pushing the idea. Now he wondered what the hell he'd been thinking. Who knew if there was anything on the island to do with Silas's death anyway.

Still . . .

He turned onto the broken tarmac that led to the wharf and the smattering of small craft bobbing on the water beneath patchy blue skies. As he parked, he saw Earl already stepping into a rowboat, a large rucksack over his shoulder that he heaved into the aft.

Okay, then. He was going.

A shiver slipped down his spine as he walked to meet Earl. The ghosts of his friends whispering in his ear.

The Blaveks' home in Cottage Grove was a small, white bungalow, in an established neighborhood, the street lined with maple trees. The grounds were immaculately groomed, boxwood hedge lining the front walk. Ravinia pulled up in front and admired the trimmed yard and inviting front porch with an actual porch swing. When she walked up the steps, she heard music from inside and recognized a popular song from the eighties. Someone was barbecuing, the scent of charred beef or pork wafting to her nostrils. When she pushed the doorbell, a trill of notes rang through the house.

It took a while, but a woman in her sixties came to the door, wearing a KISS THE COOK apron in red and white checks. Ravinia realized the Blaveks were the ones barbecuing, and belatedly she understood they had guests over.

"Hello?" the woman asked pleasantly.

"Hi. Are you Diane Blavek?"

Immediately, her expression grew cautious. "Yes."

A man ambled from the back of the house, looking over his wife's shoulder to see who was at the door. Behind the couple, Ravinia caught a glimpse of smoke from the barbecue floating past a side window and surmised they'd been on their back deck.

"I'm Ravinia Rutledge."

Their reaction was instantaneous. Their faces fell. They went from smilingly polite to shut down and nervous in the space of two seconds.

"Rutledge?" the man asked cautiously.

"Silas's sister . . ."

Ravinia wanted to kick herself. She suddenly realized that she was going to have to be the one to tell them that their son was dead. She should have given Rhodes the names and address of Silas's adoptive parents. She'd selfishly kept the information to herself, wanting to interview them without police interference, and now she was faced with a task better suited to the police. In her headlong way, she'd dismissed the fact that Silas was as much their family as hers. In fact, he was probably more theirs than hers, even though he'd tagged Ravinia as "next of kin."

Diane's hand had flown to her chest. Ravinia hadn't even thought to search her heart, and now it was too late, unless she wanted to cause them more pain and confusion, which she didn't. The man—she assumed he was Kurt Blavek—put a protective hand on his wife's shoulder.

"Has something happened?" he asked.

"Um, I'm sorry to tell you—"

"Oh, no . . ." moaned Diane, her eyes suddenly wet and blinking. "No, no, no!"

"—that Silas is dead." Ravinia felt tears well in her own eyes. The whole thing was crashing down on her in a way she hadn't anticipated. She *should've* anticipated it, but she hadn't.

Diane crumpled, taking a step backward into the cocoon of her husband's arms. "No," she whispered again as tears ran down her cheeks.

"How did he die?" Kurt demanded. "And why are we hearing this from you?"

"I'm sorry," Ravinia said again. "You can call the Tillamook County Sheriff's Department. Ask for Detective Neville Rhodes. It appears he may have drowned."

"He drowned?" Kurt asked in disbelief.

"The Sheriff's Department has all the information you need."

"Silas always said this would happen," whispered Diane, sniffing and dashing a hand to her eyes. "He knew he would die young."

"He said that?" asked Ravinia.

Diane nodded. "Oh, God."

"At some level, we've been expecting you," admitted Kurt. "You'd better come in."

He held the door open, and Ravinia slipped in ahead of him. "Your friends," she murmured, glancing toward the barbecue smoke outside the window.

"Don't worry. They're good friends of ours. They'll understand. They know about Silas," he said. To his wife, he added, "You okay?" as Diane sank into a seat at the dining table. "Yes . . . no . . . oh, of course not." But she nodded and waved him away, and he said, "I'll be right back," picking up a box of Kleenex from a side table and dropping it in front of his wife, before hurrying to the back of the house.

They know about Silas?

Diane plucked several tissues from the box, drew a breath, and seemed to get some kind of hold on herself. "Please take a chair." She pressed the tissue to her eyes for a moment before meeting Ravinia's gaze.

When Ravinia was seated, she said, "Silas told us when he left that he wouldn't be coming back. He said he had a job to do, and he knew it would be the last time he saw us. He was matter-of-fact about it. He . . . just knew himself from the time he was barely walking. He was like an adult in a child's body. We had him tested for autism and everything else. He said we would learn about his death from one of his sisters."

"He said that?" Ravinia asked again, her heart galumphing.

"You're Ravinia. I think he may have even mentioned your name."

"I don't see how. Honestly, I barely knew him."

"We lived with him for seventeen years and barely knew him," she said with a sad smile and again touched the corners of her eyes with her tissue.

"But you knew he was a Rutledge . . ."

"We learned later. It was a closed adoption. We weren't supposed to know where he came from. But he was such a different child that we did our best to find out anyway. Silas told us to stop. To leave his family alone. Insisted. But we couldn't. We learned the name Rut-

ledge and that your family lived on the coast, but that was about it
before he shut us down. He didn't want there to be any trace of contact between us and you. He made that very clear."

"Did he say why?"

"He wanted to keep you out of danger. You probably won't believe me, but he was . . . precognitive, in a way. He could see things
coming up that we couldn't. He had his whole life mapped out and
said he knew how it was all going to happen. And he was right . . ."
She pressed her knuckles to her mouth, but then shook her head at
herself. "When he left, he said it would be the last time he'd see us
and to not worry about him. We didn't believe him, but he just
walked away. Didn't take a phone. Didn't tell us how to reach him.
Just left. His last words were, 'Make a happy life for yourselves and
don't think about me.' We've managed the happy life part, but not
thinking about him? Impossible."

"Of course." Ravinia's thoughts were swirling. They didn't know
all the particulars about her and her sisters, and she didn't want to go
into everything. It wouldn't bring Silas back, and it wouldn't help.

"He had those silvery eyes," she went on, almost talking to herself. "Really unusual. It seemed like people were either afraid of him
or drawn to him. I know this is going to sound weird, but he was,
well . . . messiah-like. He was so young, but he seemed ancient in
ways."

Kurt reappeared. "The Castletons are leaving."

"Oh, no." Diane rose from her chair. "That's not what Silas would
have wanted."

"They feel that we might need some time," he started to explain,
but his wife cut him off.

"No. They need to stay." She turned to Ravinia, who'd also risen
from her chair.

"Stay and eat with us. Please," she invited. "The weather's supposed to change, but it's nice for the moment, so we sneaked this
barbecue in."

"Thank you, but I can't. I have somewhere I have to be. I just
wanted to meet you and learn a little bit about Silas." She felt bad
enough already to be the bearer of the news of his death, and though
she was hungry, she wouldn't be able to make small talk.

"We'll call the Sheriff's Department tomorrow," said Kurt.

"No need. We know he was killed by a demon," said Diane. "Like he said would happen."

Kurt said dryly, "I don't think drowning qualifies as a demon."

Ravinia had to work hard not to react. "He was washed up on the beach. It was probably a boating accident." There was no way she was going to say she believed Silas might have been prophetic.

"He was always a good student. He had his problems, but they never stopped him from doing what he wanted to do," said Diane.

Ravinia didn't ask, but the question must have shown on her face because Kurt said, "Sometimes he would be with you, but he really wasn't listening. It was coma-like, except he was walking around."

"He couldn't help it, Kurt," Diane broke in.

"I know, dear. I'm just explaining. Those 'comas' would sometimes last for days. We worried it was drugs, and when that wasn't true, it seemed like a psychological problem. But eventually it would pass, and he would come out of it."

"It got worse as he got older," admitted Diane.

"What about his remains?" asked Kurt.

"Uh, well, there's an autopsy scheduled . . ."

Diane made a squeak of protest, but then nodded vigorously. "Yes, okay."

"There's a graveyard at our lodge, and they're releasing the body to my aunt, I think. Silas's aunt."

"We don't have any say in this?" Diane questioned in a high voice.

"Well, I—"

"Let them," said her husband, then Kurt and Diane looked at each other for a long time. "It's what he would have wanted. You and I both know it." Eventually, lips trembling, she nodded. Then she cleared her throat and seemed to steel herself, her back straightening. "We . . . we need to get back to our friends."

"Yes, yes. Of course," Ravinia nodded, standing, knowing she'd learned all she could from these bereaved parents. "Maybe we should exchange numbers," suggested Ravinia, and Kurt and Diane complied, pausing in the doorway as they plugged her number into their phones and she did the same with theirs.

Two minutes later, she was saying her goodbyes and getting back in her Camry.

Though when she'd first arrived, they'd asked her to stay and join them for the barbecue, they hadn't tried all that hard to convince her when she initially refused, and now her stomach rumbled.

For the moment, she ignored it. She still had questions about her mysterious brother, but she sensed his parents had told her all they really knew about him, at least the important stuff. Any answers she still sought would have to be found elsewhere.

Maybe the Blaveks had further anecdotes to contribute about his growing up years, but they'd told her the core of who Silas had been, and that was enough. Silas had seen into his own future and followed the path laid out for him, regardless of the fact that he would die young.

Killed by a demon.

Ravinia thought about Charlie and felt cold as she pointed the nose of her car southwest toward Brookings.

The silver Outback, parked a block down the tree-lined street, waited until she was well on the road before slipping in behind her.

CHAPTER 19

Earl's strong, ropy arms rowed them toward the island. Beside the rucksack, in the bottom of the boat, were a cooler and tent poles and canvas. Nev had questioned what it was all for, recognizing even as he asked that it was insurance in case they were caught on the island and couldn't get back. Earl hadn't responded, just gestured Nev to get in, and they'd started out.

Halfway to the island and faced with some strong currents, Nev said, "Let me row." Though Earl certainly seemed capable, Nev was younger and, he suspected, stronger, though the older man was a seasoned veteran of the peculiarities that faced a trip by water to Echo.

"You'll take us back," Earl responded and kept at the oars.

The weather was changing. Nev could feel it, even though the breeze was still light, the skies still fairly clear.

"Storm's coming," said Earl, as if he'd read Nev's mind, which sent another dark chill racing down Nev's spine.

A half hour later, Earl guided the boat to what was left of the now broken-down and useless dock. He beached the boat on the rocky shore next to it, then leapt out with surprising spryness. Nev followed, and together they pulled the boat up farther onto the stony ground. "Gotta haul'er way up, otherwise she'll slip back," said Earl.

"Yeah."

Nev worked with Earl to bring the boat solidly onto dry land, farther than Nev would have done himself. He glanced to the skies again. Some darker clouds farther out. He checked his phone and saw there was no service on Echo. Not a surprise, but he would have liked to check the weather. He glanced at the older man. What did Earl know that he didn't? Nev planned to spend as little time as possible on the island.

Though Nev didn't ask for his help in his check of the island, Earl joined him on the trudge up the pebble-strewn hill to the house where Spencer had met with Mary Rutledge Beeman. Nev didn't know what he expected to see, but the burned-out shell and damp timbers were all that was left of what had once been a small cabin.

Earl stared long and hard at the remains. "Five years ago," he said, as if Nev had asked the question. "We'll camp here." He moved toward the one charred corner of wall still standing, examining the area critically.

Camp?

"Earl, we aren't camping here. I just want to check out the area. I think our John Doe was on the island."

"Storm's coming. We'll haul up our equipment."

"It seems pretty far off, still, doesn't it?" asked Nev.

Earl looked to the west, his granite face giving Nev no clue to what he was thinking. "We need to prepare."

Nev stared at him in disbelief. "You knew a storm was coming, and you still came out here?"

Earl turned his attention to Nev, his dark eyes assessing him in a way that made Nev wonder if he possessed some woo-woo, like the Siren Song women. Earl was shorter than Nev, with strong shoulders and a taut, muscular body that came from years of physical labor, but he was somewhat stooped, and it looked like he could use a few more pounds to keep up his stamina and strength. Not that he wasn't supremely capable.

"You needed to come," he answered simply, heading back to the boat.

Jesus, Mary, and Joseph. What the hell was he thinking? Nev helped him haul all the gear from the boat up to the sheltered spot Earl had indicated, all the while feeling like something was breathing down the back of his neck. He felt edgy, somewhere between angry and scared, and he had no intention of spending the night out here, if that was Earl's plan.

"Look, Earl, I appreciate you bringing me here. I'm here on unofficial reconnaissance for TCSD, but I have to get back today. Especially if there's a storm coming."

"Echo killed your friends. That's why you're here."

"Well, that's not true. It was an accident."

"You've been friends with Rand a long time. We know you need to heal."

Nev was nearly speechless. When he found his voice, he said, "Rand didn't want you to bring me."

Earl shrugged.

Nev tried another tack. "I have work in the morning."

"Work will wait."

"Seriously, Earl, I need to get back."

"What you need," Earl said firmly, "is to settle the past once and for all. Face down your fears."

"I have—"

"Have you?" Earl stared him down, determination etching his chiseled features.

Nev stared back as the wind kicked up, but he could tell there was no talking Earl Tillicum down. Like it or not, he was stuck out here on Echo with this recalcitrant man. Nev glanced to the western horizon, where storm clouds were gathering. "Fine," he said through teeth clenched tight. "How much time do you think we have?"

Earl nodded and again squinted toward the west, where storms rolled in off the Pacific. "Not much. You bring any warmer clothes?"

"Didn't have time." Nev heard the tension in his voice and took a deep breath.

"I have blankets and tarps." With that, Earl grabbed some of the tent poles and began erecting a shelter against the windbreak of charred timbers, and Nev, after a moment of internal reassessment about his current situation, bent down to help him.

Five hours. That's how long it took to drive from Silas's parents' barbecue to Brookings, Oregon, a small coastal town hugged up against the California border. Ravinia was dead tired by the time she arrived. Sleeping in this morning hadn't been enough after her restless night, broken up by Lillibeth's call.

She pulled into Brookings around ten PM, having had to give up

276 Lisa Jackson and Nancy Bush

her dream of barbecued ribs, planted in her head by her meeting at the Blaveks. Instead, she dined on beef jerky, potato chips, and bottled water from a 7-Eleven.

She filled her gas tank and used the facilities, as she had once along the way, then, using her GPS and their old address, went on her search of the Woodworths through the streets of Brookings. Of course, she could find no landline, but she had no cell number for them either.

As she scoped out the houses, she ripped off beef jerky with her teeth, chewing until her jaw ached, turning down the street to the Woodworths' address and slowing in the middle of the road in front of the address.

The house was completely dark. No lights. No one up watching television. An SUV went past her in the opposite direction, the only vehicle in this quiet area. Ravinia took her foot off the brake and edged the Camry forward, as all she would need is someone calling in a suspicious loiterer.

Was the Woodworths' house abandoned? She got that feeling for some reason. She parked and walked up to the front door anyway, knocking loudly. When no one answered, she tried again, and then searched for a doorbell in the dark. She could just make out the darker button on the wood siding, but when she pressed it, nothing happened, no dulcet chimes rang.

She grimaced, glanced around the overgrown yard partially illuminated by a streetlamp at the corner. Well, there was really nothing more to do tonight.

What a waste, she thought, returning to her car.

Sighing, Ravinia drove off in search of the motel she'd seen at the south end of town when she'd first driven into Brookings and checked out the town. The motel's VACANCY sign was splayed in orange neon script. She was glad there was a room available, and as she got out of her car and stretched, the wind, smelling of the sea, pressed her clothes against her back and legs and grabbed her blond hair out of its bun, its fingers whipping strands around her face and into her eyes.

Inside the office she checked in with a young man who could barely drag his eyes from the TV set on the counter to get her the key. Her room was only a few doors from the office, and when she let herself in, she smelled Lysol and only a slight whiff of mildew. Changing into her sleep shirt, she crawled beneath the covers, expecting to fall fast asleep, but that was not to be. Of all the things that had happened to her in a short period of time, her mind couldn't get the thought of the dream she'd had about Neville Rhodes out of her head. Annoyed, she buried her head beneath her pillow and tried to will herself to sleep. She also still felt emotional about Silas and the Blaveks, who'd clearly loved him. She wished she'd handled it differently. She wished she'd given more consideration to the adoptive family who'd raised him. She'd just arrogantly assumed that she, her sisters, and Catherine were his real family. She groaned beneath the pillow, engaging in mind-numbing self-flagellation until finally exhaustion took over.

Lucky drove past the Beach Time Inn, the basic motel where Ravinia had taken a room for the night. It had been tricky following after her all this way and remaining unnoticed. She'd had to get gas at the same station where Ravinia had stopped on the road over the mountains, and had hoped to simply stay in her own vehicle, letting the attendant help her without getting out of the car. But that proved impossible since she didn't own a credit card; she'd had to go inside the station, exposed beneath the fluorescent lights of the station's canopy, and pay with cash. She'd kept her head down and hoped Ravinia hadn't noticed the Outback. Fortunately, she'd driven to the other side of the second pump, and there had been a car between them.

Ravinia hadn't gotten out of her Camry, had seemed to be doing something on her phone, head bent over the little screen while she'd waited.

Baseball cap pulled down low over her eyes, Lucky had scooted around behind Ravinia's car.

Now she was hypervigilant. She knew she was pushing it. Ravinia already seemed somewhat alerted. Still, she'd made it this far, following her. She knew exactly who Ravinia had gone to see in Cottage Grove. Silas had told her about his adoptive parents, people he was fond of, but whom he'd never truly connected with. Lucky's own upbringing had been hellish, so, to a point, she understood how he felt. The difference was the Blaveks truly cared about Silas. Lucky hadn't been so, well . . . lucky.

She also had a pretty good idea who Ravinia was checking on now, as Silas had also told her he'd looked up Charlie's parents in Brookings. He'd never actually interviewed them, feeling like it was a dead end, so she was pretty sure Ravinia was going to be disappointed in that as well.

Now Lucky parked her Outback down the block and settled in for another night of sleeping in her car. Maybe following Ravinia was a wild-goose chase. Maybe she'd wasted valuable time in her search for Charlie. For the dozenth time, she asked herself why she'd felt Ravinia was the answer to finding him. He had to be closer to Deception Bay, because his mission was not only to lure women, and sometimes men, to him and kill them, but he also had been focused on the women of Siren Song. He was three hundred miles up the Oregon coastline—there, not here. She could almost feel it. She'd just thought Ravinia had some kind of inside track, some information Lucky was missing, but now she felt the girl knew far less than Lucky did herself.

But, in for a penny, in for a pound. She hugged her jacket close and looked up at the black sky. When it was late enough, she would cruise the area in a search for new license plates.

Nev sat on the cold tarp beside Earl, a blanket wrapped over his shoulders, back against what was left of the north wall of the house. A small piece of the west wall jutted perpendicular to the north one, so that he and Earl were in the only protected corner left. The wind was rising, serving up clenched fistfuls of rain and ocean water and throwing them against their makeshift tent's roof.

Nev had tried to reason some more with Earl, but the older man had been stoic and driven in his decision to stay on the island. Nev had suspected Earl's decision to take him to Echo had not been made on the spur of the moment. Maybe Billy or Frank or someone had called Earl and told him about Nev coming to the general store and asking about him, but Earl had to have already been ready to go. For some reason other than what he'd mentioned earlier, the older man had planned to bring him here. Nev had tried to initiate that conversation, but Earl had been silent, cocooned in his own blanket and staring straight ahead at the remains of what had once been the witch of Echo Island's house.

As if reading his thoughts now, Earl's voice suddenly sounded in the lull following a break in the wind. "You never met Rand's mother."

Nev slid him a look but could barely make out his features in the darkness. "No."

"She left when he was two. Said she couldn't bear it."

There was silence for a moment. Every fiber of Nev's being wanted to yell at him, but he pushed that down, recognizing that Earl was revealing something that might explain his motives. "Couldn't bear what?" he asked.

"That Rand might be one of us."

"One of . . . your tribe?" Of course Rand was one of them.

"Catherine's."

"Catherine's tribe? You mean the Colony?"

The older man stared straight ahead. "One of her ancestors was stolen from them and given to my grandfather."

"When you say stolen, you mean kidnapped?"

"Saved."

Well, that was one way of looking at it, Nev supposed. "You're talking about your grandmother, Rand's great-grandmother."

"She was a tortured soul. She had visions and would walk along the ridge across the road from Siren Song, above the beach." He nodded in the direction of the beach of the mainland where they'd found Silas. "Everyone thought she fell into the sea, but she was saved by my grandfather and kept safe with him. She died after my father was born."

Nev asked, "This has been a secret?"

"Catherine knows."

Nev thought, "Aha," but all he said was, "She's trusted you all these years because you're family."

There was a long beat of silence and then a shriek of wind that rattled the tarp over their heads. Nev thought about the bits and pieces he'd learned about the women of Siren Song over the years, most of it from Rand, until Silas's body had washed up on the beach and he'd started asking questions of his own. It was Rand who'd first told him about the crazy woman who'd lived on the island. Rand wasn't supposed to know about her. It was a secret, but he'd followed his father to the lodge on more than one occasion and had overheard them discussing the witch, and he knew that Earl, at Catherine's behest, rowed to Echo every so often and worked on the dock and house.

Nev thought back, remembering Earl when he was younger. His strength. His rare and slow smile. The handsome man he'd been.

A whisper of intuition suddenly slipped up his back. "You were one of Mary's lovers."

Earl's head snapped around, but he didn't deny it.

"Catherine doesn't know," said Nev.

He snorted. "Of course she knows. You don't keep secrets from Catherine."

"But you're friends with Catherine," Nev said, huddling against the wind and feeling salt spray upon his face. "How does that work? From what I know, she's not the forgiving sort."

"No, she's not." There was a hint of regret, and maybe admiration, in his tone. "When Mary called me to her I resisted . . . for a while . . ."

Nev waited. He knew pushing Earl wouldn't work. He was amazed he was even admitting to his liaison with Mary. When minutes went by and Earl stayed silent, Nev pressed carefully, "What happened?"

"Catherine wouldn't speak to me after."

From what he knew of Ravinia's aunt, Nev could imagine.

"But she came to understand I wasn't really willing. When she needed my help, I gave it to her." Nev could see his head turn in the darkness. "This house was already here, built by some of the bunkhouse men. We brought Mary to it, and Catherine let people think she died." He looked up at the tent roof. "The storms weren't as bad then."

Nev stared out at the whitecaps dancing on the black water. "Why did you really bring me here?"

"You needed to come."

"Well, yeah, but why camp out and ride out the storm?"

"Got too late to go back."

"Earl . . ."

"It's not your fault they're dead, son, and it's not the island's."

"I know that."

"Do you?" Earl's eyes were deep in dark sockets, only the whites visible.

Nev didn't answer for a moment, too surprised by Rand's father's sudden interest and loquaciousness. The man had hardly ever uttered more than five words in a row in Nev's hearing before, and now he suddenly was his what? Life coach?

"Yes," said Nev. "But the reason I came out to this island . . . okay, maybe it's to banish some ghosts . . . but I want to know if Silas was here, possibly in a fight with Charlie, who is his half brother."

"I know Charlie," he said tersely.

Nev stared at his darkened profile. Something about his tone . . . A twisted thought curled through his brain, one he could barely consider. One he had to ask, out here alone on the island. "Earl? Are you Charlie's father?"

"No." He was clear on that. "God, no."

"Are you Silas's?" Smythe had said Silas was Preston St. Cloud's son, but nothing was certain at this point, as far as Nev was concerned.

Earl ignored the question and said, "The man you call Charlie killed Silas. Here on Echo."

"How do you know that?" Nev demanded.

"They came to the island together. Silas came to kill him, but Declan Jr., Charlie, got the upper hand. They got back in the rowboat, still fighting, and the boat went down. Silas let the ocean take him to the beach, but Charlie is strong. He swam to the beach. He wanted to see Silas die and suck out his soul. That's what he does," Earl spat. "He steals souls, if he can. It adds to his strength, but Silas was stronger and denied him."

"How do you know this?" demanded Nev again. "Were you here? Did Charlie tell you that?"

Earl shook his head.

"Where is he?" Nev was angry. "You know where he is."

"He is nearby."

"*Where?*" Nev was on his feet. He had to bend over to stay beneath the tarp.

"I don't know where. I just feel it."

"You can't know what happened! Man, I'm tired of all this . . . stuff. How do you know?"

Earl hesitated under the force of Nev's frustration and anger. After a long moment, he finally admitted, "I'm only guessing."

"That's your answer? That was a pretty detailed guess."

Earl shrugged.

Nev stared at the older man then slowly sat back down, shaking his head. He didn't know whether he wanted to strangle Earl or break out in hysterical laughter. "Look, I'm searching for proof that Charlie was here and that he killed Silas. That's the main reason I'm here. I want to find Charlie and put him away for good."

"I know what you want."

"Well, of course you do," Nev muttered, irritated, cold, and stranded with this enigmatic man. "You know everything, or at least you *guess* you know."

To his surprise, he heard Earl chuckle. He'd never in his lifetime heard Earl chuckle, laugh, or even grin with amusement.

"What?" demanded Nev.

"It's just that my guesses are never wrong."

CHAPTER 20

The storm blew itself out by two AM, and Nev stepped out from under the tarp to look up at the stars, shimmering white dots flung against a slate-gray sky. The moon was a tiny crescent, offering little illumination, the wind now a light breeze.

It was strange to be on Echo Island, stranger still to be with Earl on an overnight. After half an hour of standing on what felt like the edge of the world, Nev went back to his blanket under the tarp, dozing a little, mostly awake and thinking about Spence and Duncan, for sure, but his thoughts had strayed to Ravinia.

Earl was up before the dawn.

Nev heard the older man stirring around and flung off his blanket as well. They both stood in the teeth-aching, brisk breeze sweeping off the ocean. The storm hadn't done damage, as the island was basically treeless, and the herb garden Earl had told him that Mary had kept behind the house was long gone. Echo was by all accounts just an inhospitable rock, and it probably hadn't been much more than that even when Mary had inhabited it.

Earl had his stocking cap on and was staring out to sea. He said, "You ready to row us back?"

Nev nodded. He embraced the idea of the exercise, as he wanted to work off some internal anxiety, but he'd half expected he might still have to argue the point even though Earl had agreed last night to cede control of the oars for the return trip. Earl seemed lost in his own thoughts, so Nev asked, "Something wrong?"

He shrugged.

"What is it?" asked Nev.

"Now would be a good time to look around and see what happened," Earl suggested, moving outside the footprint of the house to stand at the edge of the steep incline that led to the rocky shores of the island on all sides. "That's what you came here for, right? To investigate?"

"That's right."

Nev started with the remains of the house, looking for any shred of evidence that might support Earl's account of what had transpired between Silas and Charlie. There wasn't much to see. The weather over the last few days had undoubtedly erased most of any evidence that might be found. Dirt, stones, and small leaves and sticks from a few scraggly ground plants filled the nooks and crannies of the house's footprint and were tucked in corners in ragged clumps around the remains of the cabin's perimeter. Nev kicked at some of the debris, scattering pebbles down the face of the island, recalling Spence's slide down to the boat and his giddy proclamation.

. . . She wanted me to fuck her. Can you believe it? And, man, I really wanted to. She made me feel it! If only I'd had more time . . .

Nev looked over at Earl, who was still as death, his gaze fixed on the horizon. The older man had admitted to sleeping with Mary, but it was clear those were not happy thoughts. A far cry from Herman Smythe's fond and proud recounting of those wild days of his youth.

Nev said to him, "You know, about the story you spun?" When the older man didn't respond, he went on. "That's all well and good, but the police deal with evidence. Conjecture and guesses aren't going to cut it."

"You know the truth now. I gave it to you. What you do with it is up to you. Let me know when you're ready to go back."

Nev gazed at the man's back in exasperation. Everything surrounding the Colony was this vague "mystery wrapped in a riddle inside an enigma." He longed for a straightforward answer, like Ravinia had finally given him.

The light slowly turned from charcoal to pale gray. Nev thought about work and said, "We'd better get going soon. I have a job." There wasn't great reception on this area of the coast, and he'd checked his cell phone bars on Echo, and they were basically nil. He wouldn't be able to let anyone know that he was going to be late.

Earl started walking down the hill, and Nev automatically watched the older man's feet, worried he might slip on the pebble-strewn path. As he was looking, his eye caught on something pinkish peeking out from beneath a rock. He stepped toward it, reaching down, sliding it out from under the stone. Something smooth and rubbery. Once he'd extracted it, he turned it over in his hand.

Huh.

A prosthetic ear.

Lang hadn't left home for the station yet when he got the call from Trey Curtis. Curtis was one of his closest friends; he'd worked with him at the Portland PD, but he hadn't talked to him in a while. Whenever they got together, they would meet at a bar, and whoever saw the other one first would buy his friend a beer. Over the years, there had been a lot of good-natured arguing about who saw whom first, which amounted to more beer buying and drinking.

"Hey," Lang greeted Curtis, as he walked into the kitchen. Claire was running late, trying to get Bea ready for school, but Bea was taking her sweet time with breakfast, munching on peanut-butter toast, her legs swinging while watching her iPad.

Claire pointed to the clock and motioned that she was heading to work. Lang nodded and gave his wife a thumbs-up. He could get their daughter to school in time. Claire blew him a kiss, which he pretended to catch and slap on his butt. She half chuckled and shook her head, pushing through the door to the garage.

"Hey yourself, Stone," said Curtis. "Caught a homicide that's kind of interesting. Thought I'd better talk to you about it."

"Yeah?"

"That cult near you? The one with the dragon lady who's fighting you for custody of Bea and holds her nieces inside against their will?"

"I never called her a dragon lady. And they're not held against their will. Okay, maybe I did say dragon lady, but Catherine's just overprotective."

"Yeah, sure." Trey wasn't buying it. "You know that one of them's in Portland now, working as a PI?"

"Yes. Ravinia Rutledge."

Beatrice finished her peanut-butter toast and put her near-empty plate in the sink. "Brushing my teeth," she sang out as she sailed out of the room.

Curtis answered, "She trained with Bauer Investigations under J. D. Bauer. I've met the guy, a real pain-in-the-ass piece of work. Well, J. D. ended up dead last night in his office backyard. Apparent homicide. I've got people canvassing the area, talking to neighbors and asking what they might have seen or heard. Caught some on security cameras. And one of them, a Toyota Camry, is registered to her."

Lang made a sound of disbelief. "You're sure about that? Ravinia Rutledge?" He didn't know Ravinia well, but enough, he felt, to rule her out as a murderer. "She didn't kill him. She probably was just there going over some work or something. Maybe they had a client in common."

"You certain?"

"Not why she was there, but yeah, I'm sure she didn't kill Bauer."

But was he? He wasn't sure about anything to do with the Colony. The women of Siren Song held their secrets close. "Ravinia's not like that."

"You don't sound convinced."

"Call it an educated guess. I've met Ravinia. My partner, Savvy, ex-partner, now, maybe . . . knows Ravinia. I'm sure she'd vouch for her."

"Okay, but let me add this: The vic's wife is pointing the finger at Ravinia. Says she was there and saw her do it, which is a lie, because we know she was home the whole night. We talked to one of the neighbors, who swore the wife's car didn't move all night, and again, the camera footage backs the neighbor up."

"Any other unknown vehicles?"

"We're still running them down, but Ravinia's came right up. The way we figure it, J. D. likely met with her alone, which may or may not be important, except that, here's the kicker: there's no sign of a struggle, the body doesn't have any obvious wounds on it, but he died, that's for sure. His body was left in the backyard with his pants down and his dick hanging out, so that looks like a sex thing to me."

Lang went cold. "You're kidding." He thought of Stanford Norman lying faceup in the dunes. And Leonard Eby's dry observation: *"Pecker's out."*

"No, I am not, Stone."

"And he wasn't stabbed?"

"Nope. No signs of a struggle. That's what I said."

Lang asked, "What about a hypo?"

"What?"

"Were there any needle marks on the body?"

"He wasn't a user, if that's what you're getting at."

"Just check and see if he was poisoned, injected with a hypodermic needle."

"Body's in the morgue now. But we'll check, of course. Why? What do you know?"

"Just a hunch," Lang lied, not willing to get into it now. "Just let me know." He glanced at the clock just as Bea returned. As she zipped up her jacket, Lang motioned to her backpack, and she slid it off the back of a chair. "Okay, Curtis. I gotta go."

"Stone," he protested.

"I'm gonna call you back when I'm at the station. We need to compare notes."

"You *do* know something."

"Maybe. I'm taking my daughter to school. Call you back soon."

Ravinia woke up slowly. Light was creeping around the edges of the blackout curtains in her motel room. Her stomach growled, and she got up and scrubbed her face to wake up. She still felt groggy and unsettled, and she realized, picking through her memory, that she'd had another dream with Neville Rhodes at its center, and they had been in some kind of danger. Razor blades figured big in it. No . . . it was scalpels, she realized, heading for the shower to get rid of the cobwebs and face the day.

Fifteen minutes later, she was on the road and in a hunt for food. She found a McDonald's and ordered an Egg McMuffin and coffee, eating in the car as she drove back to the address for the Woodworths. By day, the place looked even worse. Deserted. Peeling paint, sagging roof, cracked driveway that in places had broken apart and practically turned to gravel. Nevertheless, she parked in front, wadded up the sack that had held her breakfast, and climbed out.

She picked her way up the heaving formation of broken concrete to the front door. She knocked loudly, several times, and waited.

Nothing. No footsteps hurrying to the door, no voice shouting for someone to answer it. The place was lifeless.

She glanced around the weed-choked yard, then walked back down the tortured concrete and decided maybe one of the neighbors might know something. The briny scent of the ocean greeted her as she headed to the adjacent property. Douglas firs lazily waved sweeping branches at her in a breeze that came in fits and starts, sending a ripple along her skin.

Someone's following me.

Her heart thumped, and she glanced around quickly. *Charlie?* She had an idea what he looked like from the drawing an artist had worked up five years earlier from Detective St. Cloud and her husband's descriptions, but would she know him now? If he came right up to her?

There were a few parked cars positioned in front of the houses, and she noticed a cat tiptoeing along the top of a fence separating two houses across the road.

But there was no person in sight.

No one moving.

No one watching.

Again, she eyed the house where Charlie had grown up again and told herself it wasn't an evil structure, that his spirit had long since moved away from the decrepit building with its dark windows.

Still looking over her shoulder, her nerves on edge, she set her jaw and made her way to the neighboring house, a small cottage with a neat yard, and rang the bell. It was early, but lights glowed in the windows. Ravinia wanted to catch the residents before they took off for work or school.

A woman came to the door, her face set in a deep frown. She opened the door a crack and peered out. She was in her late fifties, early sixties, Ravinia guessed. Her hair had a liberal dosing of gray, and her mouth was set in deep grooves of displeasure. She wore navy blue sweatpants and a pink and white sweatshirt in a floral design a couple of sizes too big. It swam across her slim shoulders, but she'd folded the sleeves up her arms to allow her hands to peek out. Before Ravinia could say anything, the woman announced, "I don't buy anything door to door, and don't give me any pamphlets. I got my own religion, and it's nobody's business but mine."

"I'm not here to sell or give you anything. I was wondering about the property next door?"

She glanced over toward the abandoned house, her expression sour. "He says he's going to sell it, you know, but he never does," she said.

"So, the Woodworths still own it."

"He does. She's dead. Killed herself." The woman's faded blue eyes glinted with the joy of delivering juicy gossip, and she opened the door wider. "Threw herself off a bridge. Woodworth didn't know what to do with the kid afterward. Told my Johnny, rest his soul, that he'd never wanted to adopt in the first place." She nodded to herself. "But Henry—that's the kid—he took off a few days after Ginny died, so that took care of that. Woodworth didn't have a son anymore. Poof. Just gone." She narrowed her gaze at the eyesore of the neighboring property. "You know, James always blamed the kid for the fire, but Ginny might've done it herself."

"The fire?" Ravinia said.

"A big one, shoulda burned down the whole place!"

"You said, 'James.' You're talking about James Woodworth," Ravinia clarified, and to the woman's brisk nod, "What fire?"

"Who are you, again?" the woman belatedly asked Ravinia, as if she'd finally realized she was spouting off gossip to a complete stranger.

"My name's Ravinia Rutledge. I'm a private investigator looking for Henry Woodworth." She fished in her purse and handed the woman her card.

"Oh, God, what's he done now?" She took a half step back into her house.

For a minute, Ravinia was afraid she was going to slam the door on her. "There's been some trouble. I shouldn't probably say exactly what. His family, Henry's biological family, is looking for him, and I've been hired to find him."

"What kind of trouble?" She eased back a little closer to Ravinia, her desire for gossip greater than her fear or revulsion.

"There's been a death." *Or two.*

"He killed someone," she breathed. "I knew it! You know, Ginny, James's wife, told her friend Patricia that she was scared of the kid. Her own boy. Can you believe that? Well, really, it makes sense. Between you and me, that boy was weird. Even when he was little." Clucking her tongue, she glanced down at the floorboards of the porch and shook her head.

290 Lisa Jackson and Nancy Bush

Ravinia asked again, "What fire?"

"Oh. Well. Ginny turned the cooktop burners on and filled the house with gas. She said it was a mistake, you know, but all four burners? Come on. Patricia thought Ginny was trying to kill herself, even then. Ginny was at her wit's end with that kid. Anyway, on the day of the fire, James came home and saved her but, in so doing, must've lit the burners somehow and *blam*! The kitchen went right up, and everybody got singed. I don't know all the ins and outs of it, but it set Henry's head on fire, somehow. He ended up getting the worst of it. Anyway, James put out the flames before they did serious damage, but the kid got even weirder after that. A real devil." Her eyes again strayed to the neighboring property. "They fixed up the house afterward—smoke damage, some fire damage, you know—but that's the last damn thing they did to it. Henry left a few days after it was fixed up, and Ginny took her swan dive off the bridge. I think James was relieved, not about Ginny, but that the kid was gone." She wrinkled her nose. "Tell you the truth, we all were, really." She hesitated just a beat then asked, "So who did Henry kill?"

My brother . . . my mother . . . Kristina St. Cloud . . .

"He's suspected in several homicides," said Ravinia.

"I can't believe you're a private investigator." She looked Ravinia up and down, and Ravinia could just imagine what she was thinking: this young woman, barely more than a girl, in jeans, a long-sleeved, black T-shirt, and a gray windbreaker, thinks she's a private investigator? Hah.

"So James doesn't live on the property any longer?"

She shook her head.

"Do you know where he moved?"

"Eastern Oregon somewhere, I think I heard. Or Central . . . maybe Bend?" She shrugged. "Patricia might know."

"Do you have Patricia's number?"

"It's in my cell." She gave Ravinia another considering look. "You might as well come in for a minute. I'm Carrie Lumpkin. Let's call Patricia together."

Ravinia followed her into the house, though the hairs on the back of her neck lifted, and the feeling that her every move was being observed didn't leave her. As Carrie closed the door behind her, she glanced once more down the street, but there was nothing out of the ordinary.

Once inside the living room, Carrie punched a number into the phone. "I'm going to call her. Make sure she doesn't mind me giving her number out," she said. Ravinia surmised that Carrie really didn't want to give her the number because she wanted to keep it for herself to hoard the information to be included in this new bit of excitement. "Patricia?" Carrie said, forcing a smile into her voice, her eyes meeting Ravinia's. "Hi. Good morning. It's Carrie Lumpkin. How are you doing?"

A moment passed, and Ravinia heard Patricia's muffled answer.

"Hey," Carrie said, "I'm going to put you on speaker, okay? So this girl . . . well, this private investigator is here? She wants to know about Woodworth, you know, Ginny's kid, Henry?"

There was immediate squawking, and Carrie touched the speaker button.

"—makes me sick, when I think of him," Patricia was saying heatedly. "He killed her. You know he did. I don't care if it looks like she did it herself. He's the reason she did."

"I know," Carrie said, commiserating.

"Wherever he is, I just want him to stay away from me," Patricia declared. "I don't want to stir anything up."

"She just wants to talk to James. Do you have his number?"

"No, but he lives in Salem."

"I thought he lived in Bend or thereabout, with that new wife of his."

"Rachel. Right. But they moved last March, I think. We get a Christmas card from James and Rachel, and if you give me a minute, I think I have the address."

"That would be great," Ravinia said, and then introduced herself to Patricia.

Ten minutes later, armed with James Woodworth's address and Carrie's and Patricia's phone numbers, should she need to talk to them again, Ravinia headed back to her Camry. She glanced at the abandoned house next door, thought of the fire that had broken out in the kitchen, and felt her skin prickle. Charlie and fire certainly had a relationship.

                              *   *   *

Lucky stood on the side of the abandoned house, hidden in the shadows. She suspected this was where Charlie had grown up and that Ravinia was canvassing the neighbors to gather information on him. Also, the girl was growing more and more aware of Lucky's presence. She had observed Ravinia glance around and look like she was consumed with the willies. It was time for Lucky to alter her plans.

She could go back to Silas's parents' home and talk to them herself, she supposed. Maybe learn what Ravinia had. Lucky just didn't see any reason to reveal herself to them. But she hadn't known about Charlie's adoptive family, and again, she couldn't really interview them without questions about who she was.

And that was a problem.

However, now Ravinia had background information that might help put them both on Charlie's tail, or maybe not. Maybe Charlie was far away by now. He wasn't someone Lucky had ever been near enough to get a hint of who he might be. All she knew was that he'd killed Silas, and though Silas had predicted his own death, Lucky wasn't willing to just let fate decide what happened to Charlie.

She was determined to kill him. And Ravinia was going to help her.

Lang walked rapidly through the back door of TCSD, barely giving May his customary high sign of "hello," causing her brows to lift as she watched him disappear down the short hall to the break room. "Where's Rhodes?" he asked no one in particular. May's nephew, Deputy DeShawn Wilson, walking the opposite direction, answered, "Not in yet."

"What the hell happened to him?" Lang muttered, punching Rhodes's number and waiting for the connection as he entered the break room and snagged a cup of coffee. The line rang on and on. It wasn't that Rhodes was late, yet, but Lang had already left the man two messages on his cell with no response.

The sheriff wasn't in yet, either, but O'Halloran generally showed up closer to nine.

Lang grimaced. He now had two deaths with a similar modus operandi. Before he called Curtis back with the information, he wanted to verify everything he knew for certain about Stanford Norman's death. Rhodes had done the legwork on the girl in pigtails who'd been seen running away from Norman's body. The lab work was coming in today, hopefully with a more definitive cause of death, but Lang wanted to at least discuss the homicides with Rhodes before he called Curtis back.

Back at his desk, he took a sip from his cup, sat in his chair, and punched in Rhodes's number again.

His call went straight to voice mail.

Savvy was dressed and ready to go. Baby Annabel was asleep on the bed, lying flat on her back, arms outstretched, in her little pink hat and the yellow zip-up sleep sack Savannah had purchased before she'd known the baby's sex.

The hospital hadn't kicked them out yesterday evening, like Hale had predicted, so Savannah had shooed him home against his wishes, but truthfully, she'd wanted a little time to herself with just the baby. He'd called early this morning and was now on his way.

"Hello," a female voice sounded from the other side of the open door.

Savvy wasn't sure she recognized it, and when the nurse walked into the room, she took a moment before she remembered one of the women who had grown up at Siren Song. "Ophelia, right?"

The blond nurse nodded. "I'm just coming to work, and I wanted to say congratulations before you left the hospital."

Ophelia was dressed in blue scrubs and was statuesque like her sister Isadora. They were the tallest of the Siren Song women and looked a lot alike—same length of blond hair, often pulled into a bun, like now, and similar blue eyes and same-shaped face. Isadora was the more serious of the two, possibly the more rigid. At least that was Savvy's impression the half dozen times she'd met all of them.

Ophelia gazed down at the baby. "She's beautiful."

Savvy couldn't help but smile. "I think so too. But, you know, I might be a little prejudiced."

"No. She really is."

"Thank you," said Savvy. "It's fun to have one of each, a girl and a boy. My son is five years old."

"Declan," Ophelia remarked.

"Yes. We can't seem to get away from that name, although now, with Hale's grandfather gone, our Declan is the only one left."

Ophelia nodded slowly. "Except for Declan Jr. . . . Charlie . . . but he's not really a junior or a Bancroft. My mother just named him that."

"Do you remember her?" asked Savvy.

"Not much. She was gone when Isadora and I were pretty young still."

Savvy stole a surreptitious glance to the clock. Hale would be appearing soon, but this was an unexpected golden opportunity to hopefully learn something about Charlie.

Before she could formulate a question, Ophelia said, "I spent last night at Siren Song. I have my own place now, but I wanted to talk to Catherine and see how Lillibeth was doing. She's . . . she's had some trouble sleeping—" She broke off and closed her eyes a moment, pressing her lips together, squinching up her face as if in pain.

"Is something wrong?" asked Savvy.

Ophelia ignored the question and asked, "Did Charlie contact you? That's what Isadora told me."

Savannah was surprised.

"She said that your partner came to the gates. Mr. Stone. Detective Stone," she corrected herself. "That he showed up and started asking questions."

"I believe Charlie . . . reached out to me."

"But you're not sure?"

"I'm not as sure as I was. My water broke, and everything happened kind of fast. I *think* Charlie contacted me. I don't want to be hysterical about this. Pregnancy brain on steroids, you know." She smiled, but Ophelia was regarding her with solemn eyes. "It's just that, that feeling . . . you never forget it."

"What's it like?"

"Ugh, well . . ." Savvy looked at Annabel, her perfect little features. She wanted to grab her and embrace her, hold her and never let go. "It creeps in and floods you. Overtakes you." She steeled herself to tell the full truth. "It almost feels good. Especially if you're thinking about someone you want to be with. And that's what works against the feeling too. I could think of Hale and keep Charlie out, but it took a lot of effort. It's really difficult to break whatever hold or spell or whatever it is."

"If you hadn't been in love with your husband, do you think you could have resisted?"

"No," admitted Savvy, and she saw some unnamed emotion flicker in the other woman's blue eyes. "Have you felt Charlie?" she asked, searching Ophelia's tight face.

"*No*," she stated emphatically and shook her head. "I just want my family to be prepared. You're the only one who's encountered him in person."

"Yeah, well." The thought of Charlie inside her head made her skin crawl.

Footsteps sounded in the hall, and Hale pushed into the room. "Oh, hi," he said to Ophelia.

"This is Ophelia Rutledge," Savvy introduced, seeing Hale do a double take on the nurse. It was impossible to miss the resemblance to her family.

"Ophelia Beeman," she corrected, shaking Hale's hand. "I believe my mother was married." She looked back at Savvy as she turned toward the door. "Thanks for talking with me."

"What was that about?" asked Hale, after she'd disappeared down the hall.

"I'm not sure." Savvy stared at the door as it whispered closed. "I'm worried Charlie's contacted her or something."

Hale had stepped closer to the bed and was gazing down at his daughter, his features softening. He touched the pad of his index finger to her open palm, and her tiny fingers encircled it. He looked up at Savannah, clearly enraptured.

They smiled at each other.

Hale straightened and turned his attention to Savannah. "You really think Charlie's back?"

"I don't know, but . . . yes," she admitted, hating the thought. "Yes, I think he is."

His expression darkened.

"It'll be okay," she said, not wanting him to worry.

"You think?"

"I hope."

He hesitated a second, then said, "You ready to go? I want to get home and make sure you're both safe inside with Declan and my mom."

"Safe with Janet?" she teased.

His mouth quirked, but he didn't really smile at Savannah's attempt at levity. Instead, he gathered up his daughter and tucked her into the baby carrier, and together they headed out of the hospital.

CHAPTER 21

"Not Ravinia," Nev stated determinedly into his cell as he drove to his house. He was running late after his night on Echo Island. As soon as he was back on the mainland, where he had cell service, he got through to Lang.

"Just get here, okay?" said Lang before he hung up.

Nev clicked off and dropped his phone into the console. He needed to shower and change before work. He'd barely had time to explain about Echo and no cell service, before Lang cut him off and told him about the apparent homicide of Ravinia's old boss, J. D. Bauer. When Lang added further that Ravinia had been at the scene of the crime mere hours earlier, Nev had reacted strongly, defending her. Too strongly, since he knew next to nothing about what had occurred. But he didn't believe for a moment that Ravinia was involved in a homicide.

He jerked the truck to a stop in his drive and half-walked, half-ran inside, where he raced through a shower, threw on clean clothes, and tucked the prosthetic ear into a ziplock bag. He hadn't even had a chance to mention the ear to Lang, he realized, as he jogged back to his truck and took off again.

At the station, he found Lang on the phone, pacing. Lang pointed Nev to the screen of his own computer and mouthed, "Lab work."

Nev immediately went to his own monitor, without going to the break room or taking off his coat. He put the ziplock bag down on his desk and shrugged out of his jacket, tossing it over the back of his chair, listening to Lang's side of the phone conversation.

"We put out that BOLO everywhere. Portland, Gresham, Laurelton. The whole state, the whole country. She can't have just appeared in the last few days. She's had to have killed before." Lang listened to whoever was on the other end of the call talking about the Be On the Look Out. For whom? His muscles tensed, and he couldn't believe it. Nev guessed the other party was Sheriff O'Halloran, and Lang was reporting what he'd already done. Nev logged in.

"Yeah, I think she killed all three of them," Lang was saying. A pause, then, "Ravinia Rutledge, or possibly Ravinia Beeman. Put both names out there."

Nev's head jerked up. Lang was looking at him. He could feel himself rise to Ravinia's defense again, and for a long second, his eyes held his partner's. This was not what should be happening. He had to clamp down his emotions to keep from saying something.

Jaw clenched, he forced his gaze back to his computer screen.

The lab work on the two bodies was extensive, but still preliminary.

In the report on Stanford Norman, it was noted that Norman had been given some kind of tranquilizer. Not meant to kill, apparently, but the utility knife found at the scene had taken care of that, several wounds hitting arteries, primarily the carotid, which was nicked when Norman had been stabbed in the neck.

Unfortunately, no fingerprints had been found at the scene, but the lab had been able to extract some DNA from the hypodermic needle. Now the question was, could it be matched?

As for the report on Silas Rutledge, the surprise was that he'd been administered some kind of toxin, yet to be determined, something less benign than the tranquilizer in Norman's system. A needle mark had been discovered under his arm during the autopsy.

So he too had been injected by means of a hypodermic.

The contusions on his neck were possibly from attempted strangulation, but the real question was what he'd been given. The full autopsy report was still pending.

Nev read the reports twice, all the while believing Ravinia wasn't involved. Not in the homicides. Somehow she was connected, yes, but she wasn't a killer. He would trace her whereabouts at the time of the killings and prove it.

Lang clicked off, all energy. "We're working in conjunction with Portland PD."

"It's not Ravinia."

"I don't like thinking it is, either, but we need to talk to her. I was waiting for you. Figured you were the best person to call her." He eyed Nev's cell resting on his desk.

Nev picked up his phone, realizing Lang meant right now.

Lang's gaze strayed to the ziplock bag. "What's that?"

"A prosthetic ear. I found it on Echo."

"What?"

Before punching in Ravinia's number, Nev explained further about his trip with Earl and discovering the ear before he rowed them back to shore and safety.

"Whose ear is it?" mused Lang. He picked up the bag and stared through the clear plastic.

"It's not Silas Rutledge's, but maybe it's Charlie's?"

"His face was burned in that fire when Savannah was nearly killed." He stared out the window, thinking. "Maybe Charlie did go to Echo. Maybe so did Silas."

"That's my guess," said Nev. He realized he'd missed a call that had come in earlier this morning, probably while he was in the shower. There was a voice mail, and he saw it was from the Laurelton Police Department.

Lang said, "You said Earl Tillicum is Silas's biological father? I thought it was established that Preston St. Cloud was his father."

"Earl didn't answer me when I asked, but he didn't deny it either. I got the feeling he is. It seemed like it," said Nev. "DNA should tell us."

"Call Ravinia," Lang said again, running fingers around his collar as he thought.

Nev suspected the message from Laurelton PD had something to do with the call he'd put in to Laurelton to be on the lookout for Jolene Fursberg's rampaging husband, per Ravinia's request.

Lang was waiting impatiently, so Nev punched in Ravinia's number.

Ravinia's Bluetooth answered as a phone call came through, interrupting the Camry's radio as she drove east from Brookings. She saw Nev's number come up on the screen. "Hi, Rhodes," she answered. Maybe this was the time to tell him what she was doing in regard to her search for what had happened to Silas and Charlie. She still didn't know if Charlie was alive or dead, but as she'd progressed with her investigation, gaining information, she had started to wonder why it should be such a secret. Yes, she had her own instincts to keep things hidden. Probably from years of being under Aunt Catherine's protection. Also, more than once, she'd had her investigations damn near usurped by the police. Still, she couldn't see any reason not to tell Rhodes at least something.

Are you just making excuses about this particular cop?

"Hi, Ravinia. Sounds like you're driving."

"I am. Hands free." She squinted at the phone. He sounded awfully stiff. Her fault, probably, when they'd met last week, but she thought they'd gotten past that a bit. "Something wrong?"

"Are you still in Portland, or are you coming back to Deception Bay?"

"Well, I'm on the road between appointments," she said. Maybe it actually wasn't the time to tell all. He sounded so . . . tense. "What do you need?"

"Doesn't sound like you've seen the news. There's been a homicide in Portland. A man named J. D. Bauer was killed in the backyard of his office the night before last."

"*What?* J. D. Bauer? My—my old boss?" Ravinia swerved a bit and had to ignore the spurt of fear and shock that swept through her.

"One and the same."

"But . . . How? Where? His *office*, you said?"

"In the yard behind it."

"Oh, shit. Oh, my God." Her heart was pounding erratically, her hands clenched around the wheel. "I just saw him. I was just there! Wait. Wait. Are you sure? J. D. Bauer. In Portland?"

"That's right. You were there?"

"The night before last. He called me to his office to . . ." She trailed off. J. D. was dead? She was about to turn onto the freeway and head north. Maybe she should pull over. "I can't believe it." She chased the confusion from her mind with an effort. "How was he killed?"

"Still being processed. No obvious damage to the body other than a needle mark to his neck. Possibly some kind of toxin."

"He was *poisoned*?"

"We only have the preliminary info. Lab work's coming through later. Why did he call you to his office?"

Ravinia took a moment before answering. J. D. had been killed not long after she was there. They'd had a fight. This wasn't going to look good. "He said he wanted to go over some discrepancies in my work that happened when I was employed by him. It wasn't quite true."

"How do you mean?"

She gritted her teeth. What good would it do to lie? She would be found out, somehow, and then it would be twice as bad. "He came on to me. I let him know how I felt about that, and I left. He was alive and really pissed off at me. I threw a glass of wine on him."

"Detective Curtis would like to interview you."

"Well, great, but I'm not there. I'm planning to come your way later today, so I won't be in Portland later, either."

"What time?"

"Am I getting to the beach? Later afternoon or evening. Why? You want me to come into TCSD?" She let him hear her cool tone.

"If it's later, we could meet somewhere."

He still was using his "cop" voice.

"Well, we'll see, won't we?"

"I'll be at the station till six," he said.

Ravinia drew a breath, then stated firmly, "I sure as hell didn't kill J. D., but don't get me wrong, he's an obnoxious prick, or he was. Has anyone talked to Adela, his wife? Maybe ask her what she was doing the night before last?"

"She's been interviewed," he said and offered no more insight. "Call me before you get here."

"Sure thing." She clicked off and felt her blood boil. Neville Rhodes was acting as officious and pigheaded as the rest of them. The police never listened to her. She'd been dismissed enough times to be totally pissed off at the authorities, in general, and now maybe Rhodes, in particular.

So much for trusting him.

Swearing to herself, she took the on ramp onto I-5, heading north to Salem.

* * *

"So you're meeting Ravinia at the station tonight?" asked Lang. He'd been waiting for Nev to finish his call with her.

"That's right."

"You want me to be here?"

"Not necessary. Ravinia didn't kill J. D. Bauer or Stanford Norman, or her brother, for that matter. She wants to find Charlie—Henry Charles Woodworth," said Nev somewhat heatedly.

"I know what he goes by." Lang regarded him seriously. "Look, she's very attractive. I get it. And I agree with you. I don't see how she killed Norman and Bauer, and it just doesn't seem like her to leave their dicks out, waving in the wind. But she's connected somehow."

Nev didn't answer.

"They haven't released that bit about the bodies to the public yet," reminded Lang.

"You don't have to worry about me. I'm not going to tell her how the bodies were arranged."

"You need to find out where she was, night before last."

"She admitted seeing Bauer, but left him alive."

"See if anyone can vouch for that, and we'll check the cameras again. Then find out where she was when Norman was killed. See if she's got an alibi."

"I will." He didn't like having Ravinia under the hot spotlight of both Portland PD and TCSD. "She's focused on finding Charlie. She thinks he killed Silas."

"Cain and Abel. Brother slaying brother," mused Lang. Then, "Well, Curtis wants to talk with her. Tell her that. And be careful. I'm on my way to the Norman autopsy."

Nev nodded. He was getting pretty tired of being warned about Ravinia Rutledge.

As soon as Lang left, Nev checked his voice mail. A woman's voice came on the line. "Hello, Detective Rhodes. This is Detective September Westerly from the Laurelton Police Department. You called in a warning about a Mr. Richard Fursberg. He did not harass his wife, but his body turned up in his car outside Laurelton Park this afternoon. He appears to have died behind the wheel. There was a puncture wound in his neck. Likely a needle mark from a hypodermic. No tracks on his body that were visible. Not a known drug user. Since there was no evidence of the hypodermic in the vehicle, we're treating this as a probable homicide, odd as it is. Call me. I'd like to talk over how you got your information. Thank you."

Jesus Christ! Another one?

A full-body flush heated him from head to foot. Ravinia had told him about Jolene Fursberg, but not that her husband had been administered a hypodermic.

Like J. D. Bauer.

Like Stanford Norman.

His head pounded. Was Ravinia the girl in pigtails?

No. It wasn't possible.

Maybe she didn't know about the hypodermic.

Nev replayed the message, wondering if and how all these "probable" homicides through injection were connected. And how Ravinia Rutledge figured in.

He didn't believe for a second that she was a stone-cold killer, but she sure had a way of being at the wrong place at the wrong time.

He thought of Ravinia, and his brain was flooded with images: her slanted, sea-green eyes, her dark blondish hair, the smooth curve of her jaw, the way those billowy pants caressed her hips and bottom . . .

He should call Lang, but he hesitated. He needed to think about it a while.

Damn it, Ravinia. What the hell have you gotten yourself into?

Ophelia took her lunch break alone. She drove her Pathfinder to the Drift In Market in Deception Bay and purchased a tuna fish sandwich on rye and a bottle of water. She took them back to the hospital parking lot, where she spread the waxed paper out on her lap and proceeded to eat her sandwich, not tasting a bite.

She stared out the windshield, barely noticing the clouds overhead, or the people going in and out the main doors, or the crow that cawed from one of the shore pines guarding the parking lot's perimeter.

She'd been dating Burke for over a month, off and on. He'd swept into her life and her bed so fast she'd been breathless with disbelief. Before him, she'd been dating a tech from the hospital named Brennan, and the relationship had been progressing slowly, but nicely, but as soon as Burke appeared, whammy. It was like she'd been hit by a ray gun, some extraterrestrial weapon that filled her with reckless desire.

She'd made love with Burke within hours of meeting him, minutes, really. She'd be embarrassed if it hadn't been so wonderful. When she'd heard those animalistic noises, she'd thought, *What is that?* before realizing they were issuing from her own lips.

She honestly didn't know what she thought of Burke, other than that he gave great sex. But . . . *but* . . . That great sex was turning into something else. Something not so wonderful. She'd been disappointed to realize she was losing some interest in Burke. She'd determined he should meet her family. She wasn't sure how that was going to happen, as both Aunt Catherine and Isadora forbade men past the gates, an antiquated idea that had driven Ophelia out of the lodge. Burke was hard to pin down too, however; now, thinking about it, Ophelia determined she really didn't want him on the other side of Siren Song's gates. As much as she'd railed against the walls, physical and mental, that kept the other world out, the thought of having Burke, or any man, cross into Siren Song made her uneasy. Maybe her aunt knew better than it seemed.

She'd gone to see her sisters and Catherine the night before, and Lillibeth had slept through without dreaming. Cassandra gave too much credence to the dreams, but there was no doubt they were playing havoc with Lillibeth's health. She hardly ate anything, and she was pale and wan, wasting away. Ophelia had made noise about taking her to see a doctor, but Lillibeth had refused.

Ophelia didn't blame the girl for not trusting doctors specifically or the medical profession in general. Years before, when she was very young, Lillibeth had taken a bad fall that had crushed her spine, and despite the doctors insisting she would walk again, she had ended up in a wheelchair. Ophelia couldn't remember the tragic accident, though she was older than Lillibeth. In truth, those early years, while their mother was still living at the lodge, were a blur. Mary herself was an indistinct figure.

For Ophelia, it was like everything came into focus when Mary "died" and Catherine took over. It was only years later that she and her sisters had learned that Mary had actually been isolated on Echo, and it was Charlie who'd later taken her life.

Charlie . . .

Burke was not Charlie.

He couldn't be. *Couldn't!*

She hadn't even worried he was until she'd heard that Detective St. Cloud believed Charlie had reached for her. Not reached for her, Ophelia scolded herself. That was her own term for how it felt with Burke. The detective's description was different. Not at all wonderful.

And Charlie was a bogeyman. Everything bad was caused by Charlie . . . Declan Jr. . . . Satan himself. Over the years, he'd taken on mythical proportions.

Still . . .

She wadded up her waxed-paper wrapper and then grabbed her water bottle, unscrewing the cap and gulping about half the bottle down. She felt almost ill.

Burke wasn't Charlie!

You don't even know what he really looks like.

"Yes, I do," she said aloud. There was a picture of him, passed around after his murderous rampage five years earlier, and there was also Detective St. Cloud's personal description.

She pressed her fingers to her temples and closed her eyes, rubbing. She felt out of control. She, who had always been the voice of reason at Siren Song, walking the line between Catherine's rigidity and Ravinia's impulsiveness. Taking care of Lillibeth, keeping her fears at bay. Listening to Cassandra, whose predictions *weren't* always correct, no matter how much she insisted they were.

She slammed out of the car, threw her trash in the parking lot waste receptacle, and returned to work. Her family and everyone in Deception Bay was making her crazy.

Burke was *not* Charlie.

* * *

Ravinia reached Salem a little before one. Ever since talking to Rhodes on the phone she'd thought about J. D. Bauer. Who had killed him, and why? It worried her that the police thought she might be involved, but she couldn't deal with that now. As she drove through the business section of town and into the suburbs, she thought about lunch but wasn't really hungry. She could wait. She considered calling Catherine and inviting herself for dinner at Siren Song, but she would likely have to leave a message, and that sort of pissed her off too. Isadora needed a phone *and* needed to pick up when calls came through. The whole thing made her tired and annoyed. But Isadora always served up good, nutritious meals, something Ravinia had learned to appreciate only after she left, so there was that.

She found James and Rachel's house, what appeared to be a three-bedroom ranch in the same configuration as every third home in the development. Theirs had a fresh coat of gray paint and what looked like a new roof. James may have abandoned the house in Brookings, maybe along with all the memories, but he was taking care of this one.

Ravinia wasn't sure what to expect when she rang the bell. She was already planning to leave a note on the door with her name and number if no one was home. But a middle-aged woman with dark hair and a quizzical smile opened the door. She wore a pair of black jeans and a caramel, ribbed turtleneck sweater.

"Hi, I'm Ravinia Rutledge. Are you Rachel Woodworth?"

"Well, I'm actually Rachel Finley, but I'm married to James Woodworth. How can I help you?"

The Blaveks had recognized the Rutledge name, but even though James obviously knew about the strange "cult" from which Charlie had come, his second wife clearly wasn't as familiar with all the particulars of the adoption.

"Is James here? I'm related to his son."

She stilled, and the smile fled from her face. Well, she certainly knew about Charlie.

"He's at work. Umm . . . you're related to Henry?"

"I'm his half sister."

She cocked her head, her eyebrows raising. "I understood he was an only child."

Was she unaware of the damage Charlie had caused and that he was a fugitive wanted by the authorities? Had her husband kept that from her as well? "No, there are a number of us. I'm trying to locate Henry. I just wanted to ask some questions."

"Well, I don't think James can help you," she said, looking Ravinia up and down. "They haven't been in contact for years."

"Do you mind telling me where James works? I'd like to speak with him."

She sighed, thought for a minute, then said, "Wait here." Ravinia stood on the porch, while Rachel disappeared into the interior of the house. She returned a few minutes later with a business card. "You can reach him easiest on his cell."

Ravinia thanked Rachel, who quickly shut the door on her. Ravinia heard the deadbolt engage as she stepped off the porch. She'd thought about looking into Rachel's heart, but she had a pretty good picture of her already. The woman wanted nothing to do with her husband's past life. Fine. It was James Ravinia wanted to reach. She thought about calling him, but he worked for a company called Parker Plumbing off Market Street, which was just up the freeway. Less than two miles. Ravinia drove directly there and pulled into a visitor's spot in front of the industrial, concrete building.

"Is James Woodworth here?" she asked the receptionist, a sixtyish woman who regarded her through rimless glasses. Ravinia held out the business card Rachel had handed her, as she didn't want to explain that she was there on a personal matter.

"Who can I say is calling?" The receptionist had already picked up the receiver on the desk phone and regarded Ravinia inquiringly.

"I'm Ravinia Rhodes," she lied. No need to give away her last name and possibly scare Woodworth away before she had a chance to talk to him.

The receptionist relayed the information, then said he'd be right out.

Ravinia waited in the plumbing company's reception room, which was small and fairly bare bones, although through the large, open archway, a showroom of plumbing fixtures invited customers to browse around. From her line of vision, Ravinia could see a row of sinks and glittering silver and dull gold faucets, the jewelry of modern bathrooms. Clearly, she was meant to be drawn inside, and if James Woodworth took too long, she planned to do just that.

But he was fairly fast, appearing within minutes and taking in Ravinia in a sweeping glance from head to toe. He tried on a smile and held out his hand, which Ravinia shook. "Did we have an appointment?"

James was losing his hair and kept it clipped so short the gray hair was almost nonexistent. He wore brown-rimmed glasses and was fighting twenty to thirty pounds. He seemed friendly enough, but sometimes it was hard to tell.

"No, I was just given your name. I'm building a new house and wanted to go over some plumbing ideas."

"Well, I work in the accounting department. Sounds like you need one of our salespeople. Who gave you my name?"

"Declan Rutledge-Beeman."

"I'm not sure I know him." He regarded Ravinia with that same fixed smile.

"That's odd. He seemed to know you pretty well."

"Might be a mistake. Let me get you a salesman."

Before he could hustle away from her, she searched his heart, sending him what she knew would feel like a hot ray right to his beating organ. She saw that he was basically a decent person, but his moral fiber was a bit frayed. He would always take the path of least resistance. When the going got tough, the weak would skedaddle, and that's what James Woodworth had done most of his life.

He grabbed his chest, and his eyes widened. He took a breath.

"Are you all right?" asked Ravinia.

"I'm . . . I'm . . . I'm fine." But he seemed shaken.

"Could we go back to your office? Talk some things over."

"I don't have an office, but we can talk at my desk, I suppose." Obviously still shaken, he was regarding her with trepidation.

"That'll be fine."

Ravinia practically steered him through the door to the inner workings of the company. His desk was in an alcove, behind a partition. It was semi-private from several other desks, which all stood outside the one office with a door and a window for whoever was ensconced within to be able to watch over the floor. Of the four desks, two were empty, a third filled by a man in his twenties engrossed in a phone conversation. He didn't look up as they passed.

James sank into the chair behind his desk. "What did you do to me?" he asked her, trying to hide his fear and not succeeding.

Some people, like James, knew right away that she was the cause of the sudden heat he'd felt and accused her. "You're fine," she told him shortly. "I'm here to talk about your son, Henry. I'm not really building a house."

His face froze. "I don't have a son."

"And you don't have an abandoned house in Brookings, either."

He gazed at her a long moment. "Who are you?"

"Well, let me tell you . . ." And she gave him a brief rundown of her family and how she was related to Henry Charles Woodworth and that Henry was a primary suspect in at least one murder investigation.

James looked like he was going to put his hands over his ears for a moment before he dropped them into his lap. "I haven't heard from Henry since he left. He could be dead, for all I know." He glanced over his shoulder, making certain their conversation was private. "It was Ginny's idea to adopt. I didn't want to, and I was right. You never know what you're getting."

"A lot of adoptions work out wonderfully."

He made a sound of disparagement.

Ravinia would have liked to argue with him further, but she could already see it would be a waste of energy. His mind was made up, and, in truth, the Woodworths had gotten the short end of the stick with Charlie.

"You have no idea where he is?" she asked.

"No." James shook his head. "And I don't want to know. He tried to burn down our house."

"*He* tried to burn down your house?" she queried. "I thought it was your wife."

"Well, I guess I don't know . . ." he admitted unwillingly.

"I heard you saved him from serious injury."

"He was just a kid . . . I thought." He rubbed the back of his neck, and his eyes found Ravinia's. "But he was more than that. As he got older, he got worse. Psychotic." He opened and closed his fists several times, releasing tension. "I think he killed Ginny. It wouldn't take much. She'd been having hallucinations. Dreams. About him."

"What kind of dreams?" she asked.

Color bloomed up his neck. "Bad dreams. She was scared of him. So, no, I don't know where he is, and if you find him, don't let him know where I am. I don't want Rachel, my wife, in danger."

"If I find him, I'll make sure he is taken care of once and for all."

He looked up at her hard. "You be careful. He goes after women. He went after that nanny and sweet-talked her into going away with him."

Ravinia blinked. "I thought you said you haven't heard from him. You mean the nanny who helped him escape five years ago?"

"I never heard *from* him," James clarified, "but I heard some things about him."

"How? Where'd you hear them?"

"She got our home number . . ."

"Who?"

"I don't know!" The telephone on his desk rang, and he practically fell on it in his anxiousness to get away from Ravinia. When she didn't move, he shook his head, glared at her a second, then hitched his chin toward the door, silently telling her to leave.

She tried to stick around, but he said, "Excuse me a moment," into the phone, then said to Ravinia, "I don't have anything more to say."

"Let me leave you my number in case you change your mind." She found one of her business cards, then, taking a pen from his desk, she circled her cell number several times to make it stand out. By this time, he'd turned his shoulder her way and was basically facing the wall rather than say anything further.

Their conversation was over.

She showed herself out, walking past the receptionist and outside to another overcast day, although it definitely felt a few degrees warmer in this part of the Willamette Valley than it did at the coast. Lost in thought, she made her way to her car, slid inside, and started the engine.

As she drove out of the lot and was pulling into the street, she saw a flash of gray in the corner of her eye.

A big dog leaped into the street.

Directly in front of her Camry.

Ravinia slammed on her brakes, her car screeching to a stop, her body braced for the inevitable *thud.*

But there was no thud. No howl of pain.

The animal turned to look at her, gold eyes glittering, then padded down the street.

Not a dog.

A wolf!

Her *wolf!*

CHAPTER 22

Ravinia took her foot off the brake and let the Camry slowly move forward, following the animal . . . apparition . . . whatever the hell it was, down the street. Her heart was thudding. *Oh, Chloe, he's back!*

The wolf suddenly turned off the road and ran behind a car. Ravinia stopped in the middle of the street, searching for sight of him. He was nowhere. Nowhere! He'd just dematerialized.

And then she looked hard at the vehicle he'd disappeared behind. A silver Outback. She had a full-body shiver. She'd seen this SUV before. More than once. Her mind tripped back to the woman sitting in her car, putting on her makeup. And the vehicle that had passed her last night when she was looking at the Woodworths' abandoned house. An Outback. It had been dark, but she'd swear it was silver. And somewhere else . . . where? She couldn't remember.

Whoever she was, she was following her. Had followed her since Portland.

The coffee shop! In the baseball cap. Ravinia had felt her there, but had dismissed it.

A truck came up behind her car and stopped, throbbing, waiting for her to get out of the way. Ravinia moved the Camry forward, thinking hard. Where was the driver? Watching her, even now? She turned at the next corner and drove around a long block, her eyes on her rearview. Was that the Outback way, way back there?

Her heart clutched. It was a woman following her, wasn't it? Not Charlie.

Who?

Ravinia's hands gripped the steering wheel. From Salem, she could head west toward the beach, but did she want to lead this car back to Deception Bay? Was this person connected to her search for Charlie? *Who is she?*

She reached for the phone but paused in the act. She'd been going to call Nev, but what good would that do, really?

Well, hell. If this person wanted to know what she was doing, she could just keep on following her all the way to the Tillamook County Sheriff's Department. With that in mind, Ravinia pulled into the nearest gas station. While the Camry was being gassed up, she went into the attached mini-mart and strolled around, keeping one eye on the window. Holy shit . . . was that a silver Outback passing by?

Ravinia used the restroom, then quickly grabbed some snacks for the trip back. One more meal of Doritos and Hot Tamales. Back in the Camry, she drove toward the turnoff to the beach. She didn't see the silver Outback, but she was certain it was behind her somewhere. The wolf had outed the stalker to her. He was back. He was back!

She needed to tell Chloe, but now was not the time. It occurred to her that she was going to drive right by Halo Valley Security Hospital, which was about halfway to Highway 101. This was the hospital where Dr. Claire Norris worked, Detective Stone's wife. It was also the place where Justice had been incarcerated for a time, the homicidal maniac previous to Charlie who'd tried to kill her and her sisters. Aunt Catherine had said that boys born into their family often had stronger, more dangerous powers, and, well, if her cousin, Justice, and half brother, Charlie, epitomized the male half, she was right.

But Silas hadn't been that way, she reminded herself. And her sweet brother, Nathaniel, who'd died so young, hadn't been, either, by all accounts, though she really couldn't remember him. And, also, there was no discounting the women from her clan too, who'd fallen victim to their own gifts. Her own mother, for sure. She'd heard whispers of others as well, but Aunt Catherine kept their names well hidden, doling out bits and pieces about them only when she determined it was completely necessary. So, it really was up to the gods whether they used their gifts for good or evil.

Was this woman following her some relation? Or was she some garden-variety stalker she'd picked up in the course of her work? Either way, it was dangerous.

After a few minutes of hard thought, Ravinia picked up her cell phone and called Ophelia. She, at least, would answer. Well . . . except when she wouldn't, apparently, as the cell rang and rang, and then she heard, "Hi, it's Ophelia. Leave a message."

"Hi, there, it's Ravinia," she said into her sister's voice mail. "I've been trying to chase down Charlie, but I'm heading your way." She paused. There were so many things she could say, more than she wanted to leave on a voice mail. "I'm meeting Detective Neville Rhodes at TCSD. He's helping us. Aunt Catherine knows. I would've called her, but she doesn't answer." She was rambling. Time to cut this off. "You're probably working. Call me when you can."

She clicked off, her eyes continually checking her rearview. Taking a deep breath, Ravinia determinedly headed west.

Lucky followed far behind. She'd been made. She knew it. If she was close enough to a person, she could often read their intentions, unless they were as gifted as she was, which was only members of her own family. But she'd been out of her Subaru when Ravinia had suddenly moved toward it as if directed. Lucky had literally gasped and had barely had time to duck behind a black Suburban down the street before Ravinia was glancing around, seeking her out.

When Ravinia then got back behind the wheel of her Camry, Lucky had to wait until she was out of sight before booking it to the Outback. She'd then had to think hard, anticipating where she would go next. It wasn't critical that she keep following her. She'd determined that already. But she didn't want to lose her yet, in case she did learn something new about Charlie.

She's going to the beach.

Lucky knew it as if she'd been told. That's the way her precognition worked, and she trusted it completely. So she headed west, feeling certain Ravinia was aiming for "home." Lucky kept traffic between her and Ravinia, but at one point she saw the Camry directly ahead, so she lagged back and settled behind several vehicles, keeping far enough behind Ravinia that she would be unlikely to recognize her vehicle. It was past time to switch cars, but maybe she wouldn't have to pull that off quite yet.

Since she and Ravinia were both searching for Charlie, maybe it was time to join forces?

Ravinia kept looking from the road ahead to her rearview mirror and to her cell phone.

Call Nev. Call him. Tell him someone's following you.

"And what will he do?"

Get the police involved? Send out the cavalry? Or think she's over-reacting?

The long entrance to Halo Valley came up on her right. She started to turn in and then changed her mind. There was a rest stop ahead that she knew well. She could go there instead and pretend to use the bathroom. There was a partition outside the door to the women's room that offered some privacy, but it was open on one end to the parking lot and the other to a row of box hedges. She could make it look like she was going to the restroom but just walk on through the passageway provided by the partition and hide in the hedges beyond, which would give her a view of the entrance into the rest stop.

She parked the Camry away from the restrooms, near a sorry-looking picnic area embattled by the elements. She waited a few minutes, then sauntered toward the restrooms. She hadn't seen the Outback yet, but wait! There it was. Just turning in!

Ravinia picked up her pace, bending her head to the wind. Her hair was escaping its messy bun and flying around her face. Though she was still watching the Outback from the tops of her eyes, she hoped it looked as if she was oblivious to anything but the weather.

She strode past the bathroom door and around the corner, into the hedges. Through the foliage, she could see the Outback pull into the rest stop and drive around the back of the building, but lost sight of it when it circled around to the parking area. She, in turn, sidled along the back of the building between it and the hedge. It wasn't wide enough to be a walkway. There was just enough space to edge her way along. She came out on the side of the men's room, which also had a partition. Brushing off tiny twigs and leaves, she strode past the men's room door to peek out to the parking lot.

To her utter surprise, the Outback was parked right next to the Camry.

And a woman wearing a baseball cap was leaning against the Camry, jeaned legs and arms crossed, staring in her direction. Waiting.

"Holy mother of God," Ravinia whispered.

Her stalker was out in the open.

She had her cell on vibrate, and now it buzzed in her pocket. She yanked it out and looked at it. Rhodes.

Not now. She placed the phone back in her pocket and, pulse racing, stepped into the open and started across the tarmac to greet her.

Nev hung up the phone without leaving a message. Ravinia wasn't answering, but she'd said she would be at TCSD by six.

Where are you? What are you doing?

He wanted to warn her that not only Portland PD, but now also Laurelton PD wanted to talk to her. And hell, *he* wanted to talk to her. Everywhere she went was followed by hypodermic needles and deaths.

But she wouldn't have warned you about Jolene Fursberg if she was involved. And she'd been stunned by the news of J. D. Bauer's death.

He tried to switch his mind off her. He'd sent a picture of the prosthetic ear to the lab and had heard back what he'd expected: it was a cosmetic device for someone with an injured or missing ear. "Like a burn victim?" Nev had asked, and had been told that was a very likely scenario.

Nev would talk with Lang about the ear after he got back from Norman's autopsy—Silas Rutledge's had been pushed until Tuesday—but the person he really wanted to discuss the prosthetic ear with was Savannah. She was, however, a new mother, and she might not appreciate being disturbed so soon after giving birth. On the other hand, she would want to know anything that would possibly lead to Charlie.

Pushing the Ravinia problem aside with an effort, he put through the call to Savannah's cell . . . and it went straight to voice mail. After the beep, he gave her a quick rundown of his trip to Echo Island and his discovery of the prosthetic ear.

So now what?

"Jesus," he muttered. He needed Ravinia to call him back.

His cell was sitting on his desk, and it suddenly started ringing his default tone. He saw it was from the Laurelton Police Department again. Undoubtedly, Detective Westerly was tired of waiting for him to return her call. He could well imagine how impatient she would be for an explanation. He would be, if he were in her shoes.

"Rhodes," he answered.

"Hello, Detective. Glad I got you. This is Detective September Westerly again. I assume you got my message? I would like to know who called in the apparent homicide of Rick Fursberg."

She sounded pleasant enough, but there was steel beneath her tone. Nev would have liked to talk to Ravinia, or Lang, or even Savannah before he spoke with the Laurelton detective again, but if he put Westerly off much longer there would be uncomfortable questions about why he was holding back. "Yeah, we've been busy around here." That, at least, was the truth, even if he was giving himself an excuse. "It was the private investigator hired by Jolene Fursberg. Fursberg was apparently considering divorce and was worried about her husband."

"Who was the private investigator?"

Ravinia, I'm sorry. I have to let this out of my hands.

"Her name is Ravinia Rutledge," he said, adding reluctantly, "She works on her own now, but she was with J. D. Bauer Investigations."

He heard Westerly's intake of breath as her synapses fired. "The Portland PI killed Saturday night?"

"We've been in contact with Detective Trey Curtis of PPD. Ravinia is actually on her way to TCSD now. She's stunned about Bauer's death, but I'd bet she doesn't know about Fursberg's."

"Why did she call you first?"

"We know each other. She was concerned."

Westerly humphed, then said, "I want to talk to her as soon as she shows up."

"I'll have her call you."

He'd purposely held Ravinia's number back, but it was a moot point because he was going to put her through to Westerly and Curtis as soon as she appeared. As soon as he hung up from Westerly once more, he called Ravinia's cell. Once again, he was sent directly to voice mail.

He tried texting: *Call me.*

He waited, but there was no immediate response.

"Damn."

Where the hell was she?

Ravinia felt her phone buzz in her pocket again, but it barely touched her mind. She was totally focused on the woman in front of her: About her same height and weight. Blond hair escaping from beneath the baseball cap, lighter than her own, but maybe bleached, as there were darker roots. Greenish hazel eyes.

"Hi, Ravinia," she said pleasantly.

"Who are you?" Ravinia was cold, through and through. "Why are you following me?"

"I thought you could lead me to Charlie."

Ravinia almost knew that's what she was going to say before she said it. A bit of precognition, or was it that this woman *looked* like her! Different, but there was a definite clan similarity to her and her sisters.

She immediately looked into the woman's heart. Or tried to. But there was some kind of block, although she caught a scintillating glimpse of a conflicted soul. Dark and light. Bad and good.

"I was in love with Silas, and Charlie killed him, so I'm going to kill Charlie," she stated matter-of-factly.

"You know that for a fact? That Charlie killed Silas? How do you know Silas?" demanded Ravinia. "Who are you?"

"I go by Lucky. Silas and I were . . . together until Charlie killed him." A spasm crossed her face but quickly disappeared. This was someone adept at hiding her feelings.

"You go by Lucky? That's your name? Are you related to me? *To Silas? Who the hell are you?"*

"Calm down. You want to sit in your car? I'll tell you the whole story. But let's agree on one thing: I'm going to kill Charlie for you. I know you think you want to kill him. He's despicable, evil, deadly. But you won't go through with it. Not in cold blood. But I will."

She pointed to Ravinia's car door, and Ravinia slowly pulled out her key fob and unlocked it. She didn't feel fear.

You should. You should *feel fear.*

But as Lucky went around to the passenger side, Ravinia climbed into the driver's seat.

She might not feel fear, but she certainly felt cautious.

Whoever and whatever this woman was, she was definitely dangerous.

CHAPTER 23

"You got a call just before you got in the car," said the woman named Lucky from the passenger seat.

Ravinia was half-twisted in the driver's seat so she could face her. "My phone's on vibrate," she answered inanely. She wasn't tracking well. Too much going on in her head. Too many questions.

"I can still hear it. Who called you?"

"You're related to me," Ravinia responded with a non sequitur, the best she could achieve right now. "And that means you're related to Charlie . . . and Silas."

She regarded Ravinia coolly. Whatever emotions she felt had been sublimated and were not in evidence. "My mother was known around Deception Bay as Mad Maddie Turnbull. I didn't really know her."

"You're Justice's *sister*?"

"One of 'em."

"There are more?" asked Ravinia in surprise.

"Just me and my twin, I believe. Who called you?" Lucky demanded. "Are they expecting you?"

"Yes, they're expecting me. Why? What's your plan?" In a weird way, Ravinia understood what Lucky was going to say before she said it. "You're a twin?"

"Ask Catherine about me and Gemma. She's the one who told me my work wasn't done a few years ago."

"Gemma's your twin . . . and you're Lucky?"

"My real name's Ani."

"And you're both Justice's sisters? So you're my cousin?"

"Distant cousins. Way back in the history," she said impatiently.

She clearly wanted to skip to the here and now with no preamble, but Ravinia was still processing. "Justice stabbed me in the shoulder," said Ravinia. "He was trying to get into Siren Song, and I was sneaking out." She recalled how Isadora had helped save her and felt a twinge of remorse that she'd tried so little to be friends with her older sister over the years.

"He was a psychopath," Lucky snapped. "I'm not here to make excuses for him. We don't have time, and I don't care. I've followed you to find Charlie. What did James Woodworth tell you?"

"Nothing."

"You're lying."

"I'm not lying," retorted Ravinia. "He had nothing to say."

"I can search your mind," she warned.

"If you could search my mind, you would've already."

"Like you tried to search my heart?"

They stared hard at each other.

"I can sometimes see into a person's thoughts," she corrected herself. "What did Woodworth say?"

"Nothing," Ravinia repeated.

"It was that detective who called you. The one you met at the morgue."

Ravinia's pulse spiked. She'd only met Nev the one time, and Lucky couldn't have known that without X-ray vision, that or she wasn't just boasting about reading minds.

"Ravinia, we don't have a lot of time. Silas knew it. He went to meet Charlie to kill him and knew he was going to die in the fight. But he thought he would take Charlie with him. I didn't want him to go. I thought there might be another way to take out Charlie, but Silas wouldn't listen. He drugged me to keep me from stopping him. No, it's time to finish what Silas started."

"I'm not arguing," protested Ravinia.

"You're hesitating," she shot back. "You have an idea that there's some way to get your detective friend to get rid of Charlie, but you're wrong. I have to do it, with your help."

"I don't know where he is!" Ravinia was exasperated. "My best guess is Deception Bay."

"What did James Woodworth tell you?"

"Nothing! I told you. You're kicking a dead horse."

Ravinia's phone buzzed in her pocket. Lucky's eyes went unerringly to it. "Answer it," she ordered.

"You want me to tell Rhodes about you?" Ravinia was sarcastic.

Lucky shook her head in annoyance.

Ravinia pulled her phone from her pocket to see the call was from James Woodworth. She looked at Lucky in wonder. It was almost as if she'd expected it.

"Answer it," she said again tersely.

Ravinia clicked on, her mind whirling. She wasn't sure what to think about Lucky. A part of her yearned to do exactly what she said she was going to do: kill Charlie. She wanted Charlie dead. But Lucky was right in that Ravinia wouldn't be able to kill him in cold blood. She wanted to believe she could, but she knew she would back away.

"Hi, Mr. Woodworth," she said, trying to keep the tension out of her voice.

"I took off early from work after I saw you," he said diffidently. "I didn't want to talk to you. I guess you could tell."

Ravinia felt Lucky's keen interest. She made some kind of noise of understanding into the phone. She was hardly listening to him.

"I don't know if this'll help, but I did hear about Henry a few months ago. A woman called on our landline. She found me and I wrote it all down. It was difficult to think when you just showed up," he complained.

"Who is she?"

"She said her name was Victoria Phelan."

Ravinia took a moment. Between Lucky's intent interest and her own tension, it took a moment to place the name. "She was the nanny Charlie—Henry—took off with when he disappeared."

"That's what she said. You want her number?"

"Yes, I do. Can you text it?"

"Just a minute."

In the silence that followed, Ravinia could hear the beating of her heart. Soon, Woodworth returned and carefully told her the numbers. He didn't seem inclined to text, so Ravinia memorized the digits.

"Did you call her back?" she asked.

"No, ma'am. And I didn't save the message."

"She left a voice mail," Ravinia realized.

"She said she found my name among Charlie's things. Said she'd had it for years. Thought she was safe, but said he was after her again. She asked for money. Said she needed to get away from him. Said, 'He's going to be the death of me, and he'll come for you too.' Those were her exact words. It scared my wife, and I had to act like it was nothing. A woman's ranting."

"What was the exact message? 'He's going to be the death of me, and he'll come for you too'?"

"Well, her voice was all shaky. Actually, sounded like 'he, um . . . , he'll come for you too.' She said it twice, exactly that same way, like a parrot. If you call her, let me know if I should move again."

"Okay."

"And be careful yourself," he added as an afterthought before he hung up.

"You heard that," Ravinia said to Lucky, who didn't need extra powers to overhear what Woodworth had said.

Lucky said, "The nanny was only with Charlie a short time."

"How do you know?" Then, as Lucky shifted in her seat, "What are you going to do?"

"Silas told me about the nanny. I recognize the name." She frowned. "She hasn't been with him for years."

"Don't call her," Ravinia said quickly, alarmed. "Let me talk to her first. I want to know—"

She cut herself off when she realized Lucky had extracted a hypodermic from a pocket inside her jacket. "Oh, no." Now she did feel fear. Cold terror icing her veins.

"I'm sorry," Lucky said, though she didn't really sound like she meant it. Then she jabbed the needle in the base of Ravinia's neck before Ravinia could do more than reach for the door handle.

Frantically Ravinia clutched her neck. "You—you—"

"Hopefully, it's not lethal," said Lucky.

"You can't! Oh, God. Help!"

She tried to move, but Lucky pressed Ravinia's shoulders into the seat. It was mere moments before Ravinia felt numb all over. Vaguely, she was aware of Lucky whispering something into her ear before sliding away and out of the vehicle. She heard the doors lock, but she couldn't move. Through the window, she saw Lucky bend down, then climb into her Outback.

Then blackness descended.

* * *

Lang breezed back into the station about four-thirty. "Just like we thought. Stanford Norman's death was caused by loss of blood from the stab wounds the killer inflicted. Maybe she tried to kill him with the hypodermic, and when that failed, she used the knife."

Nev looked at the clock, which caught Lang's attention. "Heard from Ravinia?" he asked.

"She's supposed to be here around six."

"Where's she coming from? Do you know?"

Nev shook his head.

"What's wrong?"

Nev was saved from an answer by his cell phone. He snatched it up but realized it was Savannah's number, not Ravinia's. With Lang waiting for his attention, he told Savannah about the prosthetic ear and the tentative theory that it could be Charlie's.

"It's Charlie's," was her flat response. "He's here. Somebody needs to warn Catherine . . . and Ravinia, all of them. Tell them about the ear."

"Ravinia's on her way here. I'll go with her to Siren Song," promised Nev.

"Don't take too long," warned Savannah.

"Savannah told you to go to Siren Song?" Lang asked as soon as Nev was off the phone.

"To tell them about the ear. She's convinced it's Charlie's."

It was Lang's turn to look at the clock. "I'll call Catherine. And Ophelia. Check in with Ravinia. See if she can get here any sooner."

Nev nodded and placed another call.

Ophelia's cell rang as she was driving to her apartment from work. She answered with a certain amount of trepidation. "Hello?"

"Ophelia, this is Langdon Stone with the Tillamook County Sheriff's Department."

"Yes?" Panic filled her. "What's happened?"

She had visions of terrible things. Acts of violence against her family. And it was Burke who did them! Burke!

Charlie . . .

But all the detective was saying was they'd found a prosthetic ear on Echo Island. It took her a moment to get herself under control, to understand they thought it was Charlie's. Then her fear spiked again.

When he added that he'd tried to call Aunt Catherine and hadn't been able to get through, Ophelia said, "I'll tell them. I'm stopping by my apartment, and then I'll go straight there." When he assured her he could meet her at Siren Song, she said, "Don't bother. Catherine won't let you in. I'll take care of it. Thank you."

She drove with concentration to her apartment. She ran up the stairs and let herself in. Dropped her keys on the kitchen counter. Realizing there was a call on her voice mail from Ravinia, she listened to it as she racewalked into the bedroom to change her clothes. She wanted a shower, but there was no time.

Ravinia's message was from hours earlier. Ophelia listened to it and then quickly called her back, reaching her voice mail. "I know you're meeting Detective Rhodes at TCSD. Didn't he tell you about the prosthetic ear they found on Echo? They think it is Charlie's. They really think he's here, Ravinia! I'm on my way to Siren Song now. Wherever you are, get back here. Call me." She clicked off, tossed the phone on the bed, and went into the bathroom to wash her face.

She looked in the mirror.

Burke was standing in the tub/shower behind her, grinning.

She froze in place. That rictus smile brought up some ancient memory, one she wasn't sure was even hers. A déjà vu from some distant relative.

Not Burke.

Charlie.

Lucky drove with studied concentration into the Coast Range. She'd called the number she'd memorized and actually gotten Victoria Phelan on the phone. All she'd needed to say was that she was searching for Henry Charles Woodworth, aka Charlie, and Victoria had broken down into near-incoherent language. Lucky managed to squeeze her address out of her, but mostly she cried, "Take him, take him, take him!"

The gloom of the day had settled like a weight on her shoulders. She hadn't expected to feel as bad as she did about leaving Ravinia unconscious in her car. She hadn't expected to receive information that might actually help find Charlie. She'd kind of written off Ravinia's quest for background on Silas and Charlie as unproductive.

But when the moment happened, when James Woodworth brought up the name of the nanny, Lucky had a searing memory of Silas mentioning Victoria too. She was the last person known to see Charlie and therefore had the most recent information on him, though Silas had told her the nanny had slipped away from Charlie . . . or more likely Charlie hadn't needed her any longer and had cut her loose. But she'd recently called James Woodworth asking for help. What was going on?

The fog lay low in this section of the mountains. She drove through thickets of brush and fir trees. Dead weeds brushed the undercarriage of her Outback as it bounced along the two narrow ruts of this long lane that led down a near-forgotten logging road. She eased up on the gas as she rounded a final curve and landed in a small clearing, where an aging A-frame cabin stood. Moss clung to its sloped roof, and a dented Jeep was parked near the front door. Light seeped around the edges of the drawn curtains over the windows.

This was the place where Victoria Phelan lived? Lucky'd certainly lived in worse, but it didn't bode well for the woman who'd once been the St. Clouds' nanny.

And Lucky hadn't liked the borderline craziness she'd heard in Victoria's voice. Something was off. She carefully checked her remaining syringes, those whose glass barrels held just enough sedative to knock someone out, and those that were more lethal. She made sure she had one of each in the inside pocket of her jacket.

Could Charlie be here? Was that what the near hysteria had been about? Yes, she'd yelled "Take him!" into the phone, but Lucky hadn't gotten the sense that she was being held captive. It seemed more like she was stressed beyond reason. Was Charlie threatening her?

What if Victoria had a gun? A person hidden away in the mountains in this part of Oregon could well have a firearm. If not a pistol, then a rifle or shotgun. She would just have to be wary and see how it all played out. If Victoria had any inkling as to what Charlie's next move was, Lucky wanted to know it.

As she walked up a muddy path to the front door, Lucky noticed that the siding around the windows was rotting; the small porch was strewn with sacks of garbage, some trash spilling onto the worn floorboards, some spread into the yard, probably from raccoons or rats or other scavengers. She kept herself from fingering the syringes as she lifted a hand to knock on the door.

It flew open while her fist was still raised.

A boy with blond hair, freckles across his nose, and wide, green eyes stood on the threshold. In faded jeans, a dirty red ski jacket, and a backpack slung over one of his shoulders, he gave her a long, hard stare. She gauged him to be around five or six.

Lucky felt it then, a tingling sensation, a wariness that ran through her blood.

Charlie's son?

"Who is it?" a woman cried from somewhere behind the boy. She was harried, her face drawn, her eyes darting to Lucky and beyond, scouring the fir-lined clearing behind her.

She was leveling a shotgun straight at Lucky's heart.

Lucky's throat tightened, and her instinct was to back away. Instead, she said carefully and slowly, "I called earlier, Victoria. Remember?"

She jerked as if jolted by a live electrical wire. "I don't know you. You didn't call. Who the hell are you?" she whispered, staring at Lucky as if she'd just risen from the depths of hell.

The boy stepped in front of his mother, and Lucky sucked in a shocked breath. "Don't shoot!" she cried. "Don't shoot!"

"Take him!" Victoria screamed. "Take him!"

The boy was unmoved by his mother's anxiety and seemed oblivious to the shotgun. Tilting up his head to stare directly into Lucky's horrified eyes, he asked, "Where have you been? We've been waiting for you."

"Oh, Burke, you scared me!" cried Ophelia. Her hand flew to her chest. "What are you doing?"

He stepped out of the tub and came up behind her, pressing his hard cock into her buttocks, wrapping his arms possessively around her waist. Fear made her heart flutter like a caged bird.

"Burke?" he questioned softly. His arms felt like steel manacles. "It was Charlie a minute ago."

He'd heard her phone message to Ravinia. Perspiration rose on her skin. She wanted to keep playing dumb, but his blue eyes glittered with malice in the bathroom mirror. He was just waiting for her.

"Okay," she said.

"How does it feel to sleep with your *brother*, whore?" he whispered.

Her stomach lurched painfully, and there was a ringing in her ears. She fought the urge to vomit. If he would just release her a little! She felt sick and suffocated.

"You'd still like it, wouldn't you?"

And then she felt that twisting sexual thrill. She tried to excuse herself. She hadn't known this wasn't normal. She'd thought this is what all people who desired each other felt.

Is that the truth, Ophelia? Didn't you purposely ignore the warning signs? Didn't you want him so badly that you made yourself believe this was love?

"Come on," he crooned, slowly releasing his hold around her waist, letting the fingers of his right hand entwine with those of her left, guiding her back to the bedroom.

Placing her on the bed, he slowly opened the nightstand drawer, pulling out the rope he'd taken from the kit in his car and used to lash her to the bed a time or two when he'd felt she was too willing and wanted to up the stakes.

"Better get comfortable. We're gonna spend some time together, Sis."

CHAPTER 24

"Put that gun down," Lucky ordered. She was going to wrest it out of Victoria's hands, if it came to that.

Victoria seemed to hear her. She dropped the end of the shotgun onto the ground with a thunk but hung onto it.

"It isn't loaded," said the boy.

Lucky flicked him a look. He was entirely self-possessed, but it was Victoria who took her attention. The woman was as pale as death, thin to the point of being bony, her hair lank and scraped back into a limp ponytail. Silas had told her she was in her early twenties, but Victoria Phelan appeared a decade older than that. "Who are you?" she repeated. Her clothes too were stained, and she nervously chewed on the insides of her cheeks, her eyes blinking wildly.

"My name is Lucky. I told you on the phone when I called earlier."

Victoria threw an anxious look at the boy. "Did she call?"

"Yes, Mama."

"You called James Woodworth a few months back and gave him your number," Lucky told her.

She pressed her arms closer to her sides and shivered. "James Woodworth . . . I found him . . . He moved, but I found him."

"You asked him for money. You said, 'He'll come for you too.'"

"I don't remember!"

"You were talking about Charlie."

Her hands trembled, and now she leaned heavily on the shotgun for support.

"You'd better sit down," said Lucky, and Victoria took several steps to sink into a dusty armchair that sent up a poof of motes. She laid the rifle across her lap. Her chin wobbled, and her teeth rattled. She glanced jerkily over her shoulder, muttering, "You don't know . . . you just don't know."

Lucky eased into the house. "Don't know what?"

"How hard it's been . . . how afraid I've been . . . how I *feel* him. The devil. Getting closer."

"You're talking about Charlie."

She pressed the heels of her hands to her temples and closed her eyes. "I—I've been trying to take care of my son . . . trying to keep Liam safe. I've been . . . a good mother. A really good one." She said it as if to convince herself. "I've been hiding for years. Moving around. Trying to stay ahead of him but now . . . he's back! I know he'll find me! I need money. I can't do this any longer." Her voice rose, and she was working herself up to a full-blown panic. "You have to take him! I can't do it anymore! He knew you would come and take him."

Lucky looked from her to the boy, who'd closed the door behind her and now was standing near his mother. "You knew I was coming?"

"I heard you," he said.

Lucky could feel apprehension feathering her skin. "You're Charlie's son," she clarified.

Victoria said, "I was with him. Charlie. Good Time Charlie." Her eyes opened, and she stared hollowly at Lucky. "I loved him. He made me feel special. Really good, and nobody else liked me. He was hurting, sick, and that brother kept scratching at his brain. I took care of him."

Silas.

"He got better, but his ear and face . . . he felt like a monster."

Lucky wanted to stop her from making excuses for Charlie. The cauldron of rage burning inside her sent up a flare. "He is a monster," she ground out. "He killed Silas."

"On the island," said Liam.

Lucky's head snapped around to regard the boy.

"He left me. And . . . and . . . as soon as he was gone . . . I woke up. I realized I'd been in a nightmare. I came home. He'd left some things, and I still have them . . ." She jerked suddenly. "You need to take him . . . what's your name?"

"Lucky. I need to find Charlie. I can't take your son."

"Charlie will find us then. Liam will call him here. Maybe he already has." Victoria shot her son a fearful look.

"I'm going with you," Liam said to Lucky.

"Did you bring the money?" Victoria looked at her beseechingly. "I have to leave after you take Liam. I can't have him find me."

"You don't need the money," he said to his mother. "They'll take care of you."

"Who?" asked Lucky.

"People from the hospital. The angel one. I called them."

"Angel?" Lucky asked.

"They will take care of her," he said to Lucky. "But we have to go. We have to go now. Before they come."

Victoria said, "If you don't take him, Charlie will, and he will twist Liam's soul to the devil."

"Who are the angels?" asked Lucky.

"They're the hospital." Liam walked to Lucky and reached for her hand. "You need to save me from him. You save boys and girls all the time."

Lucky stared at him, but he'd turned his gaze to his mother, who had tears running down her cheeks.

"I did the best I could, didn't I?" she whispered.

"Yes, Mama." He squeezed Lucky's hand hard, then looked up at her through guileless green eyes. "He's scratching at my brain too."

"You haven't eaten a thing," Catherine said, pushing aside her own plate, with barely touched remnants of roasted chicken. At the table, sharing a meal with her nieces, she was eyeing Lillibeth, who hadn't bothered taking even one bite.

"Not hungry."

Isadora and Cassandra, seated across from each other, exchanged glances, then pretended interest in their plates.

Catherine asked, "Do you feel all right?"

Lillibeth sat at the far end of the table. The girl was pale, as always, deep circles beneath her eyes, her heart-shaped face almost expressionless. "I'm okay. Just tired."

"Don't worry about Charlie," said Catherine.

Isadora had learned that calls had come in from the Tillamook County Sheriff's Department and from Ophelia on Catherine's phone. She'd listened to the disturbing news and then had them all listen to it as well. They'd collectively turned to Catherine to make sense of it, but it had been Cassandra who told about the prosthetic ear found on Echo Island, "It's Charlie's. To cover up his terrible burns."

That had sent them all into their own private, hellish thoughts, and finally Lillibeth said, "There's a fire in my dreams," which broke the momentary spell.

Now Lillibeth added, "The romance is over. I'm just worried about the baby."

Seated at Catherine's side, Isadora broke off a crust of bread and bit into it, but her eyes were on her frail sister. "We've got real problems," she said tightly. "Don't add to them!"

"Isadora."

"Do you think I'm wrong?" demanded Isadora of her aunt.

No . . . and yes . . . there was something going on, and Catherine was beginning to suspect Lillibeth's dreams somehow played into it.

"Maybe she should see someone," suggested Cassandra.

Lillibeth whipped her head around to stare at the sister who most often supported her. "You mean, like a shrink?"

"I just want you well."

Lillibeth turned her attention from Cassandra to stare into the fire burning in the grate. "Things have changed."

"Okay." Isadora spread her hands. "What things?"

Lillibeth's chin trembled, and she clamped her lips together.

"The dreams have changed?" Catherine asked her.

"Yes."

Isadora stood up abruptly and began picking up the plates. "Are you finished?" she asked her aunt.

"Yes. Thank you." Catherine eased herself back in her chair, as Isadora carried the dishes into the kitchen.

"It's . . . it's all different," Lillibeth whispered.

"Tell me how," said Catherine. Cassandra leaned in to hear, while Isadora set the plates on the kitchen counter, the flatware rattling a bit.

"He's not who I thought he was," she admitted.

Catherine tamped down her natural impatience. She was trying to understand, to be supportive, but it was difficult tiptoeing through the minefield of Lillibeth's delusional life.

Cassandra asked, "Who?"

"Must be the dream man she's in love with," Isadora stated flatly, eavesdropping from the kitchen. She returned to the dining area and arched a brow at her sister. Cassandra handed her her plate, knife, and fork, and Isadora swept them up, pointing silently to Lillibeth's untouched meal.

Lillibeth ignored her and rolled her chair back. "I'm going to my room."

"So early?" Cassandra protested.

"I'll read."

"Oh, great," Isadora muttered. "More romance."

Lillibeth threw a dark look at her sister. "Everything's just . . . different! I can't help it!"

Catherine watched Lillibeth wheel herself back to her room. In that regard, she agreed with Lillibeth. Everything was different. Ophelia had left a message saying that a prosthetic ear had been found on Echo, and Catherine had known it was Charlie's. Now the very air felt thick and suffocating. In her mind's eye, she could see the struggle on the beach between Charlie and Silas. Charlie wouldn't stop there. He'd vowed to take his vengeance on the girls who had grown up here, Catherine's charges, and she'd always worried that this day would come.

As Cassandra gathered the glasses and carried them to the kitchen, Catherine saw Lillibeth's bedroom door close behind her. No matter how dismissive Isadora was, and how much she, Catherine, had also pooh-poohed Lillibeth's nightmares, she now felt like there was a connection between the onset of those unsettling dreams and Charlie's reappearance. It wasn't just an imagined romance. The terror was rooted much deeper in the girl's psyche. Had Lillibeth's mind been plumbed? Could a twisted and romantic tale of witches and lovers and a baby be the product of ideas implanted in her willing mind?

Could years of loneliness have made her vulnerable to someone as evil as Declan Jr.—Charlie?

Catherine scooted her chair back, picked up her cane from the spot where she'd hung it on the back of an empty chair—the spot that had been Ravinia's—and stood. She glanced at the empty spaces around the long table, where once the girls had all clambered up into the chairs, some having to be propped on pillows and booster chairs. She had been able to control them then, keep them safe. But now, when it was suddenly imperative again, it felt like she was failing them.

She needed a plan.

She followed after Lillibeth, who'd managed to transfer to her bed with an ease born of long practice. She'd already laid her nightgown out and was about to slip it on when Catherine entered the room. Now she hesitated, regarding her aunt carefully, maybe suspecting she was about to hear something she didn't want to.

"Is the man in your dreams a good man?" asked Catherine.

"I thought he was, but . . ." Lillibeth picked up her braid from where it lay on her shoulder and gripped it tightly.

"And the girl?"

"She—she . . ." Lillibeth threw her braid over her shoulder and said, "No. She's not good either."

"What about the baby?"

"I don't know. I just don't think what's happening is good. Maybe I misread it all. I just don't know."

Catherine placed a hand on Lillibeth's shoulder. "Dreams are hard to understand. Maybe it's nothing."

"You understand things. You *know* things. You get messages, I know you do."

"Sometimes. Not all the time." But she was right this time. Catherine felt it. "Don't get lost in your dreams. I'll take care of things. I always do."

"I'll try. I don't want to have them anymore," she admitted.

"Leave everything to me," said Catherine, denying the ice crystals that seemed to have formed at the base of her spine.

Ravinia slowly woke from a dream where she was being chased but couldn't get anywhere because her feet were encased in shoes of concrete. Her lids felt heavy, and her mouth was dry. She realized she was sitting up. Not in bed, then. Had she—?

Her eyes flew open. She was staring through the windshield of a car. Her car.

Staring out at a darkened grassy lot and a building lit by several fluorescent lights. Rest stop bathrooms?

Oh, shit. *Lucky!*

Ravinia scrambled awake, but it was all in her mind. Her limbs felt disconnected. It took extra concentration to move her arms and legs, and she forced herself to relax and gradually get her body back on-line.

She slowly lifted her right arm and pressed it to her neck. Lucky had jabbed her with something. Her heart rate shot up. She'd thought she was going to die, but no, it was some kind of tranquilizer. She was alive. Tears filled her eyes. She was so grateful to be *alive*.

Except that bitch had shot her with a hypo needle. Relief was replaced by a flood of fury.

Lucky had played her. Ravinia had been so starved for information and almost awed by her, she'd let herself be fooled by a con artist of epic proportions.

She searched for her phone and found it lying on the floor beneath her feet, where she must have dropped it when her hand slackened.

The key fob . . . ?

"The key's under your left front tire . . ."

Lucky had whispered those words to her, hadn't she? Ravinia tried the door, and the lock popped. Lucky had locked her in? She carefully got out of the car, not really certain whether her legs would support her. Night had fallen while she'd been out. The several cars in the lot seemed somehow threatening under the dull white cones of fluorescent light from the two streetlamps on either end of the lot.

Head still clearing, she bent down and found the key fob where Lucky had said it would be. She'd meant to disable Ravinia, apparently, but hadn't planned to kill her.

She locked you in for safety.

Ravinia immediately dismissed that idea, even though it was likely the truth. She was too mad at Lucky. Didn't want to give her any credit.

And she was mad at herself for being tricked.

She got back in the Camry and switched on the ignition. She hesitated before putting the car in gear, glancing at her phone, which she'd set beside the gear shift. What was that number for the nanny? Victoria? She'd memorized it in the moment, but now was having trouble recalling it. Of course, Lucky had heard it.

Damn, damn, damn!

She couldn't *think*.

What time was it? Almost six. She was going to be late.

She picked up her phone again and saw she had a number of missed calls, phone messages, and texts. Nev had tried to call her several times. She touched on his first voice mail and put the phone on speaker while she drove. She grimaced. He was growing anxious to talk to her. Had something happened? She started to call him back, but then realized Ophelia had finally called her back.

She pressed that message and listened:

"—Detective Rhodes at TCSD. Didn't he tell you about the prosthetic ear they found on Echo? They think it is Charlie's. They really think he's here, Ravinia! I'm on my way to Siren Song now. Wherever you are, get back here. Call me."

Ravinia put a call through to Nev's cell.

"Where are you?" he demanded immediately.

"I got waylaid," she answered. "On my way now. I won't be there for a while."

"What happened?"

"Tell you when I get there." She realized she was going to sound teary if she didn't get off the phone, so she needed to cut the call short.

"I'll wait for you," he said, sounding like he wanted to say a lot more but was holding himself back. "Just get here."

He was angry at her, she could tell, but she didn't trust she could explain everything without breaking down. This was new to her. What had happened to the old Ravinia? The intrepid investigator? The drug had broken down her defenses, and she hadn't recovered yet.

Inhaling and exhaling several times, she concentrated on the two-lane highway winding out before her through the dark.

How long had she been tied to the bed? Charlie had lashed her down and then started to have sex with her, but Ophelia had thrashed and moaned and pretended to be begging for him, so he'd left her alone in disgust. Every once in a while, he'd returned to the bedroom to try and terrorize her, but she'd moaned helplessly, "I want you. I need you," which was all it would take to get him to leave her alone again.

She'd learned that well during their lovemaking.

Lovemaking? Oh, Ophelia, how you've fooled yourself!

Could she work her hands free? She'd tried, but so far hadn't succeeded. However, if she scooched up on the bed, releasing the tension on her wrists a bit, she could probably bite at the bonds with her teeth. He'd never tied them that tight before. He hadn't had to, she realized, feeling herself blush.

She worked away, nervously eyeing the doorway, listening for his footsteps, her nerves strung tight. *Come on. Come on . . .* Finally she managed to get her left hand nearly free. The right was tighter.

In a heart-stopping second she heard him returning to the bedroom and sank back onto the bed, her left hand holding the rope tight.

"Still want me to meet the fam?" he questioned with that sick, sly smile.

"I don't care who you are," she said earnestly. "We can be together always. We're made for each other."

"You'd do it with anyone, wouldn't you?" His disgust was palpable.

"I only want you, Charlie," she said piteously.

"What about Ravinia?" he snarled. "Going to the police?"

"Stay away from Ravinia." She couldn't help the sudden anger in her voice.

"Oh. I can't have Ravinia? Jealous?" he whispered, his eyes brightening.

She had to remember to play the game. She had to get away and warn her family, admit what she'd done.

"Let me tell you what I'm going to do to her," he whispered, and then he did, in excruciating detail. Ophelia closed her ears. Tried not to listen. Silently begged the powers that be to keep her from screaming at him.

But she couldn't stand to listen *any more*!

"The police have your ear. They're on to you! You won't be free much longer. They'll lock you away *forever*."

"Shut up, bitch!" His hand jumped to his injured ear, as if she'd physically smacked it.

"They'll lock you in a cell and throw away the key. You'll never get out!"

He lunged at her, wrapping his hands around her throat.

Ophelia lost consciousness. When she came to, Charlie was in the bathroom. Through the open door she could see he was looking at his injured ear. She'd never seen the vestigial remnant left from the fire before. He'd been careful to keep her away from it, but now he'd pulled back his long hair to really examine it, and she could see the scarred flesh that remained.

Her left hand was free of its rope, and her right was loose. Charlie hadn't noticed or cared. Her brain felt a bit woozy, but she reached for her cell phone, still lying near the edge of the bed where she'd tossed it.

Was he crying? As she listened, the soft whimpering crescendoed to a wail of fury and then back again.

Ophelia slowly moved off the bed. She still had her shoes on. She carefully pocketed her phone and walked swiftly and quietly to the kitchen. Her keys lightly jangled as she picked them up. Knowing he'd probably heard, she ran out the front door and down the steps. The world tilted and whirled, and she had to shake her head as she raced unsteadily across the parking lot to her Pathfinder and jumped inside.

He came roaring out of the apartment, but she was already backing up. The rear fender smacked into the garbage dumpster, and then she was moving forward. Charlie was at the driver's door, scrabbling for the handle. Ophelia floored it and damn near ripped his arm off.

He screamed after her, but she was already shooting onto Highway 101. Heart in her throat, foot jammed on the accelerator, she raced south toward Siren Song, lights from houses and buildings flashing by in the dark. Images crowded behind her eyes. Her head thrown back. Her fingers digging into his buttocks. Her back arching. Her mouth open in a scream of ecstasy.

The bile she'd managed to tamp down rose in her throat. She had to spit to keep from puking all over the car.

She shot by the small turnout for the lookout above Echo Island and slammed on the brakes, screeching to a halt and then backing up, the rear of the Nissan swerving wildly as she bumped into the guardrail above the beach. She climbed out of the car, legs shaking.

*Her brother . . . Charlie . . . Charlie! . . . her brother . . . a killer . . .
an evil murderer . . . her brother . . .*

She stood at the edge and looked down at the dark beach far
below. The surf was a hushed roar. One step and she would be over
the edge.

Echo Island was a black, crouched beast, lying in wait.

She'd warned Ravinia that Charlie was here, but had that very
warning put Charlie on her scent?

One step.

The old Fiesta rattled wildly, heading straight for her.

Charlie!

She ran for the trail. She'd seen the head of it a thousand times
but never been down it. She stumbled and fell, got up, stumbled and
fell, slid rapidly down.

"Ophelia . . . oh, Ophelia . . ."

Her singsonged name spurred her on. Her hands were bleeding,
as were her knees, her skin ripped through her scrubs.

She heard him on the trail above her, felt the dust and pebbles
cascading around her as he skidded down the treacherous path.

She was almost there. Almost down. Almost.

Oh, God, he was right above her!

He grabbed her hair. She lost footing. So did he. Wildly, they tumbled down the last of the trail. The waves were racing up the beach.
The surf had swallowed her legs. She tried to twist away from Charlie, but he had her in his grip, pulling her into the frigid water, forcing her head under the briny froth.

She was down, on her back, underwater. She blinked, looking up
at him through the blackness, but suddenly there was illumination.
Charlie had a flashlight and had trained it on her through the ever-
moving water. She knew he was staring at her, even though all she
could see was blinding light.

He wants to steal my soul.

No chance, fucker.

Shivering, she squeezed her eyes shut and waited for the sea to
take her.

CHAPTER 25

"Hey, man!"

Charlie whipped around, shining his flashlight in the direction of the voice, his grip on Ophelia loosening. Two twenty-something men were charging toward him through the darkness. They were on the beach, maybe camping out, sleeping on the beach.

Shit . . . SHIT!

He wanted to scream in frustration. At Ophelia for shutting him out. And at these two shitheads who'd foiled his plans! He had to get away fast. Furious, he scrambled back to the trail, climbing upward on all fours. If he had to, he'd kill them. He wanted to!

"Christ!" one cried. "There's a body in the water."

No time.

Willing himself upward, he made it to the top in record time, a man possessed, breathing like he'd sprinted the last mile of a marathon. The losers on the beach had no vehicle that he could see. Only his car and Ophelia's.

Ophelia's still had its lights on. She'd run in a panic from him.

He peeked inside the driver's window. The older-model Pathfinder's key was in the ignition.

He started to jump behind the wheel, then quickly ran to his own car, grabbed his kit and the rope he'd swept from the bed when he'd roared out of the apartment after her, then ran back to her Pathfinder, jumping in, throwing the SUV into gear and heading south, the direction the SUV was already pointing.

He was so full of rage he literally saw red, a haze overlaying the dark landscape. Driving wildly along the snaking road winding near the ocean, he tried to calm himself. He would need his wits about him. He shot a virulent glance toward the hedges that obscured Siren Song as he sped by. The house was staring at him.

It was time to get those whores. Strangle them one by one. Burn them at the stake. Murder them in their beds. He could turn around, sneak over their pitiful walls. Make them watch each other die in turn. He would leave that harridan, Catherine, for last.

But . . . there was one outside the gates. The rat working with the police. The one who thought she was some kind of investigator because she'd headed to southern California and found Catherine's own daughter . . . *his sister*.

His hands clenched the wheel. Her first, then.

Ravinia.

He drove as fast as he dared. Didn't want to pick up any cop as he was heading to TCSD. He smiled at the irony.

If Ravinia was already there, he'd pick her off when she came out.

Lucky headed west through the mountains, headlights dimmed against a light fog. She was just breaking through its haze when a white van passed her going the other way. Halo Valley Security Hospital was emblazoned in blue letters on its side.

The angel hospital.

From the back seat, Liam said, "They'll take care of Mama."

"Who called them?"

He hesitated.

She glanced in her rearview mirror. His eyes were dark and hard to read in the faint illumination from the dashboard. "You called them?"

"Mama thought about it sometimes. She knew the number."

She digested that, then asked, "How do you know about me?"

"He told me."

"Who? Charlie? Your, er, father?"

"The other brain scratcher."

"What other one?" she asked, then answered her own question. "*Silas?*"

"He told me," Liam agreed, turning his attention to the window and the darkness beyond. "Where are you taking me?"

"I don't have a fu—friggin' clue," muttered Lucky.

"To my dad?"

"Hell, no!"

"You're going to find him."

"Not till I figure out what to do with you." She was searching her mind, thinking of anyone who could take Charlie's son off her hands. Ravinia? Well, maybe, but how was that going to go after the way Lucky had left her? The Siren Song women? Liam was one of their own. But that would be like putting a bullseye on the boy's back, because sooner or later, that's where Charlie would land. Lucky just needed to take him out before that happened, but she couldn't risk this child's life.

Ophelia?

She heard an intake of breath behind her, and the boy said, "No. She's in the water."

"Who?"

"I can't go to her because she's in the water."

"Ophelia?" Lucky's heart somersaulted. Jesus. How good was this kid at reading her thoughts? "Ophelia's in the water?"

He'd clearly inherited serious psychic abilities from his murderous father. She hoped to high heaven he didn't get Charlie's worst traits.

"You got any ideas where I should take you?" she asked dryly.

"Somewhere safe."

"Tall order, kid."

Lucky's mind continued to churn. A thought came to her, and she flicked her eyes to the rearview once again. Had he put the thought in her mind? She wouldn't put it past him. No wonder Victoria was such a wreck. Lucky had a cold knot at the base of her spine, wondering what the future held for him.

"They're the ones," he said. "They want me."

Are you sure? Lucky silently asked, continually checking her rearview.

"Yes," he answered aloud.

It took a lot to rattle Lucky. She'd seen too much. Done too much. "How old are you, kid? *Twenty*-five?"

He just looked at her in the rearview.

She turned on her wipers against a thick, drizzling mist.

"They want another child," he said.

"I hope you're right."

She connected with Highway 26, then took the turn to Highway 101 and headed south toward Deception Bay.

Nev checked the time. Seven-thirty. Lang had hung around long past the time to leave for home, but now he took a call from his wife. Nev could tell by his conversation that Claire was working late and wondered what was keeping him from relieving the babysitter.

"Call her again," said Lang as he hung up and reached for his jacket. "Find her. She's got Portland PD, Laurelton PD, and us looking for her. I don't know what the hell she's doing, but it's way past time she showed up. Do you want me to call her?"

"She's on her way."

"You sure about that? I gotta go. Let me know the moment you hear from her."

After he left, Nev stared at his phone again. He hadn't phoned her since her call, but he would now. She'd sounded unlike herself. Weak and teary.

How well do you know her? Seriously, man. One meeting and some phone calls?

What the hell are you doing?

He placed the call to her cell, which went straight to voice mail. He damn near hurled his own cell across the room.

Lucky knew the address. Ravinia wasn't the only one she'd followed throughout her few weeks in Deception Bay. She hoped she was making the right decision. She knew from firsthand experience how childhood could ruin you, yet she couldn't think of any other option at the moment. She reached the outskirts of town, her senses heightened. The whole of the Oregon coast was dangerous for her, but Deception Bay was the epicenter of that danger.

She drove up to the road that led to the cottage perched on the hill and stopped, letting the car idle.

"I have to leave you here," she said over the hum of the engine.

He was already climbing out of the back seat.

"You're going to be okay," she said. She'd never seen anything like him.

"You have to go."

344 Lisa Jackson and Nancy Bush

"I'll wait till you get to the door."

"You can't get caught."

"Kid, I know that."

He slammed the door, then hesitated outside her driver's window. Lucky rolled it down.

"What?" asked Lucky.

"It's all happening now," he said soberly. "Goodbye."

There was something so final about that last word that Lucky drew a deep breath, aware she'd known the same thing even before he said it.

She watched as he ran unerringly to the right house and half-ran up the walk to the porch, then knocked soundly.

The front door opened, and she put the Outback into gear.

It's all happening now . . .

The Sheriff's Department was down a long drive from the highway. Ravinia turned onto it, aware how late she was. She knew she was going to face lots and lots of questions that she had no answer for.

She inhaled and exhaled as she pulled into the parking lot. She still felt shaky, as if whatever Lucky had given her had sucked up all her reserves. Anger helped, and she'd sure as hell stoked her anger against Lucky, but right now she just felt tired.

She parked the Camry, slipped her phone in her pocket, then stepped out of the car. The lights were on inside the station, but she knew that, at this time of night, most of the day staff would have left and there wouldn't be as many deputies on duty. She grimaced, as she'd ignored Rhodes's latest call, not wanting to hear anything until she got there.

She took one step forward, caught movement in the corner of her eye, and suddenly there was a long-haired man in jeans, boots, and a dark shirt right in front of her, a soft-sided tool kit in one hand, his jean jacket held casually on one finger of the other, a coiled rope tossed over his shoulder.

"Ravinia?" he asked pleasantly, smiling.

She was immediately on alert. TCSD was directly behind him, so she didn't feel particularly worried. "Who are you?" she demanded.

For an answer, he rushed her, wrapping his jacket around her head and snagging the phone she still had in her hand at the same time. He wrapped her up so fast and furiously she barely had time to inhale before he hit her hard, a fist to her face, stunning her. She tried to get her feet under her, but he dragged her to his vehicle, throwing her in the back seat. She screamed, the sound muted, kicked and fought, but the punch had taken the fight out of her.

He bound her legs with the rope. She punched back blindly, still covered by the jacket, her arms swinging and hitting nothing. He grabbed her hands and deftly zip-tied them in front of her.

It all happened so incredibly fast—and right in front of TCSD!

"They have cameras!" she screamed, her voice muffled behind the coat.

He just laughed as he slammed the door. "Goodbye, phone," he said, and she sensed he'd tossed her cell away.

Moments later, he was driving casually back down the access road.

Ravinia grabbed at the jacket with her tied hands and finally yanked it off her face. He pressed the accelerator as he turned north, and she was flung to the floor.

She shot him a bolt of heat, searching his heart . . . which was a big empty space of black.

"Charlie," she said, a shard of ice stabbing her own heart. Her senses awakened as if someone had waved smelling salts beneath her nose.

"Lovely to meet you, Ravinia. Ophelia always said she wanted me to meet her family, rest her soul."

"What? Ophelia!"

"What do you want?" she demanded, trying to keep her voice strong.

"To kill. Like you do."

"I only want to stop you."

"Same thing," he said nonchalantly.

She'd worked her way back into the seat. He was driving fast now. She imagined herself throwing her tied wrists over his head and yanking backward, strangling him. But it would cause an accident, one neither of them might survive.

Not yet, she told herself.

"Oh, Ravinia. You want very badly for me to die. You've been searching for me. Getting your friends at the sheriff's department involved.

Protecting your family against Big Bad Charlie. You're just a regular hero, aren't you?"

"You killed Ophelia. And you killed Silas." Her tone was lethal.

"Silas wanted to die and take me with him. I didn't see it that way."

Cassandra was restless. She grabbed a jacket from its peg as she headed to the back porch. Her aunt's cloak was hung next to it, though Catherine too, in the last few years, had started wearing a long coat in favor of the nearly threadbare cloak that had been her outer garment for over a decade.

Outside, the air was heavy with the promise of rain, no clear, crisp October night. She walked the length of the porch and stared through the trees. Feeling the chill of the night, she rubbed her arms. The moon, a slim crescent, peeked through clouds skimming across its surface. She stared at the surrounding trees, hearing the rush of the wind and watching the fir boughs dance and sway.

Something was wrong. Very wrong. She could feel it.

She walked back and paused at the window to Lillibeth's room, hearing a moaning coming from within. Another dream.

The back door opened, and Catherine, who had tossed on her old cloak and was using her cane, thumped toward Cassandra. "She's dreaming again," the older woman said.

"I know."

Aunt Catherine hesitated, seeming unsure, not her usual way of being. "What do you see?" she asked.

Cassandra looked at her in some surprise. Her aunt rarely asked directly about her visions. More often than not, she tried to argue about or dismiss them.

"I don't think you've paid enough attention to her dreams," said Cassandra carefully. "I don't think Isadora has either."

"Charlie's coming," Aunt Catherine stated flatly. "Do you think Lillibeth's dreams are connected?"

Cassandra felt an electrical jolt of fear. "You know he's coming?"

"Cassandra, you're the one who sees things. You don't see that?"

She automatically started to remind her that she wanted to be called Maggie, but it would only serve to fuel her aunt's impatience. "The dreams are real. I've said that all along. They mean something."

"The man of her dreams is not who he said he was. He's led her somewhere falsely."

Cassandra leaned closer to Catherine to search her darkened eyes. "You believe now?"

Catherine brushed the air, waving off the question. "We don't have a lot of time. Charlie's coming, and we need to bolster our forces. Lillibeth's dreams are her manifestation of understanding the threat."

"I think it's more than that. It's so specific and—"

"We need to call him to Siren Song."

"*What?*"

"Our strength will lure him here. He'll think it's his power that is reaching to us, but it'll really be us calling him."

"But you've spent years, decades, trying to keep him out!"

"We have to bring him to us to destroy him. I think Lillibeth is trying to warn us. She's a bellwether. The characters in her dream are not who she thought they were. Unless we destroy Charlie, he'll haunt us all."

Cassandra suddenly felt a blast of heat, as if she were too close to an inferno. "Oh, Lord," she whispered. "He's bringing fire with him."

Her aunt's free hand grabbed her arm. "You see that?"

"I feel it."

"Do you agree that we have to call him here?"

"What about Isadora?"

"I already convinced her," Catherine said, heading for the door. "She's skeptical, of course, but then she always is." She was already slipping inside, and Cassandra started after her.

By the time she had shrugged out of her coat, Catherine and Isadora were waiting by the fire. She joined her sister and Catherine. Her gaze met Isadora's, and she saw her own doubts reflected in her sister's eyes.

"It would be better if the others were here. Ravinia and Ophelia," Catherine said, grasping each of her nieces' fingers in her own and nodding to their empty hands, encouraging them to link and form a circle. "We would be stronger."

"Lillibeth's here," Isadora said.

"He's already gotten to her."

Isadora's head snapped around. "You think Charlie is her dream lover?"

"The evil exists and is manifested in Charlie," Catherine said. "Whether in her dreams or in the corporeal being Mary gave birth to, I don't know."

Catherine's hands tightened, and she squeezed her eyes shut. "Close your eyes and visualize him, then send out an invitation, tell him that you're ready."

After a long, shared look, Isadora and Cassandra did the same. Cassandra let her lids fall and then bore down in her mind, concentrating, sending out a message.

Come to Siren Song. Come now. We're all here . . .

"Who's this?" Lang asked, seeing the young boy standing in his living room.

Avery, the babysitter, held up her phone. "I was just trying to call you. I couldn't get through to Mrs. Stone. He just showed up."

"Just showed up?" Lang shot a glance out the window. It was dark, and though the wind had died down some, there was the threat of rain. He turned to the boy. "Where are your parents?"

For an answer, he slowly lifted a finger and pointed to Lang.

Bea, who'd been sitting on the sofa, bounced up and said, "He's my cousin!"

"Bzzz, bzzz, bzzz," the boy said, suddenly smiling at her. "I have a *bee* for a cousin!"

"I got homework. My mom's picking me up," said Avery, slinging her backpack over her shoulder. "I didn't know what to do."

"Yeah . . ." said Lang. With his eyes still on the boy, he put in a call to Claire.

"What have you done with Ophelia?" demanded Ravinia. "This is her car."

"I left her in the ocean."

"You *killed* Ophelia," Ravinia repeated. She felt soul-sick. This was Ophelia's car. All of her worst suspicions had gelled. The tiny bit of hope she'd held out for her sisters' safety was quashed.

"That is the plan," he reminded her as if she were a child. "We had a little fun along the way. She wanted me, and I wanted her, and it was really working out till she wanted me to meet her family. You know how that goes. Meeting the family? It's never quite as good as you think it's going to be. Now, I do intend to meet the family. Look at you. I've already started! You can help introduce me. I've already met dear old dad a number of times."

"Declan Sr. is not your father," Ravinia shot back. She didn't like the amused way he talked. It felt like it was getting inside her. "Thomas Durant is your father, not Declan Bancroft!"

"Well, see now, whoever that is, it's just not true—"

"Yes, it is. They've got your DNA. You left it at Bancroft Bluffs the night you attacked Detective Dunbar St. Cloud. Everyone knows Declan Bancroft isn't your father. Everyone but you."

"You are incorrect," he said tersely.

"Total fact!"

He slammed down on the accelerator and threw Ravinia back in her seat. She held onto the fraying leather edge to save herself from being tossed about. Fear numbed her. She counted the seconds. Expecting to die. Ophelia . . . it couldn't be. She would *know*.

Then he slammed on the brakes, and Ravinia couldn't hold on. She was thrown into the back of the front seat, knocking the wind from her, further dizzying her.

A second later the Pathfinder moved forward again, gaining speed. Ravinia saw flashing red and white strobe lights through the windows above her head. Police! Emergency vehicles! She tried to scramble back up, but before she could see out the windows, they were zooming past an accident scene.

EMTs . . . a woman's body being placed inside an ambulance. Above the beach near Echo Island.

Ophelia!

"That's Ophelia!" Ravinia screamed, pounding on the window.

"She's dead."

"She's not dead! I saw her arm move!"

"You're lying."

She was lying, but he didn't have to know it. "You're done for. She's going to pinpoint you, and you won't get away this time. You're dead, Charlie."

The roar that came out of him hurt her ears. She suddenly swooped her zip-tied hands over Charlie's head and yanked back on his neck with all her strength, the force nearly popping the skin at her wrists from the effort.

Charlie started choking. His right hand reached up and grabbed a hank of her hair, the strands that had escaped her bun. He yanked forward and jammed her forehead into the back of his head.

She saw stars. The Pathfinder swerved into the oncoming lane. Charlie jerked the wheel back but overcorrected. They slid around in a circle a full 360 degrees, and then Charlie hit the accelerator again, and they drove off the east side of Highway 101 onto the dirt-and-gravel access road that led to the Foothillers' village.

Dizzily Ravinia realized she was close to Siren Song. Less than a mile.

If she could just . . . get . . . away!

But he was off the road, into the brush. Bouncing. Careening. Tree limbs scraping the metal. Ravinia lost pressure on his neck. Charlie got one hand under the zip tie and yanked his head free of Ravinia's tied hands.

"You bitch. You're dead!"

And then they were airborne.

CRASH! SLAM! CRUNCH!

The nose of the Pathfinder smashed down hard into a large ditch. BAM! The vehicle gave a death-throe shudder and flipped onto its side.

CHAPTER 26

Nev stretched the kinks from his neck and glanced at his phone, noting the time. Nearly nine. He'd called and called, gotten no response. It was time to give up. Past time. But maybe her phone was out of juice, or maybe she was in a place where the connection was spotty. Maybe she'd been in an accident . . .

Or maybe she's standing you up.

That's obviously what Stone had thought.

So how long would he wait? He'd had plenty of work to keep him busy, reviewing reports and camera footage, making notes for his interview with Ravinia, and when May had still been at her desk, he'd asked her to wait for Ravinia while he called in a take-out order, then had run down the street to pick it up and returned to eat his ham-on-rye and chips, which he'd consumed at his desk.

Ravinia hadn't shown.

His cell phone rang, and he exhaled in relief. Ravinia!

But no, it was the detective from Laurelton PD.

"Hello, Detective," he answered.

"Detective Rhodes. Have you met with Ravinia Rutledge yet?"

"I've talked to her."

She paused. "But you haven't met yet?"

"No."

"Be careful. I've compared notes with Detective Curtis at Portland PD. We've got the same Outback at the scenes of both homicides, Bauer's and Fursberg's. Curtis had already put a rush on DNA found at Bauer's. We're looking for DNA on Fursberg's body in case she left some there too."

"She?" Nev's heart sank.

"The same killer I chased a few years back. It's her DNA. It's been found at multiple crime scenes across the country. She targets men and has used different methods, but recently she's favored drug overdoses by injection."

"Outback?" Nev was on his feet.

"It isn't your detective friend. It's someone else. I've also been in touch with the Winslow County Sheriff's Department. They've had dealings with her too. This woman's first name is Ani. If she goes by a last name, I don't have it, but her alias is Lucky. We are searching for more information on her and her full name and any other aliases, but so far that's all we have. I thought you should know. If your PI friend is involved with her in any way, she could be in trouble."

Shit!

He was half relieved, half panicked. Not Ravinia. *Not Ravinia!*

"Thanks," he said and hung up. He ran to the break room and got his coat, then out the back door to his truck. He called Ravinia again, but it went to voice mail.

Cursing under his breath he drove around the front of the station and did a double take on the only vehicle in the visitor's area. A Camry.

Ravinia's car?

He barely got the truck into park before he was leaping out and checking the vehicle.

Doors unlocked. Her purse on the floor. He glanced around. "Ravinia?" he called.

"Ravinia!"

Something had happened. She'd been here. Shit! She'd been here!

He tried her cell once more . . . and heard a ring tone from the brush that lined the parking lot. He ran toward it, bracing himself for sight of her body lying on the ground, injured by this Lucky person . . . or worse.

But there was only her cell phone, its small screen lighting up the dark. He snatched it up as he clicked off and it stopped ringing. She wasn't here. What had happened to her?

Spurred by fear, he ran back into the station, strode directly to the security unit, and demanded that the tech on duty show him videotape of the parking lot over the few hours since he'd gotten Ravinia's last call. His pulse was racing. He told himself that she was okay over and over again, as he waited for the tech to cue up the footage, but he didn't believe it.

"Here we go," the tech said, and Nev watched the image, a black-and-white recording of the parking area; cars and trucks, vans and SUVs driving in and out, moving quickly, the people getting out or into the vehicles. The images moved jerkily in fast-forward. The tech had taken the video back farther than he instructed; Nev saw county-issued vehicles parking and leaving, officers and office staff caught in the camera's eyes as day turned to night.

The lot grew less crowded. He saw Ravinia's vehicle pull into the lot. "There!" He pointed to the screen. "Slow it down," he ordered, and the tech accommodated. He watched as Ravinia, blond head visible, parked her Camry and started to get out as a man carrying a tool bag of some kind with a rope over his shoulder, holding his jacket, met up with her. The man suddenly wrapped the jacket over her face and then lashed her with the rope, yanking something out of his pocket . . . oh, shit. Zip ties. Right in the parking lot of the Sheriff's Department!

"When was this?" Nev demanded as the attacker dragged her into his waiting vehicle, threw her into the back, and took off.

"Jesus, I'm sorry. I didn't see this. Must've been when I was in the break room. I can't—"

"Enhance the license plate on that other vehicle."

He watched again. Definitely a man. Not this Lucky woman. Maybe worse . . . Nev didn't recognize Ravinia's assailant, but he believed she'd been abducted by Henry Charles Woodworth . . . Charlie.

"Blow that up. I want that license plate and the make, model, and year of the vehicle for a BOLO. Email me and cc Detective Stone."

"Got it."

Nev barely heard the chagrined tech's response. He was already leaving the security office, running down the corridor, the soles of his shoes slapping against the floor, his heart in his throat, fear that he was already too late pounding through his brain

It hadn't worked.

Catherine now felt a bit foolish. They'd called Charlie, and he hadn't come. Now, in her bed, she wondered what had possessed her into thinking calling for him would be the answer. Isadora and Cassandra hadn't believed. Their hearts hadn't been in it. Catherine had known that and hadn't let it bother her, had forged on anyway, like a woman possessed. Maybe she was a little possessed. She still felt it was the right thing to do at some level. She'd clung to her belief that, if they chanted together, he would hear them and heed their call. When that had failed, she'd argued with Isadora, who'd wanted her to sleep downstairs again, but Catherine had stubbornly demanded to be in her own room.

Now she looked around her bedchamber, sensing somehow that it might be for the last time. She reached into her nightstand drawer for the metal box that contained her journal. She hadn't bothered putting it on a high shelf again. Ravinia would find it regardless, given half a chance. Unlocking the box, she pulled out the journal, a young girl's diary, mostly, filled with young girl thoughts that were as insubstantial as dandelion fuzz.

But she'd added a separate page and stuck it inside. Now she looked it over, making sure it was as complete as she could make it. Satisfied, she tucked it back inside and relocked the box.

Closing her eyes, she bore down in her mind and called to Charlie once more.

Cassandra was drowning. The ocean closed over her head, and she looked up through the dark, icy water and saw Charlie.

With a start she woke up choking, unable to breathe. She'd fallen asleep on the couch after Isadora and Catherine had gone to bed.

Drowning? She searched her mind, gathering up the remnants of what felt like a vision more than a dream. Beach, sand, driving . . . *Ophelia!*

It was Ophelia in the water.

On her feet in an instant, she started for the stairs, intent on waking up Isadora and Catherine.

What if the vision isn't true?

She hesitated. She'd been down this road so many times before.

Where was that cell phone? She would call them from the road. She found it on the end table next to the couch and swept it up.

Then she snagged the key to the gates from its peg near the back door and ran outside, where the wind was up, the night dense and thick with the promise of rain. Once the gates were opened, she dashed to the shed they used as a garage, pushed open the door, and slid behind the wheel. She located the keys, tucked under the floor mat. "Okay," she said, starting the old Buick. She shoved it into gear and floored it, speeding through the gates and cranking on the wheel as she hit the road. She drove by instinct, straight for Ocean Park Hospital, her heart drumming, her dread mounting.

She reached the hospital in record time. "Ophelia Rutledge? She was brought in here?" she asked the woman behind the desk in Emergency.

"We haven't had a woman come in. Maybe you should check with Seaside or Tillamook?"

"No, it's . . . thank you."

Oblivious to everyone else in the waiting room, Cassandra took a seat, confused. She knew her sister was here. She clasped her hands together and closed her eyes, trying to see what had happened to her. Cassandra was certain she'd witnessed her delivery to Ocean Park Hospital by an ambulance.

Pressing her fingers to her temples, she thought she heard Catherine chanting some more. Was that Isadora too? She tried to clear her mind, but the chanting swelled and Cassandra was swept along, joining in the same song.

Annabel was asleep in her crib, and Declan was dozing on top of his bed, toy triceratops in hand. Savannah walked into the kitchen and poured herself a glass of water. Breast feeding called for fluids and lots of them. Also calories, but she'd eaten a huge meal of pasta, salad, and baguette that was now sitting in her stomach as if condensed and held in place, a product of her tension.

"You want to go, go," said Hale. "But be careful."

Lang had called her and told her about the boy who'd shown up at his house. Claire was still at Halo Valley . . . something about the intake of a new patient . . . so Lang had called Social Services, though in the end he'd decided to keep the boy with him until morning.

"I won't be gone long."

"Don't worry about it. Besides, Mom will be back soon."

"Will she?" Savannah wasn't so sure. Janet had actually connected with an old friend from high school. A widower she'd once had a slight crush on. Who knew where that was going, but Janet and the widower were out to dinner, and she'd called and told Hale and Savannah not to wait up.

Savvy climbed into her car and aimed it south toward Deception Bay.

Lucky looked over the sorry display of sandwiches in the Drift In Market's deli, skipping the tuna and egg salad for one of tofu and vegetables. She wasn't vegetarian or vegan, but she was pretty sure the sandwiches had been made for the lunch crowd, and though they were refrigerated, she wasn't taking any chances.

The market was closing. She'd ducked into it, all her nerve endings alert. She couldn't remember the last time she'd eaten a real meal, having followed Ravinia's diet of travel snacks for days.

She stood in front of the case of drinks, aware that the girl at the cash register, who'd deigned to get her sandwich, was now watching her, waiting for her to move on so she could close up. Grabbing a plastic bottle of water, she closed the glass refrigerator door and—

The ululation that suddenly filled her head nearly knocked her over. She clung to the handle of the refrigerator door, the sound reverberating like the eerie howling of a wolf. It receded slowly, but didn't quite go away. The sound echoed through her head, and it took Lucky a moment to realize the girl at the register was staring at her, her mouth a wide O of fear.

"What was that?" Lucky asked, picking up her plastic-wrapped sandwich from where she'd dropped it and carrying it and her water bottle to the counter, handing the girl a twenty.

She kept staring at Lucky as she made change. "What was what?"

"The *sound*," said Lucky. She didn't have time for this conversation. Already the girl was going to remember there was a woman in the store when their ears were blasted.

"What sound?" the girl asked.

Lucky stared back at her. She could still hear it faintly.

She shook her head and shrugged for the girl's benefit, but her heart was beating triple-time, and now the roaring in her ears was from her own growing realization that the sound she'd heard was coming from the women of her clan.

Ravinia slowly opened her eyes and stared above her head, uncertain what she was seeing. A car door? Had she been asleep? Was she lying on the floor of a car? No . . . lying on the opposite door? And why couldn't she move? Her legs were tangled up, her shoulder sore, a headache starting to throb.

She lifted her right hand, and her left came up with it. They were tied together. Zip-tied.

Memory whooshed back. Oh, shit! Oh, hell! Charlie! What had happened?

She struggled upward and looked over into the front seat. Charlie was there, one arm through the steering wheel, his head lolled against the driver's door. A purse lay on top of him, its contents spilled out. Ophelia's purse. A canvas tool kit was perched incongruously on the side of the driver's headrest.

Oh, God . . . oh, God.

She had to hurry. Get herself situated. *Get out!*

She swatted away the remnants of the loosely tied ropes and grabbed the handle to the door above her. The handle turned, and she pushed, but the door was heavy. Too heavy. Maybe it was wrenched? Her shoulder protested but she couldn't let a little pain stop her.

She pushed again. Harder. It opened a bit.

Oh. My. God.

If she'd had her full strength, she could do it, but these locked hands! And she needed her aching shoulder to get it open.

She eyed the tool kit, grabbed it up. First thing she saw was a flashlight. The second a knife.

She caught hold of the knife and frantically sawed at her zip ties. She had to work fast.

Charlie's right hand reached up onto the headrest.

Oh, no. No, no, no. She sawed more furiously.

The hand gripped on the leather harder as he sought to pull himself up.

She whipsawed the blade back and forth over the plastic ties as fast as she could. Faster, faster, FASTER. She was beginning to sweat. The plastic stretched.

The ties broke apart with a *snap*.

Charlie's head suddenly came even with hers.

He was grinning like a satyr.

And then she felt it. A snaking, climbing hot sensation that ran up her leg and inside her, into her core.

Oh, holy hell . . .

Ravinia closed her eyes and her mind, her whole body shuddering. She'd heard and heard about Charlie's pheromones, but she hadn't really believed. She was consumed by desire and revulsion.

"Hi, lover," he whispered silkily.

He started climbing between the seats toward her, and with all her remaining strength, Ravinia turned the handle and jammed her sore shoulder against the door, flinging it open to a black sky.

It's happening now.

Lillibeth's eyes flew open. The voice? Who'd said that?

She was breathing hard, as if she'd been running, and she realized . . . the dream . . . the forest . . . the woman . . . the baby.

But that voice?

Anxiously, she peered around her darkened room, her ears straining to listen, but all she heard was the sound of the wind rushing through the trees near the lodge, one branch tapping loudly on an upper-story window.

She closed her eyes again, though she didn't want to dream. Her lover was gone. It had all been a ruse, just like Aunt Catherine and Isadora and Ravinia and even Maggie had said. There was no man, no romance . . . but there was evil.

Fainter, the voice said, "You know what you have to do . . ."

She eased from the mattress, eyed the wheelchair positioned near the bed, a bit of moonlight seeping through the window to glint on its thin spokes.

She reached for it, then let her arm drop. Instead, she forced her mind to overcome her weakness, rose slowly to her feet and felt her legs tremble. But she wouldn't give in to her frailty. Not tonight. With all the mental power she could muster, she took tentative footsteps out of the room, gaining strength with each step. In the kitchen, she reached into a cupboard and found an old lamp, still filled with oil. There was a box of long wooden matches tucked beside it, and she lit the wick and watched in fascination as the little flame sprouted and grew, illuminating the room and casting flickering shadows on the walls and ceiling.

Third floor . . .

She headed for the stairs and began the ascent.

CHAPTER 27

Isadora was sleeping fitfully. Every time she came to, it felt like she should remember something just out of reach. She'd done as Catherine had ordered: called Charlie with her mind. For one moment, she thought it had worked. Somewhere out there, it felt like ears had perked up and listened.

Wolf ears? she wondered vaguely.

She fell back into a deep sleep . . . and dreamed.

Lillibeth was walking. Heading down the hall. Carrying an oil lamp.

"We have electricity on the second floor," Isadora reminded her.

But Lillibeth kept right on walking, almost floating.

Walking!

Isadora sat bolt upright in bed.

Catherine rolled over in her old four-poster and felt chilled to the bone. Had Charlie heard them? Was it even possible?

Wait. Did she hear footsteps over the rustle of the wind? She sat up, ears straining, as she listened, calming for a second, as the familiar sounds of the old timbers settling and the whisper of air swirling in the chimney reached her. It was nothing. Just her all-too-fertile imagination . . .

Was that the door at the end of the hall creaking open?

She twisted to get out of bed, and as she did, the bed sheets wound around her legs. She tried to kick them off and ended up teetering, then completely losing her balance; as she tried to break her fall, she struck her head on the bedpost, before landing hard on the floor, her head cracking against the floorboards.

"Aunt Catherine!" Isadora's panicked voice called out.

Woozily, she tried and failed to answer. Blackness was taking over, crawling around the edges of her eyesight, numbing her brain. "Isa—" But her voice failed.

And then Isadora was standing in the doorway. "Aunt Catherine!" she whispered, running into the room and kneeling on the floor beside her aunt. "What happened? Are you okay? Oh, God, you're bleeding."

"I'm fine."

"No, you're not." Isadora stood up fast and put a hand to her own forehead.

"What's wrong?" Catherine demanded.

"Nothing."

Catherine made a derisive sound. Isadora was as bad as she was. Neither of them could let go an inch. "Just help me up," she said, reaching up, grabbing Isadora's arm and squeezing as hard as she could.

"I thought I saw . . ."

"Charlie?" asked Catherine. She felt a spurt of fear. "Did it work?"

"No . . . Lillibeth . . ."

"Lillibeth?"

"It was a dream, I think. She was walking down the corridor toward the third-floor stairs, holding an oil lamp. But then I heard the door open. And it's standing open now."

"It can't be. Must be Cassandra."

"Must be," agreed Isadora, her eyes stretched wide. "Must be."

"Charlie's tricking us," whispered Catherine. "He's coming. We called him, and he's coming. Go downstairs. Get the shotgun out of the broom closet. Load it. Bring it back here."

Lillibeth eased up to the third floor, the oil lamp casting its golden glow as she slowly climbed the steps. She was a little surprised to find in her hand the key to the double doors that led to the expansive bedroom suite that had once been her mother's.

She unlocked the doors and stepped into the room, still decorated in orange and yellow, something straight out of those movies set in the sixties or seventies that Cassandra had described to her.

"It's happening now," she said aloud, waiting for the voice to respond.

But it was a different voice that answered.

You're here now, and the baby is coming.

The lamp cast flickering shadows over the wooden walls and the massive bed where so many babies had been conceived. All her sisters . . . and her brothers . . .

Something inside her stirred, a vibration, like the strings of a harp being plucked, a movement that traveled through her veins to her heart. The wooden chair, a rocker, in the corner was covered in dust, long forgotten and empty, but now it moved, slowly, back and forth, creaking.

She was in her dream again. Within the vision and also an observer, a part of it, and yet a silent voyeur. The pregnant girl was running, running through the forest, trying to avoid the horsemen. But she wasn't pregnant any longer. She'd had the baby . . .

Lillibeth could remember those labor pains, the gush of fluid as the child had entered this world.

Her baby . . . it was her baby . . . with her lover.

He materialized in front of her, standing at the headboard of the bed.

And suddenly the girl in her dreams was atop the bed, soaked in sweat, writhing, in the throes of childbirth. Lillibeth could see it again, could feel it again.

Wrapping an arm around her own stomach, Lillibeth looked at the man. Tall and handsome, with silvery eyes, light hair, and an enigmatic smile, he looked at her and then down at the woman on the bed.

"Father, help me," the woman whispered, and as Lillibeth watched, she transformed from the girl who ran through the forest to a woman with blond hair and features Lillibeth recognized as much like her own, a woman who had borne many children, a woman who had . . .

"Mother," Lillibeth said, her insides turning to ice. Not an innocent girl running from evil. A woman running *toward* it. A woman who embraced malevolence, who had many lovers and had birthed so many.

And when she stared up at the man beside the bed, his enigmatic smile twisted into a knowing leer. And Lillibeth realized he was her grandfather, her mother's father, her mother's lover, and Charlie's father.

Not my lover, thought Lillibeth with relief. *Never my lover.*

But the baby?

The Mary on the bed looked up at the man; then they both looked at Lillibeth.

The stairs were dark, only a bit of light leeching up from the open doorway on the floor below. Catherine was out of bed, but moving too slowly to the door.

Isadora's strident voice floated up from the lower floor. "Pick up! Pick up, damn you!" Isadora was yelling. "Listen, Ravinia, when you get this, call me. Immediately! I—I have the phone with me, but it's an emergency. Oh, for God's sake!" She clambered up the staircase. "Oh, God, there you are!" she said to Catherine, holding up the cell. "The phone needs charging. I don't think Ravinia's even going to get my message." She held the shotgun by its stock in her other hand. "It's loaded."

"We need to go to the third floor."

Isadora nodded and marched down the hall, with Catherine moving along slowly behind her. "Cassandra?" she yelled from the bottom of the third floor stairway. "Cassandra, are you up there?" After a moment, she tried, diffidently, "Lillibeth?"

"Wasn't Lillibeth in bed?" demanded Catherine.

"Ye–yes . . ."

"You didn't look."

"I saw her in bed. Yes. I think. She spoke to me from the dark."

They heard a thump from up above their heads, and both of them turned their eyes to the ceiling.

"I'm going up," said Isadora. When Catherine moved to the bottom of the steps, she added, "You'll never make it."

"Yes, I will."

The cell phone in Isadora's pocket stuttered. She whipped it out. "Hello? Hello? Ravinia?"

"It's Maggie . . . Ocean Park . . . Buick . . . Charlie . . ."

And then the phone went dead.

Isadora said carefully, "I think Cassandra took the Buick to Ocean Park Hospital."

They both turned their eyes skyward again, as another louder thump, followed by the sound of shattering glass, reached their ears.

Catherine said, "Give me the gun."

Lillibeth stared at the apparitions—her mother and her grandfather. As she did, her grandfather disappeared, and a younger soul took his place. Same silvery eyes, but with an earnestness that was not part of her grandfather's makeup. Silas?

She'd had it all wrong.

There was no baby. No witch trials. That was all a lie. A trick that her own mother had used on her, coming to her from beyond the grave, using her dreams to reach her. Charlie had been born long ago to the woman in the bed and the man standing and leering at her. Lillibeth had been called to make certain he died.

"You are the witch," whispered Lillibeth to her mother.

You have to burn him out, said the new apparition.

"Silas?" She turned her attention to him.

You have to burn the bones, answered Silas.

Her legs buckled.

She fell, dropping the lamp.

Glass shattered and sprayed, glittering in the shag carpet, oil seeping and running to its edge and farther, seeping into the floorboards, toward the doors, the wick still burning, catching in the soaked curtains, flickering and crackling.

Lillibeth screamed, the vision withering away. Disappearing.

She was alone.

Locked in Mary's bedroom, where the fire caught.

And her damned legs wouldn't move. Fear pounded through her veins. Trembling, she realized no one could help her. She had to save herself. "You can do it," she heard her own voice avow. And then she heard the other voices call to her, *"Burn it. Burn it down!"* Planting her elbows on the psychedelically flowered carpet, she started dragging herself toward the door.

* * *

Nev drove like a madman, a million thoughts running through his mind, most of them revolving around Ravinia. What had happened to her? Where was she? He flew through several smaller hamlets and headed into Deception Bay in record time. He didn't know where he was going, but Siren Song was in Deception Bay, so that's what he'd aimed for. His cell rang. The tech.

"Yeah?" he growled.

"The Nissan Pathfinder is registered to Ophelia Rutledge."

Nev frowned. Not sure what that meant.

But at least he was going in the right direction. He punched the gas.

Standing in the living room next to Lang, Savannah looked into the eyes of the boy named Liam, who was sitting on the couch beside Bea, both of them deep into orange-frosted cupcakes with jack-o'-lantern grins that Bea and the babysitter had made earlier. Something about him was very adult-like. *Very* adult-like. A boy wise beyond his years. "Who brought you here?" she asked him.

He licked his lips and shook his head.

"Your mama?" Savannah pressed.

He shook his head again.

"Why did you tell Bea you're her cousin? Who told you that?"

Lang stirred beside her. Avery had been picked up by her mother, and he'd been watching the children, who both should have been in bed, but, well, that wasn't in the cards yet. "We've been over this."

"And what are your answers?" she demanded, turning toward Lang.

"Don't have any yet."

"Then—"

Lang's cell phone rang, almost a blessed interruption. He listened for a few minutes, then said, "Okay."

"What?" Savannah asked when he was listening intently some more.

"It's Claire," he mouthed to her.

He'd left a message for Claire, and she'd called him back and was dumbfounded by Liam's sudden appearance. But the hospital was experiencing an unusual patient intake and she couldn't leave. She'd suggested calling Social Services, and Lang had followed through, but it was a bureaucratic wrangle that still wasn't resolved, and he and Claire had decided to keep the boy until morning. But he sure as hell had been glad to see Savannah when she walked in.

"Hey, there," Lang had greeted his wife.

"Sorry. I've got a strange case, and I couldn't talk about it, but I think it's related to the boy, Liam," she said, her voice low.

"What?"

"The woman checked herself in. She called us, or Liam did . . . I'm not getting a straight story from her. She's . . . ill. But she said Liam is her son."

It was Lang's turn to be dumbfounded. "Who is she?" he asked.

"Victoria Phelan," said Liam, apparently able to hear Lang's conversation.

Lang and Savvy both looked at him as Claire said into Lang's ear, "I'll be home as soon as I can," and hung up.

"You're Victoria Phelan's son," Savvy said in a strangled voice.

Lang dragged his eyes from Liam to look at her. Who . . . ? And then the penny dropped. Hale and Savvy's nanny. The one who'd driven Charlie away to safety all those years ago.

"Who's . . . your father?" Savvy questioned carefully.

"I'm with them now," said Liam. He pointed at Lang's chest and then at the cell phone.

Cassandra thanked the woman at the desk for allowing her to use the phone and turned toward the Emergency Room's sliding-glass doors. She wasn't sure how much had gotten through. She stepped onto the pad, and the doors immediately slid open. She heard the *woo*-woo, *woo*-woo of an approaching ambulance and then watched as it came screaming up, white and red lights circling madly.

She stepped forward as the EMTs unloaded a gurney from the back with a woman on board.

Ophelia. Who smiled dreamily upon seeing her. "Hi . . . Maggie . . ."

"You okay?" she asked urgently, relief flooding through her at the sight of her sister.

"Oh . . . I think so . . ."

"You can call me Cassandra," she said through a tight throat. Why had she fought it so long? What did it matter? All she cared about was that Ophelia was here. Alive and safe.

". . . would have drowned, but the hikers carried me up in a sling . . ." she murmured. Then her eyes suddenly snapped open wide. "Charlie! It was Charlie! Have to warn them!"

"I already have," soothed Cassandra.

Ophelia's eyes filled with tears. "My fault he's here."

"No," said Cassandra firmly, reaching for her sister's hand and walking beside the gurney as they wheeled her inside. "No one's fault but Charlie's."

They took her through the electronic doors to the Emergency Room cubicles, and Cassandra stayed behind, watching the doors automatically close.

The woman at the desk who'd offered the use of her phone regarded her uneasily. "I guess you were right. She was coming here," she said.

Cassandra just nodded. One more person who hadn't believed her.

Catherine gripped the railing with her right hand and took the steps one by one to the third floor. The shotgun was in her left. She smelled smoke and looked upward, seeing tendrils of gray mist reach beneath the door. She shot a look back down the steps, but Isadora was long gone, heading outside with the phone for better reception.

Nothing for it but to keep going.

Gritting her teeth, she moved upward.

Nev's phone rang. Deputy Wilson said tersely, "Got a call in from Ocean Park Hospital. Ophelia Rutledge is in Emergency there. Near drowning."

"On my way," he answered grimly. He pressed on the accelerator. Whatever was going on with Ophelia, he would go right by Siren Song on the way to the hospital.

"Lillibeth!" Catherine called. Two more steps. She struggled on those last two, clinging onto the rail. She looked down the hall. Smoke was an undulating blanket lying against the floor. "Lillibeth!"

Carefully, dragging the shotgun on its stock behind her, one hand pressed against the wall for support, she moved toward the double doors to Mary's bedroom.

Burn it all down. Burn it all down. Burn it all down.
The words filled Lillibeth's head as she dragged herself toward the locked doors, fighting the smoke, her eyes tearing, her throat sandpaper dry. Heat followed her, pressed down on her.
Come to us . . . we're waiting for you . . .

An orange glow glimmered beneath the double doors to Mary's room.
"Lillibeth." Catherine reached the doors, which were hot to the touch. Was that chanting? Coming from inside?
She began chanting in her mind herself.
Come to us . . . we're waiting for you . . .

Fighting whatever hell it was that Charlie was sending to her, Ravinia kicked him hard. He yowled in pain, the spell momentarily broken. With all her strength she pushed upward, holding the car door open, trying to scramble out.

Too late! Charlie's fingers clamped around her ankle and he hung on. She kicked and kicked. Connected with his face. He screamed, let go for a second and swore, "You little cu—"

She was out into the bracing air. On top of the side of the car. She'd lost a shoe. Fabric had ripped. Her hair was fully free, whipping around her face. She didn't care. Had to get away. Now!

She half fell, half jumped into the trench. Cold, cold water up to her knees. She barely noticed. Dug her hands in the side of the ditch, scrambling upward through dirt and gravel and weeds. The dank scents of mud and rot assailed her. Her fingers and feet dug deep into the wet soil, but she kept moving upward to the road, where she was on her feet in an instant. She ran into the thicket. Small sticks jabbed through her sock into the bottom of her foot. She barely felt them.

Breathing hard, searching the night, she had to get her bearings. She wasn't far from Siren Song; she knew that, but it was straight through dense brush, unless she wanted to keep going on the dirt and gravel road toward the Foothillers' community and then double back on the road that ran directly in front of Siren Song. But it was a long way. Too long.

Going through the brush would be faster . . . probably.

Splash!

Oh, shit. He was in the ditch behind her!

She stumbled, fell onto her hands and knees. She was shocked at how fast he caught up to her, grabbing her arm, spinning her around.

"You fucking witch," he ground out.

"I'll kill you! I'll kill you myself! I'll do it!" she yelled at him.

A sound suddenly filled her ears. Music? No . . . chanting? Hadn't she heard it before, or had she been dreaming?

Charlie suddenly threw back his head and screamed. Ravinia staggered backward. He threw himself around as if trying to thrust off an attacker. Was he hearing it too? What was it?

Ravinia didn't wait to find out.

She practically dove into the brush.

Lucky slowly pulled to a stop in front of Siren Song. The gates were open. She'd been to the lodge once before, but, apart from Catherine's edict that her work wasn't finished, she barely remembered it. But now she'd been drawn here. Called. Voices beckoning in unison. This is where the sound had emanated from. What were they doing? What was Catherine doing?

Calling Charlie . . .

Ahh . . .

Had someone really answered her, or was it all in her mind? Didn't matter. She was where she was supposed to be.

"911. What is the nature of your emergency?" the operator asked.

"There's a fire at Siren Song . . . my lodge . . . my home!" cried Isadora in a panic. "It's broken out on the third floor. We need help. Now!"

"What is the exact address?"

Isadora quickly answered. She was standing in the graveyard at the back of the lodge, where, for some reason, the cell reception was better. The phone hadn't picked up a signal in the front, so she'd run around to the back and finally gotten through.

"Hurry," she said, a catch in her throat, looking upward to the third-floor windows, where dark gold, scarlet, and orange ghosts danced in wild abandon.

Catherine hefted up the shotgun with what little strength she had left and slammed the butt against the lock on Mary's bedroom door. *Slam! Slam! SLAM!*

"Come on! Damn you, come on!"

She rammed the stock handle once more. With a groan and a blistering of wood, the lock broke free, and the doors flew backward. Catherine got one look into Mary's bedroom before the gates of hell opened and a wildly burning fireball blasted toward her. She cried out just as the fiery mass engulfed her.

Rand caught the movement. He spied Earl jump out of his chair and lope toward the door, as fast as his legs would carry him. Rand, in the kitchen cleaning a trout at the sink, saw his father hurry past. He too felt something. A change in the air.

"What is it?" he asked.

"Lodge is on fire," said his father. "Get the truck."

Rand dropped the knife he'd been using to clean the fish and noted his father had picked up the old Winchester he kept near the door.

Lucky walked inside the lodge's front door and looked around. Smoke scented everything. A fire somewhere. There was a faint haziness over the room: the trestle table, the kitchen on one end, a living room on the other, all covered with a whisper thin layer of smoke.

What was on fire?

She walked to the base of the stairway and looked upward. The bedroom she'd once stayed in was up and to the right, she believed. And upstairs was the source of the haze. She could feel it.

Ravinia burst from the thicket of Scotch broom and brambles, scratched and bleeding, to confront the lodge, three stories of old logs, now ablaze.

"NO . . ." She'd smelled the smoke but hadn't known it was her home.

Smoke was billowing from the third floor, and the windows pulsed, an ominous bloody orange.

Her sisters! Catherine!

One moment she was standing, the next she was down on the ground, her face buried in the wet fir needles and dirt.

Charlie had his hands around her neck and was squeezing. Hard. Her lungs burned and she struggled to breathe. Couldn't drag air in.

Panicked, she squirmed beneath him, managed to get a knee upward. The sickening, grasping, silky, sensation of his pheromones flooded her.

No! Never!

Rhodes, she thought. *Rhodes. Neville Rhodes.* His serious eyes . . . his strong hands . . . his dry tone . . . she could fall in love with him . . . loved him a little already.

Charlie roared and threw back his head once more. He staggered off her and moved toward the porch. "*You whores!*" he screamed, shaking himself all over like a wet dog. "*You can't get me to do what you want!*"

Ravinia rolled away, gasping. She stumbled to her feet and then took off at a dead run toward the side of the house.

Charlie staggered forward. They were in there. Calling to him? Expecting him to do what they wanted? They could all burn in hell!

But he was going to kill them all. *All of them!*

Stumbling up the steps, he made it inside the front door, looked around, headed for the stairs.

No! He was giving them what they wanted by going in! He wouldn't do it!

Screaming with fury, he bent double and held his head between his palms, even though the chanting had stopped. He needed to get away! Now! Fast!

Let them burn. If any survived, he would find them afterward. Take care of them, then.

Straightening, he found a woman directly in front of him. One of them. Standing just inside the door.

"Sister bitch," he snarled.

"Cousin, maybe," she said with a cold smile that sent an ice pick into his heart.

He turned around. Fuck it. Headed for the front door.

Grrrrrrr . . .

Was that growl in his head? More chanting? More—

A wolf stood in the doorway, its fur on end, its jaws pulled back into a black grimace of evil intent. Silver eyes. Charlie tried to go around it, but it blocked his way, glistening teeth bared.

"You killed him!" the woman snarled behind him.

Quickly, he spun back, and she jumped him, her body strong and agile, hanging on with a clawlike death grip. He tried to shake her off, but it was impossible. He ran against the wall, intending to knock her senseless, but her fingers dug into his flesh, her strength surprising. And still the wolf snarled, looking for a chance to pounce.

"Get off me! Get the fuck off me!"

The ceiling suddenly broke apart. Again, Charlie tried to fling her off him, but she was as determined as he, a burr on his back, digging even deeper. A cascade of flames poured over them, raining down, burning his flesh, setting his hair afire in a golden corona. He cried out, the smoke blinding him, his skin on fire, but she wouldn't let go. Her face was hard and set.

"Jesus."

Nev saw the roof of Siren Song explode in a fiery blaze, and he jerked the wheel and made the turn at high speed, barely holding onto the truck, sliding sideways in the lane before straightening out. Ravinia. Her sisters. He grabbed the walkie and called dispatch. He was only minutes away, but he knew with horrifying clarity that he was already too late.

Ravinia ran through the back door and barreled into Isadora, who was standing just inside. A blast of heat slammed into them and they fell in a tangle together.

"Where are they?" Ravinia screamed, climbing to her feet. "Aunt Catherine! Lillibeth! Cassandra . . . !"

"Upstairs . . ." Isadora stumbled upward, but Ravinia didn't wait.

She ran into the living room and saw Lucky and Charlie locked in a dance of death, with flames crackling and rising and burning their skin. She didn't have time to help as she raced for the stairs . . . and saw Lillibeth, frail as ever, standing at the top of the flight.

Standing?

"Get down here!" Ravinia screamed. "Hurry!"

From the corner of her eye she caught a glimpse of gray fur and the wolf—her wolf—launched into the fray, snarling and biting as he attacked Charlie.

Charlie couldn't believe her strength. Who was she? He clawed himself free, but the wolf bit his leg, and then the woman was on him again. Cousin . . . Ani . . . Lucky . . .

Silas's lover.

Oh, shit.

Nev screeched to a halt in front of the lodge and was out of the truck and running. In the distance, the sound of sirens. The cavalry . . . but it might be too late.

Ravinia started up the stairs, but Lillibeth disappeared into the smoke. Ravinia blinked, held her hand to protect her eyes. Did she step backward? It seemed like she'd dematerialized, it had been so fast.

A huge timber crashed down on the stairs, tumbling, shooting up sparks, narrowly missing Ravinia. She half fell back down the few steps she'd climbed and reeled back into the living room.

Through the smoke she saw Isadora coughing, doubled over.

Charlie was screaming and screaming. He was in flames, his skin spilling and charred. Lucky, in a death grip with him, was utterly silent.

The wolf streaked by them directly in front of Ravinia. He raced into Lillibeth's bedroom. Ravinia followed.

Lillibeth was in bed. Sleeping or unconscious.

What? *What?*

Somewhere in the distance sirens screamed.

Ravinia raced forward and grabbed her sister by the shoulders. "Wake up. Get up! Get out! Wake up!"

Where was Catherine? Cassandra? Upstairs? Isn't that what Isadora had said? No time to save them now. Ravinia closed her mind and concentrated on Lillibeth. She dragged her out of the bed and across the floor, her shoulder screaming in pain.

"Ravinia!"

She turned quickly. Disbelieving. *Nev*. Her heart cracked at seeing him.

"Let's get out of here!" He raced toward her. She barely recognized him. Smoke was everywhere. He hauled Lillibeth onto his shoulder in a fireman's carry. "Can you get out?" he yelled. At Ravinia's nod, he ordered, "Go now. *Now!*"

She bolted out of the bedroom.

Charlie's screaming had abruptly stopped. She smelled cooked flesh and couldn't help but glance over at the two charred bodies that were locked in a lover's embrace on the ground. Her stomach revolted, but she managed to keep from vomiting.

Another timber crashed down, blasting Ravinia with sparks and flames as she stumbled to the kitchen. Earl was just inside the back door, yanking Isadora to her feet.

Isadora chattered, "Where's Catherine? Where's Lillibeth?"

Ravinia realized Nev and Lillibeth weren't behind her. She whipped around and saw that the charred timber had pinned Nev's leg. Lillibeth lay on the floor behind him. She lifted her head but it fell back. Ravinia ran back in and hoped to lift the timber, but before she could, Earl's gloved hand pulled her back.

"Let me do it, daughter," rasped Earl, and suddenly Rand was there, and they were pulling Nev free. Rand picked up Lillibeth, and Nev leaned on Earl, and they all headed for the back door.

Ravinia shot one more look at Lucky and Charlie as the sirens reached a wailing crescendo and the fire engines came to a stop in front of the lodge.

Charlie's reign of terror and Lucky's strange mission of vigilantism had come to a final end.

EPILOGUE

*F*unerals.

Nev stood beside Ravinia as they watched the caskets carrying Silas's and Catherine's remains being buried in the plot behind what was left of Siren Song. The old lodge was reduced to burned timbers, some still smoking, charred vertical beams reaching toward a gray October sky.

Ophelia stood beside Cassandra, the sisters' arms interlocked, and Isadora stood a bit apart, openly weeping. Catherine's death had hit the stoic "Catherine devotee" the hardest. It was Ravinia who'd held them all together these past few weeks, showing the Catherine staunchness they'd all come to depend on. Several other members of Ravinia's family, notably Becca and Lorelei, two of the sisters who had lived mostly outside Siren Song's walls, had joined with their husbands to attend Catherine's funeral. The two women clustered near their remaining sisters, offering hugs and support.

Lucky's—Ani's—ashes had been picked up by a woman named Gemma Tanninger, who made Ravinia inhale on a gasp, as she was Ani's identical twin. Nev had looked at the hazel-eyed woman and been a bit taken aback when she leaned toward him and whispered, "Don't worry. You're going to marry her."

Henry Charles Woodworth's remains had been offered to his adoptive father, James Woodworth, who had given them an emphatic "No, thanks," so Ravinia had appropriated them. What was left of Charlie after the fire had been cremated and his ashes thrown into the Pacific Ocean.

Catherine's daughter Elizabeth and her daughter, Chloe, along with Elizabeth's fiancé, Rex Kingston, had flown in from southern California to attend the graveside service, and Ravinia and Chloe had been locked in private discussions about "the wolf." Nev hadn't seen this apparent apparition himself, but Ravinia had explained he'd been with her years earlier and had appeared again in her time of need. Maybe, Nev thought skeptically, but he wasn't about to argue with her.

Lang, Claire, Savannah, and Hale were also at the grave site today. Janet was taking care of Annabel and Declan, and seemed to be considering a move to the West Coast again, as she was still seeing her new friend. That news had apparently been met with mixed feelings.

Lang himself had pushed back on the idea of running for sheriff. He had too much on his plate. Catherine's death had apparently cleared the way for Bea's adoption, but now he and Claire had Liam living with them, and Liam's mother, Victoria Phelan, though getting sorely needed help at Halo Valley, seemed to still be deteriorating.

Nev moved his gaze to Lillibeth, who sat huddled in her wheelchair on the other side of Ravinia. Isadora claimed that Lillibeth had been on the third floor and she was the one who had started the fire, and Ravinia had admitted that she'd thought she'd seen Lillibeth standing on the second floor, but the girl had been found in her bed.

"Spontaneous combustion," one of the firemen had said with a shrug, when asked about what started the fire, which was no answer at all, in Nev's opinion. Just a way to say they had no clue how the lamp oil had spread across the floor and been ignited.

Ravinia was half convinced that Lillibeth had somehow gone outside of herself and done the deed, which was pure bunk in Nev's mind, though he couldn't explain the rug burns on her elbows and forearms other than to blame it on her rescue. Again, he didn't feel like arguing with Ravinia, and, well, she knew more about the Colony than he did, although he'd blown her away when he'd told her he'd been one of the would-be adventurers to try to find Mary on Echo Island and that he had been lucky to survive when his friends had perished.

But even that information wasn't as incredible as what was discovered in Catherine's journal, found faintly charred inside a metal box:

a list of Mary's daughters' fathers, on which Earl was named as Ravinia's.

Nev threw a glance at Earl and Rand, both standing solemnly by, near Isadora. He saw Earl reach into a pocket and hand Isadora a handkerchief.

"He said, 'Let me do it, daughter' during the fire, but I thought it was just an expression," Ravinia had told Nev in disbelief, and Nev remembered how Earl had never really committed to being Silas's father when they'd been on the island together. Nev had just assumed.

Earl and Rand had worked with other Foothillers to find a place for Isadora, Cassandra, and Lillibeth since their home had been destroyed. The sisters were now staying in one of the community's ranch homes as they recovered and faced a future without Catherine.

When the gathering broke up and they all left, Nev waited as Ravinia walked over to Earl and said a few words. Earl nodded, and Ravinia even managed to scare a small smile out of him.

Later, as they were heading back to Nev's place in his truck, where he and Ravinia had been navigating their relationship in every way possible—he had very pleasurable and X-rated thoughts about her—Ravinia said, "Can we stop at Davy Jones's Locker on the way?"

"Sure. Why?"

"Just do it, Rhodes."

He pulled into the back lot, and they headed in through the back door. The potholes were dry, as they'd had a spate of good weather leading up to this day before Halloween.

Inside the bar, it could have been the actual holiday. Half the customers were dressed up. "Contest," Jeff Padilla told them. "What are you? A cop," he answered himself, then turned to Ravinia. "And you?"

"I'm from the Colony," she said after a moment.

"A witch? You need a better costume."

"I'm the one who called in the order earlier."

Jeff looked at her a moment in confusion, then his brow cleared. "Just a minute."

He went in the back and returned a few minutes later. "This for him?" he asked.

"Yes," said Ravinia.

It was one of the Locker's T-shirts in his size. Nev barked out a laugh. "How'd you know?"

"I've got the gift," she said with an arched brow.

"Hah." He remembered he'd mentioned that he'd thought about buying one at one point during their myriad conversations over the last few weeks. During that time, he'd also learned a few things, like that she favored champagne and Hot Tamales; though she didn't know it yet, that was the "meal" that was waiting for her at his place.

She suddenly closed her eyes, lifted her chin, and sighed.

"You okay?" he asked.

"Just glad it's all over," she said. "I'm sad about Catherine, but Charlie's gone. His bones have been burned, and that's what she wanted to keep us all safe."

"Ready to go home?"

"Home," she said, and smiled up at him. "Yes, I am."

Liam smiled and smiled until his face hurt. He knew that's what they needed to see. A happy kid. They came back from the graveyard together, holding hands, and Buzzy Bea ran to them and threw herself in their arms. She was being adopted, and though Liam hadn't heard that term before, he understood its meaning by the way Bea acted.

He needed to be adopted too. Mama was fading from view, and he'd known for a long time this would happen.

He watched them light the candles inside the jack-o'-lanterns and tried not to be nervous. Fire made him nervous, but he didn't want them to know. They told him that children would be coming by tomorrow and asking for candy, and that had confused him too.

He knew a lot of things, more than he should, but there were big gaps too.

Scratch, scratch.

Liam looked around, worried they could hear the scratching at his brain. But they didn't seem to notice. It wasn't his father this time. His father was dead. The fire at the big house had burned him clean.

He looked at Bea . . . maybe? It didn't seem so.

There must be someone else.

Scratch, scratch, scratch.

"Come here," Buzzy Bea said, grabbing his arm and dragging him onto the front porch toward the jack-o'-lanterns.

Someone, somewhere . . .

The flame drew him, even as his stomach knotted.

Who are you? he asked, waiting for a response. And then other words came to him and sounded like they should be asked: *Friend or foe?*

The candles danced beneath a quick sputter of wind.

There's only you, he thought they said.

A SHORT HISTORY OF THE COLONY

by Herman Smythe

The locals around Deception Bay call them the Colony. Why? Because they built a lodge in the late 1800s that was named Siren Song somewhere over the years, and they've lived there together in a commune-like tradition ever since. Who are they? Well, let me tell you what I learned from Mary Rutledge Beeman, my friend, and one of the most colorful characters from the Colony's already colorful past.

It all started when Nathaniel Abernathy married his young bride, Abigail, and moved from the East Coast to the West Coast, about as far as humanly possible across North America. Both Nathaniel's family and Abigail's were rumored to be descendants of the women who were condemned to die during the Salem, Massachusetts, witch trials of the 1600s. Incidentally, the capital of Oregon is Salem and was named after Salem, Massachusetts.

Nathaniel and Abigail must have gotten a big surprise when they realized their union spawned children with extraordinary abilities. No one knows how, but it's a proven fact that Colony members— usually women—can do amazing things. How? It's been speculated that it's in the genetic code for this tribe, the result of a mutated gene, maybe. Whatever its cause, it has played havoc with Colony members and locals alike throughout the years.

When Nathaniel and Abigail Abernathy reached the Pacific Ocean, they decided that's where they wanted to live and set about buying up as much real estate as they could. They purchased a stretch of property along the Oregon coast, amassing vast acreage that included mountain forests with old-growth timber, a large rock quarry, and a hunk of coastline. In a very short period of time, their holdings stretched from the foothills of the Coast Range on the eastern edge, across the land on both sides of what is now Highway 101, to the Pacific Ocean itself (though, because of later Oregon law, the beach that was their property was ceded back to the state, as all Oregon beaches are now publicly owned).

The Abernathys cleared smaller tracts of land too, and Siren Song was erected in a spot that was clear-cut of timber. Stands of forest still abut the south section of the lodge and grounds, framing the lodge and a makeshift unincorporated "town" that is inhabited mostly by Foothillers. (More about them later.) Southwest of the lodge is the small town of Deception Bay, which spills across Highway 101 in both directions toward the timberland to the east and the Pacific to the west.

From the onset, Nathaniel and Abigail bartered and bought even more adjacent lands to expand their isolated retreat. Though their descendants no longer own that stretch of beach, or the small jut of rocky coastline directly across from the lodge called Serpent's Eye, where a now-unused lighthouse still stands (an area that's islanded when the tide comes in), they do own a larger island, Echo Island, which is about one square mile. This island is located in the treacherous waters of the mouth of Deception Bay itself—the bay the town was named after, which in itself was named for the deceptive and deadly currents and waves that swallow fishing boats almost every season.

Nathaniel and Abigail got busy right away starting a family, but of their children, only two survived: Sarah and Beth (Elizabeth). All the boys died in infancy or were stillborn, as were several other girls. Abigail was late in her life by the time Sarah and Beth arrived, and though she lived into her late eighties, long past her husband, she wasn't much of a parent to her daughters, so they mostly raised themselves. Beth, plagued by visions or sounds or sensations she couldn't handle, apparently went mad when she was in her early thirties. She had one son out of wedlock, Harold Abernathy, who was scorned by the townspeople for being both born a bastard and always acting decidedly odd. A hermit, Harold lived in sin with his young wife, an Indian shaman's daughter, who died giving birth to Harold's only child—Madeline "Mad Maddie" Abernathy—who lives in Deception Bay to this day.

Beth either fell, or threw herself off a cliff, into the sea. She was presumed dead, though her body was never retrieved from the cold waters of the Pacific. Some people think she was pushed to her death, possibly by her sister, Sarah, who got rid of Beth in order to become sole heir to the vast property amassed by their parents, Nathaniel and Abigail.

Sarah Abernathy, the surviving daughter, married James Fitzhugh in 1909, but James died in a hunting accident on their tenth wedding anniversary. A full year after her husband's death, Sarah gave birth to a baby girl, Grace, in 1920. It's been theorized that Sarah had an affair with an Indian shaman whom she seemed to fall under the spell of sometime before her husband's death. Rumors have it that Sarah and the shaman plotted to kill James, but no one knows for certain, and his "accident/murder" has never been solved. Sarah has been much vilified by the Deception Bay townies over the years, and even her descendants are suspicious of what her intentions were.

But everyone agrees that Sarah was remarkably bright and learned about the value of land ownership from her father, Nathaniel. She managed to increase the amount of acres of timber, farmland, and coastal holdings during her lifetime. Sarah raised Grace alone and modernized the original homestead into the imposing lodge it is today, although electricity and indoor plumbing only run on the main floor; the upper floors are much as they were when the place was first erected.

During Sarah's time, there was a bunkhouse on the property, left over from her parents' days of ranching and farming. Some say she enticed local men to do the work by offering sexual favors. Others fervently believe Sarah possessed strange powers, and that she used those powers to persuade the neighboring farmers, millwrights, and lumbermen to build onto the lodge and improve the grounds. Whatever the case, men seemed to come from far and wide to help out, while their wives and sweethearts stewed and gossiped about Sarah, only adding to the rumors of witchcraft that continually plagued the Colony and their supposed demon-possessed ancestors.

Members of the local community, Deception Bay, have long regarded the growing "cult" with suspicion. Fueled by gossip and the strange heritage of the Colony, the townspeople felt Sarah believed she was some kind of high priestess. It's not clear who dubbed the lodge Siren Song, whether it was the locals or someone associated with the Colony itself, but Sarah's actions seemed to be the reason, and the name stuck. Sarah's shaman lover never acknowledged that he was (a) her lover nor (b) Grace's father, but his friendship and relationship with Sarah continued until her death in 1956, shortly after her daughter Grace's marriage to Thomas Durant, a hard-drinking, good-looking, and hot-headed lumberjack who grew up in and around the Colony. Thomas was the son of one of the male workers who seemed completely under Sarah's spell. (Thomas Durant's mother, who was known by the single name of Storm, was also a member of the same Indian tribe as Sarah's shaman lover. Some say Storm was the shaman's sister, and that Thomas was really Grace's first cousin. This is the same tribe from which the sole member of the other branch of the Abernathy family tree—Harold Abernathy—took his young Indian bride.)

At the time of Grace and Thomas's marriage, Grace was already pregnant with Mary, who was born on the summer solstice, and the town gossip is that Thomas raped Grace in a night of drunken debauchery. From the get-go, Mary was a fussy, unhappy baby—the result of "nature" or "nurture" or possibly both—as the fights between Grace and Thomas were legendary. He was a womanizer, she a fiery, angry woman who could give as good as she got. (Baby Mary seemed to absorb the fury, wrath, and passion between her parents, Grace and Thomas; an unstable brew of mystical, inexplicable genetic material, she grew psychologically twisted herself, a dark personality at best, a deranged one at worst. Mary's strange behavior became legendary.)

After Mary's birth, Grace and Thomas's relationship, always tumultuous, grew even more strained. They both recognized something strange and dangerous in their daughter, though neither really addressed the issue head-on. They always spoke of it in the abstract, though, even as a baby, Mary's precognitive skills were obvious.

When Thomas inexplicably disappeared soon after Mary was born, the locals breathed a sigh of relief, as he was a notorious drinker and brawler. But then more rumors swirled. What happened to him? Where did he go? Was foul play involved? No one, however, was really interested in asking a lot of questions, not even the local sheriff, as Thomas Durant was in and out of the local jail, more often than not, always causing problems. People were kind of glad he was gone. Maybe he was killed, maybe he wasn't. A number of people said they'd spotted Thomas in the days after his disappearance, and everyone allowed that he'd probably just taken off. It was the safest assumption. Still, like Grace's Aunt Beth's body a generation earlier, he never resurfaced in Deception Bay.

Grace, free of Thomas, married John Rutledge in 1959, regardless of the question of the marriage's legality (since no one knew whether Thomas was missing or dead). From the moment of the marriage, Grace maintained that Mary was a Rutledge and never used the name Durant again. Within the year, Grace and John had one child together, a girl they named Catherine.

In 1975, Grace and John were killed in a freak automobile accident: their car missed a turn and plummeted into the Pacific Ocean at the sharp corner known as Devil's Point, a spot where the storms that rage across the Pacific hit the shore with incredible force. The funneling waters at that cove have become the graveyard for many a boater or surfer. Grace's daughters, Mary and Catherine, were seventeen and fifteen, respectively, at the time of the accident. Though Grace and John had always planned to write a will naming Catherine as the prime beneficiary—and therefore leaving her in control of Siren Song and all the other property—Catherine was too young at the time of their death, and they never fully formed their plans. Their eldest daughter, Mary, took over, and that's when the fun really began.

Mary treated her new position much as her maternal grandmother, Sarah, had: as if she were a high priestess and the only rules that mattered were the ones she made herself. But Mary wasn't as innately intelligent as Sarah, and her hot anger wasn't tempered by cold calculation, like her father Thomas's could be. Mary was a very sexual being and took lovers indiscriminately. This is a fact I'm personally aware of, as I spent time at Siren Song myself as one of Mary's many willing conquests.

But this story is of the Colony, not me.

Another of Mary's lovers was one Richard Beeman, whom Mary claimed was her husband. There is no record of this union, though Catherine insists the marriage was real. If Richard Beeman were truly Mary's husband, he certainly slipped in and out of Deception Bay and Siren Song without much more than a how-do-you-do. I'm inclined to believe he is a fabrication.

At the time of her parents' death, Mary, wealthy enough to do as she pleased, was beyond a narcissistic megalomaniac. Her mind was fractured, however, and self-satisfaction and even cruelty were her way of life. As far as relationships went, Mary slept with whomever she wanted and damn the consequences. She left behind a string of lovers and a number of children whose paternity has never been fully established.

Mary's sister, Catherine, never married. She became a midwife to Mary, who delivered children like a mother cat, indiscriminately and without much interest in the newborns once they were a couple of months old. Catherine was also called occasionally by the townies if a midwife's help was needed. They feared her less than they did Mary.

The Colony had a feel of a commune after Mary took over, during the last half of the late 1970s and the '80s, with Mary still as sexually active as ever and Catherine managing the care of the growing brood of Mary's offspring.

Beyond Catherine and Mary, there were a number of men who lived in the bunkhouse that burned down in the mid-1980s. These men were there to service Mary, and there are tales of Catherine shooing them out time and again, and maybe being the one who struck the match that finally burned the bunkhouse down. There were also a number of cottages built along the eastern rim of land that leads toward the Coast Range, where a smattering of families still live. These Foothillers, whom I mentioned before, formed their own "town," which has never been really named or incorporated. Most Foothillers are Native American, but some were shirttail Colony members, never fully recognized but bound by some ill-defined relationship. Some of them exhibited extra abilities. Some of them pretended to be special. Some of them claimed to be Mary's past lovers. Mary paid scant attention to them, as she did the later men who cruised through the bunkhouse while she descended into a darker interior world. Eventually, those Foothillers who were tied to the Colony all but disappeared.

The core of the Colony has always been women. As a rule, they possess the strongest extra abilities and seem to be the hardiest. Mary almost seemed tuned to some inner radar when it came to picking her lovers and the fathers of her children. With surprising success, she bore mostly girls, and those girls possess extraordinary abilities that seem to reach their zenith around puberty. Of the boys born during this time—if there were any—little is known.

The Colony has tried to live in relative isolation. People in Deception Bay are wary of them. They seem to be from some other place and time, especially after Catherine took over total control, somehow wresting it from Mary. When that happened, Catherine changed everything, right down to her own and Mary's daughters' daily apparel. Per Catherine's decree, they all dress as if they were from a previous century, wearing long skirts and calico prints and their hair mostly in buns. The townies live in uneasy coexistence with Catherine and watch her closely on the rare times she deigns to go into town for supplies like food and fuel. The enlightened locals of Deception Bay consider the Colony merely benign oddballs, out of step with reality and the world, young women who live with their "clan." Still, there are dissenters who consider them beyond weird, even evil, based on the lingering rumors of witchcraft and all the missing people and unexplained deaths.

The absence of men hasn't gone unnoticed, either, other than the "studs" who moved through the commune either from the bunkhouse or the Foothillers' community, or as random lovers like myself. There is definitely an element of townies who are resentful, mistrusting, and envious of the women of Siren Song and their dark gifts.

Letter within
Catherine Rutledge's Journal

To Mary's children,

From time to time, I've tried to remember and write down the names of the men who fathered you. I know you want to know. I've listed best guesses here, and, along with DNA, they should help identify some of them.

Isadora, Parnell Loman
Ophelia, Dolph Loman
Cassandra, Herman Smythe?
Lillibeth, Herman Smythe, maybe?
Ravinia, Earl Tillicum

I believe Preston St. Cloud was Silas's father, and that Thomas Durant, Mary's own father, was Henry Charles Woodworth's.

I also have a secret I've never fully admitted, but I'm writing it down now in case I don't find the right time to tell you all: There never was a Richard Beeman. He was entirely fictional. Mary pretended he existed when she realized she was in a sexual relationship with her own father. She buried the name Thomas Durant and created Richard Beeman in his place, pretending to be married to the man. In the end, I think she longed for a traditional relationship, and that's why you all were given the last name of Beeman, though many of you have reverted to Rutledge once more.

Please know that I care for you all very much and have always only ever wanted what I've felt was best for you.

Your loving aunt,
Catherine

Dear Reader,

From *Wicked Game, Wicked Lies, Something Wicked, Wicked Ways* and now *Wicked Dreams*, it's taken a lot of years and a lot of characters to finally reach the finale of the Wicked Series. Wow! We can't believe we're really saying goodbye to the inhabitants of Siren Song Lodge.

For those of you who've read all the books in the series, you might wonder how some of the newer characters in *Wicked Dreams* fit in.

Lucky first appeared in Nancy's book, *Unseen*, and then reappeared in the third of her Nowhere series, *Nowhere Safe*. Langdon Stone and Claire Norris's story began in Nancy's novel, *Blind Spot*, which also introduced the character of Tasha, whom we don't see in any of the previous books of the Wicked Series but who is obliquely referred to in *Wicked Dreams*. Nancy's thriller, *Hush*, is partially set in Deception Bay and a number of familiar characters walk through its pages as well. Though both of us planned to write more spin-off stories to complement the Wicked Series, Lisa was already deep into the Bentz/Montoya series and the To Die series when we began, and then Nancy added the River Glen series to her Nowhere series and there were a lot of stand-alone stories in between so . . . Phew! . . . we just managed to eke out enough time to finally complete the Siren Song saga.

Even so, we couldn't showcase all of the characters we loved so much over the years in the way we wished we could. Be assured we didn't forget Becca and Hudson and Lorelei and Harrison, the main characters from *Wicked Game* and *Wicked Lies*. We just left them living their own lives away from the action in *Wicked Dreams*.

We really hope you've enjoyed the Wicked Series. We've certainly loved writing it! And the question that always comes up is: Will there be another story about the Colony?

Well, at this point, we're saying unlikely . . . but strange things happen along the Oregon coast . . . and since most of the writing of these books took place in a small Oregon beach town, much like the imagined one of Deception Bay, you just never can tell.

But for now we're leaving the Colony and concentrating on our other series. This summer check out our latest upcoming books: Lisa's newest installment featuring Bentz and Montoya, *The Last Sinner*; and the fourth in Nancy's River Glen series, *The Camp*.

Happy Reading!

Enjoy!

Lisa Jackson & Nancy Bush